Praise for
The Maestro and Her Protégé

What an intricate, inspiring and rewarding novel Kate Whouley has written. Mademoiselle Boulanger, with her utter devotion to music, is an unforgettable character, and it's easy to understand why, under her teacher's outsize influence, Hannah dedicates herself to composing and conducting. But life has a way of interrupting, and the world of music remains dominated by men. *The Maestro and Her Protégé* is a dazzling debut.

Margot Livesey, author of *The Road from Belhaven*

Kate Whouley's deep dive into the world of classical music is a joy to read—a fascinating behind-the-scenes look at conducting, composing, and the making of a prodigy. I found myself completely immersed in the lives of Hannah Shaeffer and her legendary mentors, Nadia Boulanger and Leonard Bernstein, and finished the book in two days, thoroughly entertained and with a fuller understanding of a side of music I knew little about. *The Maestro and Her Protégé* is a refreshingly original story about artistry, identity, and the struggle to break barriers while staying true to oneself.

Mira Lee, author of *Everything Here is Beautiful*

❦

I loved Kate Whouley's latest, a story of art, ambition, and music, inspired by the real-life luminary, Nadia Boulanger. I adored following Hannah, a young artist becoming a conductor ... and becoming herself in a male-dominated world. *The Maestro and Her Protégé* is the perfect novel for readers who love music, Paris, and delving deeply into both.

Amanda Eyre Ward, *New York Times*-bestselling author of the Reese's Book Club pick, *The Jetsetters*

❦

What a terrific book! Moving fluidly through colorful, realistic scenes past and present, *The Maestro and Her Protégé* portrays the lifelong relationship between teacher and student through an entertaining, poignant story of a conductor at a critical juncture in her life. With her seemingly boundless knowledge of music—its structure, composition, and conducting—and her elegant, witty prose, Kate Whouley depicts the toil of mastery, personal sacrifice and personal growth, and the joy of making music at the highest level. Whether or not you're a music lover, you'll find much to enjoy in this soulful, satisfying novel.

Daphne Kalotay, author of *The Archivists*

❦

In her lyrical and emotionally resonant debut novel, Kate Whouley delivers a poignantly charged portrait of a woman at the pinnacle of her career as a pioneering conductor now facing a life-altering crossroads. Set against a richly drawn backdrop of music and memory, *The Maestro and Her Protégé* is a beautifully composed story of a woman who has as always let music lead the way, but now dares to ask what else life might hold.

David R. Gillham,
New York Times-bestselling author of *City of Women*

❦

This warm, deeply engaging novel follows Hannah Schaeffer, a brilliant female conductor who gives everything to music—so much so that her own compositions, and much of her personal life, are left behind. At its center is her demanding but inspiring teacher, drawn with affection and nuance, whose influence shapes Hannah's path in ways she can't always see. The story brings musical greats like Philip Glass and Leonard Bernstein vividly to life, capturing their quirks, genius, and impact. *The Maestro and Her Protégé* is a thoughtful, lively look at what it means to devote yourself to art—what it costs, what it asks of you, and the rare, powerful rewards it can offer in return.

Rosie Sultan, author of *Helen Keller in Love*

❦

As a brilliantly artful writer and musician, Kate Whouley weaves a soulfully engaging story of life in both worlds. In *The Maestro and Her Protégé*, readers enter a magical world where musicians are made, composers become conductors, and both happen to Hannah Schaffer, sent to Paris at the age of 10 to study with the musical genius, Mademoiselle Nadia Boulanger. The depth and breadth of their relationship is the heart and soul of this story, enriched by the enduring presence of Lenny Bernstein and other real-life musical mentors and colleagues. The novel reads like a favorite movie to watch over and over. Kate Whouley is The Maestro of Storytelling.

Karol Jackowski, author of *Sister Karol's Book of Spells, Blessings*, and *Folk Magic*

Praise for Kate Whouley's Work

Cottage for Sale, Must Be Moved

... a pitch-perfect description of both small-town life and personal anticipation...told in a voice of such good humor and thoughtful humanity ... It is not simply about the marriage of a small house and smaller cottage, but about the hope we all find in home. I loved *Cottage For Sale.*

Anna Quindlen, *Book-of-the-Month Club News*

... an odyssey of confusion, consternation, and light comedy ... there is so much here you will want to read it twice ... a cast of characters that range from interesting to eccentric, a series of misadventures that might have come from a comic novel, and a narrative style that makes you keep turning the pages. It's one of those books in which the author has taken something personal and made it universal.

David Pitt, *Booklist*

Whouley's gentle memoir...deftly explores the themes of independence, pride of place and loss ...

Penelope Green, *The New York Times*

... an almost Holy Grail quest ... highly entertaining.

Kara Swisher, *The Wall Street Journal*

Remembering the Music, Forgetting the Words

Reading Kate Whouley's memoir felt like sitting down with an old friend over coffee...As a reader, I felt privileged to be on the receiving end of such a confidence, which concerns the most important issues: family, mortality, our aloneness in the world, our connection in the face of it. I read it in two sittings and turned the last page with regret.

David Payne, author of *Barefoot in Avalon*

... often humorous and always compassionate ... Whouley is a smooth navigator.

Janet Lloyd, *USA Today*

A lovely, honest account of her mother's decline into Alzheimer's disease.

Kate Tuttle, The Boston Globe

Grab your tissues and favorite James Galway music and prepare to laugh and cry through Kate Whouley's memoir of the challenges and rewards inherent in caring for a parent with Alzheimer's disease, as well as the power of music to heal our souls.

Jaclyn Fulwood, *Shelf Awareness for Readers*

The Maestro and Her Protégé

a novel

KATE WHOULEY

A Blackwater Press book

First published in the United States of America by
Blackwater Press, LLC

Library of Congress Control Number: 2025935304

ISBN: 978-1-963614-12-1

Cover design by: Inés G. Labarta

Blackwater Press
120 Capitol Street
Charleston, WV 25301
United States

blackwaterpress.com

For Eric
who loved stories
with characters who worked interesting jobs

In Paris, you can always hope to find what you thought you had lost, your own past, or someone else's.

Italo Calvino, *Hermit in Paris*

Do not take up music unless you would rather die than not do so.

Nadia Boulanger

Author's Note

Historical figures and contemporary musicians, including Nadia Boulanger, Leonard Bernstein, and Philip Glass are characters in this novel. Other twentieth-century musicians have walk-on roles, as do some of the real-life family members, friends and colleagues of Boulanger and Bernstein. While I have honored chronology and known historical fact, *The Maestro and Her Protégé* is a work of fiction. All historical and living characters are portrayed fictitiously; their interactions and conversations are wholly imagined.

Overture

—1—

I am your duckling.

Though you resisted mothering, I imprinted on you, forming myself in your image.

Even as I had my small rebellions. *Insoumissions*, you called them.

Yes, I am your duckling, Mademoiselle.

And I've returned to you, with yellow roses.

—2—

My mother told me we were moving on the day I finished fourth grade. My father owed a man a lot of money, she explained, and the best thing we could do was to go somewhere else. "Without your father," she clarified. We would find a place where no one knew us, or our history—a place, as it turned out, I wouldn't see until a few days before I started fifth grade. Because while my father dodged loan sharks and my mother looked for new beginnings, my grandmother sent me to France to study music with Mademoiselle Nadia Boulanger.

Sending a ten-year-old abroad was not without its complications. It was June of 1959, and transatlantic air travel was brand-new—Pan Am's first commercial flight between New York and London had taken off just eight months earlier—and it was crazy-expensive. Most Americans were still boarding ships to travel to Europe. But my grandmother was determined. Once assured that a glamorous stewardess would look after me in the air, she plunked down most of her life savings on a round-trip plane ticket.

Invoking the heroine of the books we'd read and loved together, Nana told me she was sure I could be as fearless as Eloise. "But don't be as bossy!" she admonished—worried, I guess, that I would start ordering everyone around.

The ordering-everyone-around part was years away. On my first flight, I tried my best to be a picture book heroine—sophisticated, sure of herself, no adults required. I thrilled in the view out the window—the people and places on the ground growing smaller and smaller, the rise through clouds. I felt nervous—not about flying, not about being alone, not about the trip. Ten-going-on-eleven, I was already worried about the music.

It was my grandfather's long reach that permitted a precocious ten-year-old to study with the acclaimed Nadia Boulanger. Gramps was a great storyteller, and I'm told, a very good cook, but all my memories of my grandfather Jacob are musical. I remember him playing his violin, then letting me pluck the strings with my pudgy baby fingers. He brought me a beautiful wooden soprano recorder as soon as he could persuade my mother that I wouldn't eat it, and he spent hours bowing a long tone on his fiddle and asking me to find the same pitch on my recorder.

After I'd learned the notes and the fingerings on my instrument—and this before I understood the entire alphabet or could count to a hundred—we began to improvise. "Just play," he would say, "and I will follow you." In our practice sessions, we played catch, tag, and hide-and-go-seek. All these games I knew first in music, only understanding when I went to kindergarten that they could also be played without instruments.

It was always play to me, but I know now that he regarded those early lessons as essential in developing the musician he suspected I might be. And based on that suspicion, he had extracted a promise: Mademoiselle would take me on, would teach, me—assuming, at least in the version she told me—that I was worthy. It was as if he knew he wouldn't be around to do the job himself. He died before I turned six, but he'd made the arrangement right around the time he'd handed me my first recorder.

Gramps played with the Boston Symphony—he was the concertmaster—and that's where he met Mademoiselle. The first woman ever to conduct an American orchestra; she made her Boston debut in 1938. As my grandmother tells it, Mademoiselle had a hard time with many of the orchestra members—there was not a single woman seated in the BSO. This men's club of musicians was not particularly enthusiastic about following the directions of a female conductor. But my grandfather welcomed her; he showed her respect, and most importantly, he brought her home for dinner, forging the beginnings of a musical friendship that would last beyond his lifetime. Once he had set the tone, his colleagues knew to follow suit.

Still, there would be the small mean things that I am sure many players did to Mademoiselle during that first rehearsal. "Mr. Tanier," I hear her saying to the principal trumpet player, "I do not believe that note was written to be bent. Please straighten it up and we'll begin again at the double bar."

This scene is easy for me to conjure because forty years later, not too much had changed when I ran my first rehearsal with the BSO. I remember smiling at Doriot Anthony Dwyer before I lifted my baton. She was the principal flutist and, at that time, the only woman in the history of the BSO to hold a first chair. When she smiled back at me, I knew at least one member of the orchestra was planning to follow my cues.

—3—

It took forever to get here, Mademoiselle.

A car from the hall to the airport. LAX to Heathrow—flight running late. They waved me through Customs with minimal attention to the four flutes and two piccolos in my carry-on. I made the connecting flight only to get stuck in rush hour traffic from Orly. Then we had to cross the city to the 9th.

The driver was philosophical, unhurried, taking the traffic in stride.

"*Americaine--vraiment?*"

"*Americaine,*" I confirmed.

"I know I have seen your face," he declared. "Are you in cinema?"

I'd spent the last thirteen hours in the air, had been awake for twenty-nine hours straight. He couldn't have possibly mistaken me for a movie star.

"*Musicienne.*"

His eyes moved to the mirror at the traffic lights, and I caught his version of me in the rearview--untamed hair, smudged eyeliner, mascara running. An aging punk rock queen, after a long night of transatlantic partying?

He complimented me on my unaccented French after I asked him if we could stop at a florist. Then we dropped my bags at the apartment before he drove me up the hill.

"I'm sorry for your loss," he said to me as he dropped me by the gate.

I let that explain it all—the hurry, the exhaustion, the mess that was my face. I let it all be your fault, the fault of your going, the fault of your being gone. And I gave him a giant tip.

—4—

"You have great talent and no discipline." My teacher sighed, worrying her lips into a careful smile. Mademoiselle was in her seventies and without front teeth; she tried not to expose her gums. Leaning down to peer into my eyes, she would hand me a stack of staff paper. "Fill it—and no more Nancy Drew until you do."

I would do as I was told. I would write a flute part of running eighth notes, imagining the small, neat teeth that Mademoiselle must have had when she was younger. Missing my cat, Timothy, I would write a mournful clarinet part, unaware that Prokofiev, too, had chosen the clarinet to play the cat. Thinking the loss of Mademoiselle's neat teeth was also sad, I'd sketch in some horns, an oboe to bridge the quick-moving brightness of the opening with a modulation into the minor. Soon enough, the music made me realize that I needed all the strings in an orchestra to say how much I missed Nana, whose teeth were uneven and yellowing, but all her own. The pages would fill up quickly. Ignorant of harmonic considerations, I would compose from the top down, struggling to find the strong, broad bass line to contain and embrace all the breathlessness I'd written.

Turning in my work to Mademoiselle, I might be rewarded with another toothless smile before she found the weakest line in the score. "Come. You must learn the instrument."

I spent a good deal of the summer closeted in studios, trying to understand the range and capacity of instruments that were as foreign to me as the French countryside. "We are sorry to interrupt, but Miss Schaeffer has a favor she requires. Would you play for her this cello part?"

The cellist was nineteen years old, but with the unceasing patience of a much older man. I am sure that is why Mademoiselle brought me to Peter's practice room for my first lesson in her unconventional orchestration method.

"*Mais oui*, my pleasure. Do come in." A nod from Mademoiselle, and I was in the room with him, a boy-man with friendly eyes. A gentle guide, and a badly needed friend for a lonely little girl far from home. He didn't have the outward intensity of many of the young musicians at Fontainebleau. But oh, how he played. He saved it all up for his music. After he read through the unplayable cello part I'd written, Peter would ask me, "What are you trying to achieve?"

The first time he asked, I had no words to answer him. How could I tell him about my childish inspirations? How could I explain that when I put my number two pencil to staff paper the world widened, the present realities vanished, as the music rushed in?

"Listen to the cello's voice," he said, playing long, deep tones. "The cello offers resonance and body. The range is roughly the same as the French horn, but the sound has an entirely different quality. The quality of sound affects the quality of mood. The horn calls to action. It asks you to listen in a different way. Here, have you written a horn part?" When Peter played that part for me, I began to understand how I wanted to answer his question.

"Let me work on it some more. Will you be here in an hour?" When we met again, he played his new part.

"This is a mournful piece of music you have written, *petite mademoiselle*. So sad, and so beautiful. Is this what you want?"

"Yes, just that. *Merci*!" And I would rush off to find the horn player.

"It is the difference between wind and string." Emil, a

teacher in the program, had a compact belly, a mustache, and curly black hair going gray. He reached to pull his horn out of its case.

"Breath," he said, "breath is life. Wind players breathe life into their horns." I thought of Peter, and I knew he would be insulted by the unspoken comparison.

"But *monsieur*—"

"Quiet, now. Let me warm up. Then I will see what you have brought me." He fiddled with his mouthpiece, put my pages on his music stand.

"We'll talk—*ma petite philosophe*—but after we play your music."

"Hannah, I forbid you to write the melody. Only the bass until you hear it on the first play."

We were taking musical dictation; Mademoiselle would play eight measures on piano, and we would write down what we heard. She knew I had an ear for the melodic line—and I could capture the rhythms on the first play. But Mademoiselle's latest dictum meant my progress was slowed to the pace of my classmates. I would struggle through three plays, trying to block out the melody. My difficulty was not just learning to hear the harmonies; I didn't understand them. There was a lot of grounding that I lacked, basics that the other students already grasped.

One day after a particularly trying class, Mademoiselle sent me home with a Bach chorale. "Take the organ part, and work on it. We will meet in one week." She wanted me to analyze the piece, to break it down and label chords, but I knew I couldn't manage that on my own.

"This is not what I had in mind," she said, when I turned in an arrangement for string quartet with flute soloist. "But we'll work with it. Make enough copies for your classmates."

Three days later, my hand was still cramped when I passed

out the scores. There were no mimeos in Mademoiselle's universe.

"We will take this quintet to the garage." Mademoiselle had picked up odd Americanisms in her time abroad, but she also confused words. "We will lift up the roof, and take every little, tiny pipe out. Then we will put it all back together again. Hannah? Please distribute."

Mademoiselle asked me to listen and annotate my copy with the analysis markings as the class worked through the piece. While they dissected the arrangement into four, five, and one chords, debated over the odd seventh and the minor second I'd thrown in, I felt like I was riding in the backseat, listening to grown-ups talk about me as though I weren't even there.

At the end of the class, Mademoiselle passed out another bit of Bach, a chamber cantata. "Analyze this one for next week. And make sure your work is legible! Hannah, stay a moment, please." As the other students filed out, Mademoiselle studied my transcription of the class analysis.

"Very nice work. Do you understand what we did today?"

Her half-smile did me in. I began to cry, and soon I was out of control—tear drops—splat—on my desk, on my music.

"What is it?"

"You killed it! You killed the music!" I wiggled away from her and ran towards the door—landing headfirst in the softness of Emil's belly. I stayed where I was, my back to Mademoiselle, Emil's strong hands squeezing my shaking shoulders.

"What did you do to make our little one cry? Oh—you put her arrangement under the microscope today, *non*? I thought it could end up this way. You took the music out of her head, Nadia, and gave her only mathematics. Hannah can't hear notes and numbers yet, and you took away the notes."

Emil was exactly right. I was comforted, simply by his understanding.

Mademoiselle was quiet for another minute, then she spoke in French, "But you understand that she must learn to hold both in her mind at the same time?"

"*Bien sûr.*"

I started crying again; my advocate had submitted to my tormentor.

"Nadia," Emil paused, looking down at me. "She is ten years old."

"Of course, yes. You are right. But we have so little time."

"Still, perhaps there is a reason that your analysis class begins with music written centuries ago?"

"*Mais oui*, there are issues of musical era, development—"

"And when you analyze Palestrina, there is, conveniently, no one to offend."

"Hannah," she said, after a four-beat pause. "I only meant to make the analysis live for you, not to make your music die."

I remained in place, silent, unwilling still, to look at her.

"*Merci*, Emil," she said, and then she left the room.

—5—

Death, Mademoiselle.

That's what I've come to talk about today. Or—maybe, Life. I'm not sure.

Is it my age? Not necessarily. I've always had a penchant for the philosophical. You, Emil, even Peter—you teased me all the time about my need to examine, to ponder.

But speaking of age, give me a decade or so, and I'll be almost as old as you were when we met. I thought you were ancient. Of course, the toothlessness didn't help.

You know, dreams about losing our teeth are supposed to mean that we are experiencing, or fearing, a loss of power. But for me, the interpretation would be the exact opposite. I would be dreaming about coming into my full power. I would be dreaming of becoming *you*.

But back to death. It occurs to me that I've known you dead for longer than I knew you alive. You were in that terrible line-up of losses that began in my late twenties. First Nana, then Felicia, then you, and then Lenny. "That's a lot of grief to process in a relatively short span," a therapist told me a couple of years after Lenny died, when I found my way into her office. I remember being surprised by this observation. You'd taught me to move on.

"Don't mourn Rose," you told me a few weeks after my grandmother died. "Memorialize her."

I obeyed. For Nana, I wrote the first of my *Elegies*. Felicia got the second. You were the third, even though I didn't know that when I set to work. And Lenny, well, he got a whole memorial concert, a re-orchestrated Mass, and an arrangement called *Bernstein on Broadway*.

Death was just a part of life, you told me, and the main thing was to get as much done as possible before your expiration date. All right, that isn't exactly what you said, and I know you never used that term, expiration date. But you know what I mean. And besides, your English is perfect now in the afterlife, right?

Well, you *acted* as if it were all about getting the maximum amount accomplished.

Everything *important*, anyway.

But your duckling, presently, is unsure of what, exactly, is important.

Oh, God, yes, of course, the music. You don't have to yell at me!

But.

So.

Mademoiselle, my mother died.

You never really liked her, I know. You thought she held me back; you couldn't understand why she would ever question the importance of my musical training, or how she couldn't see the music in my essence, in my core—in my soul, as you used to like to say.

That bothered me about her, too. So did a whole lot of other things. If I'm honest—and what would be the point of dishonesty here, in this place of silent stone—I didn't like my mother that much either, or at least I didn't like the way she was with me.

But.

I guess I loved her.

I'm crying, Mademoiselle. Heaving, nose-dripping, where-is-coming-from sobbing.

No one will notice, or mind. That's one of the nice things about visiting you here.

Oh, look. The first cat. All black.

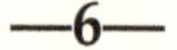

Mademoiselle's summer headquarters occupied a suite of rooms in the Fontainebleau palace, boasting the same high ceilings and elegant cornices that graced the rooms we used for classes. But this one was filled with overstuffed armchairs, family photographs, a grand piano, and glass-fronted bookcases stacked with scores. And a little gray cat stretched out on the piano bench. I made straight for her, and with feline caution, she allowed me to sit beside the bench—not on it—and rub her behind the ears. I missed my own cat, given away in the throes of relocation and family disorder.

"Ah, I see you have won over Tasha," said Mademoiselle, entering the room. I wasn't sure by the way she said it whether that was a good thing or a bad thing.

"*Bonjour Mademoiselle*," I ventured.

"*Bonjour ma chère*," she replied in a gentler tone, with the beginning of a smile, replaced almost instantly with a forehead-crunching frown. "It is essential we speak with frankness to each other."

This did not sound good. I wondered if I could get away with having this conversation from the floor, where I could stroke the cat for security. Mademoiselle, reading my mind, said, "I'll need you to sit here in the chair across from me. You can spend more time with Tasha later."

I could tell Mademoiselle was not at ease. I thought I might be getting a glimpse of that human side of her that Emil had told me was there. After the theory class incident, we'd taken a walk, and he explained some things to me.

"She can be harsh," he said, "but it is only because she has a large heart. If she let it out into the world without protection, she would not have survived her own life." He told me that her younger sister, Lili, had died young, and that her own mother was stricter with her than Mademoiselle would ever be with me. "Her mother dominated her," he said, checking to make sure that I understood the word. I could not imagine anyone ever dominating Mademoiselle.

"And add to all this that she was a woman in a man's world of music. *Bien sur*, Mademoiselle Boulanger is severe. What choice does she have? But she means well. She will, in every minute, have your best interests at heart. I do too. That's why I want to help you understand that she is human. Though sometimes, she will make you believe otherwise. Now, don't breathe a word of this conversation to your teacher!"

I felt myself sitting up straighter as Mademoiselle looked at me through her wire-rimmed glasses and began to speak. "Your grandparents were dear, dear friends of mine. Your grandfather made me feel welcome in Symphony Hall. Your grandmother invited me into their home. They were not wealthy; they were not patrons. They were open-armed American friends, and I cherished every moment I spent with them. Visiting your grandparents was like a small vacation for me. It was stolen time, time that I might have been teaching into the night, time that I might have been attending some social function that could help my career, but it always was time well spent.

"It would be a simple thing for me to accept you into Fontainebleau only on the basis of my association with Jacob and Rose. If your talent were small, I could teach you here without demanding more than you could manage. I could provide a safe musical haven for you, away from the troubles in your parents' marriage.

"But your talent is not small, and so my role changes. My

job is to stretch you past your limits, to test and expand your capacity. My job is to recover all the lost years in your musical life—I know you are only ten years old, but you have lost almost five years already, without a teacher since your grandfather passed away. I am suspicious of the word prodigy, but do you know what it means?"

I nodded. It was a question my schoolteachers had for my mother, mostly because my musical notation was consistently better than my handwriting.

"I don't know—and I don't care—whether you are a prodigy. I know your talent is huge, bigger than you are. Bigger than this palace. Imagine filling all the rooms of this palace with music. That is what you must do."

"And the stables, too?" I was thinking maybe I could get a horseback lesson out of this.

"Yes, the stables too."

"That is a lot of music."

"No more than you have inside of you." She moved toward the piano, signaling the end of the conversation, and the beginning of my first private lesson. "The only way you will ever hear the bass line is if you understand the range. You must study piano, in any case. We'll do both at once."

***

For the rest of that summer, Mademoiselle had me to her salon twice a week. I would sit beside her at the grand piano, trying not to stare at my teacher's large and powerful hands. I wondered if I would ever grow into hands like hers. They seemed miraculous and full of meaning that would only become clear when she played. But on summer afternoons in Mademoiselle's studio, I had to work to hear her play.

First, I had to muddle through my reading exercises, all in the left hand, all in my dreaded clef. Then, more piano work, some chords. Finally, she'd join in, and we would play four-hands. I felt such a relief to hear the top voices, at last; I could slip away into the music, past my poor technique and bass line frustrations. I was a miserable pianist, but I loved playing duets with Mademoiselle. I am sure I played my best when I felt her assurance right next to me.

After the four-hands, Mademoiselle would ask me to explain how melody and harmony worked together. Note by painstaking note, I identified chords, progressions, themes and counter themes. This part of my lesson was my least favorite, reminding me too much of what my classmates had done to my music. But my teacher would have none of my complaints about our musical demolitions. "We may be tearing down the music, but we are building your ears."

I touched my ears and began to giggle.

Mademoiselle heaved a sigh and attempted to look severe, but I could see a smile creeping in around the corners of her eyes. "This is very important," she continued.

I tried to look suitably serious, but a laugh sputtered out. The idea of building my ears! She reached across the piano and pinched my earlobes. "*Ma chère.* Just wait until we finish with these little ears of yours. With the talent you have and the training I will give you, these ears will take you to places you cannot imagine." This struck me even funnier—the image of my ears up ahead, leading me. Giant ears we'd built over many years at the piano. I was really giggling now, trying to squirm away from her.

"*Dites-moi*," she said.

And so, I told her about ears as big as skyscrapers leading me down the street. Ears I could climb inside. Rocket ears ready to blast off to outer space.

She listened to me carefully, as if the stories I was telling were of the greatest importance. "Write it."

"Pardon?" I said it half-French, half-English.

"For next week, write some ear stories and some music to accompany them." She was dead serious.

"Ear stories?"

"Yes silly, you just told me some. Think up some more and write the music to go with them. A little ear opera for us to play."

"Ear-opera-ear-opera-ear-opera." I began to sing and play.

"We are finished for today," Mademoiselle announced. "Stay for a snack."

***

Midsummer's Eve at Fontainebleau was sort of like a late April Fool's Day. There were no classes, and students would spend the day lounging by the usually off-limits reflecting pool, scheming up jokes to play on their teachers. That night, there would be a big party, with lots of food, dancing, even wine. The only rule? You must do no serious work on Midsummer's Eve, not a note is to be played or written in earnestness.

The teachers who starred in my Ear Opera were slightly tipsy teachers, all in costume, and I got to be the growing Ear. Mademoiselle conducted in a scarlet dress and a feathered hat, wardrobe choices to help her from taking the performance too seriously. She looked funny; I looked ridiculous; we all looked idiotic. Everybody laughed and clapped and whistled at the end.

Then, by some secret signal, the record player began blasting Elvis Presley. Mademoiselle lifted left palm to head, as if she could not bear to hear such rubbish on the sacred grounds of her school. At just that moment, Emil took her conducting hand and began dancing her around the stage. Peter came to me, and said, "I've always wanted to dance with a giant ear." Soon, everyone was up on the stage, a great and grand finale to The Ear Opera.

"You see, your teacher is human after all," whispered Emil when he cut in to dance with me. It was exactly what I was thinking.

"Why can't she be this way more often?"

He laughed. "Oh, she is human all the time, *ma petite*. That is why she takes life so seriously."

The next day was business as usual. I didn't have a lesson scheduled, but Mademoiselle asked me to come by for a few minutes after lunch. She was wearing her dark uniform and her sensible shoes, no hat. But her mood was bright. "*Ah, la petite Rossini*," she greeted me, congratulating me on the debut of my first comic opera. "A little silliness is not a bad thing."

Tasha greeted me with a leg-rub. I reached down to pat her.

"It seems Tasha is always present for your most important interviews," Mademoiselle said, before she turned serious. "We need to discuss your future."

"We are *always* discussing my future."

"Your immediate future," she clarified, "the coming school year."

"Oh." This was not a topic I wanted to discuss. I wasn't looking forward to going home to the new apartment to live with my mother and starting a new school year in a new school, no friends, no kitty, no father.

"I think that you should remain in France. Come with me to Paris, continue your studies."

Always, when I thought about the end of the summer, I felt sad. I saw myself leaving Fontainebleau, leaving my teacher. I'd tried to construct the place we would live from the letters my mother and grandmother had sent me, but I couldn't. I could only get as far as leaving Fontainebleau, taking a train to a plane, being picked up at the airport in New York. Would my grandmother come to meet me, too? I hoped so. Then I could see us driving, driving, driving to this new home. I could even imagine my grandmother's careful questions about my summer and my mother's nervousness as we got closer to the apartment. But I could not get us all the way there in my day-dreams, only closer and closer, from New York to Massachusetts, from highway to back roads—to where? I'd never lived in an apartment before. My ten-year old experience of home was the one suburban neighborhood I knew as mine.

"Hannah." She knew I wasn't paying attention. "I need to know what you think of my idea. Would you like to stay?"

"I don't know."

"Let me tell you why I believe this is the best path for you. Are you listening?"

I nodded.

"*Ma chère*, I am an old woman. I don't know how many more summers I have left at Fontainebleau. But I know that you need more than my limited attention—even if I have another lifetime of summers. You need daily lessons; you need a place to nurture your music. You need to attend concerts, to hear great music performed by the best musicians in the world. Yes, you need a general education, too, and we'll arrange for schooling when we get to Paris. I have a room upstairs at Rue Ballu, and you can live there. This is not an offer I make lightly. If you were merely talented, I would never make this suggestion. But you have shown me this summer that you are a hard worker, dedicated to learning the craft as well as the art. We have lots to do. And I think it would be best that we continue our work without interruption."

What would it be like to live with Mademoiselle? Is that what she was saying? To live in Paris? What would my mother say? Would my grandmother come to visit me? What about my father? Where was he now? Would he know I was living here, or would he turn up one day on my mother's new doorstep, looking for me, asking if he could take me out for a pizza only to find that I wasn't even living in the same country anymore?

"Think about your music." She said it as if she knew I was considering all the wrong things in my silence. "Would you like to continue our work together?"

That answer was easy. "Yes." I said it without hesitation.

"Then I will write to your mother."

I felt my small world whirring out of control. For Mademoiselle, the music was the only consideration. Even as I dreaded going to a strange apartment with my mother, the alternative I'd hoped for was happy reunion of my mother and father and a return to our old home.

She could sense, maybe, that I was having trouble processing all this on the spot, but Mademoiselle didn't offer me time, only a second chance to answer. "Do you want to stay and study with me?"

"Okay." I said. Not yes, or even no. Just *okay*.

A half-hearted assent that would change my life.

—7—

It was raining on and off all day, so I postponed my morning visit, puttering around the apartment, making lists, taking measurements. I need to lease a piano. Though that assumes I have a spare note of my own left in my cluttered brain, which honestly seems a big assumption.

Oh, stop shaking your head—you don't think I know that I am feeling sorry for myself?

On the way up the hill, I ducked into the corner bakery. I picked out a ham and cheese croissant for a late lunch, but really, I was there for the melodic, predictable exchange of greetings and thanks, the way the bakery ladies wrap up their treasures with a practiced twist of the wrist: "*Voilà*."

I paid and sang my part: "*Merci, Madame, au revoir!*"

La dee, da-dah dee-DAH—you know the melody—right?

As I emerged from the bakery, the sun came out, lighting the tops of the buildings. There's an interval, after a spring shower on a Paris afternoon, that makes you believe in redemption. Or at least an active afterlife. By the time I turned onto Rue Rachel, I had to reach into my purse for sunglasses. At the gate, another song: *Bonjour Madame/Bonjour Monsieur*, this time with the guard.

I climbed the steps. Took a quick right, then a left, following the row of stones. And here you are, on the edge of Division 33. With your mother, your father, your sister. Lily. *Boulanger*, it says in raised letters on the weathered marble headstone. The built-in garden atop the tomb needs tending. I will get to that, I promise.

In your marble vase, there's a fresh red rose in the center of the daisies I delivered yesterday. Someone must have visited you this morning, Mademoiselle. Another former student, or a student of a student.

You died without heirs of the usual kind, but generations of musical lives will be touched by your influence. The legacy of a great teacher.

Did you ever consider that while you were living? You were always so practical. You told me more than once that you had to find a way to support your mother and your sister, that the income from teaching was more reliable than the income from performing or conducting or composing. Yet, you did all those things—until you didn't. You were a gifted teacher, to be sure—look at the rose, look at the Copland overtures, the Glass operas—I could go on. But you were also terrifying. You drove away as many students as you kept. You were a one-person arbiter of musical futures, certainly the arbiter of mine. But what happened to yours? Why did you retreat to your studio?

But if you hadn't—would there be roses in your vase?

There's a grave, not far from yours, with a giant, polished granite pen, the nib stabbing the flat stone. *Writer*, it says, under a name I have never heard.

I don't think I'd want a giant baton on my grave. A little phallic, don't you think? And if that's the case—well, take this writer: is his death-pen sized to his reputation, or to his ambition, or is it just a declaration of his eternal manhood?

Eternal Manhood. What an awful concept. I guess I kind of hope we eventually escape the bonds of gender—pure spirit, right?

I remember years ago, New Year's Eve of 1979, to be precise. My father was still alive, and he and his wife were in New York, and we were visiting Lenny. All afternoon, Dad and Lenny had been riffing on jazz standards—Lenny actually bought my father a clarinet that day, when he discovered he played. Anything for a duet partner, I guess. You know Lenny—expansive, the heart of a lion—leonine appetites too. That night, it was just the four of us. And the way you do, when the year is disappearing, we were talking about time—and people—passing. Lenny was thinking of Felicia, lost a year earlier to cancer, and I was thinking of Nana, and of you. You'd passed away that October.

Joanne—my father's wife—wondered aloud if we thought you and Felicia and my grandmother were still around in some form.

"I like to believe they can hear us now, but I hate to think they can listen in whenever they want," I said. I was still in my thirties and worried about you tuning in to find me in bed with a man.

"Or watch," Lenny added, as if his thoughts were following mine. "Like we are some kind of Earth-TV."

Lenny—*Earth TV*. If he subscribes, he must have a million channels, channel surfing on some giant heavenly remote.

And you, Mademoiselle? I imagine you would seek out all the great performances; you'd be less interested in the human drama. You'd avoid long talks like the one I plan to have with you. But on the other hand, I know you won't ignore me, either.

After all—*duckling*, remember?

—8—

"Katherine, do you have to smoke in the car?"

It was before anybody knew how bad smoking was for you, but my grandmother hated it all the same. She especially hated that her daughter smoked. "So unladylike," she'd once said to me. "It is a terrible habit, and I hope to God you don't pick it up."

"Open your window," my mother said.

I sat in the back seat, watching the smoke take sides.

Hours, and several cigarettes later, we arrived at the apartment. A walk-down in a concrete building, stairs with spaces in between them, covered in ugly red-orange carpet.

"The library is right next door," my mother said. "You can borrow all the Nancy Drew you want." I stole a secret look at my grandmother. Nana had sent me the complete set during the course of the summer. And I'd read every one between theory assignments.

As my mother led us to the back of the apartment, I thought about how disappointed Mademoiselle had been when she received the reply from my mother, and how worried she was about my musical future. I'd never been sure about the idea of living with Mademoiselle, but Emil and Peter had promised they'd be in Paris, too. They gave me maps with Mademoiselle's neighborhood highlighted in yellow. Emil told me the hot chocolate in Paris was the best in the world, and Peter told me Mademoiselle's apartment was huge—the living room where she taught had an organ and a grand piano.

"Here's your bedroom," my mother said.

A dark cave, dominated by my white canopy bed, the one I'd loved and wanted so badly. My parents had bought it for me two years earlier, paying "on time." My father had made a joke of it. On the nights he was home, he'd put me to bed, telling me just how much of the bed we owned. He marked squares with his fingers; at first, we owned just a square inch; a month later, a square foot. As the months passed, he would lay his big body on the bed: first curled up, then stretching out a bit—the length of an arm, a leg. Finally, we were all paid up. If he were here, my father could lie right in the middle now, making snow angels in the covers to show we owned it all. But my beloved bed looked huge in the small room—and temporary—like it was stored in somebody's basement.

"There aren't any windows, I know, but who needs them when you sleep? There are nice big windows in the kitchen and the living room."

"Sure," I said. "Who needs windows when you sleep?" I was only echoing my mother's words, but she didn't seem to notice. She needed me to like the place, I thought, to help convince my grandmother that she'd made the right choice. I wondered how long they had argued about this move, this apartment, my staying in Paris or coming home.

We followed my mother into her bedroom. She had a new bed, smaller than the one she'd shared with my dad. "Your father needed the big bed. He's so tall. It was made especially for him."

Back in the living room, I sat on the footstool of the big chair, glad my large father hadn't claimed that too. Mom lit a cigarette. Nana wrinkled her nose and headed for the kitchen. She returned with three glasses of lemonade, fresh with real lemons, the way she knew I liked it.

"I think I might sweeten mine a little more." My mother winked at me. She was going to add some whisky to it. It was a joke my father and she used to share, sitting together, watching Ed Sullivan and drinking whisky with lemon juice.

While my mother was out of the room, my grandmother began asking me about my summer. "And how did you like Miss Boulanger?" she asked, giving me a big encouraging smile that made me want to cry.

"She is strict, but she is a good teacher. She taught me a lot."

"She wrote to say you were an excellent student, that you worked hard and that you show great promise. Your grandfather would be very proud of you."

"That's my Hannah," my mother said, walking back into the room, "wowing them on the Continent."

I smiled uncertainly in her general direction.

"I'm proud of you, too, dear, but you are too young to stay in a foreign country with some old woman we don't even know—"

"Nadia Boulanger was a friend of your father's and mine. She isn't a stranger."

"Well, strange enough, to suggest a ten-year-old stay in Paris, far away from her family."

"I don't think you realize just how talented Hannah is. Or how renowned Nadia Boulanger is in the music world. She doesn't make such offers lightly. She commands a high fee from her students. She offered to find a patron, and until then, to teach Hannah for free!"

"Of course I realize Hannah is talented. She's my *daughter.*" She placed the emphasis on *daughter*, as if that explained all of it, explained all of me.

My grandmother looked my way. "You must be starving after two plane rides."

"I am." They both looked at me expectantly, as if I was supposed to do something. But what? They were the grown-ups here. I got up, taking my glass and Nana's into the well-lighted kitchen.

"Rinse them out, will you Hon?" my mother called after me. "Now that there's only two of us, we'll need to be extra neat." This made not the least bit of sense to me, but I rinsed out our glasses. When I walked back into the living room, my mother and grandmother were just where I'd left them.

"Are we going to go eat, or what?"

"What do you want for supper, dear?" my grandmother asked. "You get to choose. It's your welcome home dinner."

"Pizza," I said without hesitation. My mother groaned.

"Pizza," my grandmother confirmed. "Well, I guess we had something else in mind, but—"

"I haven't had pizza all summer long."

"And you survived without extra cheese!" my mother waved her cigarette in my direction. "You missed your pizza." She paused a few seconds. "But did you miss me?"

"Yes," I answered immediately, "I did miss you, Mom." And I realized as I said it that I wasn't just saying it for the brownie points, or to make her feel better. I did miss my mother, sarcastic and smoky, beautiful, but always a little disorderly.

She rubbed out her cigarette in the ashtray before she looked up at me. She smiled her thousand-watt movie star smile. I smiled back, loving her in that moment—sure that if I didn't, no one else would love her for me.

***

At my new school, my classmates were learning the things I'd learned the year before.

I stayed home as often as I could. My mother was working, and I'd have the apartment to myself. I'd wander from room to room, singing the harmony exercises that Mademoiselle had taught me. I wrote letters to my teacher, but I never mailed them. I wished for a piano, but there was none, nor were there any music lessons for me.

"You need a vacation from all that," my mother said. "I don't want you to end up being one-dimensional." She would come home for lunch and make us Campbell's soup. "How are you feeling? Better?"

"Yeah, a little," I would say, leaving room for not feeling well enough to go to school the next day.

On the days I did go to school, I was the teacher's reluctant assistant. She would ask me to help with long division and reading. I hated helping because it made a point of me, but I hated just sitting there, too. My classmates were tolerant, considering. Maybe they could tell I wasn't one of those kids, always raising their hands, trying to show off what they knew. I just sat still until I was called on, doodling musical notes.

Then one day, we had geography. We looked at maps of the world, memorizing the names of countries from their outlines. Then, we had to pick a city we'd like to visit, look it up in the encyclopedia, and write six paragraphs about it. It could be anywhere in the world. I picked Paris. But I didn't look it up in the encyclopedia. I got all my information from the stories that Emil and Peter and Mademoiselle had told me.

The next day, just before recess, the teacher asked me to stay behind. Sitting at her desk, she asked me where I'd learned about Paris. I was still at my desk too, and without a class full of kids, she seemed far away. "From my friends," I said, "Peter and Emil."

"The assignment was to look up information in the encyclopedia. Did you do that?"

"I didn't need to look it up. I was practically there."

"Hannah, I know it's hard for you to be in a class where you've already learned a lot of the lessons, but that doesn't mean you can make things up when I give you an assignment that requires research."

"I didn't make anything up! It's all true. Ask Emil or Peter —or ask Mademoiselle. She would never lie!"

"Mademoiselle." She sounded tired.

"My teacher."

"I'm afraid I don't understand. I'm your teacher. Do you know what product is produced in Paris? That was supposed to be in your report."

"It *was* in there. Bread—a bakery on every corner. Bread-bread-bread-bread!"

"Yes, I have heard that is true about Paris," she conceded. "Now who is Mademoiselle?"

"I told you! My teacher! My music teacher. She lives there in Paris. And I should be living there too!"

"In Paris." Measured, articulated quarter notes, no rise.

"Yes! Don't you see?"

She didn't. "I'm going to give you some time alone. I can see you're upset. We'll talk some more later." With that, she went out to recess. And I stayed inside.

***

We didn't talk later like she said. Instead, she called my mother in for a conference.

"Your teacher says you aren't being very cooperative at school, and she is worried about your attendance. She says when you are there you have trouble following instructions. Is this true?"

"I hate her."

"That's not an answer, young lady."

"It's my answer," I said, before she sent me to my cave.

The next time my mother was called in for a conference, she couldn't go. My grandmother went instead. Afterwards, she took me out for an ice cream. "That woman didn't know a thing about you. Why didn't you tell her that you were studying with Miss Boulanger?"

"She didn't even believe me that bread was the product of Paris. In my geography report." I clarified.

"You told her bread—"

"Well, Emil told me—"

My grandmother was laughing. "Oh, my little wonder. Now how can we get you out of this terrible woman's class and back to your music teacher?"

"Mom won't let me go."

"She might—if you cause any more trouble at school." She winked at me.

The next week, I worked on perfecting my musical notation. And I got really dumb at long division.

"Hannah, I can't go to teacher conferences every week. I am missing time from work."

"I don't see why you need to go. I'm getting all A's. What's the problem?"

"She says you have an attitude problem, and I'm beginning to agree with her."

I stayed silent.

"Try to do better, okay? With just the two of us now, we both have to try harder."

Try harder. Be neater. Be more careful. Have less fun. With just the two of us. The way she talked, you'd think my father had been amputated.

"Ma, I don't know what to do with her. She's missing school, and that makes them upset. And when she is there, she doesn't pay attention. I've asked her to try harder. If her father was here, maybe things would be better."

My ear to my bedroom door, I rolled my eyes. As if my father had all the answers.

"What did the teacher say to you today?" my mother asked.

"I met with the teacher *and* the principal," my grandmother said.

"Oh no." I heard the swish of my mother's lighter.

"They said that Hannah has the classic profile for a juvenile delinquent. Smart, frustrated, recalcitrant."

"They said that? Oh my God. Do you think it's true?"

"I think she's bored. But they know better than I about those things."

"What should we do, Ma?"

"Well, they think Hannah needs discipline, and music gives her that."

"You really think she would get better if we sent her away to study?"

"It's worth a try. I can write to Miss Boulanger to see if her offer still stands."

"Maybe just for the rest of the school year, take the pressure off while I get settled." My mother's voice was drifting off.

"It's worth a try," my grandmother repeated.

"Yeah," my mother exhaled. "It's worth a try."

—9—

Emil's in a wheelchair, now—I didn't know until I saw him—or more accurately, until I noticed he wasn't standing to greet me as I approached the table. We'd set up a dinner. Parisian style, in a proper restaurant; one course following another. And another.

"Hannah, so good to see you. Let me introduce you to Inspector Jean-Luc Bourlou."

Bourlou was tall, angular, Black, and put-together in the way only French men can be: dove gray suit, white shirt, yellow tie.

"Maestro," he said to me. "*Enchanté.*"

I echoed his words, but Mademoiselle, I was not at all enchanted to meet him. I'd been so looking forward to sharing a meal with Emil, no one else. Even a handsome stranger. Maybe *especially* not a handsome stranger.

"Please, call me Hannah."

Emil jumped in. "*Oui-oui*—let's dispense with titles. Jean-Luc is a family friend. He offered to come along. It's not easy anymore for me to travel on my own."

"*Merci,*" I said. "I appreciate your kindness."

You're relieved to hear I still have some manners. You were a big fan of graciousness above all, and I was doing my best. What I wanted to say was that it would have been fine to cancel dinner, that we might have figured out a way to eat alone. Oh, I'm horrible. You think I don't know that? Impatient, too—I can't imagine where I picked that up.

"You can call me Luke," he said. "I know Americans

prefer a strong consonant."

"And you know this how?"

"I studied in the States."

"And Hannah studied here." Emil seemed pleased by the symmetry. He was comfortable in his role as host, maneuvering the conversation like a skillful driver on a narrow mountain road.

The inspector told me that he had followed my career, that he is a fan of my work, and suggested at least seven times that I ought to call him Luke. For my part, I told the stories that Emil instructed me to tell on cue. I was obedient, but barely present. Then, Inspector Luke-the-Fan Bourlou asked me how I came to study with Nadia Boulanger.

I was relieved I wouldn't have to give my "Why Boulanger Matters" lecture. In the States, even dedicated symphony subscribers are mostly ignorant of the master teacher who influenced a century of American music. I hate to tell you that. Here in Paris, you share the plaque on your apartment building with your composer-sister Lili. Together, you have a *Place*. But that doesn't assure any consistent awareness among your countrymen. When you say *Boulanger* these days, most Parisians assume you are talking about the proprietor of your preferred bakery.

Emil smiled. "She almost didn't."

The exchange led us to safe ground, familiar territory: the past, with its own unexpected twists—not always easy to navigate, but ever-leading to the present moment—which is to say, at least know we have survived it.

"My grandmother managed to persuade my mother I would become a teenage criminal if I didn't study with Mademoiselle."

Emil smiled. "Luke knows something about teenage criminals—especially the musical kind."

"Musical criminals?" I could not resist the bait.

"No—no." The Inspector smiled, folded his napkin and placed it on the table. "They haven't rushed through a rest or played a wrong note. Well—they may have—they do that all the time. But that sort of mistake is allowed when we are students, isn't it, Maestro?"

Emil jumped in. "Jean Luc started a program—how many years ago?"

"Twelve years this month."

"He started a program for young people who are—"

"They are in detention, in a home. A halfway house, they would call it in the States."

"And they play music with instruments that Jean Luc has supplied. They take lessons and they have an orchestra." His tone was full of admiration for the younger man's work. "Jean Luc plays trumpet. He's an excellent player. "

Emil said that because he knows I am a musical snob. So is he. So were you, Mademoiselle. Music is no place for part-timers, right?

"You have many lives, Inspector Bourlou." Even I could hear the edge in my voice. The anger. I knew it was one hundred percent misplaced. I mean—the guy works with troubled children—it's more than I've ever done. Not to mention he got Emil here to meet with me. And Emil seems to like him. What was my problem?

I just wasn't prepared to be "on" last night. I have to live too much of my life being nice to people I don't know, and I'd come to Paris to get away from that job requirement. No excuse, I know. But on the other hand, you were all about not wasting precious time—and well, I felt like that was exactly what I was doing.

If he noticed my tone, the inspector gave no indication. He was nonplussed, responding with effortless charm. "I'd much rather hear about your singular life, Maestro," he said.

He was not calling me Hannah. I was not calling him Luke.

I was saved from my own sharp tongue by the arrival of a dish of chocolate mousse that I hadn't ordered.

"*Café, thé à la menthe, digestif?*" the waiter asked us.

When Emil ordered port for the table, I was consumed with murderous thoughts. I needed dinner to be over. I needed to make a duet date with Emil and to figure out a way to make sure all our future meals together would be on our own. Otherwise, I imagined, there could be a string of dinners, a rotating cast of "friends of the family."

But then, after complimenting Emil's choice in wine, the inspector invited me to try out the acoustics in Saint Chapelle. I've never played there, only conducted—and that was years ago.

"Call me," he said, writing his mobile number on the back of his business card, "and we'll arrange it for a noon hour next week."

So maybe the dinner wasn't the waste of time I thought it was. But I didn't get to tell Emil what I wanted to tell him. I wanted to talk with him before I came back to see you.

Oh well, I guess I'll just let you know, right now.

Mademoiselle, it seems that—well—after nineteen years on the podium, I am soon to be fired by the Los Angeles Philharmonic.

—10—

I'm guessing my grandmother didn't tell Nadia Boulanger that I had the classic profile for a juvenile delinquent. All these years later, I still don't know what Nana wrote in that letter. But I do know something about Mademoiselle's response. She said she had two requirements before she could consider accepting me as a student again. First, my mother must write to her personally to state she wanted me to continue my studies. Second, I must be prepared to make a three-year commitment.

Nana was especially worried about that second part. She thought it was important for my mother to believe she was only sending me away till the end of the school year. When summer arrived, Nana was sure she'd be able to persuade my mother that I should study again at the American Conservatory at Fontainebleau. What was there for me to do at home? As September approached, Nana thought she'd say, "Oh, but she is doing so well there. Why disturb a good thing? Remember last year?"

Nana wrote back, explaining her alternate plan, saying how hard it would be to talk my mother into three years all at once. "Give her time," she wrote.

Mademoiselle replied to Nana by transatlantic telephone. "I am seventy-one years old. I don't have time. And I can't find her a patron unless I have some promise Hannah will be here to study and learn and perform; otherwise she would not be considered as a serious musician."

My grandmother, having drained her savings to get me to

Fontainebleau, understood the value of a patron. She wondered if this patron would be willing to fund more than my music lessons. What about paying my way home three times a year for those three years?

"Ah, Rose, you are an astute negotiator. If you get your daughter's promise, I will find a way to get Hannah home three times each year."

***

"Think of it as boarding school," Nana said, when she broached the subject after Sunday dinner at her house. My mother was tapping her fingers on the table, wanting a cigarette, but knowing that smoking was banned at her mother's table.

"Boarding school? When a kid goes off to boarding school, they are maybe a couple of states away. Maybe she would be in Connecticut or somewhere. This is Paris. Three *years*?"

"But we can't pay for this ourselves. If we want Hannah to have every opportunity, we need to agree to the patron's wishes."

"The *patron*. It sounds like something out of the 16th century. Next, you'll be telling me that Hannah's staying at a villa in Italy, playing her flute for some half-blind count or something."

"I don't think they have counts in Italy," I offered. My mother's head jerked in my direction. Mistake. She'd forgotten I was there, and now I had gone and reminded her. She stared at me, tapping sixteenth notes on her unused spoon.

"Hannah wants this," Nana said.

My mother turned her head from me to her mother and back to me again. She stopped tapping. "Is this what you want? Do you want to go to Paris for three years?"

I shrugged.

"That's not an answer, Hannah Schaefer."

"I'll get to come home for visits, right?"

"Miss Boulanger will see to that. You'll come home for the Christmas holidays, and sometime between spring and summer, and one other time—early fall, Thanksgiving, whenever you like." This was my grandmother, speaking as much to my mother as to me.

"You haven't answered me," my mother was persisting.

I knew she wanted me to prefer her company to the chance to study with Mademoiselle. And surely, I loved my mother more than my teacher. But I did want to go to Paris. I thought about all the music that Mademoiselle said was in my soul. How could I ever take it out from that hidden place if I stayed here? I needed to study, and I needed my teacher, strict and somber and demanding.

"Well, I can't go to school here," I said.

"That's the truth. You can't. Oh, I'm sorry, honey, but you'll have to go." My mother got up from her chair and stood behind mine. She leaned down, reached her arms around me, and gave me a squeeze. "Yes, darling, you'll have to go. It will be all right. Don't worry."

***

Later that evening, my mother wrote to Mademoiselle and offered me up for three years—all the while apologizing to me, reassuring me that I would come home for holidays, that I would not be lonely in Paris, that this was the best thing for me, even though it would be very hard. I went along with her version of events, though I was thrilled by the idea of returning to Mademoiselle. I remembered being afraid of Paris back when I was at Fontainebleau, but now I was fearless and ready to depart on a moment's notice. I felt the music bursting out of me, and I knew there was no place for it to go but Paris.

Once my fate was sealed, my mother took me shopping. She used my father's erratic child support checks to buy me "a few very fine things" from stores where we'd never dared to shop. I needed to make the right impression, my mother said. I remember the swing coat we bought at Lord & Taylor's: cherry red, boiled wool with a little fur collar and rounded pockets. I loved that coat. "We'll buy it a little large so you won't grow out of it so quickly. In the meantime, an extra layer will fill it up." My mother had good taste, and that coat lasted me almost four Parisian winters before I had to give it up.

We packed my new clothes, my music, and some schoolbooks my mother insisted that I take along. "I know this is hard for you Hannah," she would say again and again, "but I really think it is the best thing for us to do right now. You'll understand a little better when you're older." Or, "It will be difficult at first, but you'll get used to it, and you'll be home for vacation before you know it." I would nod and stay silent. I knew that it was important for her to believe that I was unenthusiastic about the trip.

She'd reached my father–always elusive in those days—to tell him I'd be leaving soon, and one night he came by to take me out for roast beef sandwiches. "Slice it extra thin," he said with authority to the woman behind the counter.

"I hear you are off to Paris," he said, after we slid into a red plastic booth.

I nodded.

"Well, I am very proud of you. You are quite the girl."

"Thanks," I said, reaching for my 7-Up.

He smiled and unwrapped the tin foil covering his sandwich. He shook some salt onto the roast beef and began to eat. Halfway through his sandwich he spoke again. "I don't think I'll be able to visit you over there," he said. "But who knows, maybe I will win big one day and come see you in

Paris." He pronounced it 'Paree'. He smiled across the table at me, and I smiled back at him. My father was always at his best when he was imagining what he might do when he won big.

"But just in case—in case I don't make it over there—I want you to know I love my girl." I took another bite from my sandwich. I was afraid to look at him. "How's that roast beef?" he asked.

"Extra thin," I said.

"That's the way we like it." In silence, we finished our sandwiches.

We stopped for an ice cream on the way home, and we didn't talk about Paris. I don't remember if we spoke at all. My father wasn't much for talking. He'd always relied on my mother to keep the conversation going. I guess I had too, because I felt at a loss for words whenever I was around him. Or maybe it was because the conversations I wanted to have with him were impossible. I wanted to ask him if he would ever come home again, if he had really stopped loving my mother. I wanted to tell him that he didn't need to win big in order to come back, that we were happy just to have him show up for dinner. I wanted to ask him if the stories about the loan sharks were true, and I wanted to ask did those men have big teeth and scary jaw lines? I wanted to ask him if he was afraid of them; was he ever afraid, was he ever afraid of being alone at night the way I knew my mother was?

I remember once, when we were out for pizza, when he seemed in an extra-good mood. "Good day at the track, " he said to me, winking as we ordered an extra cheese with pepperoni. On our way back to the car, I asked him to come home. He looked away from me and lit a cigarette.

"I can't," was all he said.

I didn't ask him to explain, and he didn't patronize me by saying I would understand when I was older. He just smoked his cigarette down to the bottom, then flicked it onto the ground where he stamped it out. I thought that I would continue the conversation on another of our evenings out, that I would ask him why not, that I would convince him that he was wrong, that sure, he could come back, that we could make it work. The apartment was a little small, but we could make room for him, and I knew my mother was lonely and would want him back.

But I never asked him about coming home again. I couldn't forget how sad he sounded when he said he couldn't come home, and I guess I didn't want to remind him of that sadness. I don't know if I guessed that the sadness was with him all the time. Did I never ask again to shield him from the pain of my question, or to protect myself from the pain of his response? I don't know. But the subject never came up again.

***

My mother took a day off work to take me to the airport, and my grandmother arrived the night before to make sure I was ready. In a strange role reversal, my mother seemed calm, and my grandmother seemed nervous. "You have everything you need?" Nana kept asking me.

Finally, my mother said, "Ma, she's fine. We've spent the last four weeks shopping. Trust me, she has everything she needs."

"What about your flute? You are going to carry that with you, right?"

"Uh-huh, my flute and a couple of recorders."

"Your music?"

"That's packed in my trunk. It's too heavy to carry."

"I'm sure all your luggage will be fine." I knew that what she really wanted to say was, I hope your bags aren't lost or you'll lose all your music.

"Ma, this isn't like you. You're the one who convinced me this was the best thing for her. Why are you so worried all of the sudden?" My mother and I looked across the dinner table at my grandmother. After a beat, Nana seemed to realize that she was expected to answer this question. She set down her fork.

"I know that Hannah will be just fine. I know that this is absolutely the best thing we could ever do for her. But I feel like we are shipping her off to her destiny." She paused, turning to look at me. "My mother—your mother's grandmother and your great-grandmother—came over to this country on a boat when she wasn't much older than you. Her big sister was already here, and she met my mother at the dock. They worked as maids of course—'domestics' they called them—but they made lives for themselves, found husbands, raised families, and here we are today. It all worked out. When I think of my mother now, I imagine her as a young girl, making that trip all alone, and I think of how brave she must have been. How strong and hopeful.

"Now, Hannah, you are making the journey in reverse—no, not to Ireland, but back across the sea. And I know in my bones that you, too, will change more lives than your own by going to Paris. When you're my age and you have children and grandchildren of your own, there will be something true in their lives that wouldn't be there if you hadn't made that trip. I wonder what it will be."

My mother sneaked a glance my way. I looked down at my plate, not wanting to give anything away. I was puzzled by Nana's words, but I knew she was saying something important.

"Hannah," Nana said, "Your grandfather is so proud of you." I remember that was how she said it, *your grandfather is*, not *would be* or *would have been*. That present tense startled me; I looked up, right into my grandmother's eyes. I saw tears in the corners. I hoped she wouldn't cry. My grandmother was the strongest one at the table—despite her nervous questions. If she cried, we all cried.

***

"Hannah, is your toothbrush packed?" The next afternoon, my grandmother was all business.

"My toothbrush?"

"Your toothbrush, Miss. You used it this morning. Is it packed?"

"No."

"Good. Go brush your teeth again before you pack it up. Then, check your room to make sure you haven't forgotten a tiny thing. We're off in six minutes." My grandmother never said five minutes or ten minutes, or even a minute the way people do. Long before digital clocks, she specified the exact number of minutes.

It was another long ride, endless it seemed. Nana kept the conversation going for as long as she could, but finally she gave in and suggested we listen to the radio. I thought about the last ride home from the airport. I thought about how many more times we might make this trip in the next three years. Would it become routine? *Just taking Hannah to the airport; I'll be back tonight.*

With the radio as background noise and no requirement for conversation, I allowed myself to imagine Paris. I'd pored over the pictures in the books from the library, and I knew all the highlights. But I wouldn't be living at the Eiffel Tower. I knew from studying the maps last summer that Mademoiselle lived on the north side of the river. But for all the pictures I'd seen, I couldn't really imagine what an apartment in Paris would be like. I was pretty sure, however, that it wouldn't be like our apartment here. Mademoiselle had enough space to house me, a pipe organ, and a grand piano. She held classes there, too. It must be really big, her apartment. It probably isn't in a basement, either.

Waiting for the plane, we sat in a silent row: Nana, me, my mother. But when they called my plane for boarding, we all began speaking at once, interrupted by the stewardess who had come to collect me. "I'm Tina. I'll be helping you get on and off the plane and making sure you have a good flight. Are you ready?"

My mom grabbed me first. "Hannah," she said, just my name. She gave me a kiss and released me. "You wire us as soon as you get there."

I turned to say goodbye to my grandmother. She took both of my hands into hers. "Oh, honey, I'm so proud of you. I'm so glad you are going back to study with Miss Boulanger. But I'll miss you, too! I'll write you once a week, I promise."

I nodded, holding back tears. She pulled me to her and stroked my hair before she passed me back to my mother.

"Don't forget me," my mother whispered as she released me.

Tina took my hand. We had to walk outside and up a long flight of stairs to get to the plane. On the top step, I turned, and I gave a little wave to Ma and Nana. They waved furiously back at me. And as if I were the queen of the world, I blew them each a kiss before I turned to cross the metal threshold.

—11—

Of course we won't *only* talk about death. I can see where you might tire quickly of that subject, Mademoiselle.

Death, and work. Wait, that's death and taxes—certainties in life. Was that Ben Franklin?

Love and work—Freud, right? Or Jung. Damn. I'm not sure, but I know one of those guys believed they were the essential ingredients in a fulfilling life. That doesn't sound like Freud.

And love and death: Woody Allen. But maybe Nietzsche first.

You would know all this—well, maybe not Woody Allen. Just as well, he didn't turn out to be so admirable in the human being department. How did you feed that vast intellect of yours and keep it nourished? Maybe I need to read more books and fewer scores.

Okay. Death, life, love, work. Oh yes, we're definitely going to cover love in our discussions, and you can't wait, right? But here's what I want to talk about today: is there a death of work? I mean, if the work is music, then the work is everlasting, right? Even if I lose my podium?

I know what you are thinking: If I'm not conducting, I'll have more time to write all that music you believed I had inside me. *Fill the stables.*

The thing is, I love my job. Well, I don't love the back-office politics, and yes, I would like more time to compose. But I love being immersed in the music, uncovering its essence in a score, translating notes to sound—beautiful, important, must-be-heard sound. Every day with my orchestra is a good day.

And my contract grants me a year to compose for every six I work at the Phil. There's some sort of agreement that L.A. gets right of first refusal on any new symphonic work I produce while I am away, but otherwise, I am free of commitments—no guesting, no admin tasks, no command appearances for funders. And this is year seven, the final year of the current contract. I've been looking forward to this time, a breather before I return for six more years.

Or so I thought until Mel called.

"We have a problem, Schaeffer."

You remember Mel? You insisted on three overseas phone calls before you gave him your seal of approval. "He'll be honest with you," you told me, when I was twenty-two. And you were right. Mel has worked hard for me, through the stream of endless thanks-but-no-thanks we heard for the first eighteen years after my "stellar debut." He never gave up, and he never sugar-coated the truth.

Because let's face it: Any man with my qualifications, with my reviews, with my supporters—I had Bernstein's imprimatur, for God's sake—would have been ensconced—and revered—before he turned thirty.

I know you never wanted to talk about the challenges of being a woman in this world where directorial brilliance is inextricably entwined with *machismo*. You told me that I would garner the respect I deserved, and I think you meant it both as promise and punishment. I wouldn't achieve my potential if I didn't live up to it every single day, in every musical moment.

Trust me, I took your words to heart. And you know, I was respected. By musicians all over the world where I guest-conducted, but it was never enough to persuade a Symphony Board to take a chance on hiring me for a regular gig. It seemed the powers-that be could not imagine handing over an orchestra to a woman for more than a few nights at a time every five seasons or so. Until someone—some forward-thinking individual who was prepared to fight for me—*was* able to imagine it.

You know, I still don't know who that person was. Because once they put me on the podium, once they saw me in action, once they saw the increased attention—and attendance—every member of the Philharmonic Board claimed me as his own idea.

I remember that first night at the Dorothy Chandler Pavilion. So much press, and it seemed that all of Hollywood was in attendance. *Mine*, I thought, as I ascended to the podium. It felt as momentous as a Mahler fanfare.

And you know I know my Mahler. His first and the third symphonies, I conduct without a score. They are among—oh, I don't know—two-hundred-something—orchestral works I have memorized. I wonder how that stacks up to the sheaves of music you carried in your head. I always thought you had some sort of wonder-mind. But now I understand the three-part secret is focus, desire, and time. When reporters ask, I tell them that I've built my repertoire like every other Maestro has—through decades of study, through single-minded dedication. In that way, I am the rule, not the exception.

Once, an interviewer asked, "Should we call you *Maestra*?"

I think she saw changing the last letter as a kind of feminist act—a way to signal that I was a woman at the helm.

"God, no," I told her. "That's almost as bad as *poetess.*"

After fifty-seven years of living, the fact that I am a woman no longer surprises me. (I'm paraphrasing you—and sometimes I just quote your exact words—with credit, of course.) But the truth is that my gender remains newsworthy, even thirty-five years after my debut with the New York Philharmonic. There just aren't that many of us.

I've discovered that most people—even those who have never studied music—carry an image of a conductor: dressed in tux and tails, shoulders moving, arms raised as the orchestra plays that big, final note. They can picture the audience applauding, the conductor turning around to take a bow. Do they see the face of a woman? No.

Unless they are recent subscribers to the L.A. Phil.

Asked when I was twenty-four, or thirty-six, or even forty-two—whether we'd be seeing more and more women leading major orchestras, I answered with an emphatic, assured, *yes*. But the change has been slow, slower than I ever imagined. Maron Alsop is leading Baltimore now, and there are some young women working their way up in Europe. I have to believe in ten or twenty—or surely, thirty—years, we will see a shift away from the macho-maestro connection. Yes, music-making will triumph over outdated notions of gender.

But for a long time, I was the only woman invited to play in the musical major leagues, a celebrated anomaly. And while I was continually made aware of my unique status, I never approached my job as a woman—only as the best musician and leader I could be. (See, I did take your instruction to heart.)

"They actually had the chutzpah to use the phrase, *considering a new direction*," Mel told me.

"Considering?"

"*That's* where you go?"

"Well, only after I translate *new direction* as *music director with a dick*. Pardon my language: *penis*. Oh, and no offense."

"Yep, and none taken. Look, Hannah, I didn't see this coming. You've never had a bad review. 'Attendance is flat,' they told me, and I told them to look around—the country's in an economic meltdown, and symphony tickets aren't exactly a necessity. Also, I pointed out—'*flat* is not down, and you might want to talk to some of your counterparts around the country.'"

"But—I mean is this a conversation—a negotiation—or—?"

"I haven't seen anything. Not a low-ball offer or an outlandish proposal, so I felt like I had to let you know. It's possible it's an opening gambit, but I don't know. This feels more like a shake-up than a shake-down. There are new members on the Board, too."

"The thing is, we've kind of set them up with the perfect transition scenario, haven't we? I'm away on sabbatical. A parade of guest conductors—otherwise known as job applicants—come streaming through all season long. They hire one, and—"

"Yeah, I know. And I feel like a shit for leaving you wide open like that, but I had no indication, or I would have talked to you about giving up some of the composing time and taking some guest gigs yourself."

"So—we wait?"

"Not for too long—remember we can walk away from them, too."

Walk to where?

Walk to where.

—12—

"You will go to school with the Americans and take your academics in English. But it is essential you become fluent in French. You will meet with your French tutor twice weekly. Monday, Thursday." As she spoke, Mademoiselle was filling out a block schedule for me in her crabbed handwriting. "There," she said when she was finished. "This is mine. You will copy and keep this close to you. You must know where to be and when. I advise a pencil," she added. "Your schedule may change in the notice of a moment."

The more time I spent with her, the more fascinated I became with Mademoiselle's spoken English. She had a store of half-understood American idioms, but more often, she sounded as if she were reading out of an old book. Over time, I realized that Mademoiselle *thought* in French, then translated into English. She rarely made obvious mistakes, but she never sounded completely at ease with the language.

I did as I was told, making a miniature version of her calendar, but soon enough, my weeks settled into a routine. Up early for theory lessons with Mademoiselle on Mondays, Tuesdays, and Thursdays. On Wednesday mornings, I practiced piano before breakfast, and on Friday, I played my flute while Mademoiselle taught early lessons downstairs in her salon.

We were never alone at 36 Rue Ballu. Mademoiselle's musical assistant, Annette, would begin teaching her roster of students after breakfast, which was served promptly at seven-thirty by Zita. She and her husband Giuseppe managed all elements of Mademoiselle's daily life that did not include music. Zita spoke French with an Italian accent and sent me off to school with a hug and an assortment of homemade snacks. Giuseppe drove me each morning from Paris to Louvenciennes, the home of the American School. Sometimes I fell asleep en route, but more often we swapped language lessons: remedial English for even more remedial Italian.

My American School classmates seemed worldly and at home in France. Some had parents in the diplomatic corps, others were the children of corporate executives. They swapped stories about the places they'd lived, a subtle competition always for the most exotic, the most primitive, the most interesting. As if they, not their parents, had earned their locations. I felt immediately out of place, a feeling that was only intensified by my special hours. Three days a week, I left early for music lessons and classes. I always felt as if the teachers resented my early departures, perhaps even more than the students did. I was kept inside during the recess period, when I was instructed to catch up on my work. I was rarely behind in my work—at least not my schoolwork—so I used the time to complete my assignments for Mademoiselle and for Madame Aubrun, my exacting French tutor. I didn't mind staying inside, but it meant I had even fewer opportunities to make friends.

Then, one noontime recess, I was joined by Elaine Adams. She gave me a secret smile as she swung herself into the seat next to me. I smiled back without thinking, and the teacher caught me in the act. "This is not social hour, Miss Schaeffer. You are here to catch up on your work, and Miss Adams is here because—why don't you tell Hannah why you are here?"

Elaine Adams looked right into my eyes and said solemnly, "I have socialization problems."

Without thinking, I said, "Oh, so do I."

Mrs. Lockum was not known for her sense of humor. I

knew better than to say another word. A teacher's assistant, she took her job as disciplinarian to heart. Soon, I knew, she would produce reams of paper and recite some sentence for us to write a thousand times. A sentence of sentences. I wanted to whisper my witticism to my socially problematic companion, but I knew to wait until Mrs. Lockum had given us our dictation.

"For you, Miss Adams, please write the following five hundred times: *I will behave in accordance with playground rules at all times*."

"But I was only—" Elaine began.

"Miss Adams! Follow that with: *I will not speak back to the teacher at any time*. Five hundred times." Elaine was silent as Mrs. Lockum handed her paper and a pen. I was looking down at my work, pretending to be absorbed in it. Hoping to escape Mrs. Lockum's notice.

"Miss Schaeffer." She handed me several sheets of paper. "*I will keep my business to myself*. Three hundred times." It was a silly sentence for me. I kept my business to myself unfailingly. "I trust these assignments will keep you two busy—and silent—for the rest of the playground period." That was her exit line. I waited until I heard the doorway at the end of the hall click shut.

"A sentence of sentences," I muttered to Elaine. As if I had just thought of it.

She laughed. "Very good. Maybe we should put that as the title at the top of the page."

"I don't know. Mrs. Lockum would probably just give us more sentences for that."

"She's so—" Elaine was struggling for a word. "So strict!"

"Oh, no, she's worse than strict." I knew strict, and I'd learned from Emil that strictness had its purposes. Mrs. Lockum had a gripe with the world. "She's mean. She's out to get kids. She hates her job. Maybe she hates her life." I was surprised at all the words coming out of my mouth, and maybe Elaine was too. Where was the normally quiet, verging on nonexistent Hannah? I guess I had been silently observing, and now I had some opinions to share.

"You're right! She *is* mean!" Elaine looked at me for an extra second and then took up her pen and began to write with a sense of righteous indignation.

"I have heard she has socialization problems." I said it in the serious tone I'd imagined Mrs. Lockum had used when she labeled Elaine Adams.

We held onto our desks, so they wouldn't hear us laughing outside.

***

When summer came, I moved with Mademoiselle from Paris to Fontainebleau. It was easier this second year; I felt more a part of the place. Not quite twelve years old, I was still a lot younger than the college-age students who were my classmates, but I was feeling much more sophisticated after living in Paris. Plus, the months with Mademoiselle, the Wednesday afternoons in her studio—I had made my peace with theory and analysis. The assignments that were torture for me just the summer before seemed straightforward, even basic, a year later.

I think Mademoiselle worried less about me, too. Now, she felt, I was hers. She had captured the growing musician in me, and she had negotiated at least three years to form me. This meant she almost never made a fuss over me in classes. After feeling like the exception every day at the American school, I was relieved to return to the rigid summer schedule of theory, ear training, composition, practice, and performance.

In September, we moved back to Paris, back to school, lessons, and more practice. Also, Correspondence, a favorite of Mademoiselle's non-musical lessons. Every Sunday afternoon from two to four o'clock, we sat down together with our incoming mail. Mademoiselle stayed in touch with students all over the world, with musicians and conductors and composers, colleagues and friends. She believed in the brief response; installed at her lady's desk, she could write twenty or thirty single-page letters in the two-hour span.

My letters on the other hand, were longer and more labored—or at least it felt that way. Nana had kept her promise to write weekly. Her letters were newsy and about nothing in particular, always asking about me, about my studies, inquiring after Miss Boulanger. I usually wrote back to Nana's letter first, answering her questions and asking her to write again. Writing to my mother was always more difficult. Her letters were less frequent, and she didn't seem nearly as curious as my grandmother. She always closed with, "Wish you were here—Love, Mom." The words belonged on a postcard of the Maine coast—*The lobster was delicious, weather is spectacular—wish you were here! Love, Mom.*

Did she really wish I were there? I thought a lot about it as I reread old letters, trying to think of something new to say. I knew I loved my mother, but I didn't wish she were here, and I didn't wish I were there, not really. It didn't seem like a good basis for our correspondence. Sometimes, I copied what I'd written to my grandmother, changing a word here or there, but Mademoiselle did not approve of this method. "I am sure they share your letters. How will it be when they get exactly the same news? You must be more creative."

"But she never asks any questions, the way Nana does, so I never know what she wants to me to write."

"Remark upon what she has said. Mention something that happened this week. Tell her about an upcoming performance. There you have it—*voilà—une lettre.* Don't make it so difficult."

"But she doesn't write that often. I can't remark upon what she has said when she hasn't said anything for the past three weeks!"

"Correspondence is not a strength for everyone. To maintain contact requires discipline—"

"*Everything* requires discipline with you! I'm sick of discipline!" I was startled by my own words, and frightened. I thought of running out of the room, not for dramatic effect but just to avoid seeing Mademoiselle's expression at that moment.

She waited until I looked at her. When she spoke, she sounded a little tired. "You are quite correct, *ma chère*. Everything does require discipline. Without it, we accomplish nothing."

I looked down as soon as she finished her sentence, trying to catch the sobs in the back of my throat.

"Hannah?" she said, with a question and a kindness in her voice that made me look up. She had turned sideways in her chair, had put down her pen. "Come here." And something about the way she said it sent me into her arms. I cried hard, and she held hard. She said nothing more, just waited for me to collect myself; then she offered me a tissue, *un mouchoir*. I blew my nose three or four times.

"*Bien sûr*, there is still a half hour left for us to finish our correspondence. I suggest that you take that time to rest while I write a brief note to your mother. I'll tell her you weren't feeling so well today. When I'm done, I'll come up and get you. I think we should go out for some fresh air, don't you?"

I wasn't sure I should trust Mademoiselle with a letter to my mother. Mademoiselle had never been a mother, but she had clear beliefs about how mothers should behave. I always sensed that mine did not live up to her standards. A mother, according to Mademoiselle, should recognize and seize every opportunity for her child's development and learning.

Children should not be coddled, but rather they should be challenged and encouraged, in that order. If a child shows a talent, that talent must be nurtured, explored, stretched. That my mother would hesitate for a moment in sending me to Paris to study was incomprehensible, and possibly a criminal offense.

"I'm okay," I said. "I'll finish my letters."

She gave me an approving squeeze and let me go. I walked back to my little table. On a blank page, and using my ruler, I drew two staves. I was used to composing in pencil, but I boldly inked in the notes. I pictured my mother picking out the tune on Nana's piano. At the top of the page, I wrote, "For Mom." At the bottom, after the double bar: "Love, Hannah." I folded it in half, slipped it into the lined envelope, and wrote out the address.

"I wrote a musical note," I said, pleased with my cleverness. I giggled.

"*Parfait*," she said, smiling back at me. But I don't think she understood the pun. She was humoring me, and relieved to see that my mood had shifted.

I slipped my two letters next to her stack of envelopes. Mademoiselle always put the stamps on all at once at the close of our correspondence sessions. I liked to watch her sort the letters: overseas, airmail, local. In one compartment in her desk, she would find a little green sponge in a white dish, in another she would locate all the required postage. With the certainty of a great pianist, she would dip and paste, dip and paste—and quickly.

Today, though, I didn't want to wait around for stamping time. "Can we still go for a walk?" I asked. I was hoping for a hot chocolate at the little cafe up the hill.

"Twenty minutes," she said.

"Yay, yay, yay, yay!" I think I skipped out of the room. A correspondence day triumph. I'd finished early!

***

On my way home that Christmas, I felt nervous. As if I were going to a strange place; as if I were flying away from home, rather than making my way back to it. Perhaps Mademoiselle had guessed this would be the case; she sent me with plenty of assignments and an empty music notebook to fill. I composed my way across the endless Atlantic Ocean until the stewardess came to escort me off the plane. I saw Nana first, maybe because of her plum-colored hat. Beside her, my mother, looking especially pretty in a blue outfit that matched her eyes. I broke free and ran to them, surprised at how happy I felt to be back. My grandmother stood just in front of my mother. I landed in Nana's arms.

"How we've missed our Hannah," she said, whispering to me as she squeezed me in close. My mother began to move toward us, and I saw that she was also moving away from a man—a tallish man, an older man, balding, a man whose hand she had been holding. *Who was he?*

"Hello, honey," my mother said.

I hesitated a moment, and Nana sensed my pause. "Go to her," she whispered.

My mother hugged me as if I were a fragile thing. It crossed my mind that she did not want to wrinkle her dress. "It's good to have my daughter back," she said, moving away from me, taking me in, measuring, I knew, how much I had grown, probably trying to assess whether that little red swing coat still fit me. She led me by the hand to the man, introduced him. "Hannah, this is my friend, Bill. He was kind enough to drive us to the airport today to pick you up."

"Good to meet you, Hannah," he said. His voice wasn't too deep, a tenor for sure. "I've heard so much about you."

And I've heard nothing about you, I wanted to say. But I didn't. Instead, I stumbled. "Uh, yeah. Hello." Then I imagined

Mademoiselle, stupefied by my lack of social graces in this situation. Had I learned nothing from her? I straightened up, pretended he was a stranger, which really, he was. A stranger holding my mother's hand, a stranger who was kind enough to drive my mother and grandmother to New York to pick me up. *Yuck*, I wanted to say. *Go away*. But I remembered my manners in time. There was barely a pause before I said, "Pleased to meet you, too. Thank you for coming to pick me up."

My grandmother smiled, and my mother gave me a wink before she turned back to Bill. "Can you take Hannah's bag?" she asked him.

"Oh, of course—I am ashamed you had to ask me." He moved to take my bag, and I realized I didn't want to relinquish my flute to him. Not because he seemed untrustworthy. Not because I imagined him as an evil stepfather. I hadn't even made that connection yet. I just didn't like him. It was his blandness I didn't like, his evenness, his willingness to be friendly and helpful. Or maybe it was none of those things, but merely the fact that he was not my father.

***

"He's *not* your father," my mother would say to me later that evening, after Bill had left us to our cellar apartment. "He's calm and easy-going and—"

"And boring!" I blurted out.

"Yes, he is a bit boring, honey. But your dad was a little too much excitement for a little too long. I need somebody steady, now, somebody who doesn't gamble away the mortgage money. Bill is reliable. That's what I need. A reliable man."

"He's *your* boyfriend," I said, turning, shrugging, digesting her revelations about my father.

"Yes, he is, and I hope you will come to like him."

We were talking in my bedroom, now her studio, too. My mother had moved her sewing machine into the corner of the room, and during her off-hours from the insurance agency, she'd taken up dressmaking again. I loved looking at all the exotic fabrics—she bought mostly remnants and fashioned them into her own designs—but it felt a little crowded in the room, between the four-poster bed, bureaus, and sewing center.

"I'll leave you now. You must be very tired. Do you like your new coverlet?" She'd made it, I could tell, out of little scraps of silk. It was beautiful, and I told her so. I knew she was pleased as she kissed me goodnight. "I'm glad you're home," she said.

"Uummm," I said, sleepy, unsure, noncommittal.

In the morning, I found my grandmother at the kitchen table doing the crossword puzzle. "Six letter word for very fast," she said as I entered the room. "Ends with *o*."

"*Presto*," I answered.

"That's it!" she said. She put down the newspaper to make me breakfast, chattering, asking me a million questions, not always waiting for the answer before she went onto the next query. "My sleepyhead," she said as she presented me with a stack of thick blueberry pancakes and a pitcher of warm maple syrup, some bacon on the side.

The food did its magic, and I began to wake up. "What time is it?" I asked.

"Eleven o'clock! Almost lunchtime!"

"Mom's sewing again," I said, a statement and a question.

"It is very good for her to have that outlet."

"Outlet?"

"For her creativity."

For her frustration, more likely. I remembered my mother sewing madly when she was angry with my father, sewing with vengeance, literally. There was a pair of curtains she made for our house that I always associated with the big fight they had when he finally showed up late that evening. In this context, I figured Nana hoped her sewing would keep my mother off the lemonade and whiskies. Not the cigarettes, though. It was a tribute to her eye and hand coordination that my mother never burned a hole in any of those fragile fabrics.

"She has a talent, a wonderful sense of color." Some of my mother's designs were being sold in a Boston boutique, Nana told me. I felt proud of her, and so did my grandmother. But Nana worried about my mom, too. Even surrounded by lovely silks and beautiful patterns, even as she was in her element, pinning something up on one of the three dress forms that now occupied my bedroom, my mother projected a need for protection.

Maybe that was why Bill was here now. He spent most of the holidays with us, and he was careful with me, never pressing me, as if he sensed that I was unsure of him. "Please don't mention Bill to your father," my mother asked me on Christmas Eve, just before Dad was due to pick me up.

"Mom has a boyfriend." I said, before we were out of the apartment complex. Flat out with the facts, I thought. I was still hoping my father would come back and rescue us.

"Oh, that's nice," my father said as if we were talking about the weather. Clearly, he did not understand the implications here.

"His name is Bill," I continued. Maybe if I mentioned a name, he would realize the gravity of the situation.

"Bill," he said. "Where did she meet him?"

"At the insurance agency. He works there too. His wife is dead."

"Oh, that's too bad," my father said, drawing in on a cigarette, holding the wheel with one hand. This conversation was not going the way I'd hoped. Why wasn't my father upset? Why wasn't he making a U-turn right now, heading back to the apartment, bursting in to tell my mother how much he missed her, missed us, loved us, how he'd finally realized what a big mistake he'd made? Instead, he seemed to be taking in the momentous news about my mother—his wife—as if she were a stranger, or, at best, some distant relative.

We drove around, looking for someplace to have dinner on Christmas Eve. Most of the restaurants were closed. We ended up at a Chinese place, where we shared a Poo-Poo platter and some pork fried rice. He produced a package for me after we'd finished our dinner. It was flat and soft to my touch, wrapped in peppermint stripes with red ribbons. I read the matching tag, *To: Hannah. Love, Your Dad.*

"I do love my Dad," I said, before I opened the package.

"And I love my girl. Open it." I did, and inside I found a beautiful leather case with handles and a shoulder strap tucked inside. "It's to carry your music in", he said. "Your flute should fit in the outside pocket."

"Oh, thank you Daddy," I said. "I love it."

He told me the case was hand-made, that he'd gotten the exact measurements of my flute case and made sure the zippered part would hold larger pieces of music. "It will last you a long time," he said. "And I hope you'll think of your old Dad every day that you carry it."

He sounded lonely when he said that. I didn't know what to say. "I have a present for you too."

"I was hoping you might." I passed him the small package, and he opened it slowly, carefully, trying not to rip the wrapping. I think he was just trying to make me squirm.

"Daddy!" I protested.

"Want to make it last, kiddo. Delayed gratification. Do you know what that is?" I rolled my twelve-year old eyes in response. Finally, he slipped the little blue box out of its wrapping and undid the Scotch tape, opened the lid. Inside was a tiny Eiffel Tower tie tack. It was silver, and meticulous in detail. I'd seen it in a jeweler's window in Paris. I told Mademoiselle about it, and she went with me to negotiate a price and a payment plan. Then she proceeded to line up some small paying performances so I could afford this gift for my father.

"Look at that—a little piece of Paris to remind me of my girl," my father said. He grinned as he ran his finger over the little silver struts. "And I have just the place to wear it."

"On your tie, Daddy." He was already pinning it onto the lapel of his jacket.

"Tonight, I'll wear it on my collar, but I promise I'll wear it to work on Monday. I have a new job, you know, and I have to wear a tie."

"That's great," I said, realizing for the first time that the tie tack might have been entirely useless if my dad didn't have this new job. "What kind of job?"

"It would be better if you didn't mention this to your mother," he said, not answering my question.

I found my mother bent over the sewing machine when I got home that night. "How was your visit?" she asked me.

"He has a new job," I told her. After all, I'd told my father about her boyfriend. I owed her this information.

"What kind of job?"

"I don't know. He wears a tie," I offered.

"Well, that sounds promising. Maybe I'll start getting checks more often."

That seemed to be the end of the matter. Once again, my plans had backfired. I'd hoped that my mother, realizing that my father was, after all, steady and dependable, and still much more interesting than her reliable Bill, would rush to the phone, call him up, invite him to Christmas dinner.

"Bedtime," my mother said, turning off her sewing lamp, kissing me goodnight, reminding me to brush my teeth. "Sleep tight," she said, as she left the room, her gauzy pink bathrobe billowing after her.

—13—

I don't just visit you. I come up the hill to feed the cats, too.

And they are beginning to recognize me. Especially the two black ones—I call them *La Petite Noire* and *La Petite Noire Nouvelle*—and the creamy gray tiger—*Le Chef Gris Avec Crème*. He's the cat in charge in the Boulanger *Division*. The older of the black cats is his first wife. The younger—the sweetest and most friendly of the three—is their daughter. The relationships I am learning by watching, and from conversations with other cat-feeders.

I make that little chhchchhchheeing sound that crosses all language barriers between cats and humans, and these three run to me. *La Nouvelle* jumps right up to sit beside me, asks for food and petting. Her mother is more distant, but she flirts and rubs against the stones and sits, blinking at me from only a few feet away. *Le Chef*, he comes close enough to sniff my fingers, but no petting yet. He's still a little wary of my movements, but he follows me on my rounds. I suppose he feels I am his responsibility. In turn, I feel as though he and his little family—and the many other cats who share their territory—are mine. On some days, they are quite well fed. I find food in all the little hiding spots I have discovered on my walks. But other days—and I cannot detect a pattern to this—the food dishes are empty, and the cats are hungry. I make a point to come prepared.

I spoke to Elaine last night—you remember her—even if you were stumped by our connection—after all, she didn't sing or play an instrument. Maybe that is the very basis of our forty-something years of friendship. She's never been a part of my musical world. When the discipline was too much—when *you* were too much—and later, when, honestly, I was too much—Elaine was my refuge. She offers living proof that there is a different way to move through the world, indisputable evidence of another kind of life.

Elaine married her college sweetheart. They have three children, more animals than I can count, an apple orchard, and a shared veterinary practice. There have been times when I wished for elements of her life—the husband, the family, the peacefulness of place. You are shaking your head. Did I learn nothing from you about the singular dedication required for a life in music? Oh, I learned plenty.

Elaine, the veterinarian, only conditionally approves of the cat feeding, and she is even less sure about the daily graveside visits with you.

"Don't you remember? Cemeteries here are different," I said.

"What makes you think I spent my teenage years in Paris visiting graves?"

"Yeah, I guess we were too busy shopping or talking about boys. But remember Mademoiselle used to come up the hill every Saturday, to visit her sister's grave?"

"Yes, and we agreed it was morbid."

"Well, here I am—and it's not. It's more like coming to a park. Flowers everywhere. Graves are cared for, tended. There's a woman about our age who comes every day—just a few rows over. Last week, I saw her wiping down the gravestone with a damp cloth." I paused, realizing I still wasn't giving Elaine the right picture. "Not everyone there is in mourning. Construction workers sit on benches and have their lunches. Old ladies meet to gossip. And it is so quiet. I can think."

"Couldn't you think at a sidewalk café like the rest of the

artistic types who go to Paris?"

"Cafés aren't for thinking, just looking, really."

"Yeah, we did a lot of that when we were kids, didn't we? Sitting side-by-side, sipping *chocolat chaud*, and watching the city walk by," Elaine remembered.

"I've been wondering if Mademoiselle fed the cats when she came to tend to Lili. She had a soft heart for cats. You know, Tasha was once a scraggly stray. Mademoiselle found her hanging around at Victoria Station. She scooped her up and took her home on the train to Paris."

"I never knew that."

"Oh, guess what? I've planted a garden. Now, that's the opposite of morbid."

"You? Gardening?" Elaine lives on a small farm in Vermont. I helped her plant some bulbs on a visit a few years ago; if she hadn't intervened, I might have planted thirty purple tulips upside down.

"Yes, a lot of the graves here have little gardens." She sighed, but I persisted. I described my plants, the arrangement.

"The impatiens—are they New Guinea? Then, they'll take sun. Begonia is a good choice. You're in a temperate zone. Heather might look nice, and it would give you some color next spring."

"I knew I could at least count on you for gardening advice."

"Damn you!" Elaine laughed.

"But you see it isn't all about death?"

"Yeah. But—your mom, and now maybe your job? It's a lot. I mean, you've had more than your share of loss in your life. And you always respond by throwing yourself into work, by getting busier. But now—loss plus uncertainty—have you heard any more from Mel?"

"Nothing good."

"That sucks. Well, how's the composing going?"

"Next question?"

"The notes will come back. It's bound to be hard for a while."

"But I will grow strong," I offered, trying to soften the edge in my voice.

"You already are strong, and that's not what I meant. Maybe you need to be soft. Be sad. Let it sink in this time."

"Yes, Dr. Elaine."

"Well now that I have permission to analyze you, I think I see what you're doing with this new cemetery routine."

"What do you mean? I always go up the hill whenever I'm in Paris. This isn't some new thing."

"Yeah—but those were short visits, occasional visits. This is every day, rain or shine. But I know what's going on. As long as I've known you, you have had a busy schedule. Even when we were kids, you carried that little calendar of all your lessons and assignments. Now you're far away from home and work, and you don't have a routine to follow—unless you make one. So, you visit Mademoiselle Boulanger every day, make a garden, and feed the feral cats. It all makes you feel like you have to show up."

I realized she was onto something. I do take comfort in the ritual, the walk up the hill, the feeling there is somewhere I have to go in the morning. "Hmmm," I offered. "Maybe."

Before we hung up, she told me not to be afraid to move the plants around. "That's half the fun of gardening—it's like rearranging your living room."

Elaine is right. I am moving the begonias to the four corners of the garden so I can plunk a small rose bush into the center now. *Orange Symphony*, according to the tag. How could I pass that one up?

Double roses for you today, Mademoiselle. I brought some long-stemmed red too. Mixed with baby's breath, and beautiful in your white marble vase. The buds are just beginning to open; this bouquet will last awhile.

I'm back with the watering can, and I must say I feel pleased with the way your grave is looking. Though I do need to go shopping for a new frame for your photo. This plexiglass thing is hideous, not to mention caked with dirt.

Ah, you've already guessed. All the roses are a clue, and I've been promising we'd talk about love. It's among your least favorite topics—romantic love, anyway. I was never actually sure about your position on familial love or what it was that you felt toward me? Duty, responsibility, I know. You taught me for the sake of the music. Too many times, you reminded me you were not my mother. Was all your love contained inside the music?

In my life, I've found that some of it seeps out.

Maybe more when I was younger.

Now, well, I find myself of two minds. On the one hand, I cannot imagine, any longer, another life for myself, or a place in this life where I could fit another human. But on the other hand, I feel more aware than ever that I operate alone in a world where most people pair up. I question myself, my choices. One in particular. His name was Geoffrey Lassman.

It was 1998. I was five years into a nine-year contract, with a seven-year extension already negotiated. I was settled. Content. Maybe—I'm not sure—I had some extra space between my ears that morning, which is to say I didn't wake up thinking about a viola part I would need to hear at rehearsal. I woke up slowly, groggy with a half-remembered dream, and in that pause between stretch and rise, I found myself thinking about life, about time passing, about the ones we love, and those we lose. All the things we've been talking about lately. Which is interesting, because now that I consider it, I rarely have that kind of thinking space—not in L.A.—and surely not when the Phil is in season.

It wasn't that I wondered if there was something larger

than the music. You and I agree on this: the music will always be bigger than everything. But I felt a sort of reverse-nostalgia, feeling wistful for a life that wasn't ever mine.

A shower and some strong black coffee, and I felt my focus returning. Doing my best not to get any crumbs or peanut butter on the score for the new work I was going to be rehearsing a few hours later. By the time I reached the hall, I was my single-minded self, rehearsal-ready, looking forward to hearing the piece.

Then, Geoffrey Lassman walked onto the stage.

"Good morning, Maestro. Thanks for the chance to play." There was a depth, a resonance to his voice that grabbed my attention. I wanted to hear it up close, to put my ear to his chest as he spoke, to feel the rumble I could sense beneath the sound.

My response was crisp, professional and several beats late. "Welcome to L.A.. Shall we review some tempos?"

We discussed a few transitions before he adjusted his music stand and I took up my baton. I flashed him my Maestro smile. His return smile revealed itself in slow motion. Eyes first; then lips; then finally showing his teeth. I took this to mean he was ready, and I prepped the downbeat.

It was a new work by Philip Glass. He had written it for unaccompanied sax before he got in touch with me to ask if the Philharmonic might consider commissioning an orchestral version.

Don't get me wrong: there's nothing like a great jazz tenor, but saxophone with orchestral accompaniment? It's nothing I would have thought to commission. But assuming you follow your students from the great beyond, you already know that Philip is perhaps the most prominent living composer in America, and only recently has he written more work for full orchestra. It seemed important to me at the time. And Geoffrey Lassman is a big name, too. He's a crossover artist in almost every way—playing clarinet, every kind of sax, and flute—in genres ranging from classical to jazz, new music to world beat.

Before I went to the board, I asked Philip if he'd be willing to write something new into the saxophone part. I wanted to be sure we could call the performance a premiere. "No problem. Just what I'd like to do. Oh, and you'll love Geoffrey Lassman," he said. "What he can do with a saxophone will make you cry."

That morning, on my stage, the soloist didn't make me cry, but I knew what Philip meant, even on the first read. The strings tapped their bows on their stands, the winds put their horns down and began to clap. "Mr. Geoffrey Lassman," I said, Ed Sullivan style, gesturing towards him. The orchestra stomped their feet, and our soloist smiled in slow motion again.

"There are a few sections I'd like to review, if that's okay with you," I said. We went back to work—tearing apart, reassembling—for another twenty minutes before we ran through it twice more, start to finish. It's a beautiful, inventive, richly textured piece. You would have approved. But I would never say that to Philip. In interviews about his influences, he tends to play down your role. That's always bugged me.

When we finished, Geoffrey Lassman shook my hand one more time, and then walked down into the darkness of the auditorium. I heard the squeak of the hinges as he took a seat. I could feel his eyes on me, and I knew my concentration was compromised. I shook my head, as if to shake him out of it, and broke the Copland into tiny pieces, perfecting entrances, polishing transitions. The musicians were surprised at my rigor, I suspect, but I rewarded all of us with a run-through of an early Haydn symphony we would be playing in our next series.

In concert, the Glass soared. Geoffrey Lassman played

beautifully; the interplay of solo and orchestra was balanced, responsive, just right. It was the kind of performance that we wish for every night of our lives, and we achieve—if we are lucky—one night out of three or five or seven. We were clear, open, and ready to experience this one, singular piece of music, no thought of technique or pitch or phrasing, and at the same time we were filled with our collective past experience and the deepest knowledge of every piece of music we'd ever played.

There was that stillness before the applause. You know, those few seconds of silence, the hesitation that signals the audience has been inhabiting the music along with us, that they are reluctant to leave the place of understanding and connection. When they remember where they are and realize what has happened, they will breathe again, inhaling, exhaling, sighing and clapping, all at the same time.

That night, the applause was loud and long. The audience knew that something magical had happened, and they were part of it. I acknowledged their appreciation, stepping off the podium and walking toward Geoffrey Lassman. I sent an open arm his way, directing the applause to him. He gestured back to me, and I to the orchestra. They stood as I reached his side. I stuck out my hand to shake his.

I gave a quick nod to Philip in the second row to let him know he was next, before I followed the soloist offstage.

"We need Glass," I said to the stage manager.

"It's arranged. He's coming now."

I checked the monitor, saw Philip moving toward the stage.

I turned to Geoffrey Lassman. "I need you to get back on that stage and make sure Philip stays up there with you, okay?"

A minute later, I joined them, said some words about how honored we were that Mr. Glass had chosen us to debut his new piece, thanking the board, patrons and friends for making this commission possible, and thanking Mr. Lassman for his stellar performance. Philip shook my hand and clapped our soloist on the back before he returned to his seat.

"We have experienced a very special musical event tonight," I said to the audience. "Thank you all for being part of this evening."

More thunderous applause: my cue to depart. I tilted my head in the direction of the wings. Lassman caught my signal, and we headed offstage.

Just beyond the curtain, he asked me to dinner.

I said no.

—14—

When I was thirteen, my mother married Bill and changed her name to Audrey. "I'm getting a new last name. Why not a new first name to go with it?" It was late August, and I was home for the wedding.

"How did you decide on Audrey?" I asked.

"Designs by Audrey. It has a ring to it, doesn't it?"

"I guess." She still hadn't answered my question.

"Bill and Audrey sounds better too."

"Didn't you like your old name?"

"Don't you like the name Audrey?"

"It's okay," I shrugged.

"Bill thinks it's beautiful. He says it suits me."

"What about Nana?" I asked. "Does she know?"

"Oh yes." My mother took a drag on her cigarette. "She knows." She exhaled the smoke through her nostrils and sighed. "It would help if you would call me by my new name, too."

"You want me to call you *Audrey*?"

"Sure. You're a teenager now, and you live away from home most of the time. Don't you think it would be more grown-up if you called me by my first name?" She squeezed my hand across the table. She didn't wait for my answer; instead, she stood and turned to survey the contents of the refrigerator. "I wonder what I can pull together for dinner."

Bill came for dinner that night, and they talked about the wedding. White roses or delphinium with the red? *Who cared?* I worked on a piece of music in my head, trying to figure out the best way to transition from minor back to major.

"Hannah?" I heard my mother say. "Were you listening?"

"Umm, I guess not." My mother—*Audrey*—rolled her eyes. "She does this," she said to Bill, smiling at him apologetically.

"What?" I said.

"You don't listen."

"I didn't know you were talking to me."

"Well, if you had been paying attention to the conversation at the dinner table, you would have known you were being addressed." My turn to roll my eyes. Nothing worse than my mother when she is acting like the queen. *She does this*, I felt like saying to Bill.

"I was saying that it would be lovely if you played your flute at our wedding."

I almost choked on the piece of chicken in my mouth. In my opinion, it was enough to ask me to attend their wedding. Kids aren't supposed to even be alive for their parents' wedding. Never mind provide entertainment.

"Would you like that?" she asked.

I took a sip of my coffee milk, pretending I was considering my response. *Would I like it? No, I would hate, hate, hate, hate it.*

"Don't you think you are putting Hannah on the spot?" It turns out the groom was more observant than I had given him credit for. I glanced at my mother, gauging her reaction.

"You don't think she should play?" my mother asked.

It's a trap, I wanted to tell Bill, but since when was I on his side?

"Uh—" he said. As good an answer as any. I studied my peas, wishing I could make them disappear without swallowing any.

"What would you want me to play?"

"Oh, I don't know. You could pick."

"Do you want to play, or not? Be honest." It was Bill.

"Oh sure," I said, staring at the table. When I looked up,

he was staring right at me, earnest, I could tell, and meaning well. Bill wasn't a bad guy, but I couldn't give him the satisfaction of having a role in this family. My grandmother would say I was cutting off my nose to spite my face.

I saw a flicker of resignation in his eyes before he sliced himself another piece of chicken.

***

"When you are a professional musician," Mademoiselle had told me, "you will have to play something you don't like. Or you may play a piece you love for an audience who does not understand it at all. But even if the audience isn't paying attention, God is listening." So I played a Mozart rondo that day, but not for my mother or Bill or my grandmother, or the handful of people who were scattered in the pews. When I was done, I was surprised by the applause. Everyone was looking at me, even my mother, still holding her bouquet and standing at the end of the aisle. Bill's arm was around her waist. I bowed my head then lifted it again, the polite acknowledgement that my teacher would suggest for such an occasion.

Nana patted my arm as I squeezed by her to retrieve my case. "Beautiful," she whispered. There was a shuffling as people filed out, greeting and kissing my mother, shaking Bill's hand. "We should go join the receiving line."

"I need to clean my flute and pack up," I said. "Don't wait for me."

Nana hesitated only a moment before adjusting her hat and posture to meet my mother and Bill. I watched as she gave my mother a kiss, then covered Bill's hand with both of hers. She joined the line, standing tall, smiling, making small talk with each person as they approached. My mother was already looking tired from it all, leaning into Bill. He nodded a lot, looking right at each person, listening as if they were giving him important advice. I stayed where I was, cleaning my flute, polishing each key, swabbing the headjoint again and again. I waited until the line dwindled, and stood just in time to slip out the side door of the church. There was no way I was going to the reception. I'd already made plans with my father for the rest of the afternoon. He was parked just across the courtyard.

"How was it, kiddo?"

"It was okay," I said. I leaned over and gave him a kiss on the cheek. He reached out and tousled my hairdresser-perfect curls before he put the car into gear. We drove in silence to the roast beef place.

"Sliced thin?" he asked, as we approached the counter.

"Is there any other way?"

***

It took almost two years before I got used to calling my mother by her new first name. I don't know if the transition would have been any easier if she'd asked me to call her Katherine. I doubt it. In my heart, I think I was insulted that she had relinquished her maternal title with such ease. For a while, I just didn't address her at all. My letters would start with a cheery "Hi!" or sometimes, "*Bonjour*," but never "Dear Audrey." When I was home, it was less convenient to avoid calling her by name, because it meant I couldn't yell from one room to the next in the large home that she and Bill now shared.

My grandmother, despite her reservations, honored my mother's wishes. "A rose by any other name," my grandmother would quote, when I questioned her. But I didn't agree with my grandmother. A mother by any other name is—apparently—an Audrey.

I remember the first time I called my mother by her new

name. Bill was away on a business trip, and I was home for a break between the end of the school year and the start of Fontainebleau. My mother and I had been living on take-out Chinese and frozen dinners, the way we did that first year on our own. I was digging into Swanson's turkey and mashed potatoes, my favorite. My mother was picking at fried chicken. When I took my first bite of cherry cobbler, my mother spoke.

"Did you know I used to play violin?"

"You did?" I managed, my mouth full.

She didn't say anything then, just nodded, lit a cigarette, and walked back into the kitchen. I finished my dessert and followed her. She was pouring herself another whisky and water with a squirt of lemon juice. I threw my aluminum dish into the trash.

"Come join me in the living room," she said.

We sat in opposite corners, in oversized white wing chairs. I wanted to ask my mother more about her violin-playing, but I knew it was better to let her tell me in her own time. But the silence, and the suspense, was killing me. I decided to try a low-key approach. "So, you played violin, huh?"

"Yes," she said, exhaling smoke. "And I was quite good, you know." She paused and looked right at me, to see if I believed her. "But I was also very nervous about playing in public. Do you get nervous?"

I thought about this for a minute. The answer was yes and no. Yes, in advance, but no at the moment, or within a moment of when I begin to play. I decided the safest answer was *yes* in this circumstance. She nodded, as if she'd suspected as much.

"Your grandfather was my teacher. He began teaching me when I was very small. I could barely hold a quarter-size violin. I remember how heavy it felt. But I wanted to please him, so I held it up to my chin and tried my best to do what he told me. He corrected my position, asked me to listen for the pitch, frowned when I wasn't getting it, and never complimented me—just gave me a nod when I got something right. I was desperate for his attention, and so I practiced that much harder."

I thought of my own early lessons with my grandfather, and how they seemed like play to me, how much I loved them, how much I missed them after he died.

"He was different with you," she said, as if she'd read my thoughts. "Maybe because of the terrible mess he'd made with me." She dug her cigarette butt into the ashtray, putting it out as a form of punctuation. As she pulled out the silver lighter with her new initials, my mother looked at me, assessing the impact of her words.

"There were five of us you know, and he worked his way up to concertmaster. Money was tight. There wasn't enough to spread the music around. He had to pick, and he chose me.

"Sometimes my father and I would play duets after dinner. I don't remember now if I was nervous in front of the family—I don't think so—or maybe it was just that I wasn't so nervous when I was playing next to him. He could cover up any mistakes I made, even while he noticed every pitch, every bowing, every rhythm.

"When I was nine or ten, I began to have my lessons with him over at the conservatory. I was his first lesson of the day, and we would ride the train together on Saturday mornings. I liked those train rides." My mother paused.

I imagined she was remembering sitting next to my grandfather as they rode the trolley down Huntington Avenue. I'd taken that route with him myself before he died. I loved those rides, the trains half-empty on our way in, jam-packed on our way home. Sometimes, he'd teach late, and there wouldn't be time to go home. He'd take me to dinner with him, then bring me backstage at Symphony Hall. Nana would meet us there and we'd sit in his special seats for the evening concert.

"Did you ever go to Symphony Hall with Gramps?" I asked.

"Oh yes. You weren't the only favored child." I was startled by the edge in my mother's voice.

"Freshen my drink, and I'll tell you the rest of the story. Two inches of whisky and just a splash of water. There's a plastic lemon in the fridge. Just squeeze a little in, okay?"

I didn't like her drinking, but I wanted to hear the end of this story, the end I suspected would be horrible, the kind of ending I didn't want to imagine, but couldn't help wanting to know.

"Thanks honey," she said, as I handed her back the glass. "You make a stiff drink." She lit another cigarette, blew a few smoke rings, and smiled. "Would you like to hear about my debut at Symphony Hall?" I nodded eagerly. Maybe this story wouldn't end so badly after all.

"It was a group recital, and I was in the middle of the program." Another pause; another drag on her cigarette. "Waiting in the wings, I felt the anxiety spread from my stomach to my chest to my throat. When my name was called, I realized that even my legs and arms were sort of numb and tingly. I don't know how I made it across the stage. I put the music on the stand, held my violin up, and lost control of my fingers, my memory, my ability to recognize a note on the page. The accompanist looked up at me. I knew he was waiting for my nod. But I couldn't move my neck. He began to play. There were sixteen measures of piano before the violin entered. I can still picture the staff, the number sixteen just over it in bold-faced type. I stared at that rest and tried to count, tried to remember a single thing I knew about playing the violin."

"Well, of course I missed my entrance, but the accompanist was experienced, so he repeated the opening for me. I should have walked off the stage without playing a single note. Just let the pianist play his part. Instead, I joined him the second time, and I played the piece as badly as anyone could ever manage to do. As if I hadn't spent months practicing it, as if I hadn't spent years learning the instrument. It was the most humiliating four minutes of my life."

"I bet you didn't play that badly—"

"Well, you'd lose that bet, baby."

The knife was back in her voice. But I couldn't help myself. I wanted to know. "What did Gramps say?"

"Oh, he said just what you said—that I didn't play as badly as I thought, that it was natural to feel a little nervous, that he should have talked to me more about stage fright, that we'd work on it for next time. But I could see the disappointment in his eyes. I knew I'd failed him."

"And I hated him." My mother's voice was almost a whisper. I felt stung by her words, as if she'd said she hated me. "I never played again." She said the words with finality. The end of the story, no question-and-answer period to follow. I was silent. She lit another cigarette, waved it toward the stairs. "Give me a kiss and go to bed. It's late."

When my mother gave a direct order, there was no choice but to follow her instructions. I stood up, walked over to her, breathing in the mix of whisky and tobacco, lemon, smoke, and a trace of Chantilly. I wanted to say something, do something, to try to reassure her about her recital. I gave her a quick hug and a kiss on the cheek. "Goodnight Audrey," I whispered just before I pulled away.

***

On that same trip home, my Dad took me to a fancy restaurant where we were met by a woman he introduced as his future wife. "We're celebrating, tonight," he said, squeezing my hand across the table, "order anything you like."

"You order for me," I said to my father, a technique I'd

learned in Paris when I was confronted with a menu too difficult to unravel. Tonight, the menu in front of me could have been written in an ancient, indecipherable language. I could not manage it on my own. Joanne seemed nice enough, but I had been looking forward to spending the evening alone with my dad, and I hadn't seen this coming.

I surprised myself with my appetite for the food that came at my father's confident command. By the time the dessert arrived, I was happy that Joanne had come along, grateful for the way she seemed to make my father come out of his silent shell. I couldn't remember the last time I'd seen him so engaged and engaging.

At the end of the evening, Joanne told me how pleased she was to finally meet me, how proud she knew my father was of me. "Now that I've met you myself, I know why he loves you so much, sweetie!" I didn't know what to say to her, but I gobbled up her reassurances of my father's love, her kindness to me, her warmth. She gave me a quick hug, kissed my father on the cheek and zoomed away in her Volkswagen bug.

"You don't have to come to the wedding," my father said as we were driving me home. "We'd both love for you to be there, but if you'd rather not, it's okay." He knew how much I'd complained about my mother's wedding.

"Oh, but I'd like to," I said.

"Honey, I know this might be hard for you—" he began.

"No, Dad, it isn't hard, not this time. Joanne seems nice. I'd like to come, as long as I'm home."

"Well in that case, we'll plan to get married when you're home. Maybe Christmas?"

"Christmas it is," I said. Already I was thinking about what I would play.

"You know I'll always love you more than anyone in the world."

I couldn't respond. I felt a tear go plop on my left cheek.

"Sweetheart?" my father asked across the expanse of the front seat. He drove a big Chrysler then, gold with a black vinyl roof. "Are you okay?"

My father pulled over, reached across the bench seat to wrap his arm around me. "It's okay, honey. It's okay," he kept repeating, until my sobs turned into hiccups, and he suggested hot chocolate for a cure. We went into an all-night diner and sat across from each other in the bright light.

"Joanne doesn't like roast beef," he said to me. I was holding my nose, sipping the glass of water that the waitress had delivered. I waited for him to say more. Was he going to complain about Joanne the way my mother sometimes did about Bill?

"So that means we'll still go out for our roast beef sandwiches, just me and my girl," he said.

I smiled at him. My hiccups were gone, and the inexplicable sadness that had gripped me in the car had evaporated, with the mere expectation of eating roast beef sandwiches, just me and my dad.

—15—

A fallen chunk of granite, a missing pane in the glass window of a mausoleum. These are the entrances to the village beneath the tombs—tunnels connecting to tunnels, exits marked by the light that enters from above. I picture the cats down there sheltered from storms and heat, and close to the dead.

The other day, I watched a funeral two rows away from your grave. I'm not sure why, but I felt compelled to visit the deceased's resting place after the mourners left the cemetery. A dark-striped kitty, still as a statue, was already occupying the only patch of polished black granite in the carpet of fresh flowers. Soaking in the morning sun, welcoming the new arrival, she was mindful, yet fearless of my approach. I left some food nearby, but the guardian did not leave her post. "*C'est là*," I told her. "You can eat it when you take a break."

You know, I'd like a little feline company when I die.

Though I'm not sure I'd want to be buried.

I need to figure that out. Three years from sixty, with no instructions for my funeral. And no one to take care of everything the way I did for my mother. She was similarly unprepared, it turned out, and Bill, shocked and devastated, was no help at all. It wasn't expected, but what death ever is? Even knowing my father was losing the battle against cancer, even seeing you—barely conscious, and literally shrinking before my eyes—I was still surprised by the inevitable endings, unready for the phone calls.

I don't think we're ever really ready, even when we think we are.

With Audrey, it wasn't life-preserving denial; we had no warnings to ignore. She went out shopping one morning, and never came home. A truck speeding through a stop sign, my mother creeping across the intersection, her driver's side exposed to the full impact of the crash. She didn't have a chance. Which many might construe as a blessing. It was not an accident that you would want anyone to survive. But she and Bill had never discussed her wishes. She was seventy-seven, and you would think she'd have made some provisions. Or at least I had thought. When I was a youthful fifty-five, I found myself feeling annoyed that she had left the deciding up to me. But here I am, two and a half years later, my affairs in a similar state of disarray.

It isn't that I expect to live forever, or that I don't think death is something that will happen to me. Really, I should get on it. I wonder if there is any room here. I wouldn't mind spending eternity with you and the guardian cats.

Unless they have space under Sainte-Chapelle. That's where I was earlier; that's why I am late today, Mademoiselle.

***

I met the inspector outside Le Palais de Justice. An odd place to hide a beautiful church—inside those forbidding walls.

"*Bienvenue*, Maestro Schaeffer. A pleasure to see you again." He guided me toward the security post just inside the double doors. I opened my instrument cases for inspection before I passed through the metal detector. "I'm not sure I mentioned at dinner that I am the concert coordinator for the police *prefecture*. We cannot fit your Los Angeles orchestra, but we can accommodate you and your flute and perhaps a small chamber group if you would like to play a concert here."

"You run an orchestra for wayward children, and you coordinate concerts? What *is* your job?"

"We are fortunate not to have as much violent crime as you have in America, so I have time to arrange some music, but most often, I am a cop."

He used the American word with emphasis, but also with a Parisian accent: *cup*.

"Here is my mobile, Maestro. Call if any problem should arise or if you need the doors unlocked."

"I'll be locked in?"

"Yes. We must be sure you are secure. All the workers in Paris will be on their lunch break while you are playing your flute." A guard opened the doors to the chapel, and I was immersed in beautiful, filtered light, the ancient stained glass glowing above me. Before I could even say *merci*, the inspector was gone.

"We must secure the chapel, Madame. You will be all right? If you have any trouble or there is an emergency—"

"I have his number, ça *va bien*."

"*Ah—bon! Au revoir, Madame*!" The man smiled as he closed the doors, relieved, free to eat his midday meal without worry for my fate.

There was a music stand by the altar. I moved toward it, thinking I would start there, but I knew I'd want to hear the space from all the angles.

Reaching into my bag, I grabbed the Louis Lot. In giving me your sister's flute, and in coaxing me to play my grandfather's violin, you taught me that every instrument has its own life, a life that is passed from one set of hands to another. And during that life, an instrument absorbs something of its players, and in this way, every player has some connection to the others. I have cared for this flute, minding the thinning tenon, and allowing only my lips to touch the plate, thinking of Lili, and of you. If she hadn't set aside the flute in favor of piano, and to focus on composition, I wonder if you would have ever entrusted this treasure to me.

I began with a low F. I heard the room take the note and carry it back to me, circling. I jumped the octave and felt the space around me shift. The zing kicked in when I played the C. Down a third, and the A was clear joy. To C, to the high F. Wow. *Wow*—just—wow.

I loved the way the sound rang out in the space. The lower octave sounded amazing. And this on the Louis Lot, a chamber flute, really. Wondering what a modern flute would do in the space, I pulled out my Powell.

Stronger, the Powell sang like a happy bird in springtime. I moved back to the Lot, improvising something light and small and French, and gentle. Then, returning to the Powell, I played the same thing just to hear the difference.

It's now or never with the Bonneville, I thought. I opened the case and stared at the flute for a long beat.

The Bonneville is a karma tube, even more than Lili's handmade French flute. I'm not sure you've ever heard me play it—at least while you were living. Peter and I found it, abandoned, pads swollen with an ill-advised immersion—someone must have tried to clean it—tarnished and unplayable, at *Les Puces*.

Oui, Mademoiselle, there is more to the Peter story than you know. But another time for that.

The Bonneville was an astonishing flea market find and a huge project to reclaim. On my own, I would have bid it a sad farewell and left it behind. Peter, though, was determined that I have a companion to the Louis Lot. He snapped it up, began his research. He found a specialist in London, shipped it off to be rebuilt, and presented it to me for my birthday six months later.

But the plot thickens. Remember the Glass premiere I told you about, the saxophone player, Geoffrey Lassman? Like a lot of sax guys, he played flute too. But unlike a lot of sax guys, he played flute beautifully. I discovered this when I let him play the Bonneville. So, this afternoon when my lips touched its plate, I couldn't help but think of him.

Just to recap: the known history of this instrument with a mysterious past begins in a Paris flea market, travels to a London master technician, comes back to me via Peter, and the only other person who has played it in this century is some guy I never even dated. I don't know what I was thinking, or not thinking, to let him try that flute. He just got to me. Even as I rebuffed him, drawing solid, impassible lines around our roles: Maestro and soloist.

"You can't be me," Lenny told me, not long after my debut with the New York Philharmonic. "You can't be as casual. No blurring of boundaries. Not now, maybe not ever." It wasn't because he thought I'd take a false step. No, his advice for me was in response to something that happened *to* me. On a conducting fellowship—those short stints abroad designed to serve as stepping stones to more guesting gigs.

I wasn't exactly welcomed into the fold in most of the cities I visited, and I understood that I'd have to prove my worth, to run a rehearsal or two, to show my capacity in front of any given orchestra. But there were no guarantees I'd even get that chance. One well-known Maestro called me Little Girl, and sent me on errands, never letting me near his players. Another praised me, promised me recommendations, said he would help me secure guesting offers. When he asked me to come to his conducting quarters to review a score, I thought nothing of it. How many hours had I spent doing just that with Lenny?

But.

Maybe I should have known?

I still question myself thirty-something years later. Was there a signal I missed? Or did I give him the wrong impression?

I tried to be polite, to invent a boyfriend, a fiancé. He said something about puritanical American values, and how he would help cure me of those, so I could tour all of Europe. I laughed, tried to charm my way out of the room that seemed to be growing smaller by the minute. I loved my fiancé, I told him.

"Don't think of this as cheating. Think of this as getting what you deserve."

"Right now," I said—trying my best to sound breezy, "I think we both deserve a drink."

He smiled—certain his machismo was having the desired effect. He was wearing a crimson silk robe, belted at his hefty waist as he moved across the room toward the small bar. As soon as he turned away, I ran for the door. Up the stairs and out of the hall. I took a cab to the airport, grateful for the Amberson credit card Lenny had given me. I flew home.

And I told no one. But Lenny guessed. Returning a week early, no bags, no scores, no explanation. He was furious on my behalf, but he didn't argue with my instincts.

"Men can be dogs," he said. "You need to be, well, maybe a little prickly and cold."

Really, it wasn't bad advice. It was of the era, I guess. Making women responsible for the control of men's uncontrollable appetites. Has much changed since? I don't know, but we have terminology now: sexual harassment, sexual assault. If I had had the words then, would I have been able to use them in a sentence?

More useful—or practical—was the career decision Lenny made for me after he saw to getting my things shipped back to me: No more fellowships or assistantships. We would only accept offers for principal guest conductor gigs. In the meantime, I would start touring with Lenny—assisting him to keep my arm in shape, working on my repertoire.

Why didn't I tell you?

You were so certain that only the music mattered. You

were so certain I could rise above gender, reminding me that my femaleness was not, ever, to be an excuse. I think I worried you might have blamed me even more than I already blamed myself.

The villain in the story, by the way, is now deceased. I like to think his red silk bathrobe is daily singed by the fires of Hell.

So, the flute. The lines. Maestro and soloist. That's what got me thinking about all this, all these years later. I tried to take Lenny's advice, but I was never very good at being prickly. I found that if I shut down to the musicians, I risked closing out the music. But I did find this way to be friendly, polite, but distant, and cool in every exchange that was not musical.

The Bonneville has a nice sound—round and focused. Different from Lili's Louis Lot, but they could pass for cousins. It filled Sainte-Chapelle, fitting it just right. I played a years-old melody that I haven't fit into anything yet. I traveled up, up, up, testing the limits of the instrument. When I drew a breath, I found myself gasping the way you do when you are crying really hard. Again? But why?

Kleenex. A drink of water.

Better.

I heard the door open. Bourlou. He nodded, then took a seat at the back, facing away from me. I stared at the colored windows, the light coming through them. I faced the altar, and I picked up the flute again.

I began small and soft, allowing the sound to linger in the lower register. I let the sound be sad.

Did you know they have recorded humpback whales, deep in the waters, calling to each other with long, mournful notes? It's called sounding. I think that's what I was doing. My own musical voodoo, a sounding to reach across time, maybe space. Maybe beyond death. Did you hear me?

A modulation was called for. I moved to the major, stepped up the tempo, worked in some jazz riffs. Then: applause.

"I hope I didn't startle you, and I am so sorry to interrupt. But it's almost two—"

"Oh, I lost track of the time!"

"*Pas de probleme.* I recognized some Mozart, but after that? Was I hearing your own work?"

"Some of it, yes."

"Beautiful—and sad."

"Thank you—and thank you for the space. What a treat to have it to myself!"

"*De rien.* Would you like to come play again at the noon hour? It's lovely to hear you during the quiet of the day."

"Oh, but so much trouble to arrange, I'm sure. I appreciate—"

"*Non*, no trouble at all. Would you like to play here again tomorrow?"

"Tomorrow?"

"Or perhaps Thursday—or next week—whenever you like."

"You are offering me the chapel to myself, again tomorrow?"

"I am offering you the chapel every day if you like, between twelve and two."

"Every day from twelve to two?" *Talk about a practice room.*

"If you wish it, it is done."

I wished it, Mademoiselle. I wished it.

—16—

As soon as the cranky, inefficient furnace at 36 Rue Ballu roared to life, I began to wheeze. It happened every year.

Mademoiselle moved me downstairs to the spare bedroom, saying she could keep a better eye on me there. This made no sense to me, as she only visited me for a few minutes early in the morning before her first lessons began, and for a few minutes more before dinnertime.

It wasn't only that my teacher's rigorous schedule gave her no time to attend to me: she knew nothing about the care of a sick child, and she would tell me so in the same tone she used when she was irritated with a student who asked superfluous questions. If I'd had more strength, I would have felt guilty for inconveniencing her. I remember not wanting to move or to speak, wanting to sleep, and sleep some more. In a way, she honored my feelings, never making any effort to break through with affection or warmth.

It was Emil who would knock gently on the door and peek in to see if I was awake. It was Peter who would tell me jokes, and it was Zita who would bring me warm soup, apple sauce and ginger ale—American ginger ale that Emil's wife Ghislaine found for me. Sometimes Ghislaine would deliver it herself. She'd sit on the bed, coaxing me to drink lots of fluids, sweeping her hand across my forehead, checking my temperature in the absentminded way that experienced mothers do.

"*Ma petite*, everyone is so worried about you. We want you to get better right away, okay?" She said *okay* in English, and always with a smile, as if she were pleased with herself. "Let me brush your hair, and you will feel better."

Ghislaine was the sickroom angel that Mademoiselle could never be. But she also had children of her own and couldn't visit if I was contagious. So, when I was the sickest, I was mostly on my own. But poor Zita was charged with getting me out of bed to walk around the apartment. Something to do with the movement keeping any pneumonia from settling into my lungs. Twice, my usual bronchitis did turn into pneumonia, walks or no walks.

After the first bout with pneumonia, I went along willingly with the daily walks around the apartment. If moving around could prevent me from being isolated and without visitors, I was more than happy to accompany Zita—as we made the circuit, three times, of the bottom floor.

Hearing from Mademoiselle that I was sick, Nana would call on the telephone, and my mother would get on the line too, "You have to get better in time for Christmas," she would say.

"Okay," I managed. I realized when I heard their voices that I didn't like being sick this far away from them.

"Do you need anything, honey?" Nana asked.

"No, I'm fine," I'd assure them, but my cough would usually give me away.

"I don't like the sound of that cough," my mother would say.

"It's breaking up. That's a good sign." Nana.

"I suppose." My mother didn't sound convinced.

Then they would remember I was on the line, too. "We don't want to tire you out, so we'll go now. You just get as much sleep as you can, and you'll start feeling better soon." My grandmother, gently ordering me to get well. "We'll see you soon. Only a few weeks to Christmas!" We'd hang up, and I'd feel sad that they were so far away, a sadness I remember feeling only when I was feeling ill. I'd move from the living room, where I'd taken the call, back into the extra bedroom, to curl up under the covers.

When Mademoiselle came in to see me, she would just sit in the chair by the bed and hold my hand. It was comforting in a way, but still strange. I could tell in her wordlessness that often she was far away from me; her thoughts were taking her someplace else entirely.

Once, she spoke, and I had another glimpse into that human side of Mademoiselle that Emil had tried to tell me was there.

"This was my sister's room," she said.

"Lili's?"

She nodded. "It was sometimes difficult for her to manage the stairs, and this room is closer to the center of the house." I waited, but she said nothing more, only stared into space. I knew her sister had died young. I wondered if she had died in this room. The thought made me shiver.

"Are you okay? Do you need more blankets? Do you have a fever again?"

"*Non—merci, Mademoiselle.*"

"*Ça va bien, ma chère,* I hope you are feeling better soon." Her exit line.

Once, Mademoiselle came to sit beside me late at night, fingering a rosary and murmuring prayers, her voice a drone, deep in the dark. After three Hail Marys, she requested protection for me. Then, she requested patience for herself. I liked hearing her pray beside me. I felt the protection she requested in her very presence, in the repetition of her words, in the heaviness of her tired, end-of-the-day self.

I mentioned my teacher's surprising late-night visit to Zita the next morning. "*Mais, ma chère, elle vous vient chaque soir—après vous êtes dormi.*

Mademoiselle sat with me every night? I had no idea.

But the presence of my teacher always registered when I began to feel a little better. "When do you think you'll be able to do some harmony homework?"

"Not today."

"I hate to see you missing your lessons like this."

"I know. I'll be better soon." In the end, it was always me, reassuring my teacher that I'd be well, rather than the other way around.

There would be an interval, just before I was well enough to resume my schedule, when I almost enjoyed being sick. I was allowed to read mysteries and fashion magazines sent over by Ghislaine and take as many naps as I liked. A day or two later, Mademoiselle would replace the magazines with scores, and soon after that, I would be well enough to move back into my room to catch up on my composition homework.

I would usually be better in time to fly home for the holidays. I always felt bad to leave Mademoiselle behind, wondering if she'd feel lonely on Christmas. More likely, she enjoyed the break and the time alone. She usually spent the holiday with Emil and Ghislaine, but she had plenty of other invitations, too. She kept quite a social calendar, and I knew she attended a number of concerts during the season, because she always saved me the programs—complete with her notes—to study when I returned.

From the States, I would call her on Christmas morning, long-distance, a call underwritten by my grandmother. "*Joyeux Noel*," I would say as soon as she answered the phone.

"*Oh, merci, ma petite chère. Joyeux Noel à toi, aussi.*"

"I just wanted to wish you a Merry Christmas," I would say, restating the obvious in English, at a loss for what else to say to my teacher.

"You are so precious—to call me like this."

"I miss you."

"I miss you too, Hannah. Hurry back to Paris!" she would say, and between the crackles of the transatlantic connection, sometimes I thought I could hear just how much I meant to her.

***

"Are you very fond of the American School?"

We'd just finished the piano four-hands, and the question caught me off-guard. Mademoiselle filled the pause. "I know you have friends at school, but I think it would be better if you were to go to *lycée* here in Paris."

I'd learned by then that my teacher was quite self-contained. She had connections all over the world, and kept up through letters with many of her former students. She welcomed musical visitors passing through Paris on tour, and she hosted recitals in her apartment, but she was just as content with only herself for company. It seemed to me that she never sought anyone out; rather, people came to her, and she made them feel at home, if not needed.

I was not fond of the American School or the long drive every morning and afternoon. My only real friend was Elaine, and I was bored in many of my classes. But a *lycée* in Paris? If I couldn't fit in with a bunch of overachieving American kids, how could I hope to survive in the throngs of fast-talking French teenagers I'd seen hanging out in front of the school just down the street?

There was an awkward pause. The conversation was not proceeding the way my teacher had hoped. I'd learned a little bit about Mademoiselle in the almost five years I'd known her. On one hand, she expected me to do whatever she asked; on the other hand, she didn't like to tell me what to do. She wanted me to volunteer to change schools. It was a subtle sort of manipulation, and it worked much of the time. But

I wasn't ready to say yes, or to act as if I thought this was a great idea. I wanted to put her in the uncomfortable position of telling me rather than asking me to change schools.

I changed the subject. I asked her if she knew about my mother's violin playing.

"Yes, your grandfather mentioned it to me."

"Did he tell you about her recital?"

"He told me your mother was very nervous, very frightened. He blamed himself for not realizing she would be afraid on stage, for not preparing her."

"Did she play as badly as she says she did?" I asked.

"I don't know. I know she stopped playing after that, and Jacob never forgave himself."

I didn't say anything. I thought back to my mother's initial rejection of Mademoiselle's offer. At the time, I had known nothing of my mother's disastrous recital, but Mademoiselle already knew the whole story. I wasn't sure how to interpret this new information. Did it explain her unwillingness to accept anything less than a three-year commitment in writing from my mother? And had my mother's reluctance to let me study music been her way of protecting me? Was she afraid that I might fail as she did? I did get nervous, but not like that, not the way she described, not so nervous that I couldn't move my limbs or read a note. Not yet anyway.

"Do you think that could happen to me?" I asked the question I'd been thinking about since my mother first told me the story.

"*Non, ma chère, non, non. Jamais.*" She looked at me, perhaps to see if I believed her. "Don't let your mother's story frighten you. You are not your mother. Think of it. She was a small girl—younger than you were when you first came to me. She had never performed on a stage in front of others, and her father—her idol—had never mentioned that nerves could be a problem. She was quaking, scared beyond death, and worst, ashamed. She had no history to reference, no reassurances from her teacher or within herself that everything was as it should be, that she would survive. And so, she didn't. Or at least her music didn't survive that performance. She never played again. A pity, because your father said she was quite talented.

"But talent is always tested. Underneath whatever we find remarkable in a person, there must be layer upon layer of dedication and practice and work, work, work. Always work. Pride is the enemy of talent, even while it pretends to be a friend. It was her pride, her fear of failing again—especially her proud fear of failing in front of others—that caused your mother to abandon her music.

"And there is something else too, a grain of necessity that some of us feel, and others do not. There are those of us who simply would not, could not walk away. No matter the circumstance, we would be called back by our gifts and by the knowledge that our art is our life.

"That is the real difference between you and your mother. You are seeded with the inner necessity of music. To play it, to write it, to be in it in every way. And for me, it is my job to grow that seed in you, to help you care and nurture it until the necessity is so strong that you cannot ignore it, even for a minute. For it is that seed that will drive you, and that seed that will send you back on stage, no matter how well or badly you perform the night before.

"We all have nerves before a big performance. It is simply a signal that we care about our work. Think of all the notes you have played already, all the concerts and recitals you have given. When you have a moment of nervousness, a moment of insecurity, recall all the successes you have had, every note you have played well in all your life, and trust—trust in yourself and your ability and the music inside you. Trust in your training and your talent. Forget your pride, and remember you are never playing alone. The angels play with us as surely as God listens."

I was quiet after she finished; thinking mostly about the necessity she said was the difference between my mother and me. I could imagine it was true. For what I could not imagine, the part of the story I could not, for the life of me, understand, was the fact that my mother never, ever played again. Even if she hadn't wanted to perform, she could have still played, or if she didn't want to play the violin again, she could have started with another instrument. There was the piano in Bill's house that she could learn as an adult. But she didn't play or sing, or even invite much music into the house. I had no idea that she'd played an instrument until she told me that story. Yes, there was some fundamental difference between us, and maybe Mademoiselle was right. I needed music in a way my mother must not.

"Hannah, about the *lycée*," Mademoiselle interrupted my thoughts. "You'll think about it?"

"Okay."

"I do think it would be best," she said.

"I could still see Elaine on weekends?"

"Yes, of course. Saturdays will remain your own, so long as you fit in your practice time."

"*D'accord*," I said, realizing that it didn't matter to me—not one bit—where I went to school. "If you think it's best."

***

Saturdays remained my own, just as Mademoiselle had promised. I'd practice early and meet Elaine by 10:00 or 10:30. We'd ride the Métro, jostling with weekend shoppers, and sticking together so we wouldn't get lost in the crowds. Sometimes we'd join other girls from the American School, but mostly we were two—sharing confidences and giggling, talking in code about boys we knew, teasing and sshhshing each other in turn.

For me, it was a relief to have one day when I was allowed to act my age. The rest of the week, the little agenda that I still carried was full—classes and lessons, practice and rehearsal times, and—more and more—paid performances on flute. Many weeks, it was the prospect of Saturday, of seeing Elaine and feeling a taste of teenage liberty, that pushed me through the days of endless obligations.

One Saturday afternoon when we were almost fifteen, Elaine and I tried out kissing—practicing for the day when one of us might be kissed. We planned our experiment for a day Mademoiselle was away. We sneaked a bottle of wine and two glasses upstairs. We lit a candle, purchased specifically for the occasion on the recommendation of an article we'd read. We drew the curtains, sipped the wine, and finally, awkwardly, kissed.

"I don't get it," Elaine was the first to admit.

"If one of us were a boy it might help."

We sipped some more wine, wondering if being in love held the key.

"Maybe you need to pretend I am Thomas Holland." He was a boy at school I knew Elaine liked.

"You are *not* Thomas Holland," she said emphatically.

"No, because Thomas Holland has the most gorgeous deep brown eyes. And his hair is so wavy, and wouldn't you just love to touch it? And Thomas Holland has big strong hands. Wouldn't you love to hold them? And Thomas Holland's lips—" I was imitating her dreamy voice, and I was about to get carried away.

"Stop!"

"Admit it. You think about his lips! I think they're a little big for his face, myself, but you go for those lush lips! Lush Lips!"

"I don't think about his lips!"

"Lush Lips!"

Elaine tried her hardest to act mad at me before she dissolved into giggles. I collapsed onto the floor, joining her. So much for the kissing experiment. But we did discover a helpful new code name—LL—for Thomas Holland.

"Ouch! My cheeks ache from laughing so hard!" More giggles, and finally, the realization: "Mademoiselle will be home soon. We'd have to clean up before she gets here!"

We gathered up the evidence and dumped it far from Rue Ballu, and when I returned home that evening, I returned as a quiet, serious young musician. Mademoiselle didn't ask me how I spent my day; she never asked questions on Saturdays. She allowed me my small social life, but she stayed separate from that part of my existence.

"I am too old to be a mother now. You must be wise for yourself while you are here in Paris." She had set me straight within hours of my arrival.

Yet I cannot imagine a deeper relationship than ours. Sometimes I felt hurt by her lack of curiosity, her tendency to ignore my life beyond the walls of her studio, but in time, I came to understand. Music—Mademoiselle believed—was the only life I had.

***

I was fifteen when my grandmother wrote to say she was selling her house. "There are many happy memories here," she wrote, "but it is time for me to find a place that is smaller and easier to manage." The news came as a blow: Nana's house had always felt like home to me, the one true, unchanging home. When I stayed with my mother and Bill, I felt like a guest in a friendly hotel. I rarely stayed with my father and Joanne, but their house, too, felt strange to me.

By then, I'd spent way more time at Rue Ballu than I'd ever spent at Nana's house. I lived there. Was it my new home?

I wasn't sure. And I definitely wasn't sure that I wanted to spend Christmas in Paris when Mademoiselle first suggested it.

"I will call your mother to explain it to her." Mademloiselle told me that I'd have any number of opportunities to play my flute, and more importantly, a chance to conduct at a Christmas Eve choral concert at Trinité. "We'll also attend many concerts. It's a busy season in Paris."

We were never casual concertgoers; before and after every concert, we would study the scores in detail, and often we would have one across our laps in the hall.

I was torn. On one hand, Mademoiselle's idea of a holiday sounded like just that much more work. On the other hand, it was work that I loved. I wondered how we would spend Christmas Day. Would there be presents?

I remembered the first time I'd given Mademoiselle a gift. "You are never to spend money on me, again. *Jamais*," she had told me. I was eleven, and I'd saved for months to buy her a birthday present. She wore the scarf occasionally, but she held to her dictum. Would she change the rules if I were in Paris on Christmas?

My mother surprised me by going along with the plan. "You'll come home for Thanksgiving instead," she said, when Mademoiselle passed the phone to me.

"We'll just have Christmas early," my grandmother chimed in on the extension.

"*D'accord*," I said, without thinking.

"What?" My mother and grandmother, in unison.

"Okay," I said. "Okay."

***

I flew into New York, wearing my unaccompanied minor badge, on November 20, 1963. Two days later, President

Kennedy was shot. I was poring over the choral scores for the Christmas Eve concert when my mother called with the news. "I'm coming home right away," she said.

The phone rang again. My grandmother. "Are you okay? I'll be over in twenty minutes."

My father arrived without calling first. And so it happened that on the day that President Kennedy was shot, my father sat between my mother and me on the living room couch, an arm around each of us, as we listened to the radio. My grandmother arrived and squeezed in next to me. Bill picked up Joanne on his way from work, and when they arrived, my parents rose to greet their new spouses. But when everyone found their places, my parents were back on the couch, side-by-side, in a sad and silent version of the reconciliation I had hoped for years before.

Like people across the country, we were circling the wagons. People gathered in mourning, but also out of a sense of personal fear. The death of a young president seemed to mean we all were in danger. The right response was to check in with everyone you loved. The news traveled around the world quickly, and Mademoiselle, unable to get through the busy international circuits, sent a telegram: "I am praying for you and your president."

The funeral seemed to last for days, days of black and white images on the television, flickering in the living room. I felt bad for John-John and Caroline, losing their father that way. Having to attend his funeral on TV, on display for the whole country to see. My mother and grandmother watched Jackie intently. "We met her," my grandmother said, remembering a tea for the BSO wives when my grandfather was still alive. "She is a very gracious lady. Imagine losing her husband—so young—such a tragedy."

I don't know if it was because we could see it all on television, but we personalized this loss. We identified with Jackie,

Caroline, John-John, and the whole Kennedy family, and I don't think we were unique. Somehow every family in America felt they had lost an important and dear—if distant—relative.

That Sunday, there was a memorial concert. The sound was horrible, all shrunken into the television, but still, I was mesmerized as I watched Leonard Bernstein conduct the New York Philharmonic. I'd studied the Mahler songs, but this was the first time I'd heard the Second Symphony. Maestro Bernstein spoke before the orchestra began. He said that he chose the Resurrection Symphony because it was important not only to mourn our loss, but also to honor the hope that the president had symbolized for this country. He talked about music as a response to this terrible act of violence. It made me think about the fact I hadn't picked up my flute or played a note on the piano since Thursday.

As I listened to the Mahler, I closed my eyes. Watching a performance made me think about technical issues; by closing my eyes, I could experience the sheer emotional power of the music itself. I think it might have been in the few seconds between the second and third movements that I realized, I too, mourned this young president. Up until that point, I had almost felt like an intruder, someone who had walked into the wrong wake at a funeral home. I understood and felt a part of the general aura of sadness; I felt bad for the survivors, but I felt as if I didn't know the deceased. And really, I didn't. Not the way other people in America knew him. I'd been living at a distance for so long.

The power of that symphony, the strength of that chorus. Something in me broke, and then, something in me healed. I began to understand what Maestro Bernstein had in mind when he selected this piece. And I realized then that home wasn't Rue Ballu, even if it was.

***

Thanksgiving was subdued. After days of memorials, Masses, and music, a turkey dinner seemed almost a sacrilege. In fact, my mother wondered out loud whether we ought to just hold off having a big dinner. Nana bristled. "After a great tragedy like this, it's even more important to take the time to remember all that we are grateful for," my grandmother's words an echo of Maestro Bernstein's. It turned out to be a very important dinner. For the first time in six years, my parents shared a Thanksgiving table. My grandmother had invited my father and Joanne.

Surrounded by the people who loved me, I did feel grateful, most of all to my grandmother, for making sure we all held hands to say grace. I thought of Mademoiselle while my father said a halting prayer of thanks, and I knew I was also grateful for her, and for the music in my life. Music, Maestro Bernstein had said, must be our response to violence and to sorrow. What he didn't say was that music can be a call as well as a response. Music can be violent and sorrowful and gentle and joyful, and sometimes all those things at once.

When my father finished saying grace, and while we were still holding hands, I began to sing. It was an old hymn with a haunting melody and words that I barely remembered: "We gather together to ask the Lord's blessing." My grandmother joined in first, then Bill, next Joanne, and finally, my father and mother—an octave apart, but in unison.

Reverie

—17—

The piano has arrived. Arranging the delivery was complicated in that uniquely French way that requires long conversations, obscure paperwork, and—in this case—a preliminary visit to my apartment by the piano mover. "We must, of course, understand the place where the piano will rest," a big, muscled man named Dominic explained. He arrived, clipboard in hand, dressed in a dark suit that strained in the shoulders when he reached for the measuring tape attached to his belt.

"*Bien sûr*," I said, showing him where I planned to put the piano.

"*Ici?*" he asked, surprised that I wanted the instrument in the foyer. He suggested that I would want it to be in the living room, or the dining room, even in the bedroom. He was concerned about acoustics, about humidity, and about where I would seat an audience if I wanted to give a small recital. I attempted to quell his musical concerns by reminding him that the delivery would be that much easier if he didn't need to move the piano through any other doorways. "Ah—but of course this is my expertise," he reminded me. "I can locate your piano anywhere. You only have to choose the proper place."

"*Là*," I said with emphasis. "This is where I want it. This is where I work."

"As you like, Madame." He said with a shrug that let me know he would yield to my wishes despite his better judgment.

Dominic returned this morning, driving a delivery truck

with a little lift built in—it was like an exterior elevator, designed to hold a piano. He was wearing overalls that allowed him the freedom of movement his suit had not. He parked the truck in the courtyard and came upstairs to announce the delivery, asking me to sign some papers.

"*Ici*?" I noticed a barely perceptible shake of his head. "Or you have changed your opinion? I can place your piano anywhere in your apartment."

"*Oui. Merci. Mais je le voudrais là.*" In some strange way, I felt pleased that I was defying his piano-placing conventions.

I stayed upstairs to watch the lift rise up three stories, pausing just above my balcony. With the piano suspended there, Dominic and another hefty man came upstairs to meet it. With one man on the platform and two on the balcony, they used a combination of ropes, advanced geometry, and brute strength to maneuver the instrument down, over the railing, and through the double doors.

Dominic offered me one last chance to change my mind before he and his helper positioned the piano next to my desk. Then they unwrapped its swaddling clothes. There were layers and layers of blankets to protect the fine ebony wood. When the instrument was finally revealed, Dominic pulled another piece of soft cloth from a pocket and began polishing.

The piano gleamed its own invitation to me. Before the piano movers had made it downstairs, I was installed at the keyboard. I felt a funny mix of exhilaration and nervousness—I wanted to get that first touch between us right. But before I could sound a note, the phone rang.

"How's the piano, kiddo?"

"Mel—how did you know? It just arrived!"

"Word travels fast. Or more to the point—invoices do. They emailed me the delivery receipt. I passed it to your mysterious patron, and his lawyer just called to see if you needed anything else. Do you? He has money to burn, or so it would seem."

This patron reminds me of my first—the one you found for me, Mademoiselle. She wasn't anonymous, but I never met her. When she died, we attended her funeral at La Madeleine. Cavernous, packed with people, and you and I were in the very front, listening to my music being played. I was maybe sixteen, confused by it all. A woman I hadn't known at all had known me, and my music. She had specifically requested the composition that was played at her funeral. She even left money for me in trust to complete my education. Who was she?

And who is the piano-giver?

"Mel, do we know the donor's a *he*?"

"We don't know for sure. The attorney who calls is always careful to say *my client*. But his client wants to know: do you need anything else to complete your next masterwork, Schaeffer?"

"A sense of job security would be nice."

"Ah—yeah. I don't have any news there. But I think we might want to talk about walking."

"You think it will look better if I resign the podium, right? But doesn't that kind of let them off the hook? And it's not like I have some big plans to announce."

"Not yet. But if we let them know that you're considering other options and they don't make any effort to stop you, we have our answer. And either way, it's better if you leave on your own terms."

"You mean it's better if it *looks* like I am leaving on my own terms."

"Yeah, that too. Look Schaeffer, I know this sucks. And there isn't a single logical reason for them to find a new music director. You are fuckin' beloved by your orchestra, your subscribers, all of L.A., for God's sake. It's lousy Board politics, and we all know how much you love that part of the job. With these two new guys—"

"But I still have advocates on the Board, too—"

"Yeah, but do you want to feel like you have to fight for your job? Everything about this is wrong, Schaeffer. I know. But—"

"You want me to break up with them before they dump me."

"Pretty much. We have to think long-term."

"Okay."

"Okay—like, yes?"

"Yes, like yes. I trust you. If you think we need to do this, then let's do it—and maybe we'll call their bluff."

"Maybe. But you can't count on that. You understand?"

"I do."

"So—to be clear—we're walking?"

"We're walking."

"I'll email you the language—something about relinquishing the ongoing responsibility of leading the L.A. Phil in order to spend more time on your composing work. Sound okay?"

"Sounds great," I said. *What a lie.*

I hung up the phone, moved back to the piano. Bach? Brahms? Beethoven? Cole Porter? George Gershwin? Vince Guaraldi? Boulanger? Bernstein?

Hannah Schaeffer. Wasn't that the point of this piano?

No, not yet. First, I must meet the instrument.

You taught me that.

I began with scales.

—18—

While I was finishing up at *lycée*, Mademoiselle was planning my return to the States for the next stage of my studies. She wrote to Walter Piston, composer, professor emeritus of music, the author of the essential textbook, *Harmony*, and—perhaps most significantly—a former student of hers. He was semi-retired from Harvard, teaching a single class and a few private tutorials. If Mademoiselle had her way, I would be one of them.

Professor Piston agreed to review my composition portfolio, and I began working on my application to Radcliffe, Harvard's sister school. I was stymied by the application, feeling ill-equipped to state why I wanted to study at this prestigious institution. "Using specific examples of your past achievements, explain why you believe you meet our selection criteria." I wasn't sure I did. Mademoiselle would brook no complaints about the application, but she did suggest that Peter, now a graduate student himself, might help me with it.

"You're brilliant. Of course, you meet their criteria. We just have to come up with a way for you to explain how bright you are without sounding either too egotistical, or maybe worse, in the Ivy League, too self-effacing."

"But Peter, I'm no great scholar. All my achievements have been in music. And look, here's this whole section that asks me to list my extracurricular activities. What do I say? Flute lessons, theory lessons, composition lessons, sight-singing-lessons, solfege, conducting lessons? Or are those my inter-curricular activities!"

"Calm, Hannah, calm. We'll figure this out. There is no question you should be admitted. We just have to answer the questions so that it is apparent to the selection committee."

In the end, I suspect my application played only a minor role in my acceptance. It was the composition portfolio that did it. After Professor Piston had inspected my work, he used his influence to implement a master plan for the next five years of my life. I would officially be a Radcliffe student, following an undergraduate core curriculum. By special arrangement, I would pick up whatever Harvard graduate level classes in music that made sense, mostly history and literature, where I was not as well-learned. Finally, I would study privately, for graduate level credit, with Professor Piston. If I did everything right, I'd have a bachelor's degree, a master's degree, and my doctorate within five years.

"The dissertation requirement for a composition student is a juried recital of your own music. That will be no problem for you," he'd said, the first time we spoke on the phone. It was clear to me he had inherited some of Mademoiselle's ways: the same high expectations and no-protests attitude that I knew so well. If I'd hoped to escape my teacher's demanding style, I had come to the wrong place.

I learned on that same phone call that Walter Piston intended to use me as a teaching assistant. He viewed my teaching as a continuation of the learning process. "I learn something every time I work with a student," he said, "and that is how it should be. If you stop learning, you stop living." Surely, he and Mademoiselle would agree on the second point, even if their means to an end were different. So I became a teaching assistant. Unusual for a Radcliffe undergraduate, especially since the class I would be assisting was a graduate level harmony course in the Harvard curriculum.

Leaving Fontainebleau that summer for Cambridge didn't feel so different than going home for my usual break between summer classes and *lycée*. My schedule would be reversed. I would return to Paris for holidays now, studying with Mademoiselle and playing concerts over Christmas and Easter. And next summer, I would return to Fontainebleau. I didn't clear out my room at Rue Ballu, leaving at least half of my scores in Paris. On the day of my departure, Mademoiselle and I didn't even say *au revoir*. I gave her an American style hug, willed myself not to cry, and whispered, *À bientôt*. See you soon.

***

Professor Piston smiled more often than Mademoiselle Boulanger, and he made little jokes, but he was not a man you'd want to disappoint. He kept me busy, but aside from the private tutorials, my classes were not rigorous. Perhaps he had forced the teaching issue with Mademoiselle because he'd guessed I'd be challenged in that realm. And I was. I found out just how difficult it can be to explain something you know intuitively. But as Professor Piston pointed out to me, much of what I knew now only *seemed* intuitive. "Think back to those early days at Fontainebleau, when you felt like a Martian dropped into the middle of an analysis discussion."

Teaching taught me what I knew, showed me how far I had come, and also forced me to express my knowledge in concrete, understandable terms. It was good for me, just as the professor thought it would be. Still, it was good like vegetables are good for you when you're seven or eight years old, and you'd rather have ice cream for dinner. I never felt confident in the teacher role, never knew how to balance the demanding impatience that I had learned from Mademoiselle with the caring teacher that I wanted to be. The fact that I was younger than most of the students in the class didn't help matters either, at least not for me.

But if teaching was not my forte, I did find my strength

in Cambridge, and quite by accident. When the conductor of the Harvard Wind Ensemble became ill, Professor Piston recommended me to take over the rehearsals. I'd had plenty of conducting classes, and several conducting experiences in Paris. But they were smaller instrumental groups, some singers. Not a sixty-piece band with an excellent reputation and certain expectations about their conductor.

I was terrified at that first rehearsal, and I was relieved to see that the rehearsal podium had a chair built into it. I sat down while the musicians filed in, unpacked, set up. Seated, I could exude the false sense of relaxation that I could never pull off if I had to stand. I pored over the score, sipped a cup of coffee, and made some notes for myself. I didn't watch the band members get ready, at least partly because I knew they were busy watching me.

They were polite and attentive enough when I began to speak. They were withholding judgment, at least until after my first downbeat.

"As you know, I said, "Professor Walker is ill, and in the hospital. The reports are good, but he will be there for a while, and there will be some recovery time before he can conduct again. My name is Hannah Schaeffer," I said, "and I am your shoddy substitute."

That got a few smiles.

"I have a get-well card, here at the podium, that you can sign after rehearsal," I said. "Let's tune before we tackle the Persichetti."

The oboe player obliged with a B-flat. *Right,* I reminded myself—*a band, not an orchestra*. I'd been expecting an A-natural. "Woodwinds first, then brass," I said, hoping to learn something about the group from their ability to match pitch.

The first piece I planned to rehearse was a Vincent Persichetti piece for winds called *Pageant*. It was a relatively new piece of music, but thanks to Mademoiselle, I'd analyzed it on a particularly difficult Black Thursday—one of Mademoiselle's notorious weekly theory classes—at Rue Ballu. So, I knew the work, but I hadn't conducted it until about forty minutes before the rehearsal when I ran through it in a practice room.

"From the top," I said, "Think smooth, legato." The horns sounded good, but the balance wasn't right when the trumpets entered. I asked the horns to play alone, asked the trumpets to listen. "You need to enter below that," I said. "Don't announce your entrance. Just come in quietly and build with the rest of the band, and it will be much more effective when we reach the *fortissimo.*" Nods in the trumpet section, a smile from the lead horn. They were listening, and they knew I was too.

Soon enough, we were doing some of the dissecting work I'd come to love. Taking it to the garage, as Mademoiselle had said many years before. But in my mind, there was a difference between my garage and Mademoiselle the Mechanic. I put things back together again. Finally, we ran through the piece again, stopping only once for a missed entrance in the lower woodwinds. I looked at my watch when we were finished and was amazed to see that an hour had passed. The second hour passed almost as quickly.

I found myself looking forward to band rehearsals in a way that I anticipated no other classes in my schedule. When it became clear that Professor Walker would be out for the whole semester, I was thrilled to give away my post in the harmony class to take over the band. I loved working with a larger group, and I loved the rigor of rehearsing. The band responded well to my style of disassembling and reassembling. They were listening more carefully, playing with a sense of ensemble, and they were getting used to following me. The downbeat may be in the same place, but every conductor's style is different. After ten weeks of rehearsals, we were in synch with each other.

By the end of the semester, I had conducted the Wind Ensemble in two concerts. We'd melded into a working unit, and the performances were well-received. I found myself dreading Professor Walker's return and feeling dejected at the thought that I would no longer be a part of this organization. They threw me a big thank-you party a few weeks after the second concert, presenting me with a baton and the score of a new piece for winds by Professor Piston.

"Read the note," said Sean, the piccolo player.

Dear Hannah,

Thank you for taking over the band while I was sick. What a luxury for me to recover in peace, knowing that you were doing such a great job. You already know how impressed I was at that first concert, and the second was even better!

I'm feeling like myself again, but the doctors say they don't want me conducting for more than one hour at a time. I've talked with the powers-that-be, and they have agreed to hire an assistant conductor for the next semester. I'd like you to fill that position.

Walter's piece is a bribe. We commissioned it two years ago, and it will be a premiere. If you'll help me out with the band, the piece is yours to conduct at the spring concert.

Come see me on Monday morning in my office, and we can discuss all the details.

With thanks and best wishes,
James Walker

"Will you do it?" asked Morrie. He was one of the trumpet players I had asked to play more softly in that first rehearsal.

"You all know about this?" I asked.

"Why do you think we gave you a baton?" Kevin, the baritone horn was smiling at me.

"Everybody wants you to stay." A representative from the clarinets weighed in.

"Well, thank you, and thank Professor Walker. I was feeling really sad about leaving this band behind. I'd just love to stay—"

Before I could finish my acceptance speech, there was a trumpet fanfare—a real one—courtesy of Morrie, followed by a round of applause and chanting: "Cut the cake; cut the cake, cut the cake."

***

Mademoiselle believed in a single-minded dedication to the music that left room for nothing—and no one—else. While I was living with her in Paris, she kept me too busy to worry about boys. And thanks in part to her training, my seriousness of purpose would keep even the boldest suitors at bay. But Elaine Adams, budding matchmaker, could not be held back. She was back in the States for college too, and she would invite me for weekends at Cornell where she was majoring in animal science. She raved about the ratio of men to women. "Five-and-a-half to one! Come here, and we'll get you a date."

I looked forward to those weekends at Cornell, where I could drop the musical identity and just hang out with Elaine and her many friends. I loved Elaine and could listen to her talk about her veterinarian dreams for hours at a time. But I found it much harder to muster the same excitement as I sat across from a man discussing the latest techniques to increase herd production.

"Elaine, what are you thinking? Why do you always fix me up with the future farmers of America?" I asked her after an evening spent hearing about the latest technology in milking parlors.

"Oh, you're right. It's just that those farm management majors are the nicest guys, don't you think? Didn't you have anything in common?"

"Well, he said he was thinking of doing his thesis on the effects of music on milk production. He asked me if I might be willing to play sometime while he was milking at the dairy where he works."

"You're making this up!"

"I swear!"

"Oh my God!" Elaine slapped her forehead. "I see you playing wearing one of your concert gowns. Cows in a line."

"Big eyes. Cows have big eyes. I think they would be a tough audience to play."

"You're going to do it?"

"With your help, I'll never see Mr. Greenjeans again, but I did promise him a tape."

"Hannah Schaeffer's *Music for Cows*. Could be your first really big commission."

"Well, it's the least I can do for those poor overworked cows with infected udders and dry skin around their nipples."

"So, he gave you the blow-by-blow."

"It was all I could do not to keep my arms folded across my breasts the whole time. *Yuck*!"

"Okay, we rule this one out."

"This one, and the next ten guys you are even thinking of introducing to me. I think I need to meet someone outside the animal science program."

"Landscape architecture?" she asked.

"I don't think so."

"Okay. I'll keep my eye out in my elective classes. Maybe I can find a nice liberal arts major who will talk about Sartre over dinner."

I wasn't sure Sartre would make the best dinner conversation either, but then what did I know? Elaine was sending me on my first dates ever. Maybe I shouldn't be so picky; maybe I should just go on a few dates with one of these guys and then sleep with him. Get that over with. I was intensely aware that

I was still a virgin in an unfolding atmosphere of free love.

"Don't worry, we'll find somebody you like."

There already was somebody I liked. I'd see him that summer at Fontainebleau: Peter.

"He's a lot older than you," Elaine warned. "And you don't know anything about his life."

"Mademoiselle would kill me." We were listing the reasons why I should not pine for Peter.

"But do you think he likes you?" Elaine asked, in spite of herself.

"I don't know. How would I know?"

"Well—when you play together, does he ever stay to talk afterwards, after everyone else has left?"

"Oh, always, but it has been that way since I was ten years old."

"Maybe he's had a crush on you since you were ten years old!"

"That's gross!"

"It is," she said, laughing. "But I think you've had a crush on him at least that long!"

I *had* noticed Peter during my first summer at Fontainebleau. His white blond hair and intense blue eyes. His gentle manner with me and the fierceness in him that came out when he played. I probably did have a little girl crush on him even then.

Once, a girlfriend of Peter's had come to a public concert, and I inspected her as if I were his mother. I wanted her to be perfect for him, exactly right, beautiful and smart, talented just like Peter. I was thirteen, and like a true student of Mademoiselle, I believed I could become Renée, if only I just studied her closely and long enough.

"She is a waste of his time and focus," Mademoiselle declared. "If they marry, I will have to send a sympathy note."

The thing was, she meant it. On the occasion of the marriage of a particularly promising student, Mademoiselle Boulanger was rumored to have sent a note of condolence on black-edged stationery. She could be happy enough for the students whom she did not envision as lifelong musicians, but from those of us with promise, she wanted vows of celibacy. Music must come first and last, and it left no room in the middle.

Peter didn't invite Renée to another concert, but they continued seeing each other. I'm not sure what went wrong, but I remember Emil patting Peter on the back after a rehearsal a couple of summers later. "Don't take it too hard. When it is meant to be, it will happen."

These, the words of a happily married man who believed in true love. For some reason, Mademoiselle allowed him this departure from her policy.

When I was sixteen, and Peter was between girlfriends, I wondered if I could ever fill that role. But he was in his twenties, and I wasn't even out of *lycée*. It seemed an impossible gap to bridge. Two years later, the age difference seemed much smaller. I was eighteen; he was twenty-four. And as far as I knew, he wasn't seeing anyone.

That summer, after my first year at Radcliffe, and after too many fixups with Elaine's farmer friends, my long-running consciousness of Peter turned into hyperconsciousness. His presence in a room was almost too much to bear, and when he was seated close to me in rehearsals, my skin tingled. I could maintain my concentration if we were playing together, but if there were only words and no music between us, I was lost—hopelessly at sea—no lifeboat, no glimpse of land or safety.

I had no idea what to do. And I had no idea if Peter felt anything toward me. I tried to remember what Elaine had told me. "Does he look you right in the eye when he speaks to you?" she'd asked. "That means he's interested in you."

The next time I saw Peter after a rehearsal, I noticed he

asked earnest questions to my arm. My left arm, my elbow in particular.

I reported this to Elaine in an overseas phone call I made from Emil's studio. The agreement that Nana and Mademoiselle had negotiated with my first patron included an allowance for travel and phone calls home. When the patron agreed to these provisions, I'm guessing she imagined a lonely little girl wanting to hear the voices of home. But that summer I used up all my allowance the way any teenager would—to call her best friend and talk about boys.

"Oh, then he probably likes you."

"But you said that he should look right into my eyes."

"I did? Oh, yeah, well—sometimes. "But sometimes, they are so shy or embarrassed or something—well, they can't even look at you."

"Really?"

"Oh yeah. That's what happened with Donald." Donald was Elaine's boyfriend. And he would become her husband. She was crazy about him, and he about her.

"He didn't look at you?"

"Not for weeks. He looked past me, over my right shoulder. Sometimes I felt like I should turn around in my seat to see if there was something really interesting going on behind me."

"So, you think this could be a good sign?"

"Definitely. I do."

"But what should I do?"

"What do you mean?"

"I mean, how will he know that I like him?"

"Oh, he'll figure it out. Just listen to him when he speaks to your elbow, ask him a lot of questions. Eventually you'll say something that makes him look up. Your eyes will meet, and—"

"Then what?" I interrupted her, eager for some resolution.

"He'll kiss you."

"Just like that?"

"Yeah."

"Is that what happened with Donald?"

"No. He didn't look me in the eyes until after he kissed me."

"Then what happened?"

"He kissed me again, silly."

"Oh."

"It will be all right. Just don't let Mademoiselle catch you."

"There's nothing to catch." I was suddenly more practical. Was it the mention of Mademoiselle?

"There will be."

"You think so?"

"*Definitely*." That was Elaine's favorite expression lately. Since she'd found Donald, her life seemed much more definitive. "Really. I think he likes you. And I know you like him. Call me when he kisses you."

"That could be a while."

"I don't think so. Two weeks, tops. You don't have much time. If you are going to have a summer fling, you'd better get on it. I'll be waiting by the phone."

"You will not!"

"You're right. I won't. I hope to be in bed with Donald."

"You're bad!"

"Uh-huh." I could hear her smiling. "You only wish you were as bad as me."

"I do," I admitted.

"You will be. He's an older man. You have to tell me everything he teaches you."

"Elaine!"

"Promise to call?"

"Promise."

—19—

Mums today, pinkish red, with yellow centers. The impatiens are growing leggy, and yes, that is a proper gardening term. I've been visiting the flower market by Sainte-Chapelle, talking to the vendors. One in particular has taken an interest in my grave garden. She suggested that I dig up the impatiens and plant some mums now that the weather is changing.

I have to move your vase to dig. White marble, a vase for the dead, it will last for all eternity. It weighs a ton. And I'll need to make at least four trips with the watering can to moisten the grave garden. New plants need extra water. I've learned this too. I can hear you laughing at me, and yes, it's funny. Me, getting into gardening. Next thing you know, I'll be planting vegetables. Where? Maybe here. But not until spring.

While I dig and pull and plant and water, I can tell you about my lunch date yesterday with Philip Glass. When he called a few days ago, I had no idea why he would want to share a meal with me. Even when I premiered his piece, we didn't eat anything more substantial than hors d'oeuvres in the Founders' Room. But I agreed to a late lunch in the little café across the street from Sainte-Chapelle.

He gave me a European double air-kiss hello before we settled into a booth toward the back of the restaurant. The conversation moved from the unusually sunny Paris weather to touring to—I'm not sure I would have predicted this—the heartlessness of Nadia Boulanger. Now don't be offended. Just listen, okay?

"There is no doubt that she was a great teacher," Philip

said, "but I can't imagine how you managed to live with her! I mean, she wasn't a very nice person."

"How can you say that? She saw to my musical education; she opened up her home to me in Paris."

"Her home, yes, but never her heart. I don't think that old tiger had a heart."

I laughed in spite of myself. I remembered those early days. You were daunting, formidable. I wasn't sure you had a heart then, either.

"Do you remember Emil? The French horn player? He taught at Fontainebleau, and he was around the apartment in Paris from time to time?"

"Mustache? Good player, too?"

"Wonderful player. He's still around—and playing. Emil may have been the kindest person at Fontainebleau. He taught me—when I was only ten years old—that Mademoiselle Boulanger had a larger heart than most of us. The way he put it was she had to protect her big heart, and that was why she acted the way she did."

"And you believed him?"

"I don't know if I believed him right away, but I came to understand that what he said was true."

"Really?" Philip leaned in, giving me his full attention.

"Yes. Mademoiselle was a dear to me. She was horrible and strict, sure, and she could reduce me to tears with a single glance, a casual remark. But underneath that—driving that, even—was her love for the music."

"I never said she wasn't dedicated to the music." He was disappointed with my answer.

"But more than that, she truly cared about her students."

"Musically," he clarified.

"Musically and otherwise."

"Well, you were a lot younger than I was. When I came to her, I had already graduated from Julliard. I had my own ideas. Most of which, she informed me, were ill-conceived."

"You were always fighting her. Even I can remember that from the Thursday classes."

"Oh, Black Thursdays. Don't remind me!"

"They were awful, weren't they?"

"Were private lessons any better? I remember being late once, having been stuck in a demonstration that held up the Métro. I arrived ten minutes into my lesson time. She asked me why I had bothered to come at all. I began to tell her about what had happened, why I was late. 'I am uninterested in your stories. I am uninterested in demonstrations. Politics have no place in my studio. Here, we have music.' Then she walked me to the door. "'Next week, Mr. Glass, I will see you promptly at ten, or not at all.'"

"Were you ever late again?"

"God, no!"

"Then, her strategy was effective." I couldn't help smiling.

By the way, classic *you*, Mademoiselle. I'd never heard that story before.

Philip didn't let up. "But—I mean—how did you handle it—did you rebel when you were a teenager?"

"I didn't have time to rebel. I was too busy practicing."

"I guess we all were. But I think if I had lived with *Mademoiselle Le Tyran*, I would have felt obliged to have some escapades."

"*Insomission.* Rebellion. We had a talk about it when I turned fourteen. She essentially told me that it would be unproductive for both of us, that there was no need to rebel, that I should save my rebelliousness for my mother. She reminded me that she was not a parent, nor had she ever tried to act like one. She'd impressed that point upon me before."

"Telling a fourteen-year-old who has lived with you for—what, four years?—that you are not in any way to be confused for a parental figure. I'm not sure that is kind. You haven't convinced me that Nadia Boulanger had a heart."

So, I told him the Ear Opera story.

"She really wore a scarlet hat with a feather and danced?"

"I swear."

"It's a wonderful story. The way she caught onto your silliness and helped you create something from it, and then was willing to assemble a performance, all in the spirit of your work. But she did it in the service of music. She even said it—that she was building your ears."

"You're right that it always came back to music with Mademoiselle, but the Ear Opera shows you something about her heart, too—doesn't it?

"Maybe. I'll cede to you on this round. But I bet I can round up a lot more stories from former students that support the no-heart theory than you can share to show me I'm wrong." He smiled, seeming pleased with himself.

I smiled back, thinking he probably wasn't wrong—about the stories, not your heart, Mademoiselle. Clearly, a subject change was in order. "I'm guessing you didn't invite me to lunch to talk about Nadia Boulanger?"

"No, I wouldn't have even guessed she'd come up. I'm here to ask you to conduct the *Serenade for Saxophone and Orchestra* again. With Geoffrey Lassman. I think of it as his piece, and in a way, it's yours too. You two were remarkable. Of course, it's been a few years, and won't be the same with a different orchestra, but it's a perfect gig. You don't even have to leave Europe. There's a last-minute opening at the Royal Albert that Colin Davis can't make. They double-booked him or something."

"Wait a minute—Sir Colin Davis was going to conduct Philip Glass?"

"No—God, he's past eighty now. My music would do him in for sure. It was an all-Beethoven program."

"And instead, you plan to give ye old loyal subscribers to the

London Philharmonic a dose of Hannah Schaeffer and Philip Glass? Instead of Sir Colin and Beethoven? Are you crazy? We'd have a riot on our hands! Who made this decision?"

Philip was laughing. "No—no—you've got it all wrong. They are shuffling everything around, and Michael Tilson Thomas—who was going to do a new music concert—is taking over the Beethoven series. And because of some arcane contractual issues, that leaves the new music concert without a conductor. So, they called me."

"To conduct?"

"No. To offer me the unique opportunity to be heard at the Royal Albert, and to rescue their series. The original program consisted of a new John Harbison piece, which it turns out won't be ready in time. They figured what's the difference between living American composers? Maybe they could get some Philip Glass and a conducting recommendation, make everyone happy. I suggested the *Serenade* and you."

"Philip, I'm not even guesting this year. I'm focused on composing."

"That's what Mel told me. And that's why it works out so well. I told them you'd have a piece for the concert too. We can share the bill. Do you have something ready?"

"Ready?"

"For the concert." He didn't wait for an answer. "You still have six months. They won't need the score until late March. Shall we order dessert? I love eating dessert in Paris."

"You order." I excused myself and headed to the ladies' room.

I lowered myself, fully clothed, onto a hard little seat in the cramped café toilette, considering the bizarre unfolding of the lunch. Philip Glass, offering me a commission from the London Phil and the chance to conduct my own work. It's been a while since I've been able to play that dual role—not since I've been full-time with L.A.

The Royal Albert Hall. Not exactly a hot new music venue. I remember the first time I heard a concert there with you. I was eleven, and it felt royal indeed. All the red and gold. We sat so close to the stage that I could read the first violin part.

Honestly, though, I don't enjoy conducting there. I don't like sharing with the audience the many secret looks and motions I make to my orchestra—but this wouldn't be *my* orchestra. (Ignoring the technicality that I no longer have an orchestra to call mine anyway.)

Oh, yes, the soloist: Geoffrey Lassman, on stage, playing his mournful, lovely, heartbreaking horn. And in case you weren't paying attention, this is the guy who—well—I guess he's the guy I turned down. But I still let him play my Bonneville.

It was after the third concert of the series in L.A. He was talking to the flute players backstage, chatting about wooden head joints and old flutes, and Carl—our principal—motioned to me. "You want to talk old French flutes, you need to talk to the Maestro," he said. Maybe he said it because he wanted to slip out of the conversation, or maybe—I don't know. But soon enough, it was just Geoffrey and me. In my conductor's quarters—his lips on my flute. (Wow, that sounds like nineteenth-century porn or something.)

It was a fluke that I had both the Bonneville and the Louis Lot with me. I'd given a demonstration earlier that day at an early music conference. Something Mel asked me to do *pro bono* to benefit—you know, I'm not even sure what the benefit was for. No matter. I had two old flutes. We were two flute players. We played duets. Duets, late at night, exhausted and yet keyed up, after another amazing performance on stage. Fueled by Thai takeout the stage manager had ordered when I told him I'd be staying, I even lent Geoffrey a spare toothbrush after we ate so we could keep playing. It was strange and wonderful, and I don't know what else.

We barely spoke. We didn't touch. We just played until about two in the morning. Then, I offered him a lift to his hotel and went back to my apartment. The next afternoon, we played the bonus concert, an invention of the L.A. management that I could generally live without.

"Thanks for everything," he said, all packed up, a car waiting to whisk him to the airport. I might have been imagining it, but I thought there was something about the way he said the word—*everything*—something private or—I don't know.

"One-hundred percent pleasure," I said, shaking his hand. Maestro, soloist, no more.

And then, he left. Or I let him go. Or none of the above. I mean it isn't as if he's reached out to me since—or me to him.

But.

Something.

Or not. Maybe just music.

Never *just*, I know. Only music, you're reminding me. Philip Glass is suggesting a subscription concert and new work of my own. Yes, Geoffrey Lassman's on the program. And yes, I have lingering questions about declining dinner almost a decade ago. Leading to lingering embarrassment, especially in front of you. I mean, I am a little old for unrequited—not love—infatuation, no—fascination, overstated—curiosity, yes, that's all it is. *Was.*

Focus on the music. I am, I promise. But maybe this invite, inconvenient and badly timed, could be—oh, I don't know—fate? An answer to a question I feel silly even asking?

"I'll speak to Mel and have him phone you with the details," Philip said when I returned to the table. "He'll need to get the commission worked out with the London people. And you'll have to hear all the specifics before you can make up your mind. I understand. Don't give me an answer now. We'll leave that business to the business managers. Now tell me about the piece you are working on."

"I'm working on my *life*," I heard myself say. A real conversation stopper, and not anything I planned to share. I tried for the save. "It's just that these past twenty years, I've neglected my writing in favor of conducting."

"You're a stellar conductor. I'm not sure you are neglecting anything so long as you keep getting up on that stage and making the music happen."

"Don't patronize me. You know as well as I do that it matters whether the music is your own."

"I drove a cab until I was forty-one years old. You conducted the BSO in your thirties. You expect me to say *poor you*?"

"I know. I don't mean to sound self-indulgent. I have a great life. An amazing life. But it just hasn't felt—like my *own* lately. And by the way, did you ever for a moment want to conduct the BSO?"

"Okay, point for you. Truth is I liked my cab-driving composer life."

"Because driving a cab required none of the same energy that you needed for your musical life. I've given out so much on that podium, and now what do I have left? I've heard so much. How can I possibly hear my own voice?"

"Oh, you don't want to find your voice but lose it. That's what I tell all the young composers. I don't want you to think I sound like Philip Glass; I want to surprise you."

"Fine, Philip, surprise me. But when I was a kid, I was full of my own music. Now, I am full of everyone's music but my own. Do you get it yet?"

"Yes," he said. "I get it."

But really, he didn't, because I didn't tell him that one big thing: that I don't have my own music *or* my own orchestra now. There was no way I could tell him: Nothing's official yet. And I want to tell my players first, before anything goes public.

Dessert arrived. "*So* good," he murmured. "Food is either

the best or the worst part of being on the road. In Paris, it is the best part."

"Other than the music, you mean."

"Oh—yeah—the music." He grinned at me. "Oh—yeah," he repeated, snuffling with laughter—"the music."

I'm not sure why it struck us so funny. You would never approve—music as an afterthought. But laughing together returned us both to good humor.

You know, that may have been the first serious conversation I've ever had with Philip.

The truth is, commissions and earned respect aside, I never warmed to him. He always seemed as if he was too good for the rest of us at Rue Ballu. Always making a point of his studies with Ravi Shankar. Acting as if he had other, much more tasty and interesting fish to fry. And his early work, though I have always admired the concept of it, has struck me, too often, as conceptual, period. Nothing to connect with below the shoulders. All mind and no heart. It's funny: that was his complaint with you, Mademoiselle.

He has revealed so much more of himself in his recent work. I didn't just admire *Serenade;* I loved it. Phil said over lunch that he could never have written the music he writes today if he hadn't gone through the evolution from his strictest, most minimalist days. I wonder: all those years, was he shielding his heart? Why? And what changed? How did he find safety?

Safety. The kind that gives you courage to take risks, to make *unsafe* choices. I was sure all I needed was a podium of my own. But somehow that became the remarkable thing, the rocket that was my career, not the launch pad to create my own music.

It's true that my head has been mostly filled with other people's music, but well as long as there's an orchestra in front of me, I'm mostly okay with that.

—20—

"Do you believe in God?" Peter asked me, all earnestness, a contemplative look directed—again—at my left elbow. It was a week after I'd solicited Elaine's advice.

"God?"

Maybe it was the surprise in my voice that made him look up. Because there we were, eye-to-eye, with the existence of God between us.

"Think about Bach," he offered, still holding my gaze. "All these cantatas, written for church services. Every week, he wrote another piece of music! Do you think he believed in God?"

First my beliefs; now Peter was asking me to speculate on the belief system of a dead composer. My field of vision was filled with those shockingly blue eyes. But I could tell that he wanted an answer.

"Some people say that it was God that gave Bach the music."

"But what do *you* think?"

"I think he wrote a lot of music. It came from somewhere."

"God, then?"

"Someplace that was like God."

"Are you ready?" He meant, I presume, was I packed, ready to leave the rehearsal space. "Here, let me take your bag."

"Would you like to come in?" I asked when we arrived at my room.

"Yes, very much."

"Alright, I'll make a snack," I said, as if we had done this a million times before. I found some fruit and cheese in my little fridge, cut up a baguette I'd stolen from the dining room earlier in the evening. I wished for wine but served the only beverage I had in the fridge: Coca Cola in curved green bottles.

"A feast," he said. He was sitting on the floor with his back up against my bed.

Peter resumed our earlier discussion. I wasn't sure where I stood on the God question. Mademoiselle was a devout Catholic, and I'd attended Mass with her for most of the Sundays I'd spent in Paris. At home, my mother had become an occasional Episcopalian since her marriage to Bill, and my grandmother, Catholic by birth but married to a Jew, never made her religious loyalties known to me. During my time in Cambridge, I'd read the existentialists, the nihilists. I'd learned how to disprove the existence of God in two hundred words or less. But I didn't spend too much time with it. After all those years in Paris, I was an old eighteen in America, and too immersed in music to join in the kinds of discussions that most college kids find so pressing.

"If there is proof that God exists," Peter was saying, "I think it is in the music of Bach." He looked at me expectantly.

"Mademoiselle Boulanger would probably agree with you on that," I said, immediately regretting the mention of my teacher. "Hey—do you want to go on a picnic tomorrow?" I asked, a diversionary tactic.

"Sure. With instruments?" he asked.

We had a longstanding tradition of taking a basket of food and some music into the woods at Fontainebleau, making our sounds in the forest, eating some food. When I was younger, Emil often organized these events, and Ghislaine provided the food and sometimes came along with us. A student of Emil's might come, or a girlfriend of Peter. Sometimes Mademoiselle joined us, too.

"What would it be like to have a picnic without music?" I wondered aloud.

"With only ourselves for company." There was a pause before Peter filled it. "I'll arrange the food."

"What shall I bring?"

"Your lovely self," he said, unfolding himself from the floor to his full height. He extended his hand to help me up. "I have to go now," he said.

"Okay." I heard the upward inflection in my voice, as if I were asking a question. A question Peter answered with a light kiss to my forehead before he closed the door between us.

***

The next day, Peter arrived promptly at noon. He'd borrowed Emil's gray Peugeot, and he'd laid in plenty of supplies.

"You brought your cello?"

"Yes, I thought we might want to play once we got there. Why don't you bring a flute?"

My disappointment was immediate and surprisingly deep. On this day, I felt the instruments were a distraction, and I wondered if that was exactly why he'd decided to bring them along. Was I kidding myself, thinking that he might be interested in me? But Elaine, who knew all about these things, had said—*oh, Elaine's never met him or seen us together, how could she know*?

I took my time choosing a flute as I participated in this debate. Peter was standing awkwardly at the doorway, not in, not out. I suddenly felt angry with him. And myself. Did he even know I'd invited him on a picnic with the suggestion of romance? He probably just wanted to play Bach. Maybe he was hoping for some miraculous revelation from God, proof of His existence. Maybe Peter was turning into some religious fanatic, and he was planning this afternoon to convert me. Maybe—

"Hannah?"

"Uh-huh?"

"You look especially pretty today."

I spun around, flute under my arm. "Thank you," I said, an automatic response, a smile. I'd been trained by my grandmother and by Mademoiselle to accept every compliment gracefully.

"No, thank *you*," Peter said, as he smiled back at me and winked, just like the old Peter, the young man from Holland who'd been so kind and sweet and careful with the young girl from America. I felt so glad to see him again, the old Peter, and relieved that I wouldn't have to spend the afternoon with the uncertainty that had sprung up between us this summer. He was right to bring instruments. He was right to pitch this event down a bit. It wouldn't be right, I realized. Peter and I were friends, almost family. We could never pull off a date. What was I thinking? What was Elaine thinking?

What was Peter thinking? That's what I really wanted to know. "Let me take your bags," he said. "You wait here." I couldn't imagine why I should wait, but I did, watching while he loaded my stuff into the car. I felt foolish standing in the doorway when he came back up the stairs.

"Why did you make me wait?"

"To see if you would."

"Is this some weird sort of personality test?" I asked. I was feeling annoyed again.

"No. I was just hoping you'd be willing to wait."

"What am I waiting for?"

"For this." He kissed me ever so lightly on the lips. "I forgot to ask—may I?" he stepped back to look at me.

I nodded, no words.

He took my chin into the palm of his hand and kissed me

again, softly, carefully. He stepped back once more, staring at me, another question in his eyes. I moved into his arms, looking for a hiding place.

"Is this okay? I know it is a little strange. I mean—we have known each other a very long time, but you have been a little girl."

"But now I am a big girl," I said, trying to sound light and breezy. Nineteen in less than a month, I kept thinking. But I was as frightened as the ten-year-old who came to Fontainebleau that first summer, uncertain of her future.

"Are you scared?" He paused only a moment before he said, "I hope you are at least a little scared, because I am pretty frightened myself. And not just of Mademoiselle."

"She'd be appalled," I agreed. I couldn't help but smile thinking just how appalled she'd be.

We grinned stupidly at each other for a few seconds before I took the initiative, kissing him as gently as he had kissed me. "Oh, please don't go," he said, as I began to pull back. He kicked the door shut. "The car is locked," he answered to my unasked question. "The instruments are safe. Besides, this is Fontainebleau."

It was my first real kiss, the first kiss I really wanted. Sure, there had been awkward goodnight kisses with Elaine's farmer friends, but nothing like this. Nothing sustained, nothing with a bass line. I would write this kiss long and low and deep, a chord carried across bar lines, *basso sostenuto*, with little fluttering sixteenths in the upper voices.

Finally, as if by mutual agreement, we broke from it, stood back. I felt disoriented, unsure. There was no hiding now. I wasn't the ten-year-old girl anymore. And he was no longer my friendly comforter. But who were we now?

Peter took control of the situation before my thinking grew any more desperate. He whisked us out the door and drove us into the forest. He chatted all the way, keeping the air filled with nothing special, but leaving no room for that awkwardness to get into the car with us.

The afternoon was beautiful: weather perfect; food delicious; music—yes, we did play music—effortlessness, light. We went for a walk, holding hands. Peter showed me a special tree, an ancient oak, round and tall. Peter hugged the tree, his arms reaching around the trunk.

"Try to reach me from the other side."

I put my arms around the tree, stretching to reach his fingertips. I couldn't. We found this hilarious. He edged over to one side, took my fingertips and kissed them one by one.

"Time to go back," he said as the sun dropped over the trees. "It's getting dark." We packed up the car and drove back to the grounds. He walked me up to my door, stepped inside for a goodnight kiss. But it wasn't the kiss I'd been waiting for all day. It wasn't the kiss to finish the music we'd written before the picnic.

"A Coke or something?" I wanted him to stay.

"Oh—I can't. Gone all afternoon, here last night—too noticeable, you know?" I did know. Fontainebleau was a very small place. Word traveled fast, and rumors of romance even faster. We needed to be careful, especially if we wanted to keep our secret safe. Still, I was disappointed, and maybe Peter could read that on my face.

"I have an idea. Wait here." He turned to gauge my reaction, the second time he'd asked me to wait on my doorstep that day.

"Not again," I said rolling my eyes.

"I assure you: once more, it will be worth the wait." He returned a few minutes later with his cello, a music stand, and a pile of music.

"Camouflage," he said with a wink. Then he produced a few LPs, one of which he dropped onto my turntable. "Unaccompanied Bach. It's Jackie Du Pré," he said, "but through the walls—who's to say it's not me?"

***

Peter and I kept our romance under wraps. No doubt the secrecy added to our excitement, but it also made me sad. I wanted to tell the world—including my teacher—how wonderful I felt every minute that I spent with Peter. It wasn't that I wanted her to know what was going on between us, but I wanted Mademoiselle to recognize a change in me, a change, I thought, for the better. But what she noticed was my daydreaming.

"If you don't intend to be present during our lessons, there is no reason for me to attend either," Mademoiselle declared.

"I'm sorry. I'm just a little tired today," I said, a sort of truth.

"And every day this week. You think I am not tired? I am sixty-one years older than you are! If I can make it to every lesson, I expect you can do likewise. Understood?"

"Yes, Mademoiselle," I heard myself say, the frightened ten-year-old again. I couldn't say why or how my teacher could inspire fear, but it seemed I was still afraid of her, or perhaps more accurately, I was afraid to lose her.

"Despite your tired state, you have managed a very nice sonata here. Let's have a closer look at the third movement; I want to ask you a few questions." She would lead me to better voicings, help me identify a lost theme.

"Make something of this," she would say not infrequently, referring to a melodic bit I'd introduced but never developed. "You have such an ear for the melody, but sometimes you drop a few notes like crumbs on the floor. Pick them up; build on them. Or cut them out and expand the harmonic treatment. But don't leave them unsupervised.

"Every note must carry intention. There must be a reason for being. *Raison d'être*," she said. It was a philosophy she carried far beyond the musical realm. For Mademoiselle, everything and everybody required a reason for being. She failed to understand the drop-ins, the wanderers, the aimless ones in life, just as she failed to understand those notes without vocation.

I may have dropped a few notes that summer, but I was writing furiously, and for that reason, I knew Mademoiselle would not abandon me too readily. She took a childlike delight in reading through my pieces, taking out her pencil and marking up my manuscripts with question marks and exclamation points, stars and crosses, her personal lexicon of symbols to guide our lessons.

"I think Radcliffe has done you some good," she said at the end of one lesson.

"Oh, it isn't Radcliffe; I am mostly bored there. It is coming back to you, to Fontainebleau. This place feels like home to me."

This was true, but also it was coming back to Peter that was driving me. I was in love, for the first time ever, and my feelings flowed naturally into my composition. Composing had always been easy for me, a spontaneous act. Instead of keeping a journal, I wrote music.

"But there is a new depth to your work. I think Mr. Piston has had a hand in that. You are more consistent now, fewer notes for me to mop up. You are putting your old teacher out of work!"

"Never!" I said it with a smile, but I meant it with all my heart. I could not imagine working so closely with anyone else. As much as I liked Professor Piston, as much as I admired his work, and appreciated his advice, we weren't really close. It was impossible that I would connect with him in the same way.

I don't know if my especially warm feelings towards my teacher that summer were an outgrowth of my feelings for Peter. It can be that way when you fall in love, that you find yourself loving everything and everyone around you. I remember once almost taking Emil's hand when we went for a walk. I caught myself as I reached out to him, an unconscious gesture of closeness that had become so much a part of my vocabulary with Peter.

No doubt some of my new appreciation for my teacher came from being away, from being in Cambridge, from understanding just how much she was willing and able to give to each student, even in her own peculiar way, and at her advanced age. I worked hard for her, out of love and out of fear. I wondered how much more time we would have together. She would turn eighty in September. As spirited as she was, Mademoiselle was beginning to show signs of frailty. Her vision was impaired by cataracts, and her movements were less certain. As her physical body grew less reliable, however, her mind seemed only that much more formidable. Her memory was remarkable; her curiosity was still insatiable, as was her appetite for good music.

That summer, I finally and fully understood why my grandfather had extracted that promise those many years ago. He knew what Mademoiselle Boulanger had to give me, and he knew she would offer it all up, selflessly and effortlessly for the rest of her life.

"Your music is a gift to me in my old age," she said one afternoon, after we'd worked through a score on the piano.

I didn't know what to say.

"You must protect your talent, always. You must promise me this." It was an old theme, the idea that I must protect myself, my music, but I wasn't sure where she was going with it today. Did she know about Peter? Was this a roundabout reference? But the Mademoiselle I knew was never indirect.

"Are you listening?" she asked, a little testiness in her voice.

"Yes, but I am not sure what you mean."

"We have spoken many times about the dedication

required by the musical life. And you have shown a large capacity for dedication and single-mindedness in the years I have known you."

"Nearly nine years," I inserted. Half my life.

"But there will be distractions. There always are. Even your own mind can lead you off course at times. You may feel hemmed in by the narrowness of your path, especially now that you are in Cambridge, surrounded by intellectuals and the student life."

I began to protest, but she silenced me with her hand.

"Maybe it won't be college life that tempts you from your course. Maybe your test will come later. But there will be disturbances, and there will be choices. I cannot tell you what choice to make, and I will probably be long dead when you face your largest challenges in life, but I can tell you this." She removed her glasses for emphasis, looked me in the eye. "You must never let your music die. Preserve a space for it, nourish the soul that makes it, and attend to it daily."

She stared at me long and hard, as if she could see right into that soul and read the music herself. I knew she could barely make out my form without her thick glasses, but I felt exposed, and yet not concerned, by my nakedness.

As I sat in her studio that day, contemplating the disturbances she promised, and thinking of the trust between us, I told her I was seeing Peter.

"I know," she said. No inflection.

"I know you disapprove, but—" I began.

"You know my attitudes about men and women and music. You know that I believe music must be primary in your life. As for you and Peter, I will disapprove if I see that your music is suffering. So far, I see and hear only the best work you have ever produced. You make it very difficult to reinforce my own prejudices." She smiled her face-crinkling, toothless smile.

"You think I may prove you wrong?" I asked, grinning

back at her.

"Oh no. I am unwavering in my views. But I am willing to grant you your romance if you continue to complete your composition assignments on time." Her tone now was offhand, a little distant. That moment of understanding, compassion—had I imagined it?—it was gone now. I felt disappointed, and a little sorry that I had confided in her.

"Next week—something for cello, and Peter to play it for me."

"*D'accord,*" I said, as I gathered my music together. I understood I was dismissed.

"Good lesson today," she called out, just before I closed the door to her studio.

—21—

"You can't take her home, Maestro Schaeffer. She is wild, and needs her *famille*." That's what Inspector Bourlou said about *La Petite Noire Nouvelle*. I had lunch with him yesterday.

"How do you spend your days here in Paris?" he asked me after we'd placed our orders.

"Most mornings, I visit the cemetery."

"Oh—which cemetery?" He said it as if he knew several people with the same routine and wondered if I've ever run into any of them.

"Montmartre—it's where Nadia Boulanger is buried. I like to spend time there, and I feed the cats."

"And you have become attached to them?"

"Yes—one in particular. She runs to see me and likes to be petted and loved. I think about adopting her." That was when he told me I couldn't do it.

"But what about the winter? It will be cold; will she survive?"

"The cats in the cemeteries of Paris are strong. *Très forts*. She will be fine. Besides, you will be watching over her." He paused before he switched gears to address the matter at hand. "Thank you for listening to Marie today."

Marie is a young girl from the music program the inspector manages. He'd asked me earlier in the week if I'd be willing to hear her play. There's no question that she has potential. But she never made eye contact, even when she answered my questions. It was kind of bizarre. But then, who knows what her life is like—or was like, before she landed in detention?

I asked her to play a chromatic scale in quarter notes, moving from the bottom to the top of her range.

She made it from a low *d* to a high *a-flat*, pretty good. The low notes were whispery, and the high notes were a little honky, but her intonation wasn't bad at all. "Can you go any higher?" I asked.

"Yes, but not with good pitch."

I liked that answer. "How long have you been playing?"

"Two years."

She's fourteen now, so she'd started late. "Tell me about your flute."

"Oh—it isn't mine."

"It is loaned to her," the inspector clarified. "It's part of the program we have. Marie has earned a nice flute with her steady practice and her excellent attendance at lessons and rehearsals."

I turned back to the girl at the front of the chapel. "Do you ever play anything that you make up?"

"*Quoi*?"

"*Les improvisations*?" She wasn't familiar with the term. The inspector asked the question a different way.

"Not really," she said, shyness in her voice.

"But a little bit?" I asked, pushing the point.

"A little," she agreed.

"Could you do something for me now? We will turn away from you, and you turn away from us. Imagine you are alone in this place, with the beautiful glass and the lovely sound here, and play us something you don't already know. Just see if any notes come into your head and play. When you stop playing, we will all turn around and face each other again."

"*Mais*—"

"Try it, Marie. Try to do what Maestro Hannah asks you."

Some minutes passed before she began to play—tentative notes in the middle range. Then she played a descending scale, picking up her speed. Modulated—though I doubt she knew what she was doing—and moved into something slower, with a hint of melancholy. She paused to take a noisy breath, then played some staccato eighths, pointed at first, then brighter and light, finding her way into triplets and soon, a 6/8 march with an Irish feel to it. She lost her thread for a bit, but her rhythm stayed lively, steady. At last, she found her harmonic center and ended with a trill to the tonic. A nice resolution of the problem she had set for herself.

"Beautiful, Marie. Thank you so much for indulging me with my request."

Finally, she looked at me. "*De rien*," she said. *It was nothing*. But we all knew that wasn't true. She packed up her instrument quietly, taking her time cleaning and caring for it.

The inspector broke the silence. "I know I didn't ask you this yesterday, but would you mind if we stayed for a few minutes into your practice, so Marie can hear you play?"

They left about a half an hour later; he returned just before two o'clock to help me put everything away.

As we walked to the café, Inspector Bourlou had steered the conversation to the weather—sunny today after so much rain—and to the luncheon habits of Parisians—always so prompt, tending towards long. He was happy enough with a sandwich. Did I know he often ate his lunch while he was faced away from me, listening? I had no idea. I never heard a crunch or a crinkle of paper. "That is why I face away from you," he explained.

"I thought you were just giving me some privacy."

"But also privacy for me!"

Small talk, cemetery talk, and still there had been no discussion of Marie. Then, the food arrived, and he asked me about you.

"I was surprised you knew of her that first night over dinner with Emil."

"*Bien sûr*! Anyone who knows anything about the musical life in Paris has heard of Nadia Boulanger, *non*?"

"Even now? I fear she may be forgotten."

"Soon enough we are all forgotten. But you keep her alive with your memories."

"*C'est vrai*."

We were speaking an interesting mixture of French and English. "I view you as an opportunity to speak English with a real *Americaine*. You already speak perfect French, which means you need less practice than I do. Perhaps, we can go back and forth." He smiled. "Tell me. How did you find Mademoiselle Boulanger as a teacher?"

"She was my first and most important teacher. But she wasn't easy, or even consistently encouraging. She could make you cry and show no sympathy. Some of the students hated her, and we all feared her disapproval. But at the root of every action and every word she spoke, there was a true dedication to the musical education—and musical life—of her students."

"Ah, the best kind of teacher, demanding yet caring."

"Yes. And you, *Inspecteur* Bourlou, what kind of teacher are you?" I'd learned from the girl that he had been giving her flute lessons. To say I was surprised would be an understatement.

"What kind of a teacher am I?" Repeating my question, he was stalling for time. "Well, I try to be a good teacher. But with Marie, I am teaching an instrument that I do not play. I can only go so far with her on technique. I can teach her about pitch and tone, and I can tell when her technique is off, simply by what I hear when she plays. But I don't always know how to fix it. Though I know when I get the right results. Sometimes I think I am more scientist than teacher with her,"

"Why didn't you mention this earlier?"

He shrugged, then smiled. "If you knew that I wanted you to listen to a promising young flute student of a trumpet player—"

"Okay. You're probably right. How do you manage to teach an instrument so far away from your own?"

"It's in the wind family, Maestro. At least I am not trying to teach her how to play the cello."

"Have you taught cellists?"

"Not well."

"What is it you aren't telling me? How is it that the chief *Inspecteur* has come to teach music to the wayward children of Paris?"

"Music Education drop-out. Eastman."

"And then you became a cop?"

He nodded.

"But you still play. And you teach."

"*Oui*. But let's talk about Marie. What did you think?"

"I think she does have something, some sense of the instrument that is beyond her time with it, and she has an ear. Her rhythm was right on. I can understand why you would like to see her take her studies further. I'll do some research and find her a great teacher—"

He interrupted me. "*Non*—no. To the question of who will teach Marie, there are only two possible responses: One: you. Two: me."

"But—"

"And you have admitted that she needs a teacher who knows the instrument. She is past the stage of learning flute from some lousy brass player!"

"Oh, I'm pretty sure you aren't lousy."

"I'm okay. But I am not a flute player. You are. Don't give me an answer now, but just consider taking her on. I know you could teach her a great deal. And there's no need to do it on a volunteer basis. We can find funds for her to study with you."

"Forget about funding—use it somewhere else in the program."

"Does that mean you'll accept her as a student?"

I considered launching into my standard why-I-do-not-take-students speech. (You remember it Mademoiselle—you practically taught it to me.) But then, I thought about the practice room he'd provided, and all the strings I am sure he pulled to make the space at Sainte-Chapelle available to me every day. And I figured—why not? How much harm could I inflict in less than a year's time? "Okay," I said. "Yes—for now."

"Then for now, I will call you Hannah. Let's celebrate with dessert. Or are you pressed for time?"

"I'm fine with time."

We talked about schedules and lesson times and the rules of Marie's captivity until the waiter delivered our dessert.

"You've told me about your days," he said, breaking the crust on his crème bruleé. "What do you do at night?" He raised his eyebrows, insinuating, but mocking himself at the same time.

"Nights, at home, mostly. Dinner in Paris can take so long. Sometimes I eat dinner out at this little Indian place around the corner from the apartment, where they don't act like I've committed high treason by refusing an after-dinner drink. But usually I eat in. Read some scores. Spend some time at the piano."

"You are working on something?"

"I am working on about ten somethings, but none of them seem to be turning into anything."

"Writer's block," he said. In English.

"I hope not. It's why I am here—on sabbatical, to compose."

"Ah."

There was a pause.

"When do you play?"

"You mean perform?"

"No—I mean—practice for two hours on your flute at lunchtime. Read scores over dinner. Compose at the piano at night. All work, no play."

"Makes Hannah a very dull girl."

"Oh no. Not dull at all. But perhaps she is too dutiful."

"You sound like my friend Elaine. She's always telling me I'm 'too good.' Whatever that means."

"I know exactly what she means. You do what you are supposed to do. I bet you never miss a deadline or an appointment. You are unfailingly reliable. Your colleagues, your family, your friends—they all depend on you. I see your type all the time in my work."

"You do?"

"Yes, though usually they are older than you; they have lived a long life, following the rules. Then, one afternoon, they feel an incredible urge to do something really bad. So, they rob a bank."

"They rob a bank?"

"Yes. And that will be your fate. I can see it. Trust me. If you do not start misbehaving now—in small ways, of course—you are destined to become a late-life criminal."

"A late-life criminal." I repeated, transported by the idea of myself, white hair, black mask, demanding the cash from a teller.

"I have a proposition. Let's go for a drive. It's a rare cloudless day in Paris, and we should take advantage of it."

"Well—"

"Oh please, it is my duty. Some play to protect you from a life of crime."

He was charming. And funny—in two languages. Oh, and he drives a convertible.

We headed east—past Versailles. He pointed things out to me, and I made affirmative noises, but I wasn't paying much attention. I felt lulled by his accented English, and comforted by his manner, and found myself trying to recall the last time I had done something so simple, so purely pleasurable as taking a drive in the country.

In the early evening, he walked me up to my apartment. Thanked me for my company, admired the piano from the doorway, and kissed my hand goodbye.

"Late lunch again next Friday," he said, smiling at his own presumption and slipping out the door before I could give an answer to the question he had chosen not to ask.

Well, Mademoiselle, I may have to start calling him Luke.

—22—

Peter was surprised by Mademoiselle's assignment. Surprised and suspicious. "I don't trust her," he said, "not with this."

"She said she didn't have a problem with us so long as I kept turning in my composition assignments on time. Maybe her attitude is softening as she gets older. Or maybe because she's known us both for so long—" my words drifted off. I didn't know how to express to Peter the warmth I'd felt for Mademoiselle earlier that day.

"Mademoiselle Boulanger!? She'll never soften with age! I think you are the one who is going soft." He reached for my hand, following the lines in my palm, playing with my "flute pads" as he called the rounded undertips, the place where my fingers covered the holes in the keys.

"I am going soft," I admitted.

"Me too," he said. Then he smiled. "Well, at least in my heart. Other parts of me have been growing hard."

We'd only recently been able to acknowledge that sex was something we'd like to do together. We joked about his state of excitement when we kissed, and sometimes I was bold enough to push my hips forward into him when we were standing up. But we had yet to remove a single item of clothing, and this concerned me. I knew he was probably waiting for me to take the lead, but I hadn't a clue how to do that.

The sexual revolution was in progress; love was free, but I was busy writing chamber music.

I consulted with Elaine. "Well, yours is a special situation. He's a lot older. I mean we aren't talking high school here.

The first base, second base thing probably doesn't apply."

"Elaine, I do not want to return to Radcliffe as a virgin!"

"Yeah, you do need to solve that problem—but maybe you shouldn't do it with Peter."

"What?"

"I mean, you care too much about him, and you've known him so long. Maybe you need to get some experience with someone else and then come back next summer to seduce him."

"You can't be serious."

Silence. She *was* serious!

"Well, just a thought."

"Have another thought, and hurry! I can't run over my phone allowance!"

"Okay. Try this. Sometime when he comes over, go braless, obviously braless. Have a nice bottle of chilled wine, and make sure your sheets are clean. I think your problem will be solved in a few hours."

"Braless? But why braless? Couldn't I just have the wine and the bed ready and …" *And what? I had no idea.*

"Braless because they always like to start with breasts. It's just guys. I can't explain it. But if he knows your breasts are available—and you have to wear something that makes that clear—he won't be able to stop himself from making a move. And one thing will lead to another and oh—you *have* to call me right afterwards!"

"Elaine—I can't!"

"Can't what? Go braless or call me? Okay—call me the next day."

The next day. Would he sleep over? How would we pull that off in this gossipy place? But if Mademoiselle already knew we were seeing each other, maybe we didn't need to be so discreet.

"Are you still there?"

"Yeah, I was just thinking about discretion."

"Oh, very bad. Do not think about discretion when you are thinking of offering up your breasts to the man who may be able to solve your virginity problem."

"What should I wear?" I asked, trying to imagine a single item of clothing I could wear without a bra.

She was ready for the question. "That pale green sleeveless dress you have—it looks so great with your hair, and it matches your eyes. And it will just show the ridge of your nipple, just enough for him to want to see more."

"I think you're missing your calling. You should be some sort of sex advisor. Forget vet school; you could be the Dear Abby of Sex. You are awfully good at this."

"I know I am," she giggled. "But I don't think I could give this kind of advice to strangers. Okay, now: green dress, no bra, sexy underpants, no panty hose, some little sandals, preferably with heels. Got it? Now there's the problem of the wine. I'd ask Emil for that if I were you. He's a romantic. I have to run. Donald is due any moment. Call me!"

***

I didn't have a chance to follow Elaine's advice right away. I was too busy writing. We had seven days to prepare; we agreed Peter would have four to practice the piece, and I would take three to write. "You write quickly, and I will need time with the music. You don't write the easiest stuff in the world to play."

"Shall I try to make it easier?"

"No, you should try to make it good." Realizing how that sounded, Peter apologized. He was sure that Mademoiselle had a secret agenda, and he refused to believe that our teacher's attitude may have changed.

"You know what," I said, "her motives don't matter. What

matters is that we make compelling music together." He only rolled his eyes and told me I was sounding like a combination of Pollyanna and Mademoiselle at her clichéd worst.

I set to work as soon as Peter left my room, and by the time I went to bed, I could hear the birds at the edge of the forest waking up. The sound made me think about writing a flute part to go with his cello, but I was too sleepy to write another note. I had to be in Emil's studio for a chamber music session at 11.

In the daylight, I remembered my bird thoughts and came up with a whole new scheme for the piece. I would write the music of our picnic in the woods. The birds, the forest, the sun coming down through treetops. Was it too corny? I did have these longstanding programmatic tendencies that I needed to curb. But, I thought, unless I call it *Picnic in the Woods*, no one will be any the wiser. And I could hear just what needed to happen, the interplay between flute and cello, the resonant sureness of the strings, the light staccato notes in the flute part. A piccolo? I wondered. No, too much. Maybe even an alto flute instead?

"Hannah," Emil said. "You are overanticipating that entrance. There's a *ritard* just before you come in. Please let us stretch that out a bit. It's uncomfortable for the other players to feel you breathing down their necks!"

"Oh, yes, I'm sorry." I said. What he couldn't know was that I'd been composing in my head and suddenly had come to attention, worried I was about to miss my entrance.

"Stay for a minute," Emil said to me after we'd finished the quintet work. "Did you sleep last night?"

"Not too much," I admitted.

"Are you working on something?"

"Yes, a piece for flute and cello. Due in six days, performed."

"Flute and cello," he repeated. "Peter?" he asked me, the

trace of a smile playing under his mustache.

"Yes, he'll play the cello part," I said, all business.

"Look at me," he said. I obeyed, and he looked, it felt, right through me, for several seconds. Then he smiled again. "Do you mistake me for a very stupid old man?"

"No. No to stupid, no to old."

"Well, then. Okay. Look. I am happy for you and Peter." He paused. "But I am not happy with the way you played today in the chamber session—"

"Oh, that wasn't Peter," I said, interrupting him. "That was this piece I am working on."

"You were composing while we were working?"

"Uh, yeah, I guess so. In my head."

"You were a very talented girl when you first came to Fontainebleau. Now you are a very talented young woman. I am willing to make some allowances for you. But I can't allow you to check out of chamber class in order to finish your composition homework. Think about it. There were four other musicians here, ready to play. Sure, everybody has an off day. Henri messed up the oboe part on the Schumann something terrible last week. But at least he was here, in the room, with the rest of us. If you are going to play with other musicians, you need to show up."

I felt awful. Emil lecturing me. Emil, so right of course. I was thoughtless and inconsiderate. I'd probably ruined the rehearsal, and I didn't even realize it. "I'm sorry," I said. It sounded weak, and incomplete.

"I know you are—now. But I had to point this out to you, do you understand? It is part of the lesson."

I nodded.

There was an awkward moment. Then he left me with a wink and a little squeeze on the shoulder, suggesting I use his studio to work that afternoon while he was out. I went back to my room, gathered up what I'd written the night before, and parked myself at Emil's piano, planning to raid his supply of peanut butter, Ritz crackers and orange juice. It was a food combination that Emil and I both loved, and he always asked me to stock up on the American brands on my visits home.

I worked until dinner time, salvaging some of my night's work. I decided to go with the flute and cello, and I was debating a piano part when Peter came by. "Who would play it?" he asked. "On such short notice, in front of Mademoiselle Boulanger?"

"It's only a reading, Peter."

"No reading is 'only a reading' in front of her." He wasn't in a good mood. Peter wasn't happy about the flute part. He wasn't sure we should play together.

"But we play beautifully together. We always have."

"Sure—for ourselves, and in the company of friends." He left me, and I felt uncomfortable with the distrust in the air between us. It was directed at Mademoiselle, but I felt as though it were meant for me.

I only noticed after he'd left that he hadn't suggested dinner together. I'd been hoping he'd stop by, imagined we'd take a dinner break together, and then maybe read through what I'd written so far. I decided not to stop for dinner by myself. I'd eaten enough to tide me over for a few more hours.

At about nine-thirty, Emil knocked and let himself into the studio. "I saw the light, and I wondered if you were still here. How is it going?"

"It's going."

"Would you like me to be going, then, too?"

"Oh, no, sorry. I'm just a little cranky. Probably should have had dinner."

"It isn't that I don't admire your dedication, but no sleep last night and no dinner tonight. These are not the kinds of sacrifices required by your art."

I smiled. "Will you look at it?" I asked.

"Only over dinner. Let me take you home. Ghislaine will feed you, and you can stay the night at our place tonight—I mean unless you have other plans—"

He meant Peter.

"Are you sure Ghislaine won't mind?"

"Mind seeing you? Are you kidding?"

I slept well that night, tucked into their guest room, and knowing I didn't have any commitments the next day at Fontainebleau. Emil was up before me, playing some of the cello part on his horn. It didn't sound half bad, though I'd heard the cello when I wrote it.

"Beautiful, *chère*, and I like the flute line, the way they play together. You're almost done, I think. But there are a couple of spots—" He looked at me, a question in his eyes: did I want his opinion?

"Tell me," I said, and he did, as Ghislaine brought us hot chocolate and some apple *chaussons*. I was touched that Ghislaine was feeding me the favorite food of a much younger version of myself. I gulped the chocolate and got my hands sticky with the *chausson*, and fell under the spell of Emil's words, just as I'd done when he'd introduced me to the French horn in his Fontainebleau studio all those years ago. His observations about the piece were right on the mark, and his suggestions helped me find my way to the ending that had eluded me the night before.

"Thanks so much," I said as I was leaving that afternoon. "I couldn't have done it without you."

"Of course you could have, *ma chère*. But it is kind of you to let me believe otherwise."

***

"She's up to something," Peter said at our first trio rehearsal, and he began to act as if I were part of the conspiracy too. He requested note changes, complained about my dissonances, told me I needed to understand the cello better if I were going to write for it. He was packed up and on his way before I had my flute swabbed out.

I'd played once or twice with Peter in a performance setting, and I'd never thought of him as difficult. As we rehearsed this piece, this piece I'd written with love and care, Peter was the *prima donna* that Mademoiselle and Emil had warned me not to be.

It wasn't that unusual for several busy days to go by without seeing Peter, but that week I felt sure he was avoiding me. In fact, he seemed to be avoiding all of Fontainebleau. And he wasn't answering his telephone either. The day before we were to perform for Mademoiselle, I was finally able to speak to him for a few minutes after our third and last rehearsal.

"Wait—don't go just yet. I feel like we haven't seen each other in so long."

"We have been seeing each other every day at these interminable sessions."

"Is that how they feel to you, interminable? Is the music that bad?" I asked.

He didn't answer right away, and I waited, afraid of what he might say. I was very much influenced by his opinions. Finally, he walked toward me, and leaned down, kissed me on the forehead. "No, the music is beautiful, almost as beautiful as you."

When I looked up at him, he was looking away from me. "Peter, is it my imagination or have you been avoiding me all week?"

He sat down at the piano bench, played a d-minor chord. "I've been avoiding you, I guess."

"Why?"

He added a diminished seventh to the chord, then moved up to e-flat minor, leaving the d in place.

"And why are you avoiding me now?"

"I can't explain," he said, releasing the note.

"But Peter—"

"Shhh—" he said. "I can't talk now. Let's just get through the performance tomorrow." He began playing a bit of his part on the piano now, improvising a bass line with his left hand. He smiled at me from the piano. "It is a beautiful piece of music," he said. "Maybe add a string bass part when she has you do it over."

"You think she'll make me rewrite it?"

"Doesn't she always?"

"Maybe a revision here or there, sure, but—do you really think she'll make me do it all over again?"

He shrugged. "You know her better than I do," he said—but he said it in such a way that made me think he knew her better than I did. "Gotta go," he said, as he slipped out from behind the bench. He walked back to me, lifted me up from my chair, and gave me a full kiss on the lips. As I moved closer to him, he pulled away, squeezing my hands. "Really must go."

I cleaned my instrument slowly, thoughtful and unsure of what was happening. Why was Peter staying away? And why did he get so testy whenever Mademoiselle's name is mentioned? What did he mean when he said the music is almost as beautiful as I am? I wasn't feeling very beautiful right then, not at all. But still, he kissed me.

The next group arrived all at once, boisterous and joking with each other. A string quartet. I thought about our strained little trio rehearsal, and then put it out of my mind. We're under a lot more pressure—that's all.

***

The next day, we assembled at the appointed hour. Silently, we unpacked and set up our stands, got our music ready. It felt strange to have no banter, no last-minute exchanges before the music began. Monsieur Houle gave us a tuning note from the piano. Peter's eyes met mine as we matched our pitch, but I could read nothing. He was closed, shut tight. Had I missed this about him before? Is this the way he is before a performance? The quality of his playing always feels so alive, so open, and yet he was as shut down as I have ever known him to be.

As I worried about Peter, and Peter worried about whatever it was that seemed to occupy him, Monsieur Houle exuded calm and clarity to save us all. He smiled at Mademoiselle when she entered the room; his *Bonjour Nadia* was full and strong. As soon as she was seated, he asked us with a glance if we were ready. Peter nodded ever so slightly; I smiled before I swept up and then down with my flute, using it to give the downbeat. We began, and I could hear Monsieur Houle, steady, rhythmic, and sure. Peter entered, playing *obbligato*, sweet notes dropping, rising, each beautifully defined. As he launched into a *legato* section, I joined in, referencing the earlier *obbligato*, taking it into a full-blown melody, trying to play it as lightly as I'd written it. Peter's cello was broad and deep beneath me, and the piano was the glue that held us all together. It was working.

There were a couple of rough transitions—not enough rehearsal time—but mostly, we played well. Well enough that I can't remember very much. It's funny how you can recall every wrong note, every detail of what didn't go smoothly, but you cannot describe what happens, or maybe you barely notice when you are playing well. I was able to forget I'd written the music, and just play it, just concentrate on hearing my part, fitting it into the trio. I was absorbed enough that I wasn't worrying about Mademoiselle's reaction. Maybe that was why I wrote a part for myself.

While I rested at the beginning of the *adagio* section, I looked across at Peter. This was not the Peter that played cello in the forest. There, he was relaxed, at ease. Here, all I could feel was his focus, which was tremendous. His playing had a quality of intensity that I recognized from recitals he'd given. Monsieur Houle, on the piano appeared to be at ease, but his concentration was evident as well. *Pay attention*, I commanded myself as I prepared for my entrance.

The slow dance of the flute and cello in that section felt sad that day. It felt like a parting, a goodbye. I didn't remember writing it that way, but that's the way it came out. Even Monsieur Houle's part—almost a *continuo*—had a quality of yearning, loss. I heard him hesitating with each release. It was a beautiful interpretation.

Finally, we came to the last section, a complete change of mood. The piano set the tone, lightening up, frolicking in the upper register. Peter's was almost a comic entrance; the flute following behind him. I glanced at Monsieur Houle, and he smiled at me over his music. I looked over at Peter, but his expression was unchanged. His head was buried in his music, his brow looked troubled, and his shoulders were tense. Yet his sound was light, almost frivolous, as if he were dashing off the part for fun.

We finished with a flurry of notes, a tumbledown ending with a delayed last note that we managed to play exactly in unison. I remember looking up at my teacher as we played that last note, and she looked absolutely surprised by it. I felt in that moment that the piece had succeeded. It was just that look of pleased surprise that I had hoped to elicit.

"Do you like the ending?" I asked as soon as we were through. I couldn't contain myself; I was a little kid again, looking for approval from my teacher.

"It is effective," she said. It wasn't exactly a ringing

endorsement.

"Especially when we play it together," joked Monsieur Houle, referring to the many times we'd rehearsed the timing of that little eighth note.

"How many rehearsals?" she asked.

"Three," I said.

"You have the ending down, but you still need to work on those transitions."

"There wasn't much time," I offered.

"There never is." I'd forgotten that the mention of time was always a sore point. My teacher was ever conscious of the diminishing nature of time. As I think back on it now, I realize that she probably had a right to be a little angry with a young woman who complained about a lack of time. In her aging eyes, I had all the time in the world. Yet she was vigilant that I not waste a second.

"Tell me why you didn't write a part for string bass."

"Peter suggested that," I said, not really answering the question.

"It's not a suggestion." She was already halfway out of the room. "It is an assignment. For next week. Expect an audience."

More than once, I've wondered if Mademoiselle missed her calling as an actress. She loved making an exit—even more so as she got older, as her own body became less cooperative. She used her strong mind and sharp tongue to defy the uncertainty in her movements. She would grow more dependent on others as she aged, ceding some control over the details of her daily life. But on that day, and on so many days thereafter, her words would leave no doubt as to who was in charge of the life I called my own.

***

I ended that summer at Fontainebleau with my virtue sadly secure.

It was after the second performance of the trio piece—rewritten, as requested, to include a string bass—that Peter told me, "It just isn't going to work, not here, not now."

"What isn't?" I asked, even though I knew what he meant. I wasn't ready to give up, especially now that we'd gotten through the performance. "We played well, today," I added, as if this should make up for all the tension of the past two weeks: his silences; my anger when he questioned a note or ignored a dynamic marking.

He sighed. "Yes, we played well." He was looking down, not at me, or even straight ahead.

"You mean us," I said. I felt as if it took every muscle in my body to force those words out of my mouth.

He nodded, looked up at me. "I'm sorry. I truly am. Maybe if we weren't here at Fontainebleau, working together, studying together, well. I don't know, but I think it would be different. It's too much here."

I don't remember anything I said. I remember staring into the reflecting pool as if it would offer a clue, and I remember Peter sitting next to me, patting my hand, kissing my forehead, trying to comfort me, reassure me. He apologized several times. I remember thinking he was just as miserable as I was, wondering if love always ended up this way: two miserable people, sitting on a bench, crying.

I stood first, reached for my flute. "See you at class," I said, almost lightly before I turned away. I left him sitting there, and he let me leave him. It was a small concession to my pride, a way to help me believe that I'd been the one to go away.

We avoided each other as much as possible for the next two weeks. If Mademoiselle knew what had happened with Peter, she gave no indication, but only demanded more of me. She loaded me up with impossible assignments and asked me to correct the homework for the first-year theory students. I wasn't left with much time to contemplate my failed romance, and perhaps that was what she had in mind for me. I wrote to Elaine to tell her what had happened—bad news didn't merit an international phone call—and it was as if I were writing about someone else, someone who'd been not disappointed, but rather, mistaken in love. None of it seemed real to me any longer.

Letter and heart sealed up, I opened my door and found Peter poised to knock.

"Hannah," he said, and my defenses crumbled, just to hear my name spoken, the tenderness and sadness in his voice. When I stepped into his arms, I was already crying hard. "No, no, no," he said. "Don't let me make you cry. Please." He held me, comforted me, gave me his hankie, kissed my hair, wiped my cheeks. "Please, no tears, no, no. Hannah, no, no." His lilting accent made his repetitions musical, a lullaby to quiet me.

At last we sat in silence, his back against my bed, my back against him, his arms wrapped around me. "I do love you," he said, finally. "And I miss you like you wouldn't believe. We have to find a way to be friends again. All these years. We can't throw them away." I was quiet. I wanted more than his friendship. "I was wrong to start something with you—"

"Peter—" I began to object.

He interrupted me. "I'm older, and I should have known better. It's not just this place, and Mademoiselle, but it's who you have to be. You have to think of your career."

"Now you sound like her!"

He laughed. "I do. Strange, isn't it? Imagine that Mademoiselle Boulanger has converted me to her way of thinking! But I've given this a lot of thought. Being with me would only hold you back."

"How can you say that?"

"It's true. Allow me to be old enough to see your potential, to see you have so much ahead of you. It's been true since you were ten years old, and you came into my studio with that cello part for me to play. Do you remember?"

I nodded.

He gave me a squeeze. "Be my friend. Please say you will, Hannah. So I won't have to give you up."

—23—

I woke up this morning foggy, stranded in a dream. My grandfather: he was handsome, young, with mischief and light in his eyes. His beard thick and dark, not a gray hair on his head. It was Gramps before I knew him—Gramps when you knew him, Mademoiselle.

He gave me a flute, and asked me to play something for him. He handed it to me with such care, holding it so as not to press a key inadvertently. Then, he gave me a rag, a violinist's chin rag. I remember the pattern, bright and colorful with red tulips on it, and I recognized it from his collection. Nana used to find odd scraps of material and fashion them into chin rags for him. He never used them in concert, but he loved looking like a gypsy fiddler when he practiced.

"But I don't need a chin rag to play the flute," I tried to explain to him.

"Shh," he said. "Just play."

I placed the red-tuliped cloth on my shoulder—just to get it out of my way—and took a deep breath. I looked at him; he was smiling, anticipating the sound that would come out of my flute. I started low and began swirling around the bottom of the range. It was a flute with an embracing lower register. Funny that I started that way, as if I were warming up—easy on the instrument, waking up the sound from sleep. In a dream, you would think you could begin anywhere; zip right up to the top of the instrument, thirty-second notes flying in all directions, but here I was with low d's and f's and a's, making my careful way to the middle register.

I turned away from my grandfather, listening to the instrument, making small adjustments. Then, I turned toward him and began to play. It was a lovely melody, and I remember thinking—with that part of you that sometimes lives at a distance in a dream, "I should be writing this down."

But that distant, dreaming-self had no time to take dictation, because the flute was getting bigger—or was I getting smaller? As I shrunk, my young grandfather seemed to grow. Seeing that I was struggling with the size of the flute, he took the instrument from me as carefully as he had handed it to me earlier. He showed me—the small version of me—how to clean the flute, how to pack it away. He placed it on a shelf beside another, smaller case, and from that, he pulled the most beautiful wooden recorder—an alto I think—and handed it over to me.

My child-self—I couldn't have been more than four or five judging from my size—needed no coaxing. I began to play. The music rippled into the room, running notes like dancing gnomes, graceful, but silly, almost tipsy.

I didn't see Gramps take his violin out of the case, but there it was, tucked under his chin, a yellow bandana replacing the tulip cloth we'd packed away with the flute. And we played, chasing each other around the room, playing hide-and-seek with instruments, just like we did when he was alive. I was his young and talented granddaughter, and he was my grandfather, vigorous and overflowing with music.

Where were we? I remember bare wood floors and sunlight flowing into the room, the windowpanes shadowed on the floor, three over three. Tic-tac-toe. There was the bookcase that held the flute, filled with books and piles of music, sheets and sheets. Somehow, it felt like a room in New England. A room white with winter sun.

I don't think there were any more words in the dream, only musical conversation, and lively, too. I woke up with the darting melodies in my head. Made some morning coffee, tried to write some of it down.

The music was so bright; why do I feel so sad?

Gramps seemed so real, so alive. God, I think I miss him. I knew so little of him really, despite all the stories that Nana told me through the years. You told me a few, too. But at heart, I have a child's knowledge of a life, a version of him that centers only on me, my three- and four- and five-year-old self. Oh sure, I know about his life, his musical career. When interviewers ask me to tell them about him, I can recite dates like when he emigrated from Czechoslovakia, when he joined the BSO, when he was promoted to concertmaster. But the man with the impressive career, the immigrant musician carving out a life for himself and finding a wife in America, is not the man I know. I know the man with the gypsy cloths and the dancing music—the man of my dreams.

What do you think it all means? My youthful grandfather? Musical tag? My shrinking child-self?

Could it have something to do with Marie? Was I anticipating our second lesson?

Last week, I asked her to commit to practicing at least forty-five minutes a day for six days a week. After our deal was sealed, I sent my new student home with only her headjoint to play. "Tone," I said. "I want you to work on getting the best possible sound. Think of nothing else."

"But I'll only be able to play one note," she protested.

"*Non*," I said, and I reminded her that she could use her lips to change the register, showed her how she could cover the opening with her hand to change the pitch too. Still, she balked at the limitations.

"For forty-five minutes a day?"

"If you had the whole instrument, I would expect an hour from you." Maybe I picked up more from you than I realized. I could hear your trademark stern humor in my response.

This morning, I heard a difference in her sound, a fullness that now must be supported with her breath.

"Good work," I told her as she played the rhythms on the page with only her head joint. "*D'accord*, I want to show your something. Put your hand right here, on my belly."

The girl who doesn't make eye contact looked at me as if I were crazy.

"Just place the palm of your hand, right here." I took her hand, laying it flat against me. "Close your eyes, and focus on what you feel through your hand.

"First, I keep the breath in my chest. Now, I let it go to my belly. Now, I push it into my belly, to make even more room in my chest. Do you feel it?"

"*Oui, oui*. Oh, your stomach. It is getting very large, Mademoiselle—and hard!"

I laughed; she seemed so serious and horrified.

"You need to get the breath all the way down into your belly to support your tone on any wind instrument.

"Listen. I want you to hear the difference. Turn away from me. Close your eyes. I am going to play the same note, octaves. Three times. First shallow, then a little more breath, and finally deep from my belly."

"*Oui, oui, j'écoute maintenant*!" She was a little undone when I didn't return her flute to her at the end of the lesson.

"One more week with the headjoint. First, practice your breathing. Hold onto your stomach: push it out; fill it with air. Find the breath in your belly. Pant like a dog on a hot, hot day."

She looked up at me and stuck out her tongue, in her best imitation of an overheated canine. When she giggled, I realized it was the first time I've heard her laugh.

Progress, don't you think?

Though I still feel like an imposter. On several fronts: A Maestro without an orchestra, a composer without notes, and now—a teacher without pedagogy.

And a cat feeder without cats. That's right. I have not seen a single cat—oh—it's starting to rain. These cats are weathermen, aren't they?

Well, no need to water the mums.

À bientôt, Mademoiselle!

—24—

"You must be Hannah Schaeffer," he said, rising from his seat at the piano. "I'm so glad you're home. Your teacher and I can't agree on the interpretation of this Ravel. You need to cast the deciding vote." He smiled, enjoying my confusion before taking a drag on his cigarette.

Mademoiselle took advantage of his inhalation to make a proper introduction. "I would like you to meet Maestro Bernstein."

"Oh, no Maestros here. Please. Everyone calls me Lenny." He held out his hand. I was returning from a gig, and I had to juggle my flute bag and a folding music stand to shake his hand.

"Do you appreciate Nadia enough?"

"Uh—I think I do."

"Good, good," he said. "She is the most amazing person I know. And I trust her musically the way I would trust no one—*no one*—else." He paused for a moment. "Why don't you sit?"

I looked over at Mademoiselle, saw her smiling at the Maestro as if he were her favorite child. I put down my stuff, took off my coat, and sat in the chair closest to the piano.

"Now Nadia, you give your argument first; then I will give mine, and Hannah will be the arbiter of good taste."

I paid close attention as my teacher spoke, her authority on the subject self-evident in the tone of her voice; her enjoyment was just as obvious.

When the Maestro spoke, he filled up the room. Even this

high-ceilinged parlor, the room that could contain thirty students and a grand piano, the room that housed a pipe organ and a composition class, felt small in his presence. He alternated his focus, moving his gaze between us, as if we were conducting a joint interview. Despite his charisma, I could not award him the prize, at least not without musical examples. "I need to hear it, not just hear *about* it," I said.

"Ah, Nadia, you are right as always! Perfect! Hannah, can you come with me to rehearsal tomorrow morning? I'd like you to assist me."

"Assist you? With the Ravel?"

"Oh, we'll solve the Ravel problem later. I need help with a rehearsal in the morning. Shall we look at the score together now?" He crossed the room and opened a briefcase, brought some music back to the piano and patted the seat next to him. Mademoiselle and I were bookends to the Maestro as he read through his score of *Dumbarton Oaks*, noting his markings, explaining his thinking about tempo, noting the points where the orchestra was liable to miss an entrance or misplay a chord.

Mademoiselle chimed in, "You've missed this, Lenny," she said pointing to a section where the winds joined the strings, ascending together. "It must be *pianissimo*, and it never is! More instruments: more sound, but Stravinsky asks for less. It is much more powerful if this section is just a whisper."

"A whisper—exactly! And you show that with your shoulders," Maestro Bernstein said. "Like this!" He slid off the bench and moved quickly to the center of the room. "You are the orchestra," he said to us. "Nadia is the string section, playing along, and you, flute-player, are just about to enter. Now watch my cue!"

He looked at me, almost wincing, and pulled back his shoulders, his arms, all the way down to his fingers, until his hands were almost flat; only a gentle curve of his fingertips told me he wanted any sound at all. There was no mistaking his signals. After my imaginary entrance, he moved his whole body even further away, his beat grew even smaller. A *decrescendo* from *piano* to *pianissimo*, the whisper-quiet sound that the piece required.

"Do you see it?" he asked me, still standing.

"Yes. Clearly. Beautifully," I said.

He smiled at me as if I were the happy center of his universe. "You've played the original, right? And conducted it?"

"Part of it—for a class."

"Well, Hannah Schaeffer, tomorrow you will conduct all of it! I'll leave the score with you. You can study it for a few hours more. Rehearsal isn't till eleven." He reached across the piano, found a pencil, and scrawled an address and a phone number on the cover of the score. "The address is for tomorrow. The phone number is for tonight. I never sleep. Just call me if you have any questions." He helped Mademoiselle off the bench, crushed her into an embrace and kissed her full on the lips before he helped her back into her chair. "You have no idea how much you mean to me," he told her. He moved toward the door, winking and promising me that we would have fun in the morning. "*À demain*!"

"He loves a dramatic departure," Mademoiselle observed. She said it fondly, smiling in the direction of the door.

I had a million questions. First: "Who am I conducting tomorrow?"

"*L'orchestre Nationale*."

"*Pourquoi*?"

"Why not?" she answered. "Shall we look through the score again together?"

"But—you don't understand. I mean—I don't understand."

"It's simple. Clearly you have a talent, perhaps even a calling to conduct. You need more than the Harvard Band; you need to learn more than what I know. I asked Lenny to try you out."

"Is this an audition?"

"After a fashion. But there will be no jury, very casual. Just Lenny. Maybe I will come too. Would you mind?"

"Would I mind? You're telling me I will conduct a new arrangement of Stravinsky in less than eight hours, with no time to sleep if I want any time with the score, that I will conduct the piece —that, by the way, you premiered yourself—in front of possibly the most famous conductor in the world, and then you ask me if I mind whether you are in the audience? Does it really matter?"

Maybe it was the lateness of the hour, or maybe it was the lingering effect of that kiss from Maestro Bernstein, but Mademosielle let out a little chuckle. She lifted her hand to her mouth, as if to stop the laughter, and she looked over at me. I rolled my eyes, and it was all the encouragement she needed. Her laugh moved to her belly and crossed the room, rolled over me and broke down my resistance. After all, if I didn't laugh, I'd cry.

***

I got to the *Théâtre Mogador* around 10:30, too early. It was all locked up. I installed myself across the street in a café to watch the stage door. I didn't want another cup of coffee. I'd spent half the night studying the score and the rest of it worrying about conducting for Maestro Bernstein. I was nervous and excited and in need of more artificial stimulants. I ordered a *chocolat chaud* and sipped slowly.

At about quarter to eleven, a man in a long trench coat unlocked the stage door. Immediately musicians began to file in. Where had they been waiting? How had they known the signal? I watched them, instruments in tow, chatting on their way in. My stomach leapt to my throat. I'd been so nervous at the prospect of conducting for the Maestro that I'd virtually forgotten I'd have an orchestra in front of me. An orchestra expecting Leonard Bernstein.

I paid my check as a cab pulled up across the street. The Maestro emerged, then leaned back in, extending his hand to Mademoiselle. I watched the care that he took, the deference he paid to her. She smiled at something he said. She must have replied as she turned toward him. He threw back his head, laughing, extending his arm to her.

When I entered the hall in a line of musicians, it was almost eleven, but the stage was only one-quarter full. "They are notoriously late, this little orchestra." The Maestro had materialized at my elbow. "They are also not the most professional group I've conducted. They usually need a little discipline; you'll see. I was thinking I'd let you have them first. Do you mind?"

"Uh—"

"Don't worry. I'll introduce you, tell them to pay attention or risk my wrath. You'll be fine. Nadia tells me you've been conducting the Harvard Band."

It seemed a question. "Yes," I said.

"And you like it?"

"Oh, yes."

"Well then, you'll *love* this. Just wait." He smiled broadly and squeezed my arm before he walked over to the concertmaster. It was past eleven now, and most of the orchestra was on stage, but not all the instruments were out of their cases yet. The rehearsal was unfolding at a leisurely pace, musicians chatting with their neighbors, playing a few warm-up notes, adjusting their stands. Leaning over to say a few words to the players in front of them.

The Maestro didn't seem to mind this social club atmosphere at all. He was making the rounds, saying hello to the musicians he knew, hugging some of them, laughing and patting others on the back. Smoking a cigarette down to almost nothing, he took a moment out of his conversation with the string bass section to realize his fingertips were in danger. Would he drop the butt on the stage and stomp it out with his foot? No, a savior appeared, arm outstretched, ashtray in hand.

Bernstein clapped his hands together, gave me a nod, and walked to the podium.

"*Bonjour mes amis*," he began. In fluent French, he outlined the program, reviewed the concert schedule, and gave a short speech on the importance of paying close attention to every note, at every rehearsal. "It doesn't matter whether there is an audience out there or whether we are playing for ourselves," he said. "We are here to make music." The players looked a little bored, but he continued. "I especially need you to pay close attention to the Stravinsky today. You may not know that the original version of *Dumbarton Oaks* was premiered by the esteemed Mademoiselle Nadia Boulanger. She's here today to assist with the interpretation of my new orchestration." He gestured to the house, and the orchestra broke into applause.

"Mademoiselle Boulanger's protégé, Hannah Schaeffer, will conduct the Stravinsky today. She is a young and—I think you will agree—formidable conductor. Please grant her your attention and courtesy. Hannah?" He smiled at me so broadly that I could not help but return his grin. "The podium is yours," he said, though he did not leave his place as I walked toward the front of the stage. He reached out to me, took both my hands in his, leaned in close. "They won't be warmed up," he said. "They will need some scales before they tune."

I couldn't imagine asking professionals to play warm-ups as if they were a student orchestra. As I stepped up to the podium, I knew the scales were as much a test of my ability to get what I wanted from an orchestra as they were a warm-up for the musicians in front of me. How would I manage it? I opened my score, smoothed it with my hands, looked up to find every eye on me. I smiled, dropped my shoulders as I took a deep breath. "Who has played the chamber version of this piece?" I asked. Only a few hands: the concertmaster, a cellist, the oboe player. "You three know that we have some interesting harmonic progressions to play today. The rest of you have a treat in store for you. It's early Stravinsky, but it has shades of the dissonances and experiments to come in his later work. We can't play it cold, unknowingly. Let's warm up our instruments and our ears with some scales, scales in the style of the composer."

"We'll begin in unison. Concert e-flat minor; please hold each note until I release it." I lifted the baton and horns were raised to lips, bows were raised to readiness. I gave the downbeat. Bernstein was right. They were not even close to tuned. "Listen," I said as we approached the flatted third note of the scale. I stopped them. "Hear the minor," I said. "Descend to the tonic. Now back up to the third. Follow me. Between those two notes only, please." And so we moved slowly between e-flat and g-flat. "Adjust," I said, a command, loud enough to be heard over an orchestral *mezzo-piano*. I was irritated, just a little, that they would need this warm-up from their conductor. Weren't they supposed to be professionals? But I saw in their eyes that they were serious of purpose, that they were listening, adjusting, and at last the interval was in tune. I had them play the ascending scale in unison. When we got to the top, I stopped them. "Winds, on the downbeat, you will descend the same scale. Strings, you begin at the bottom again and ascend."

For fifteen minutes, we played relevant scales in as many configurations as I could dream up. I had the flutes begin on the second against the clarinets on the tonic, the trumpets ascending from the third, with all the strings descending. We played one key against another, ascending together, descending by section. And I noticed we were beginning to sound a little like Stravinsky.

"Let's move to the score." The Maestro had told me I could take up to an hour of rehearsal time. Last night, that seemed an impossible amount of time to fill. Now, I felt pressed in my remaining forty-five minutes. But the warm-ups paid off; the group was with me, and I had lost track of the fact that Leonard Bernstein was watching, listening. We tore the leaves off *Dumbarton Oaks* that day, examined the bones of the trees. I was a little ruthless with the group; perhaps I overworked the transitions, stopped to ask them to listen a time or two more than needed. At last, we ran through the piece without stopping, and the orchestra achieved a smoothness I'd have not believed possible just a half an hour earlier.

"Brava," I heard behind me. "Excellent work." It was the Maestro speaking.

"It *was* excellent work," I said to the group. "Thank you for your time and attention." The players surprised me with applause. Bernstein extended his hand to me, faced the orchestra.

"Isn't she marvelous?" he asked them. "And an American too—but of a French teacher of course!" The musicians laughed, and the Maestro helped me move off the podium as if I were descending from a great height.

***

Plans were made over a late lunch in the café where I'd been sipping my cocoa that morning. I felt dazed by their details, unable to focus, unable to eat. But Mademosielle and the Maestro barely noticed me. I would move to New York in the fall. The Maestro needed the spring to convince the Symphony

Board to sponsor me. Mademoiselle, meanwhile, would work to find another patron to fund my incidental expenses.

They spoke quickly—mostly in English—about where I would live—*with us or as close to our apartment as possible*, and how he would introduce this new apprentice to the Board—*they have no choice in the matter, but I have to make them believe that they do*, and whether Mademosielle would be able to find supplementary funds for this new phase of my musical education—*it is harder now, but there are still some believers who may answer my call.* I listened to the conversation as if they were speaking of a mutual friend, as if all this planning were not on my behalf. I could not comprehend that in the span of an hour this morning, I'd become apprenticed to Maestro Bernstein.

I thought of the band at Harvard, how I had gained their trust last year, the premiere we would play this spring. I'd conducted two concerts on my own last year while Professor Walker was sick, and this season I'd shared the podium on two more. I knew I wouldn't be guaranteed even a rehearsal with the orchestra.

"Hannah?" The Maestro was speaking to me. "Are you with us?" He was smiling, and I could not help but feel his warmth touching me across the table. I smiled back, but I had no idea what they had been discussing. "Please tell us your thoughts on all this, before we plan your future away. Do you want to study with me?"

"Yes—of course!"

"Something is bothering you, though. I can already read you. What is it? What were you thinking about before I asked the question?"

"The wind ensemble," I answered.

He nodded as if he understood, but Mademoiselle looked at me as if I were certifiable. She began to scold me, but he interrupted her. "Nadia, we need to make certain that all our plans are right for Hannah." He looked at me. "You'll miss

Harvard?"

"Yes. I guess."

"And?"

"It isn't that I'm not grateful, or that I don't realize what a tremendous opportunity this is, but what will I *do* in New York?"

"Stay up late into the night with me studying scores. Go to bed exhausted, your head full of music. Get up a few hours later to observe my rehearsal with the orchestra—"

There was the word: *observe*. How many years of observation would it take before I could conduct on my own again? Before I could stop myself, the words were out: "But I don't want to observe. I want to conduct."

"So much the better," the Maestro said. "You will be even more motivated to learn." He'd pulled back from me now. I was no longer in his personal envelope of warmth and laughter. Mademoiselle, for her part, looked horrified at my bad manners. I didn't know what to say.

Bernstein lit a cigarette. "You told me she was strong-willed, Nadia, but you didn't warn me she was after my job." He grinned, forgiving me, exhaling smoke.

"Here's the honest truth. There are several assistant conductors at the Phil. I was one once. Like you, I was impatient. I wanted my chance. It took years, but eventually I got it, and so will you. In the meantime, there are a half-dozen young men in front of you in line. As it is, they won't like you joining their ranks. You are younger, more talented and also you have the misfortune of being born female. No, they won't like it a bit." He smiled again. "Under the circumstances, I can't offer you a concert with the Philharmonic. Not this season anyway!"

"I didn't mean—I mean, I know I have no repertoire to speak of, and I know there is plenty for me to learn, and of course I am honored to have you take me as a student. I'm sorry that—" I rushed to repair the rift I felt I'd caused, but Bernstein interrupted.

"No apologies required." He winked. "Are you in?" he asked me. I thought for a moment of my father, his now-curbed tendency to gamble away the mortgage money. Under Joanne's influence, my father's days at the track were over, and his only poker games were with me. We played for M&M's.

"Yes," I said, understanding the stakes on this game were much higher. "I'm in."

—25—

Emil says I am not the imposter I think I am. I saw him yesterday, after I visited you.

"*Mais oui*, you are a teacher. Every time you conduct, you are teaching—a way of listening, a sense of music and sound, the importance of discipline."

"No, I don't think so. The Phil's musicians are among the best in the world. They need very little from me."

Emil tried another approach. "Didn't Luke say just the other day that he was learning by listening to you practice?"

"Yes, but—"

"And did you set out to teach him anything? No, you are there for your own sake. But you are a natural teacher. *That's* why Nadia steered you away from teaching—because she knew that you had that capacity, and she hoped to save you from her fate. She sacrificed a lot to become the teacher she was to you and thousands of other students. She saw that you might not need to make the same sacrifices. Nadia discouraged you from teaching, not because you would be a bad teacher, but because you were potentially a great one. And though you may not call yourself a teacher, you teach every day. Every time you pick up your flute or step in front of an orchestra.

"Weren't you paying attention all those years you spent working with Bernstein? Try to tell me he wasn't as much teacher as conductor."

"Oh, but that's Lenny. He couldn't help himself."

"And you are Hannah, and you can't help yourself either.

But forget the music for a moment. Aren't we *all* teachers to each other? Only some among us are more gifted, we carry understanding to others, sometimes even understanding about themselves. You will teach this girl flute, and you will do that beautifully, but more, you will teach her about herself; about what she has inside of her. Maybe even some music—who knows—but these lessons aren't about music. You must know that. What is that American expression—*role model*—that's what Luke wants you to be to that girl, don't you see that?"

Truly, I hadn't.

"You think he wants you to teach her the proper use of trill keys, how to triple tongue? *Mon dieu*, it is good that you have your old Emil as a teacher too! You can be a very slow student!

"Ah, you're laughing—a good sign. *Ma chère*, lately you are—"

"A ray of sunshine in your day? That's what Mel called me yesterday. I'm sorry. I know I've been short on patience –and—"

"Heartbroken. You forget how long I've known you."

His tone, his concern, his sweetness, and the truth of what he was saying. I bent over, as if to protect myself, and then the tears began. Again? But I am not a crier! *Was* not a crier? Damn.

Leaning on his cane, he got up and moved slowly out of the room. He came back with a blanket. He wrapped it around me, pressing it gently to me, making sure my heaving shoulders were covered. This was not a short cry. I was out of control.

He left the room again, returning with a box of tissues. And after the last slow trip, he placed a glass of water on the table next to me. He said nothing. He stood beside me for a moment after he put the water down, and with one hand holding the back of the chair for balance, he rubbed my shoulders with the other. I could feel the age in his hand, but also the strength in his fingers.

I was thinking *I* should be taking care of *him.* I've allowed myself to neglect Emil, rarely visiting, for too many years. But he forgave me my absence, invited me to play duets, and welcomed me back as if I'd never been away.

I told him about the contract troubles, how Mel encouraged me to walk. And how I have no idea where I am walking. How there is this part of me—it may be your voice—that sees how being relieved of my orchestra might give me the space I haven't had to compose.

Emil nodded, listened, made tea, delivered chocolate-covered biscuits on a blue glass plate.

"But the worst thing—the absolute worst thing—is that I can't seem to write anymore. That's never happened to me before. I mean all those years. I built my conducting career, and I managed to compose—maybe not as much as I would have if I'd spent less time on the podium—but still—a respectable output. But lately—it's all fits and starts, and I just can't seem to get anywhere."

"How long?" he asked me.

"Maybe a couple of years."

"Your mother—she passed away—when?" He already knew the answer.

"But we weren't that close—and besides, wouldn't you think the grief would come out in music? I mean I wrote the *Elegies* and the tribute to Lenny—"

"Out of love, not sorrow. You wrote the first Elegy as a tribute to your grandmother—not because you lost her. Because you loved her. The same for Felicia and Lenny too. And of course, for Nadia."

"But—I think I loved my mother—even if I didn't always like her—or her way of doing things. But I guess—this is going to sound absurd—I feel like an orphan now."

"Why is that absurd?"

"Well, it's not like my mother was ever into mothering—and I'm a long way from a dependent child."

"Something changes when your second parent dies—no matter how old you are. I felt it when I was in my seventies and my father passed away at ninety-six. And Ghislaine was still alive then, and I had Marcel, too. I was not alone. Still, I felt—well—disconnected."

"I *am* alone. Single, no spouse, no siblings. It bothers me lately. It never did before. It's like someone flicked a switch. Elaine says it's hitting me so hard because I'm losing my orchestra too. I mean it's hard even for a grown-up orphan to feel alone when she has a hundred and ten musicians waiting for her downbeat."

"Orchestra or not, you're not alone. And even without our parents, we're never really alone."

"Please don't tell me I should join a church."

"No, we'll keep God out of it for now." He smiled, then he grew thoughtful. "I miss Ghislaine every day. And I still miss Nadia. But seeing you, it is almost as if Nadia is in the room with us. When Marcel and I play together, I feel like Ghislaine is just in the kitchen, making us a snack, as she listens to us. If I've learned anything in my old age, it's this: love outlasts us all. Surely you know that too, or you wouldn't spend your mornings tending to Nadia's grave."

He set his teacup down. "I want to play something for you."

Emil pulled his horn out of the case and rustled through some music on his stand. He warmed up for a few minutes, listening to his intervals, adjusting, playing a few minor scales to suit the mood. Then he played a slow, mournful melody—a beautiful piece, so perfectly suited to the horn, to him. The high notes were open and full, and he sounded as though he were reaching, reaching for something—something just beyond the music. I found myself coming to attention. The mood of the piece shifted, and the horn started having fun, playing a game of tag with itself—a scherzo—or maybe a rondo.

Then, Emil stopped playing.

"Oh, continue, please. It's a great little piece."

"Isn't it?"

"I can't wait to hear where it goes," I said, trying not to telegraph my impatience.

"Don't you remember? You gave this to me for my birthday one year. You were twelve at the time. You promised me you'd finish it, and I am still waiting."

I could hear my way around the problem that the younger me hadn't solved in the scherzo. And I heard a new theme—something reflective and matter of fact, and kind, just like Emil. And maybe an allegro opening movement, too.

"Can I take it with me?"

"Oh, I'd never let this original out of my hands. You'll have to copy it," he said with a sly smile. He meant copy it by hand. I could only think of you. You always said we learned more by copying music by hand. I still sketch that way, but I do a lot of work with midi keyboard, too. I am almost certain you would not approve of these electronic methods.

Handing me a notebook of staff paper, Emil told me where to find some pencils. He put his horn away and excused himself for a nap, told me to help myself to anything in the kitchen if I got hungry.

"Emil?" I said, just before he left the room. "If I finish this for you, would you consider playing the premiere?"

"Something at Sainte-Chapelle with you?

"No—I'm going to write it for horn and orchestra."

"Ah—the kid's orchestra," he said. He knew I'd promised Luke I'd write something for his group.

No," I said, trying not to laugh. "With London. At the Royal Albert."

"The London Philharmonic? What can you be thinking? Anyone in that group could outplay me! I am an old man—"

"But would you do it for me?"

"You are crazy." *Folle*, he said.

"You are not answering me. Would you like to do it?"

"A solo performance with London? *Bien sûr*! But that is a younger man's dream."

"Dreams never age."

He smiled at me from the doorway, leaning on his canes. I saw the younger Emil inside the old man with the bad legs, and I'd been hearing the ageless Emil whenever he picked up his horn.

"I'll explain everything when you wake up from your nap."

In my tone, I heard the confidence of the twelve-year-old girl who had sketched a sonata in the span of a morning for a birthday present.

Emil left me, and that little girl and I got to work.

—26—

While the Maestro worked to persuade the board that I was a worthy apprentice, I worked to increase my repertoire. Every Friday afternoon, I took the train from Boston to New York. I'd arrive at the Bernstein apartment while the Phil was still in session. The Maestro's wife, Felicia—she insisted I call her by her first name—would usher me to bed before he came home. "You know Lenny will keep you up all night, and you need your rest." She was right. I learned quickly that I couldn't keep up with the Maestro's boundless energy unless I used Friday nights for sleeping.

Felicia was like no one I'd ever met. So glamorous, so *effortlessly* glamorous. She was beautiful and perfectly poised; her lipstick never smudged, her patience with Lenny and the children apparently unceasing. Though my lessons were with the Maestro, I wanted to learn Felicia's secrets, too.

On Saturday mornings, I would rise before the rest of the household, make my way upstairs to the Bernstein's piano room and practice my flute. In a crazy scheme the Maestro had hatched, I would get an artist's diploma from Curtis Institute. Curtis would credit my studies with Mademosielle and Professor Piston, my work with the Harvard Band, the results of the endless theory tests they had administered to me in February, and three compositions for the instrumentation of their choice. I'd already submitted the compositions, and now I had to meet one last requirement: a flute recital.

I loved those Saturday mornings, just my flute and me, upstairs in Lenny's studio. It smelled of cigarette smoke, and there were scores everywhere, but I didn't have to worry about them, not until later in the day. In the morning, it was as simple as playing my flute. It hardly seemed like work to me. The program I'd selected included traditional recital works—a Bach sonata, Mozart flute and harp, Hindemith, Ibert, and the piece I'd written at Fontainebleau for flute, piano, cello, and bass. The Bach sonata I'd played since I was fourteen; the challenge there to play it freshly, new, to avoid the trap of playing it the way I'd first played it. Same with the Mozart, though I'd added it to my repertoire more recently. The Hindemith was new to me, and I loved it—the unexpectedness of the harmonies with the piano and the blunt, openhanded feel to the work. The Ibert was so French, and so playful. I could play it all day long and never tire of the twists and turns. It made me smile. I thought I'd probably close with that.

Around 11, Felicia would send one of the kids to summon me. Bernstein breakfasts were late morning gatherings over heaps of pancakes, giant omelets, or waffles topped with strawberries and cream. The conversation was lively and sometimes difficult to follow. Often, there were guests—a visiting soloist who was a friend of the family, one of the Maestro's business partners, a recording executive from CBS. Not so different from the rapid-fire French exchanges at Mademoiselle's formal table; I felt grateful for her social schooling.

After breakfast, Lenny and I moved upstairs, where we'd spend most of the afternoon. We'd begin at the piano, with the scores for that evening's performance. He'd review my markings, ask me to conduct a section from memory. It was an odd experience, moving my hands in the air, no sound, except what we could both hear in our heads. He'd interrupt often, reminding me of my omissions—a *decrescendo* not clearly indicated, an accent written which I had not conducted. Sometimes he would stop me to ask about something

I had done, rather than what I had neglected to do: "The horns," he'd say, why are you asking them to play *legato* there? Do you mean that? Or do you want them to announce themselves with more separation between the notes?

"Every move you make must communicate your clear intention; you must desire a result, and you must remain in control of the interpretation. So long as you hear in your head—even a split second before you give that cue—what it is you want to hear, you are in control. Never allow an entrance to surprise you. One moment of fatigue, of inattention, you'll lose command of the orchestra.

"That said, you must be open to a fresh interpretation every time you conduct. Music happens in the moment, and the best musicians live in the present and the future simultaneously. We hear the next note as we intend to play it—or as conductor, to instruct the players how we want it played. At the same time, we need to hear every note as it happens—be with every note, give every note life, in the present. And while that's happening, we are also with the next note, and the next, and so it goes. Do you understand?"

I nodded. He lit a cigarette as I considered the truth of what he'd said. He blew smoke rings at me, smiled a fire-breathing dragon's grin. "Are you sure you want this job, kiddo?"

I was sure. And he knew it. He could tell from the way I studied the scores, the way I peppered him with questions after we listened to his recordings, the careful interpretations I brought back to him from Boston. I had a seat, courtesy of the Maestro—and an assignment—for every Thursday BSO concert. Each week, I picked one piece to study in advance. After I listened to the concert, I had to mark the score from memory—tempo changes, dynamics not in the score, any indications that would show how it had been performed that evening.

The following weekend in the Maestro's studio, one or

both of us would conduct from my marked score. "It's time to be Leinsdorf," Lenny would announce, after we'd tackled the Philharmonic music for the evening. It was the signal to have some fun, especially if it was the Maestro's turn to play the conductor. He imitated his colleague's stance and movements, sometimes even pretending to walk across the stage and acknowledge the imaginary audience in Boston before he began to conduct from my score. My job, when he was the conductor, was to recognize his Bernstein moments and correct him, turn him back into the BSO conductor. Leinsdorf's movements were compact; he was quietly authoritative, and the beat was always where the beat belonged. Lenny's style was larger, more dramatic; it was easy for him to slip into type.

"I'm forced to conduct as myself," he would scold, "because there are no markings here, at this critical transition. What can I do, but fall back on my own bad habits?" I'd lean over his shoulder, stare at the score, and try to remember what it was that Leinsdorf had done at that unmarked moment. If I wasn't sure, he would ask me to change conductors. "Be Koussevitzky," he would command. It didn't matter that I had never seen Koussevitzky conduct. He was a point of reference in almost every lesson. He had sponsored Lenny's conducting career, advised him, and recommended him to his first post at the Phil. Lenny's respect for the conductor who had nurtured him as a young musician ran deep. Whenever he was in doubt about an interpretation, he told me, he would ask himself how Koussevitzky would conduct that passage.

Several Saturdays into this conducting exercise, we ran across an unmarked passage where I could not recall the conductor's interpretation. "Then show me how Hannah Schaeffer would interpret this," he said. On the imaginary podium, I prepped the downbeat with his admonition in my ears: "Don't be *Bernstein*, now!"

***

As Lenny had predicted, the fact I was female was not sitting well with the conservative symphony board. They thought themselves open-minded enough to have hired an American at a time when most major orchestras would only consider Europeans. Hiring another American was not out of the question, but hiring a woman—a young woman—that was another matter. They were not ready to be so forward-thinking, and they told him so. Could the Maestro be serious in his intention to work with me? He assured them that he was. "Your students are your business," one of the officers told Lenny at the following meeting, "but the decision to hire one of your students as an assistant conductor is ours. We have no interest in hiring this girl."

The Maestro reported back to me in detail, "You need to know what you are up against," he said. Still, he championed my cause, perhaps because in some ways he identified with me. "I'm an American Jew; two strikes against me," he said once when we were talking about his own struggle to find a podium. It was late, after the Saturday night performance, after a big dinner out with friends of the Bernsteins. Felicia had gone to bed, but I was sitting up with the Maestro.

"And then there are my 'rumored homosexual liasons,'" he said.

I said nothing, sat very still. *Too much whisky*, I thought.

"You see they don't care if I have a mistress, if I cheat on my wife with another woman. That makes me more macho, more the man in charge, more deserving of the baton. But they have a much harder time thinking I might seduce young tenors." His voice was bitter, and thick with alcohol. I didn't know what to say.

"Does that bother you too, Hannah Schaeffer?" He was looking right at me, and I knew this was an important question. This was not a moment he'd forget in the morning, or maybe ever. I'd heard the rumors, but I never believed they were true. Why was he bringing this up? What was he telling me, and what, really, was he asking me? Yes, it bothered me to think that the happy home I'd visited every weekend for the last three months might be disrupted. It bothered me on account of Felicia, for the sake of Jamie, Alex, and Nina. On the other hand, I didn't see they loved him any less, and he loved them more than life.

I thought about how Mademosielle adored Lenny, even in his excesses. "He lives too much," she told me once, but she smiled when she said it. What would she say now? She would tell me I was here to learn from Lenny, musician to musician; that was that.

"Oh, *now* I get it. You're telling me the board won't hire me because they think I'll seduce the tenors too?"

He laughed. The tension was gone.

"Nadia was right." he said. "You are a treasure." We sat in silence for a few minutes. "Don't you worry. We'll get you hired."

***

There was one more Harvard performance that spring, my last. I was conducting half the concert, including the Piston premiere, *Tunbridge Fair.* Walter's composition was a lively depiction of a town fair, complete with circus fanfares and a marching band within a band. It was challenging, but the ensemble dug in; they had worked hard in rehearsals, and they played flawlessly—and musically—in concert. As I lowered my baton, I heard a *Bravo* from the center section; then the audience was rising. A standing ovation. Professor Piston came to the stage.

"I'd like to thank Harvard University for commissioning this piece, the members of the Harvard Wind Ensemble for their excellent performance, and I would especially like to acknowledge the young woman on the podium, who has brought the piece to life. A perfect interpretation, Miss Schaeffer.." Professor Piston shook my hand.

Professor Walker joined us on stage. "A few words, if you please," he shouted. The audience settled back into their seats. "Over the past two years, Harvard audiences have come to know Hannah Schaeffer. I don't mind telling you that she single-handedly saved this ensemble last year, stepping in while I was sick—taking over rehearsals, guiding the group through two seasons, conducting three concerts that would have otherwise been canceled. Conducting a college band isn't an easy job, and conducting the Harvard Wind Ensemble isn't a job, some said, for a nineteen-year-old girl. But this young woman is an exceptional musician and a natural leader, already a talented composer, and a gifted conductor. We are honored to have her with us.

"Earlier this year, Miss Schaeffer caught the attention of an important Harvard man, the great Leonard Bernstein. He has invited her to work with him in New York. This is the last concert Miss Schaeffer will conduct with us—at least until we can coax her back for another premiere—but I can assure you, this isn't the last you'll hear of Hannah Schaeffer.

"If you'll beg my indulgence, I'd like to thank Miss Schaeffer for her service with two gifts." He handed me a long silver box; I knew right away it was a baton, another one. I opened it: a little Harvard emblem engraved in the wooden handle, which was just exactly the right size for my hand. As I gripped it, he said, "We'd also like to give you something to conduct with that Harvard baton." He nodded stage left, and Lenny appeared. His was the voice behind that *Bravo*.

Recognizing the famous Maestro, the audience went wild. He faced them for a moment, smiled, and bowed before he gestured for their quiet. He held out a folder: conductor's score and all the parts, his signature on the front. "It's a little suite for band. I hope you'll like it." As he handed me the score, cameras flashed all around us. He wrapped me in a big hug. "Look photogenic," he whispered. "This is your American press debut."

Lenny's presence at the concert, his gift of the score, and the picture which made the front page of the Boston papers and the arts section of Sunday's *New York Times*, forced the hand of the board. Their Maestro had given me his imprimatur in public. I had been recommended by Walter Piston. I had reviews (!) that foretold of a promising future. And just to be sure, Lenny had dragged along two board members—Harvard men—to the concert.

Lenny filled me in later. "They said the band never sounded better. 'Tell that to the rest of your board,' I told them, 'and hire Hannah Schaeffer before Leinsdorf steals her for Boston.'"

***

That summer, I returned to Fontainebleau and to Mademoiselle. We spent long hours in her studio with the scores for the coming Philharmonic season. Seated beside her at the piano, all the years melted away. I was ten years old, and in awe of my teacher.

"This passage," she would begin, playing a few bars from memory, "you have one clarinet, one flute, and an oboe, against all the strings. Her large hands, gnarled with arthritis, became violins and violas, cellos and basses. "You can't let them overpower the winds." I marked my score dutifully, reminding myself to subdue the strings, to signal their supporting role. "Show me," she would say, and I was back in Lenny's studio, conducting in silence, the music playing only in our heads.

Mademoiselle's conducting style was less showy than Maestro Bernstein's. She used small movements, conveying as much through her eyes and face as through her body. I recalled Lenny's words before I'd left: "Learn as much as you can from Nadia; she is a genius."

I quizzed Mademoiselle about her experiences—all those years ago—conducting in New York, Boston, Washington. What was it like, being a woman on the podium in 1938? The first woman, ever, to conduct those orchestras, and to this day, the only woman—how did it feel?

"They were more gracious in Boston than in New York," she told me. "Still, they tested me. You'll need to expect that. That's why it is essential you know your scores thoroughly. Because you can be assured that the members of the orchestra will try out their composition skills on you. If you don't notice, and notice right away, they will not show you any respect."

"It sounds like the early days at Harvard, but those were college boys. These are grown men, mature musicians—"

Mademosielle laughed. "They have no reason to act or play maturely for you."

"Because I am a woman," I sighed.

"Man or woman, you have to prove yourself."

"But I have to prove myself even *more*; I have to be better than a man."

She would have none of it. "You have to be the best musician you can be every moment. If you follow that rule, you will gain the respect you deserve. If you falter, you will also gain the respect you deserve." Mademoiselle's universe was essentially just, but there was an emphasis on punishment for those who didn't live up to their potential.

"I do not consider that I am a woman," she had told the members of the Boston press in 1938. "I was born so, and it does not now astonish me."

I imagined a much younger Mademoiselle: her long dark skirts, her tiny wire-rimmed glasses, her large hands directing the orchestra. Probably because she had so much experience leading choral ensembles, she preferred to conduct without a baton. She would be serious, and stern, and she would know every note by heart. But could she convince the men in the orchestra to forget she was female?

Watching her on those rare and precious moments when she would stand in her studio and conduct a passage for me, I knew exactly what she wanted, at every moment. Her style was so self-contained, and yet so communicative. More than that, she was commanding. She'd lost a few inches to age, but even as she approached her eighty-first birthday, there was something in her stature, in her very presence, that ensured I'd pay attention.

I've been asked in interviews what it was like to study under Boulanger, under Bernstein, to be a student of two great but very different musicians. I usually say something about feeling grateful I had the opportunity to know them both, that from each I learned an enormous amount about commitment and passion. I've realized only recently that despite their huge differences in style, they were not so different in substance. As teachers, they were both rigorous and demanding. They expected from me what they expected from themselves. When the lesson was over, either one of them could speak passionately of world events, ancient philosophies, great literature. They were brilliant, both of them, and fascinated by the world around them, a world that dropped away as soon as the music began. Bernstein, like Boulanger, was a natural and gifted teacher. And Boulanger, just as easily as Bernstein, could, through sheer force of personality, command one hundred and ten men to play—shhh—quiet—*pianissimo*.

—27—

Love outlasts us all. I've been thinking a lot about what Emil said. And wondering: is love the reason I visit you? I find myself going back to the duckling theory: I imprinted on you. I followed you around—musically speaking—all your life and mine until you arrived here.

But you were never easy to love.

Now—Lenny—he was lovable. But I'm not hanging out in Brooklyn at Greenwood cemetery, am I?

He doesn't have a garden, just a flat stone set into the grass. But there is a bench nearby. And Felicia's there too. I have visited, yes. Okay, it's not like I have to come to your grave to talk to you—or to hear you—commenting on my musical—and life—decisions. You're always with me. Lenny's in my head, too. But his voice tends to tell me to go for it—whatever *it* is. You, on the other hand, are often the voice of pause. Of reflection. Of looking before I leap.

Have I ever leaped? I mean taken a huge, giant, leap of faith? When I think about my life so far, I see a girl—and then a woman—who was directed. Guided by my grandfather, by you, by Lenny, by Mel. I wasn't coddled—you saw to that—and I have worked incredibly hard. And of course, I had this tremendous ambition. Otherwise, well, my life would not have unfolded as it has. You told me once that my music would be my protection. But I've been protected, too, by you and all the people you made sure were around me.

Working with Marie, I wonder: Who looks out for her? No one. Lately, I'm so weepy. I talk to Emil about feeling alone.

But Marie? She seems to me to be a deeper kind of solitary. The other day when she laughed, I felt like it was the first time she really let me in. But I won't be here forever. It would be dangerous to let her imprint on me.

Could music be her protector? Or does she need a human to step in?

Luke, maybe.

Every Friday lately, he stays to the end of my practice session. He puts my stand away after he stacks my music, lining up all the edges, and placing it next to my bag. While I clean out my instruments, he busies himself with other small tasks, sometimes making a quick call. He never reveals any details or mentions a specific case, but I am growing familiar with the refrain: *Are you certain of this?*

"We must be nothing less than certain," he said yesterday, snapping the phone shut.

"I've noticed you always mention certainty when you make your calls. Do you ever entertain doubts?"

"Certainty is important to my work—yours too, don't you think? Imagine a conductor who was unsure of the beat. A disaster. You *are* the beat."

"And you are the Law."

"Oh—no—I am Law's representative. And only human, and for these reasons, it is all the more important that I am sure of every case. Instinct is involved. Often the first suspicions are borne of intuitions, feelings. The *gut*, as you say in America. But we have to support every case, make sure we have grounds for every arrest. I am not speaking of vagrancy or minor crime. On the big cases, if we arrest and—God forbid—convict the wrong person, we have not only stolen the freedom of someone who was innocent, but we have let the criminal be free—and then, we have endangered the community."

"I didn't mean to be making light of your work. I'm sorry."

"No, I am the one taking things too seriously here, lecturing you."

"Big case?"

"Yes. There is pressure, but I am not ready to make an arrest. Lots of circumstantial evidence, nothing of substance."

"Would you feel better skipping our lunch to work on it?"

"In Paris, even crime can't keep us from our midday meal."

Before the food arrived, he asked nonstop questions about my work. Was he trying to keep me from asking questions about his? From what Emil has told me, Luke's position, although affiliated with the Paris police, is more like what we call a District Attorney in the States. If he is worried about a big case, I bet it is truly big.

"What does it feel like on the podium? How does it feel to have all those musicians at your command?"

"You make me sound all-powerful. It's not like that."

"Isn't it? You hold the beat in your hand."

"It's more like I hold the music in my head. A good conductor is a translator, that's all."

"You are underestimating your role."

"No—I think that many conductors overestimate their role. I just do my job up there. Really, it isn't that much different from going into the office. I could manage some small company, 110 people. Instead I run an orchestra. And really, I don't have to worry about half the things I'd have to worry about if I were a CEO. My job isn't so hard."

Wasn't so hard, I thought.

"If you say so. How long have you been conducting?"

"A long time. Over forty years, if you count my student days."

"What did it feel like the first time you directed? I bet it didn't feel like going into the office then!"

"The very first time? I was fourteen. I was here, in Paris, studying with Nadia Boulanger. I'd been sitting in on a conducting class at the Conservatoire. Mademoiselle would quiz me on scores we were studying, and soon, she began to add conducting lessons into our weekly schedule. She was a masterful conductor, and she taught me a lot.

"The first group I directed was a string ensemble at the Conservatoire. I was worried about working with all strings, coming from a wind background—I was just starting with violin.

"You play violin?"

"Not well, and rarely."

"What was the piece?"

"Barber's *Adagio for Strings*."

"How did it *feel*?" Luke was looking at me intently.

"God, it was so long ago. I remember being terrified at the first rehearsal. I was sure I would lose my place, miss a time signature change—it moves between 5/2 and 4/2 and 3/2. I was worried about conducting such strange measures—the half-note gets the beat, and it all moves so slowly! The players tend to rush, and it was my job to hold them back. Do you know the piece?"

"Oh yes, it's one of my favorites. I would have loved to have heard your concert."

"Oh, I am not sure I would have wanted you in the audience. The performance was even more frightening than the rehearsals. If I screwed up in a rehearsal, I knew the players would forgive me; they made mistakes too. But in concert! A dropped beat would be the end of my world."

"Did you drop any?"

"Beats? No, I don't think I did. The performance went well. But I was glad I took Mademoiselle's advice and wore a long, full skirt. It was less evident to the audience that I was shaking the entire time."

"But now—now conducting a concert is as blasé as office work." Luke grinned.

"Well—no. That isn't what I meant, exactly. I could never feel blasé about performing or conducting in a performance situation. What I meant was that it isn't about glamour; it is about work. Sure, if I'm lucky, I find moments that are sublime. There are moments when I feel I am working outside my body, outside my mind—moments when the music is transporting me somewhere else, and I am able to carry the whole orchestra with me. In those moments, I understand why I do what I do; I am reminded of the power of the baton. But it isn't my power. It comes from somewhere else."

"But your mind memorizes the music, and your hand holds the baton. Your body gives the signals."

"Yes, true. And maybe because conducting is such a physical act, you forget—at least over time—just how much mental rigor is involved. How many years of learning the music and studying scores, all the decades of accumulating repertoire."

"How big is your repertoire?"

"From memory—around two hundred works. A few hundred more I know well enough, but I'd want a score in front of me."

"What a mind you must have, to be able to fill it with so much music! And still have room for anything else!"

We were silent for a minute. I was thinking about everything that I *wasn't* saying, and looking for an easy way to change the subject.

"I dropped out of Eastman before I could take a conducting class," Luke said. "But there's still a part of me that wishes I had finished music school."

"Tell me how you ended up at Eastman in the first place."

"By accident. My father was offered a position in New York to develop a French American exchange program. It sounds crazy now, but it was after the war, and it seemed that France and America were determined to share everything—even police procedures.

"I went to high school in Manhattan. I played in the band, led the trumpet section, and I loved it. I thought I wanted to be a musician, and my parents—maybe because we were living in the States—were willing to humor me. Sometimes, I wonder if they were counting on my not getting in—but I got accepted into the music ed program, and off I went. Blissfully unprepared. I was a pretty good trumpet player, but I'd never had a theory class in my life. I didn't have a clue how to build a chord, never mind hear one, and I couldn't read the bass clef. I had an ear for the line I'd always played, but the rest of it was indecipherable for me."

"Sounds a lot like me when I first came to Mademoiselle."

"Perhaps, but I was already eighteen years old. And I had nothing like the talent that you possessed at ten!

"Music school was hard for me. I kept at it. I practiced all the time, and I spent hours trying to understand my theory homework. But I couldn't train my untrained ear fast enough. I just wasn't cut out for the place, and that was pretty clear to me, almost from the beginning."

"Did it get any easier?"

"Everyone always told me that it would, so I stuck with it. Until my father died. He died at the beginning of my second year—suddenly, and in the line of duty. I left school as soon as I got the news, and I never went back."

"Oh, Luke, I'm sorry."

"Thanks, but it was probably for the best. Not that he died, of course. What I mean is he was openly skeptical I could make it as a musician, and I was determined to prove him wrong. Once he was gone, I think I gave up the struggle. I lost the need to prove anything to him, or anyone."

"What about your mother?"

"She wanted to go back to France. She couldn't face being in America without her husband. I don't blame her. My mother had emigrated once already—from Tunisia to

France—and she knew how hard that had been, even after she met my father. Interracial couples weren't that common in France then, and they both faced prejudice. But in Paris, we lived in the 10th—it was a lot easier to blend in there than it was on the Upper West Side. That's where they housed the exchange officers and their families. So, Black, alone, a French-speaker with minimal English skills? New York was a scary place for my mother, even if she was living in one of the safer neighborhoods in the city.

"She encouraged me to stay, to finish my degree. But it was my first real experience with death. It changes you, especially when you are still a teenager, and you realize that your parents—the infallible immortals that raised you—have the capacity to die. My world was shaken up. I wanted to go back to Paris with my mother. I knew by then that I wasn't cut out for Eastman. I don't know if it was giving up, exactly—"

"Well, you still play, right?"

"Never stopped. Not even at the police academy. Used to drive my bunkmates crazy."

"Well, then—you haven't given up a thing. Except maybe a career option."

"The chance to hold the beat."

"The chance to manage an office of cranky musicians, each one of them wishing they had a solo career and often pretending that they do. Trust me, you are not missing as much as you think."

"But those transcendent moments—what did you call them—sublime?"

"Yes. Those. I have been lucky with that."

"I know. It is lots and lots of work, and years of practice."

"And many, many moments when you are exercising, just working your way through a passage, re-playing a section, making sure the clarinet is listening to the horn when she enters so that their dialogue doesn't degenerate into a musical argument. And we haven't even begun to discuss the off-stage politics that have to be mastered to hold down a podium. Seriously, if you are thinking about a career change, I would look elsewhere!"

He laughs.

"But you love it, don't you?"

"I do."

"*Parfait*! I have a wonderful opportunity for you to keep up your skills with a young orchestra while you are on sabbatical." He smiled. "No, I'm joking about your skills—but if you are free on Monday night, would you consider coming over and meeting some of the kids and listening in, maybe give me some pointers?"

"The group Marie plays in? You're the director?"

"Oh God, no. I'm only filling in, so we don't have to cancel rehearsals. Getting out is so important for the kids. We're working on recruiting a new volunteer from the Conservatoire."

"So you're inviting me to your conducting debut? How can I say no?"

He shrugged and threw his hands in the air—a gesture that gave him away as a Frenchman. Then he leaned across the table. "You have a great laugh, Maestro."

Was he flirting? I have no idea. And you'd be the last person I would ask for an opinion on that. Not to mention—*aging*. I'm evolving into my singularity, finally, reaching that point where I am mostly invisible to men. So probably not flirting. But the way he said it made me think about how I felt when Marie had laughed—just a nervous giggle—when she was touching my belly: as if a single brick had been removed in the wall she has constructed around herself, allowing me a glimpse of the girl inside.

—28—

Leaving Fontainebleau that summer, I was excited and terrified in equal measure—certain of what I wanted, and scared silly that my ambitions would prove impossible to achieve. I remembered my grandmother, all those years ago, talking about shipping me off to my destiny. I'd been back and forth so many times since, but this crossing felt a lot like my first. I'd just turned twenty, and in New York, I would be an official member of the New York Philharmonic family. My title was Assistant Conductor—one of several, and as Lenny had promised—at the very back of a long line of eminently qualified and highly competitive young men. It was clear I wouldn't be doing much in the way of assisting on the podium for some time to come, but the affiliation meant I was paid a small stipend to study with Lenny and was granted unlimited access to Philharmonic rehearsals and performances, not to mention the music library.

"My repertoire is your repertoire," Lenny told me over dinner on the night I arrived. "And you have picked a perfect season to be here. I've already warned the press and the public that there will be a little bit of our own century in every concert. That means you won't be stuck studying only the old warhorses—many of which I imagine you already know."

"But knowing and conducting are two different things entirely."

"Touché," he said, "but you can't do one without the other. I know you'll feel frustrated by the amount of time you'll spend off the podium, but I promise we won't waste a minute. And you still have some conducting to do at Harvard, right?" He meant the piece he'd written for me.

"And maybe we'll find a chamber group for you, just to keep your arm in shape. But meanwhile, try to be patient. Be patient and learn."

"This from the paragon of patience," Felicia said, as she urged seconds on me.

Lenny smiled. "It's good to know I can rely on my lovely wife to keep my ego in check." He said it without a trace of sarcasm, then turned back to me. "I don't mean to sound like some guru. I remember what it was like for me as a young assistant conductor, always hoping, waiting for that break. Your day will come. You have my word of that. But I can also promise you that it won't be this year. You may as well bury your head in scores and soak in as much as you can. And I think it's a good idea for you to continue with Thursdays in Boston. That way, we'll have more to study and discuss."

It was a frenetic schedule, busier than the year before. I took the early morning train up to Boston every Thursday, arriving in time to grab a quick lunch before I had to run to rehearsal at Harvard. From Cambridge, I would take the subway back to Boston, where Lenny had arranged not one, but two seats for me at Symphony Hall. "Make sure you invite Rose to a few concerts. I'm sure she'd enjoy that."

"You never told me you knew Lenny," I said to my grandmother.

"Oh, but I don't—he knew Jacob, that's all. I know he conducted several times while Jacob was with the symphony."

And he remembered the concertmaster from all those years ago? And recalled his wife's name? Thinking how Lenny seemed to be on a first-name basis with many members of the *Orchestre Nationale* last year, I realized that—of course—my new teacher would have spoken with, even befriended, my grandfather. I could imagine them swapping stories and jokes after rehearsals. It was something about Lenny that I wasn't sure I could emulate. He had a quality beyond charisma. He really cared about the people around him, and he wasn't afraid to cross professional boundaries in the name of either music or friendship.

"Would you like to come with me to the Symphony next week?" I asked Nana.

"I'd love to—what a treat!"

I would often squeeze in dinner with my mother and Bill, or Dad and Joanne, but my grandmother was the only one I invited to the BSO. She was good company, and we balanced each other out. Nana would sit back in her seat, relaxed, transported by the music. Beside her, I sat hunched forward, hands on knees, brow furrowed, visualizing the score that I would mark as soon as we got back to her apartment—before I went to bed, and while the music was still with me.

Early the next morning, Nana would send me off with a hug and a kiss, breakfast, lunch, and a thermos of coffee. I relied on the coffee to keep me awake on the train, where I would study another set of scores—the music for that evening's performance of the Philharmonic. I'd arrive in New York with a head full of music and a strong desire to play it out. Friday afternoons, I spent in Lenny's upstairs studio with my flute, Lenny's piano, and my grandfather's violin. Under Mademoiselle's tutelage, I'd grown into a passable pianist. As a violinist, I still had a long way to go. I'd picked up the instrument not quite five years earlier, when Mademoiselle decided I needed a first-hand understanding of the string section.

"I would wish for you the cello, for you to play in a range apart from the flute's, but it would be criminal to let your grandfather's violin remain unplayed." I was surprised that my grandmother let me borrow it, but I was grateful for the beauty of the instrument; the depth of sound made up for my awkward bowing technique and motivated me to be a better player.

During my second year at the New York Phil, on a Friday afternoon, the phone rang in Lenny's studio. I answered it, as I had been instructed to do.

"Miss Schaeffer, the Maestro is ill and unable to conduct this evening. He has asked that you take the program." The general manager didn't check my availability; it was required on Friday and Saturday evenings as part of my contract.

"Maestro Bernstein tells me that you have conducted the works elsewhere. Is this true?"

I nodded, before I squeaked out a yes. "This past summer," I managed to add, willing my voice to pitch down. I'd rehearsed and conducted the Fontainebleau Orchestra for a Stravinsky festival. Over the course of several days, we'd played everything on tonight's program.

"Very well, then. We will send a car at six-thirty."

Six-thirty. I glanced at my watch: 4:30 already. I was debating my next move when the phone rang again. Felicia.

"Have they called you?"

"Yes."

"Good. Lenny isn't well, or he would speak to you himself. He asked me to call. Do you need anything?"

"A day's notice, a long rehearsal—nothing that you'd be able to provide."

She laughed. "You'll want a little snack. Right about now. Otherwise, you won't be strong enough for the second half. I'll bring something up in a few minutes. And you'll need help getting ready."

"I have a wardrobe of concert black and white in my closet but I am already panicking over what to wear."

"Don't worry. I'll be right up."

She brought me little meatballs. "Protein is very important," she said, handing me a plate, fork, cloth napkin. "Now about your costume." She winked. "Lenny, Nadia, and I have done a little shopping."

"Mademoiselle?"

"Yes, she actually did the shopping. She knows all your sizes. It's your birthday present—a little late. You eat, and I'll be right back."

Despite Felicia's urging, I wasn't sure I could eat—or whether I should eat—but the meatballs smelled delicious, and there was crusty bread, too, and a little salad. By the time she reappeared with two large boxes, I had put away most of the food.

She pulled a long black skirt and a little bolero jacket from the bigger box. I recognized the work of my teacher's dressmaker. The sleeves had the same swirling pattern that I'd admired in the photograph of Mademoiselle with Stravinsky. Instead of sequins, the pattern was sewn in gray-black piping just a shade lighter than the jacket itself. The skirt, full and beautiful, was decorated in the same subtle swirls. Out of the second box, Felicia pulled the most gorgeous blouse I'd ever seen. A cascade of white ruffles, and I could tell even without touching it that it was silk chiffon.

"How did you know?" I asked.

"Oh, we didn't know. Or we would have had it pressed already. But we knew you'd need something like this eventually." The phone rang again. "That will be the doorman. I told him to call me when the dry cleaner arrived."

"Felicia, how can I thank you—I mean, you've thought of everything—"

"Until you get yourself a wife, let me take care of things for you." She gathered up my new concert clothes, handing them to the man who'd appeared at the door. "We need these back within the hour," she said, in a tone that demanded obedience.

"Okay, now," she said, turning to face me. "I have a few instructions from Lenny."

"Oh God! I hope so! I've only led the orchestra on *Dumbarton Oaks* in rehearsal."

Lenny had asked me to assist earlier this week, a surprise move that felt like a repeat of his gesture with *L'Orchestre Nationale*—minus the warm-up scales. "Are his scores here? Maybe I could review his markings. Especially on *The Rite of Spring.*" The very idea that I would conduct this without a rehearsal was patently absurd.

"Lenny told me to tell you to conduct it your way. 'Tell her not to be Leinsdorf or Bernstein,' is what he said. He said you should use the scores you marked for Fontainebleau. But he did suggest you call the concertmaster to review your interpretations. Why don't you do that now, and I'll come back up when your clothes are ready?"

And she was gone, leaving me with only my nerves for company.

***

Less than two hours later, Felicia and I were in the back of a black limousine, en route to Lincoln Center. I was still in street clothes, though I was wearing more make-up than I ever had in my life.

"Trust me on this," she had said, her stage experience speaking. "There's a good chance you'll be photographed tonight, and you don't want to look washed out."

I felt another lurch in my stomach when I considered there might be press at this performance. But I heard Mademoiselle's voice in my head. *You are playing for God.* And Lenny's helpful commentary: "She's right. So only worry about God's opinion. Screw the critics."

Thanks to the concertmaster, who was also my violin teacher in New York, word had already gone out to the orchestra that I'd be conducting. When I spoke to him earlier, David Nadien had offered to call the principals of every section. "I think it will be easier on you if they are prepared to see you instead of Lenny," he'd said. "What would you like me to tell them?"

"Just remind them my movements are smaller than Lenny's. And I'm likely to move through the slower sections more quickly than he does."

"The orchestra has a sense of you from the rehearsal this week. By the way, Lenny never rehearsed us on his own on *Dumbarton Oaks*. And he conducted your interpretation in concert last night. So you should feel really confident on that one."

"Too bad it's on the second half of the program!"

"Do you want to speak to anyone else before the concert?

"The percussion principal, for sure. And the bassoon soloist on *Rite*. Damn, I wish I could talk to *everyone*!"

"Well, I could try to convene—"

"No, it isn't practical. Just beg them on my behalf to watch me. And reassure them I have played and conducted everything on the program. Even though we haven't played this stuff together, we all come with experience. Oh—and let them know I want to hold back—just a little—on every piece. Save something for *The Rite*."

"That's very un-Lenny," he laughed.

"On his orders, I am not to be Bernstein tonight."

"Excellent advice. I am really looking forward to playing under you."

I could tell he meant it, and I didn't know what to say. Getting me onto David Nadien's student roster had been a strategic move on Lenny's part. He'd lent me a powerful ally in the orchestra.

As the stage manager unlocked the guest conductor's headquarters, I wondered, not for the first time, whether Lenny was actually sick. It seemed unlikely he was so ill that he couldn't speak to me. And it was unusually convenient that he would call in sick for a program that I knew so well. I thought about the stories he'd told me of his own debut, stepping in at the last moment for Bruno Walter, to conduct this orchestra twenty years ago. Lenny told me, one late night in his studio, that he always wondered if Maestro Walter had planned his illness in order to give Lenny his first big break.

"Every time I brought it up, he would thank me for taking over on such short notice and commend me for doing an excellent job. He never gave me more than that. I still don't know the truth of the matter."

And I'd never know the truth about tonight.

Felicia unzipped the two garment bags that held my skirt, jacket and two blouses. "No one sweats as much as Lenny, but you'll still want a fresh top for the second half," Felicia told me, when I realized the chiffon came in duplicate. Once I was dressed, she turned her attention to my hair before she gave me my good luck charm. "From Lenny," she said, handing me a Star of David on a gold chain. "He always wears it when he conducts Mahler." I grinned. Lenny was always teasing me about my mixed religious heritage. He knew I'd wear his necklace alongside the gold crucifix from Mademoiselle. If there had been any question about whose God might be listening tonight, at least two bases would be covered.

***

We were opening with Stravinsky's *Scherzo Fantastique*, a lesser-known piece that dates to 1908. It's a good warm-up for the audience, gives them a clue of what's to come, but doesn't push them to the back of their seats the way his more contemporary work can. Mademoiselle had introduced it to me—and to Lenny—in a piano four-hands version the summer before I'd started with the Philharmonic. Lenny resolved to program it, and suggested I do likewise. "It's perfect for the Fontainebleau group," he'd said.

Crossing the stage, mounting the podium, acknowledging the applause, I let a memory of that Fontainebleau concert flash through my head. I was following Mademoiselle's instructions for conquering nerves: "Remember all your past performances, all the experience, the musical successes you carry within you."

I stood for a moment facing the orchestra. *The New York Philharmonic*. Yes, I was anxious, but I was also thrilled by the sight of them, by the sound I knew would soon fill the hall.

I smiled. I lifted the baton. They lifted their instruments. With my left hand, I touched my temple, index finger extended to the corner of my left eye: *Watch me*. Then, I moved the hand in front of me, flattened my fingers and pressed down the air. I brought thumb and index finger within an inch of each other—asking the players to hold back ever so slightly. We were ready.

Lifting my eyebrows and baton in tandem, I prepped the downbeat—and then, it arrived.

—29—

There's enough room on Monsieur Ferrot's grave for all of us—*Le Chef, Noire, Nouvelle, et moi.* If only I could move this china posy that is attached in the middle of your neighbor's flat stone. It looks silly—out of scale, and a poor substitute for a living garden. Not to mention the sharp edges on those little glazed roses. The cats and I must be careful.

Do you want to hear about my evening with Luke's little orchestra?

He collected me in his roadster—top up, it was raining—and we drove over to the 15th. An ancient *concierge* answered the bell at an even more ancient school building.

"*Bonsoir Monsieur*. Your room is ready. I have tried to give you a little heat, but you know the building—"

"Oh, all those teenage bodies will heat up the room," Luke assured him. "Let me introduce Mademoiselle Hannah Schaeffer," he said, sensing perhaps that the man was staring at me.

Funny, when I told Luke to skip the Maestro, I never expected Mademoiselle instead. In shops, in restaurants, in all my daily errands, I am presumed to be *Madame*. It's a matter of age, a sign of respect as much as an assumption about marital status. But in truth, like you, I am a Mademoiselle. But when Luke introduced me that way, I was thrown for a moment. It's not like you are the only Mademoiselle, but I've called you that forever, and I kind of think of it as your name now.

"Where are the kids?" I asked Luke, after the guard

squeezed just my fingertips.

"They come over on a bus. Security issues, you know."

I wondered: Are any of these kids actually dangerous?

"No armed robbers." Luke said, reading my thoughts. "But one or another might think to run off, and that would ruin everything. Even after all these years, there are people who would like to see this program stopped. They don't believe in rewarding kids for bad behavior, and that is what they think I am doing."

"Because you teach them music?"

"Because they get special treatment. They are excused for music lessons, and if they play in the group, they are allowed out for evening rehearsals and weekend concerts. Naysayers object to the free instrument program, saying these delinquents are given instruments that 'good' kids could use instead.

"But we have kept the program running for fifteen years, despite the critics. And we have had only one runaway, and he didn't really run at all. He was hiding in his room because he hadn't practiced his part."

"The kids are that serious?"

"Some are; some aren't. You'll see." Luke opened the door into a large room, already set with chairs and music stands. "Will you help me out tonight?"

"Help you how?"

"Maybe you have an exercise or two we could do with the kids? Or maybe you'll have some ideas, or hear something I miss. Will you take the baton from me if I am doing badly?"

"I am sure you will do fine."

We could hear the kids in the corridor. "I work with most of these kids one-on-one—"

"And that is why they will work with you now. They respect you on an individual basis."

"Yes, but just promise me. If I need to pass off the baton,

will you take it for a few minutes?"

Was the apparent insecurity real, or an act?

"Hannah?" I could detect a sincere note of desperation in Luke's voice.

"You really are that worried?"

"I'd rather face an armed man in the street right now."

The kids started to file in, ragtag and clumsy with their instrument cases. They were loud, and excited as they found their seats. Beside me, Luke was turning green.

"Do you have your trumpet with you?"

"It's in the car."

"Introduce me, and then go get your horn. I think we need some help in the brass section."

"You'll take the rehearsal?"

"Uh-huh."

"Oh, *merci, merci mille-mille fois*!"

Then he handed me one of my own batons.

Before I could say a word, Luke was calling for the group's attention. "We are honored tonight with the presence of Maestro Hannah Schaeffer. She conducts the Los Angeles Philharmonic Orchestra."

The kids appeared to be supremely unimpressed.

"She has made CDs, and you can download recordings online." The kids looked a little less bored as they took in my electronic qualifications.

"How many downloads?" asked a big kid holding a French horn.

"More than you can count," Luke to the rescue.

I walked to the front of the room. Kicked away the shag-carpeted podium, and adjusted the conductor's stand. "Who knows how to play a b-flat major scale?"

Most of the hands went up.

"Okay, does anybody know what I mean when I say I want you to play a b-flat major concert scale?"

No hands.

I asked the flutes and violins to play a b-flat. On the chalkboard, I illustrated the difference between a C instrument and a B-flat instrument before I asked the clarinets and cornets to join in. We worked the transposition puzzle on the board, adding instruments until everyone understood the notes they were to play.

We began with a half-note scale. I could feel the concentration in the room as we made our way up to the top and back down again.

At the bottom of the scale, I held the tonic.

"Listen." I said. "Take a breath if you need to—and come back in. But find the pitch."

As the note moved close to some tonal center, I released it.

"Now, I want you to follow me. I will cue in each section, and we will hold that note until we are in tune. Then we will go onto the next note in the scale. *D'accord*?"

Starting with bass instruments, I cued in sections until I got to Marie, who was playing piccolo.

"Okay, I said, releasing the pitch. "Did you hear how the note sounded better as we worked with it? Could you hear the difference by the time we stopped?"

All quiet.

"What happened when we added new voices? Anybody?" Silent stares. Attentive, but hesitant to volunteer a wrong answer.

"Well, I'll tell you. Every time we added a new section, we lost the pitch for a few seconds. We had to adjust. And you did adjust. By the time I let go of the note, we were in tune."

"But it took *forever*," Marie said out loud, before she turned red because she had let the words slip out.

"It did take a long time. But if you practice together at every rehearsal, you'll learn to make the adjustments more quickly. Now let's play some of the music you have in your folders."

Luke had left a rehearsal outline for me on the music stand, and I followed it gratefully, wondering only between pieces whether he'd planned it to happen this way, or whether he had intended to run the rehearsal himself. He doesn't strike me as faint of heart, and yet, I sensed he truly was afraid to lead his delinquents. But he never got his trumpet from the car, either.

From the back of the room, he signaled me to wrap it up. How long had it been—an hour, two?

"Please practice your parts for next week! And practice your scales!" I shouted after the kids as they were heading for the bus.

I noticed Marie, taking a little longer, swabbing out her flute and her piccolo. "Nice playing tonight." She is head and shoulders above the rest of the group.

"*Merci,* Maestro." She was intent on cleaning her piccolo.

"Marie! Hurry!" a voice from the doorway, a clarinet player, I think. Marie was up and out of her chair in a flash.

"Will she be in trouble for being late to the bus?" I asked Luke.

"Oh, she's always in trouble. She is too much the exception to the rule," he said. "Quite a rehearsal. I learned a lot myself."

"So, you are ready to take over next week?" I asked Luke.

"Don't you want to see how well they practice their scales for you? Don't you want to rehearse those pieces until they get them right?"

"Maybe I do. But I'm feeling a little peeved with you, too. You planned this. You stole my baton!"

"It was just lying there, next to a score on the piano. You ought to watch out for your things, Maestro." He flashed me a crooked smile. "Honestly, I just thought I might need you to conduct some part of the rehearsal. I planned to run it myself—*vraiment*—but I was hoping you might jump in if I needed help."

"But you acted so frightened."

"No, that was not an act. I was—what is that expression—scared stiff!" When I smiled at his pronunciation—*scare-steefe*—he thought I wasn't taking him seriously.

"Vraiment! I was already afraid I couldn't control so many kids at once. And then I had you, world famous conductor watching me. I couldn't imagine what I had been thinking, inviting you here. I was sure I'd make a fool of myself."

He tucked the conductor's folder and baton into my bag and hoisted it onto his shoulder. Then he reached for my hand to lead me through the now-dark hallways. He still had me by the hand when the concierge let us out. "*Bonne soirée, Mademoiselle*. I hope I will see you again."

"Next week," Luke said. "You will see her next week."

So it seems I have a replacement orchestra.

Not exactly. I can't read you on this one. On one hand, you'd be appalled by the collective sound of the group. But on the other—wouldn't you want to take that music apart and put it back together again? Oh, maybe not. At one point, you would have told me this is a gargantuan waste of my time and talent. But I have more time now.

And talent?

Well, we're way past that.

Rhapsody

—30—

"Brilliant, Hannah Schaeffer, you were brilliant."

Lenny, smiling and apparently fully recovered from his mysterious illness, was already seated at the head of the table when I arrived—a little late—for the traditional Bernstein Saturday morning breakfast.

"Have you read your reviews?" He didn't wait for an answer. He turned to Ronald Wilford, an agent from Columbia Artists who was once more trying to convince Lenny that he would be better off with their representation. "Have *you* read her reviews? Shame on you for letting this marvel slip through your fingers." He gave me a broad smile, a smile that included me in his mischief, a smile that said we are in this together, a smile that made me relax, even in the presence of the agent who believed women like me were to be heard but not seen.

"Give up your fantasy of the podium," he'd told me, when Lenny first introduced us almost two years ago. Wilford didn't say it in an unkind way, but rather as if he were my father trying to persuade me he knew what was best for me. "You'll never get a conducting job that's worth your while. And you're a talented composer. Stick with that. If we promote you as H. Schaeffer, no one needs to be the wiser. What's your middle initial?"

"Is the fact I am a woman that much of a problem for you?"

"Not for me, but for the whole world, Miss Schaeffer, yes. Look around you. How many women conductors do you see?"

"Nadia Boulanger conducted the Phil in 1938," I said, feeling a surge of defiance.

"And how many times since then has a woman conducted the New York Philharmonic? The answer is zero. Zero times. And zero times zero equals zero. In case, during your outstanding musical education, your mathematics were neglected."

His words hung in the air, his meaning clear. Not only would he never represent me as a conductor, but he thought my chances of success were nil.

"Ahhch—I don't need Wilford and you don't need him either!" Lenny had said when I repeated the conversation to him later. "What a *schmuck*. How can he think I'll ever sign with him if he treats you like this?"

"Are you considering signing with Columbia?"

"No. But they handle a lot of the artists I work with, so I can't be as rude as I'd like to be. I'm done with outside agents. But you're early in your career. We need to find you an agent with clout and connections—but someone who is still hungry."

Lenny posed the problem to Schuyler Chapin, one of the most thoroughly decent men I've ever met in the music world. Schuyler and Lenny were good friends as well as long-time colleagues, and he was as dependable as he was diplomatic. His diplomacy was critical, especially now that he would be directing the activities of Amberson, Lenny's new production company. Despite his effusiveness and good intentions, Lenny the artist could be difficult, temperamental, and demanding. This morning, Schuyler was sitting next to a newcomer at the Bernstein table, Mel Rieder.

Mr. Rieder, I'd been told, was interested in representing me, and judging from the way he was putting away Felicia's blueberry pancakes, he qualified as hungry. I glanced over at him while Lenny was sparring with Wilford, and he must have felt my eyes on him. He turned his attention from his plate to me. He winked, lifted his fork as if it were a glass, toasting me before he brought it to his lips. I couldn't help myself. I speared three layers of pancakes from my plate, and returned his salute.

***

The reviews were enthusiastic, but I still had trouble reading them. I felt like I was reading about someone else. Some other young woman who had stepped in for Leonard Bernstein at the last possible moment. The inevitable comparisons to Lenny's own debut were made, and of course there was plenty of commentary about my age—I was just 21—apart from the fact I was also female. I remembered Mademoiselle's words to that reporter in Boston. I wondered whether I could simply quote her when the press asked me the same questions.

"My only regret," Lenny said, as the plates were being cleared, "is that I was ill for Hannah's debut." Everyone laughed. "I'm serious," he said. "Of course, it couldn't be helped—last night—but at least I will be able to see her tonight."

"Tonight?"

"Yes, my dear. I am feeling so much better, but still not quite up to conducting. And it's Saturday night at the Philharmonic. Always the best night of a series."

"You mean—tonight—I—me?"

Lenny laughed. "Yes. Tonight. You. I have it all arranged. It's great publicity for the Phil. They were pleased to have you return to the podium. It was a little tougher to persuade our Amberson backers, but you can thank Schuyler for that."

"You'll be filming?" This was getting to be too much for me to take in. Another night of conducting? And television equipment, too?

"We'd already arranged to film tonight's concert," Schuyler explained to me. "We don't have any specific plans to air it, but we thought it would be a good trial run. We already have all the contracts signed, including the orchestral permissions, so we thought it would be best to go ahead with it. That is, assuming you'll agree to be filmed."

"Uhh—"

"Mr. Rieder is happy to represent you on this."

"As your unofficial representative, he squeezed twice your annual salary out of the board for tonight's performance alone," Lenny piped in. "I'd say Mr. Rieder is a pretty astute negotiator."

"It's Mel to you, Maestro Schaeffer." He extended his hand across the table. "Pleased to meet you."

"Likewise."

"We don't need to make any formal arrangements yet. Wait and see if you like me."

Mel had a strong New York accent and a down-to-earth way about him that made me feel instantly at home. I already knew I liked him.

"Are you in?" It was Lenny, reminding me of the question he'd asked me almost two years ago, when he and Mademoiselle Boulanger had arranged my future over cocoa and croissants.

"I'm in," I said. "For sure, I'm in."

***

Felicia followed me to the door. "You'll need sleep."

"God, yes." I had never felt more tired in my life. Aside from the unwavering concentration, the physical act of conducting music is like running a marathon on your arms. They say the regular aerobic exercise and upper body movement is one reason why so many conductors live so long.

"I'll get your clothes cleaned and pressed, and I'll make the calls."

"Calls?"

"Your parents, your grandmother. You'll want them there tonight, won't you? Lenny's arranged the tickets. You just rest until I call you. I'll get you a snack and bring up your clothes then."

"Felicia, I can't impose on you like this."

"It would be really good for you to get a massage before tonight's performance. Even just neck and shoulders. Maybe backstage. I'll see if I can arrange it."

"Felicia—"

"Shhh, shhh. Just sleep. Sleep."

The exhaustion was bone deep, deeper and stronger and more demanding than my nerves. I fell asleep right away, and slept until the phone rang at 4:30.

"I gave you an extra half-hour, but now we have to move at a good clip. You have to be at the hall by 6:30 so they can confirm the camera angles with you and the orchestra. Why don't you hop in the shower now? When you get out, I'll have a snack ready for you. Oh, and a hair stylist will be with me."

"A hair stylist? Were there complaints?"

"No-no-no. It's for the filming."

The filming that night gave me a chance to work with the orchestra. We were all in place with instruments. They needed sound checks, a sense of where to place the cameras. The orchestra was being paid. Playing eased the tension all of us were feeling under the lights. We worked through a couple of transitions, and I was able to talk to the group, to thank them formally for the great performance the night before, to review some passages. It was less about music and more about musical bonding. Nearly as important under the circumstances.

The evening rushed past me, much like the night before. I was both more and less nervous. Less worried about the orchestra and their response to me. I'd proven myself in their eyes and ears. More worried about my own capacity to pull it off two nights in a row, especially knowing I would be judged more critically this evening—by the press who had been alerted to attend, and by the Philharmonic management who were paying me for my services tonight. I was aware too that, somewhere in the audience, my parents and my grandmother might be listening. I wasn't sure who would have been able to make it on such short notice. Felicia had asked me if I wanted to see anyone before the performance, and I'd said no.

"What about at intermission? Press? Family? Lenny?"

"If it is possible, I'd like to have the intermission to myself."

"Done. I'll let the stage manager know."

"Will Lenny be offended?"

"I think he would do the same thing in your place. He'll understand."

It was Lenny who led the crowd backstage after the concert, after the applause, after the standing ovation for *The Rite of Spring*. He had his arm around my grandmother. In their wake, members of the press, quizzing him, adoring him. I spotted my mother and Bill, and Dad and Joanne in the middle of the media melée. I wanted to run and hide. But I heard Mademoiselle's voice in my head, scolding me. Telling me that I must be in command, whether on or off the stage. But with Lenny just twenty paces away, I wasn't sure how to act. *Be Hannah Schaeffer*. I wondered, momentarily, who she was.

Felicia materialized by my side, giving me a hug just before Lenny swooped in, embracing us both.

"Wonderful concert, Maestro Schaeffer," he said, loud enough for the press to hear his form of address. He leaned in to kiss my cheek, lowering his voice to whisper: "Now prepare to bask in the limelight."

—31—

It's not only the orchestra I'll miss. It's the hall.

I love that damn hall. It took so long to build, and there were times when it seemed it might never be finished. I don't mean the usual construction delays you'd expect on any big—giant—construction project. I mean there was a period of time when everything just stopped, and there was no certainty we'd be able to continue.

In 1987—the year before I was hired as music director—Lillian Disney gave the L.A. Philharmonic a gift of 50 million dollars for a new concert hall. Some said her generosity was closer to a curse. It came with conditions. She wanted a role in the selection process for the architect, and the gift was contingent on breaking ground within five years' time. Reasonable enough, if there were no property disputes around the site, or if all the neighbors were a hundred percent on board with the concept. But there were layers of issues that began with the very ground to be broken. And it quickly became clear that Mrs. Disney's munificent gift was not nearly enough to fund the project. Millions and millions more dollars had to be found—partnerships, grants, fundraising drives. And, of course, the longer it took, the more money it cost.

We finally played a concert in Disney Hall in October of 2003. Sixteen years and a century later.

But God, it's beautiful. The sound, Mademoiselle. It is beyond stunning. It is indescribable. Though I have to admit that first rehearsal—I was worried. You know there's almost a tradition of difficulty with new halls. It happened in Berlin and in Philadelphia. And of course, I'd heard from Lenny about all the issues he'd had with Philharmonic Hall, how difficult the move was from Carnegie Hall, how long it took to get it right. It also took a ton of money.

Still, a part of me was pretty certain that everything would be okay. Frank Gehry, the architect, had called me—after the stage was built but before the seats were in—to see if we might try some music in the space. We'd met the next day, me hauling a couple of flutes and my grandfather's violin. I spent so much time on the site over the years that I had my own hard hat. It was hot pink—if you're already a woman in a man's world, why not let everyone know you're here? (Oh, and my hat went missing for about 24 hours in late 1999, during which time persons unknown applied gold glitter, forming the word *Maestro* on the brim. I suspect it was a joint effort involving the percussion section and the project manager.)

So, there I was, strapped into my glamour-girl hard hat, trying out flutes.

The sound was spectacular.

This unofficial event was on the down-low—the last thing we needed was an audience, or word of our sound-check getting out to the press. I couldn't assemble an orchestra to test the range of sound. But I wanted, at the least, to hear wind and string. I asked my always-discreet concertmaster to meet us there. Malcom played his own gorgeous instrument, filling up the hall. Then, I asked him to play Gramps' violin, too. I may be a barely serviceable violinist, but I know the sound of that instrument by heart.

All of us—Frank, Malcom, me—found ourselves teary in that cavernous, unfinished space. It was the beauty and resonance of the sound, but it was also, I think, the awareness of just how long it had taken to reach that point. We still had a way to go, but it was a huge moment. As memorable for me as opening night, really. And you know, if Frank hadn't suggested that we meet, I might have waited until our first rehearsal.

Our first, close-to-disastrous rehearsal. It didn't go well.

But our secret sound-check meant I knew the aural potential of the space. I felt relatively assured that all the many things that were going wrong, all the imperfections and the hiccups, were of the human variety. There would, of course, be a process of settling in, adjusting. Even though we were playing music that was familiar—every musician on the stage was hearing something he or she had never heard before. Truly, the acoustical precision and depth of the hall is astounding. Astounding enough to throw more than a hundred professional musicians off their game. Our game. My game.

Sure, we play in halls that are unfamiliar whenever we go on tour. But they are well-established venues. We arrived with a sense of security that was borne of history of all the ensembles who had played there before us. After years of anticipation, we found ourselves ensconced inside a twenty-first century architectural marvel. There was not a person on that stage who didn't feel a bit intimidated by the unabashed modernity of our new digs.

The wavy aluminum exterior would have had you hand-clutched-to-heart. And the organ—well, that's a story in itself, and thank goodness we had a maker who was both open to Frank's wild designs but ever mindful of the practicality and sound. So many conceptual drawings were tossed, and still, it is like nothing that would have been built in your lifetime. It's as much a sculpture as a musical instrument. I can imagine your beautiful expressive hands on the keys. You would love it. And you'd love the concert hall, too, once you caught your breath. It's beautiful and inviting; the seating hugs the stage. What never felt right to me at the Royal Albert is perfection at Disney Hall.

Opening night felt like a second debut with the orchestra. Again, a parade of glittering Hollywood stars, a red carpet, and enough press to fill a small recital hall. As I contemplated the newness of it all, I remembered my first concert in L.A., reminding myself that everything that night felt brand new, too. For extra reassurance, I had my somethings-old: your photo, Lenny's, my crystal votive holder—the ritual objects required for my pre-concert meditation. Peter was there—he'd come over from Amsterdam, and Elaine. My Dad had passed away before the hall was finished, but Joanne came with my mother and Bill. Emil sent flowers and regrets. The trip would have been too difficult for him.

You would not have exactly embraced the program. There was a strong pop element in the first half. Hollywood, remember? But I know you would have approved of my final selection: Stravinsky, of course. *The Rite of Spring*. How could I premiere a new hall without our old friend?

In my convoluted cosmology of the Afterlife, I assumed you were there in some form—hearing the exquisite sounds that were produced that night. Lenny, too. My grandfather, Nana, Dad, Felicia—the celestial line-up of the close-and-departed.

Lenny told me all those years ago that I needed more ego in order to take possession of the musicians in front of me. But that's not it—really. It's time, and familiarity, and shared commitment. In the same way that the L.A. Philharmonic became my orchestra, Disney Hall became my hall. Mine, because they are my home.

Were my home, I guess.

People change houses, right?

–32–

"After I debuted with New York, Arthur Judson called me into his office, showed me a pile of contracts, and told me all I needed to do was show up for every engagement," Lenny said. He was looking at Mel Rieder as if it were entirely his fault that we weren't drowning in offers.

"We all know it isn't going to be that easy for Hannah," Schuyler said. He was playing the diplomat as usual, trying to protect Mel from Lenny's intensity of purpose.

"Because I'm female." I heard myself sigh.

"There's that," Mel said. "You're also really young—even younger than Lenny when he debuted."

"But she already has a larger repertoire," Lenny pointed out.

"Maybe you can mention that in the next few interviews you do," the ever-practical Schuyler Chapin chimed in.

"Have there been any calls at all?"

"A few. But nothing from the majors."

"Don't they read *The New York Times*? Idiots. What about the Phil? Did they ask her back?" Lenny was more worked up about my nonexistent career than I was.

"They committed to one series. We haven't worked out the program."

"Well, that's something. I just don't want Hannah relegated to the minor leagues." We'd had many discussions on this subject. It was the opinion of Lenny, Mel, and Schuyler—the official guardians of my conducting career—that if I were to accept a job with a lesser orchestra, I would be stuck there forever, with little hope of moving up.

"An official guest conductor gig with the New York Phil will be a good, high-profile job," Mel said. "Meanwhile, I'll talk to San Francisco, Pittsburgh, St. Louis. Maybe L.A. But we can't expect to fill her dance card right away."

"Even on the strength of her debut—with these reviews?"

Mel shrugged his shoulders.

"*Damn*," said Lenny.

***

When he left the New York Philharmonic the following year, Lenny asked me to come with him. He wanted me to assist him in his many guest conducting assignments, and to work with his Amberson associates on the various film and television projects they planned to produce. "You get any better offers, I want you to take them," he said to me. "But meanwhile, I'll guarantee you conduct at least six concerts a year, and as many rehearsals as we can manage. We'll be building your repertoire and your resume. Mel and Schuyler can work out the details."

It was an arrangement that lasted for several years. It was exciting and exhausting. Lots of travel and lots of hotel living. But I had the chance to conduct in Vienna and Amsterdam, in London, and even in Tokyo. I ran enough rehearsals to keep my arm in shape, and I studied every piece that Lenny conducted—including a lot of opera that was new to me.

I told Mel I wanted to take flute work, too. I wasn't prepared to lose my original instrument in my quest for a podium, and it was easier for him to keep me playing than it was for him to secure conducting gigs. But with each new strong review, I was getting noticed, and Mel's phone began to ring with new requests. By the time I was in my mid-twenties, my schedule was filling out with guest-conducting engagements all my own.

Mademoiselle followed my career closely, and despite her advanced age, she managed to surprise me backstage after more than one European concert. "I am so pleased to see you on the podium," she said, the first time she saw me conduct, "but I want to hear your music, too. You must not forget that little girl with enough music to fill all the rooms and stables at Fontainebleau."

I knew she was right. It was all too easy to get caught up in the whirlwind of guest-conducting. With my teacher's voice in my ear, I made a habit of writing on airplanes and in the wee hours of the morning. I sent my work to her, and she returned it to me with comments and the familiar hieroglyphs alongside the notes. With her encouragement, I managed to crank out several chamber pieces and a tone poem for orchestra that I premiered with the Pittsburgh Symphony.

Nana, too, was always eager to hear about my latest work, my upcoming conducting assignments. "I am so proud of you. I know I didn't invent you, but it's okay if I brag about you, isn't it?" Perhaps because she felt I was self-sufficient in my musical career, she took it upon herself to worry instead about my romantic life. "It's fine to wait. I married late—twenty-eight, very late for my time. But remember, there is nothing in this world that matches the love of a true and good man."

She was talking about Peter. He'd surprised me backstage after my conducting premiere at the Concertgebouw. "I am here to welcome you to my home country," he said, handing me a bouquet of red roses. A photographer snapped a picture. Peter was an up-and-coming international soloist, and much revered in Amsterdam.

"Why thank you so much." I matched his tone almost precisely even when I asked him if he were free to join a group of us for an after-concert dinner.

"It would be an honor to join an old friend who has brought such beautiful music to our city."

We laughed at our reporter-ready exchange later that night, after the large dinner party had disbanded, when it was just Peter and me, sitting in an all-night bar, talking of music and Mademoiselle, about our careers, our travels, and—as the night became morning—our feelings about each other.

"I still love you," he said. He looked down, swirling his brandy, not registering my startled reaction.

"Peter?"

When he looked up, I could see in his eyes the painful truth of his words. "But you—you were the one who ended it. You—"

"I know. I really thought it was for the best. And it's worked out for both of us—in terms of our careers."

"You think if we'd stayed together that I would be following you around the world, making sure your tuxedo is pressed?"

"More likely I'd be seeing to your concert attire." He smiled, and I realized that I missed him. I had avoided him at Fontainebleau, while I pretended the relationship hadn't mattered—that *he* hadn't mattered. Then, I focused my attention on my studies with Lenny, and on building my career, one engagement at a time.

"I'm sorry I have been out of touch," I said. It was a weak apology for my abandonment, and it wasn't at all what I wanted to say. "I just didn't know how to be friends with you."

"I understand." He touched my hand. "Do you still have flute pads?" He turned over my fingers, touched my fingertips one by one. "You do." He traced the lines in each of my palms. "Your hands are even stronger now."

I couldn't think of a thing to say. The heat from his hands to mine had left me without words. It passed through my mind that I needed to excuse myself, run to the phone booth by the ladies' room and call Elaine for a whispered consultation. I laughed at the image.

"Tell me," he said.

"Oh, I was thinking about how my friend Elaine used to advise me about you. She told me that I should wear my green sleeveless dress without a bra if I wanted to get you to sleep with me."

"I remember that dress. It matched your eyes. She was right. I would not have been able to resist temptation. I'm having a tough time of it now."

"Why try?" I asked him as I leaned in for the kiss. The kiss with a sustained bass line, the kiss with a tremolo in the violins, the kiss with deep round notes from the middle voices and articulated sixteenths in the upper woodwinds. I paid the check. I brought him back to my hotel room. I played the Maestro, the woman of the world. I've conducted the New York Philharmonic, I told myself when my courage faltered. Surely, I could manage sex.

"Umm," I said, as we made our way to the bed. "Umm."

"You have a boyfriend?" Peter asked, pausing only a moment in his quest to remove my bra.

"No, no."

"And I'm not seeing anyone either, so we don't have any worries on that score." He lifted up my hair and started kissing the back of my neck. I shivered.

"Cold? Do you need me to warm you up?"

I didn't want to ruin the moment, to admit to him that I was twenty-four years old and still a virgin.

"Are you okay?" he asked when I looked away.

"Ah, yeah. I'm great." I sat up. "But remember how we were talking about how we've both put all our focus on our careers?"

"Yes." I could tell he was completely puzzled. The seductress suddenly wanted to have a deep conversation about life choices.

"Well, in my case, I really have put all of my focus on my career. I mean all of it. I mean no time for relationships. No time for—uhh—sex."

"Oh, so you're a little rusty. So am I. Don't worry; it's like riding a bicycle." He slipped one hand under the front of my underpants.

"Except—I've never ridden this bicycle before."

His hand moved toward my belly button, and in a hurry. "You mean—"

"Yes. The sex bicycle."

He moved his hand to my side, pulling back from me, looking at me.

"Well, this is an unexpected development. You sure don't kiss like a virgin. I mean that with all admiration and respect," he added.

"I want to do this," I said. "I just wanted you to know—in case I do something stupid or wrong or something—"

"Shush," he said putting a finger to my lips. "Don't worry." He paused. "You're telling me you want to learn how to ride this bicycle?"

"Yes," I said. "I am. I do."

***

Peter was a good teacher, a generous lover. For five days in Amsterdam, we left behind the demands of our lives, the memories of Fontainebleau, even the music, indulging only each other. For three years after those five days, we arranged our schedules to incorporate time together in the cities where we played. It was a crazy, international relationship, and although we told each other—at odd hours, and usually from different time zones—that we loved each other, we also promised ourselves the freedom to live our separate lives in music.

He tired of this arrangement before I did. Peter was older, ready to settle down. He wanted children. He wanted stability, a home base, a wife there to greet him after a long tour. Our break-up felt like a repeat performance: Peter, telling me that my talent was too large to be contained in the domestic life he craved, that he couldn't hold me back. Me, stunned, and soon after that, angry with myself for falling in love with him in the first—or second—place.

I took on more work, kept a schedule that punished me, and gave me not a moment to spare. My grandmother, watching me from afar, could see into my heart.

"Hannah, honey. I'm so sorry it didn't work out with you and Peter. You know I liked him. But it wasn't meant to be. There's someone out there for you. I'm sure of it."

"Sorry to report the men aren't lining up at the door," I told Nana.

"Can they even find the door? You keep yourself so busy with your work."

She was right. I was hardly in one place long enough to meet someone, never mind sustain anything resembling a normal relationship. And even when I felt ready to take a chance again, most of the men I met were members of the orchestras I conducted. Not exactly the ideal scenario for a first date.

Still, she persisted, bringing up "the door" in almost every phone call.

"Is the door unlocked?"

"Unlocked, and ajar," I reported.

She laughed. "Well fling it wide open! But don't let any loonies in!" I wondered when she said this whether she was thinking of my mother and father. Probably not. By this time, I had come to realize that my grandmother regarded their failed romance as an anomaly. Love makes you happy, she believed. I want Hannah to be happy. Therefore, I want

Hannah to be in love. Her logic was skewed, but her heart, I knew, was always in the right place.

"What about your door, Nana?" I dared to ask her once.

"My door?"

"Yes. Don't play innocent with me. You know what I am saying."

"I'm much too old for new romance."

"False," I intoned solemnly, echoing a game we'd played when I was a kid. "Look around—your friend Judy just remarried, and she's older than you. And not nearly as interesting. Not to mention you are a beautiful woman. I bet the handsome widowers would be lined up at your door, if only they knew your address!"

She chuckled, and I thought I almost had her. But then she collected herself. "You are sweet to say so, but I have had my grand romance.

"I am free in my old age, and that is a sort of blessing too. Why would I want to take someone on now, so late in life, so much work, so little reward? No thank you. Your grandfather meant the world to me, and no man can measure up to him in my heart. I'd pity any man who came to my door in search of love. Even if I loved someone else, that someone would always be playing second fiddle to your grandfather."

"Everybody plays second fiddle to a concertmaster," I said.

"I didn't even think of that," she said. I knew she was smiling.

"The truth is you like to date at the top."

"I've never dated a conductor," she teased me back.

"I could introduce you to a couple of Maestros who are just about your age. And in good health, too."

"What about finding a Maestro who's *your* age?"

"A little young for you don't you think?"

"Oh, you are *impossible*." We laughed and said our goodbyes, Nana asking me to promise to keep my eyes open for romance, me asking her to promise to spend more time with her girlfriends and less time alone in her apartment. Neither one of us willing to promise a thing.

—33—

No flowers today, and not enough energy to change your water, so just as well. But I can dump this faded bouquet. And feed the gathering cats.

Have you missed me?

Have you worried?

All those Novembers I spent with you. I should have expected this. But I guess I thought I'd outgrown that tendency to bronchitis when the heat comes on.

The first night—or really the third, I guess—I remember hoping that whoever was pounding on the door would go away.

"Hannah? Hannah!"

I tiptoed toward the door, willing the sloping floorboards not to creak. I could hear Luke on his phone.

"When was the last time you spoke to her?" Pause. "I don't like this, Marcel."

Marcel? Emil's grandson? Damn, I'd forgotten to cancel the Mozart rehearsal with his quartet.

"It just isn't like her to miss the youth orchestra. I got her machine when I called earlier—twice. She isn't answering the door. I'm worried. I am going to break in."

Can you imagine the scene with my landlord, me explaining that the place had been broken into—by a cop—while, yes, I'd been home, not answering the door?

I decided to call Luke's mobile.

"Bourlou."

"Hi—I'm here. Sorry. I was sleeping."

"I'm sorry to intrude, but Marcel and Emil and I were worried about you. You missed rehearsal tonight—"

"I just realized that. I'm terribly sorry. I guess I just slept through it."

"And our calls, too? Are you very ill?"

"I'm fine." It was an obvious lie.

"May I come in?"

"I just have a little flu. I'm okay. I don't want you to catch this thing."

No response from the other side of the door.

I looked through the peephole. *Resolute* is the word that comes to mind. Phone to his left ear, Luke was looking straight ahead, as if he could make the door open on its own if he just stared at it hard enough.

"And I'm vain. I don't want to be seen like this."

"I won't look." I could hear him through the door several seconds before his voice reached me via the telephone.

"But the germs—" I was leaning up against the door. He could probably hear me in duplicate too.

"I won't breathe, either."

I slid down the wall, landed sitting on the carpet.

"I am coming in."

No doubt he uses those the same words when informing lawbreakers they are surrounded, that they have one last chance, their best chance, to turn themselves in, to go peacefully.

A key turned in the lock.

"How—"

"The *gardienne* was very willing to provide a key when I produced my credentials."

"Oh, great." I reached up to open the security latch.

"Why are you on the floor?"

"It was the most convenient place to sit."

"Ah." He joined me. It was clear to me, even in my feverish state, that his cop training had not prepared him for a sick, recalcitrant, aging-out-of-middle-aged American woman sitting on the floor of her apartment, and apparently happy with her position. "The floor is cold," he observed.

"Let me help you back to bed." He grabbed both my hands. I found myself dizzy with the effort of rising.

"I've called a doctor."

"Thanks, I've been meaning to do that. I'll see him tomorrow."

"No, she's on her way right now."

"Oh right, France. They still make house calls in this very civilized country." I felt irrationally angry at Luke—for barging into my space, for calling a doctor without consulting me, for treating me like a child, for seeing me without makeup, and for being so conspicuously healthy and energetic.

"You should have called me."

"I know—I feel terrible about the rehearsal—"

"That isn't what I meant. Why didn't you call me over the weekend and tell me how sick you were? Why didn't you let me know that you have this tendency towards bronchitis and—

"Oh, the hell with it," he said, interrupting himself. "If you didn't want to call me, you could have called Marcel or Emil. You have Emil very worried. I mean really, what are you trying to prove?" He didn't wait for my answer. "You need to rest until the doctor comes. I'll make some tea." He deposited me on my bed and disappeared into the kitchen.

I was left to contemplate my alleged selfishness.

Oh, be quiet. Besides, selfishness is a job requirement in my line of work. You'll love this: The doctor prescribed antibiotics, rest, plenty of fluids, and walks around the apartment every three hours. God, Mademoiselle. All those circuits around Rue Ballu. Remember?

"You live together?" the doctor asked me.

"Oh—uh—*Non.*"

"Oh, then I will call the hospital. You cannot be left alone."

"*Non, s'il vous plait, non*! *Je ferai le promenade*! I will set my alarm, and take my medicine, and get up to walk."

"No, absolutely not. Too dangerous."

"I'll stay," Luke said. He didn't say it to me, or phrase it like an offer. He declared it, to the doctor, adding, "I will see to everything."

"If her condition should change, if her breathing becomes more difficult, go directly to the hospital."

"*D'accord.*"

I meant to protest, to tell Luke he didn't need to stay. But the next time I was awake, we were walking around the apartment, and it was midnight—then, three, six, nine in the morning.

"Don't you have to go to work?"

"Not today."

Today, yesterday, tomorrow. I lost track of time. I don't remember being this out of it when I was sick as a kid. Maybe I just settled into it, feeling safe and protected and prayed over. Mademosielle, thank you for that.

God, I'm a sweaty, filthy mess. That was my first coherent thought when the fever finally broke. "I feel much better," I said to Luke. "I'm going to take a bath."

"Not alone."

"Well, not with you."

He laughed. "*Bien sûr*—not with me! But you are very weak. You haven't eaten anything substantial in days. You could fall."

I fought him with all the energy I could muster, but he was stronger and healthier and ready for every argument.

"This is so completely embarrassing."

"I won't look."

"You said that the night you broke into my apartment."

"I didn't break in. You were delusional. I used the key."

"You've been looking at me for four days now, and I have looked my worst. You lied then, and you're lying now."

He sighed, crossed his arms, centered himself on his legs.

"This bothers you? The way you look when you are sick? That I would see you at your worst, as you say?"

"*Vraiment*, it bothers me!"

We compromised. He ran the bath for me—a bubble bath, one of my favorite things about Paris—and he helped me to the bathroom, placed two towels within reach, and stationed himself outside the door.

I used the chair he had moved up against the tub as a railing. The water was just the right temperature. I leaned back against the little plastic pillow I'd bought at Monoprix.

"Are you okay?"

"Fine." The water was cold. I must have fallen asleep. I added some hot to the mix.

"Hannah!?"

"Out in a minute,"

I got serious about soaping up, rinsing, shampooing, rinsing. Applied some conditioner, sat back to let it soak in. That time, I caught myself before I drifted off. As I rinsed my hair, I considered the impossible task ahead of me: getting out of the bath.

When I grabbed the edge of the tub and started to stand, I was instantly dizzy.

"Ummm—I think I need a hand, but—"

"I won't look."

"How many times are you going to say that?" I asked him through the door. Why do I feel so shy around him? It's not like he hasn't seen a naked body before—but he's never seen *my* naked body.

I covered myself in an armor of bubbles. "If you could just help me up—"

He was through the door in a second, had me standing in two. He turned his back, instructing me to lean on the chair for support while I rinsed. Still facing away from me, he passed me a towel as soon as I shut off the sprayer. A magician of linens, he produced another, "For your hair," he said.

I know women who can wrap a towel around themselves, tuck one edge in, twist, and *voilà*—they can sport their *après le bain* attire all day long. I lack this skill. I wrap, tuck, twist, but the towel never stays put. This deficit was at the front of my mind when I admitted I'd need help getting out of the tub.

Luke spun around, offering his arm as if we were on the way to the opera. With one hand holding my towel and the other fastened on Luke's forearm, I was escorted to the center of the bathroom floor.

And I was exhausted. Just like I am now. My ride's here, anyway. I was going to take a bus, but Luke insisted on sending a car for me. A police car. I was dropped at the gate, allotted forty-five minutes for a visit, and now my time is up.

À demain, Mademoiselle. Au revoir, mes petits chats.

—34—

"Let me turn down the music." I heard the clunk of the receiver on the kitchen counter. Nana was listening to Gramps playing Beethoven. In her younger days, she kept my grandfather's recordings stashed away like the family jewels, taking them out only on special occasions and to share with me as part of my musical education. "That is your grandfather playing," she'd say. "You can thank him for your talent and your education. He asked Miss Boulanger to promise that she would teach you."

"If I was a worthy student." Mademoiselle's version of the same story emphasized my worthiness, as if I were a fairy tale heroine called upon to prove myself through a series of difficult tasks and death-defying feats of endurance.

"Honey, that was never in question. I think your grandfather always imagined that he would teach you himself until you were old enough to study abroad with Nadia. Though sometimes I wonder if he had some premonition that he might not be around."

"You think he knew he would die young?"

"I wonder. But I don't wonder about how much he loved you and wanted the best for you. I wish you'd been able to know him better, that he'd lived just a few more years, to see you and hear your music."

"Maybe he does?" I ventured, thinking of how often my grandmother referred to Gramps in the present tense, as if he were still at her side.

"Oh, sure he does. But it isn't the same."

Lately, my grandmother hadn't been waiting for my visits home to listen to her record collection. She took out my grandfather's recordings and played them again and again, sitting alone in her small apartment. I came to expect to hear my grandfather playing Brahms, Mendelssohn, and Mozart in the background of our phone calls.

I didn't worry at first. I chalked up her nostalgia to her advancing years and told myself it was normal. I read up on how the memory works, and realized it was easier now for her to remember the time with my grandfather than it was to remember the details of her day. She was always happy to hear from me, and eager to learn about my life and my career. But her stories were more and more about my grandfather, and though I loved hearing them, I wished there was more activity in her daily life to anchor her to the present. I noticed, too, a note of sadness—wistfulness—in her voice that I hadn't heard before. Almost thirty years after losing him, my grandmother was missing my grandfather more and more each day.

***

As I entered my thirties, Nana entered her eighties. I kept up with the phone visits, and she kept up with my career, but I began to hear her confusion about how all the parts of her life fit together. Sometimes she would brag to me about her talented granddaughter, telling me stories from my own childhood, as if the woman on the other end of the phone was not the same person as the little girl she wanted to tell me about. Sometimes I listened without telling her that she was telling me stories about myself. And sometimes, when I was resistant to what I feared was happening, I would let her know. "Nana, you know that little girl, your granddaughter—that's me."

There would be a pause. I felt as if I could almost hear her processing this information.

"You're Hannah," she might say. Sometimes with an upward inflection, asking for confirmation, sometimes with a strong downward inflection, a proclamation, a sense in her voice that she had triumphed, made the connection, merged the young girl and the young woman.

"Yes, I am."

"Of course." At this point, she would always assert her certainty.

She had stopped asking me about my love life. I wasn't sure if it was because she could no longer make the connection, or because she didn't like Ted or the fact that we were living together, unmarried, in New York. He was a jazz trombonist with his own quintet. We shared late nights and early mornings, practiced and wrote very different music at desks in the same living room, and had satisfactory, if not great, sex. "We are calmly compatible," I liked to tell Elaine.

"How is your mother?" Nana would ask instead, as if my mother didn't live down the street from her, as if my mother didn't drop in each day, as if they didn't eat lunch several times a week.

"You tell me," I would say, when I wanted to press the reality into her.

"But, dear, I haven't seen her in so long."

"Who took you to lunch yesterday?"

"Yesterday? Oh, you know I can't remember things like that. I can't remember what I had for breakfast an hour ago."

"Yes, but you have lunch with her three times a week. You know who."

I could almost hear her straining. But usually, she came up with a tentative, "Audrey?"

"Yes. Audrey. My mother."

"Oh, Audrey is your mother. Of course."

"So, you tell me—how is Audrey?"

"She's doing just fine. A little bossy though."

"Well, she owes you some bossy. You bossed her around enough!"

"I did?" A giggle.

"Yes, ma'am. You were the boss of all of us!"

"Well, I am the oldest!"

Nana never lost her sense of humor, even as she lost touch with the world around her. Returning to the present, she arrived with a wry remark. And while her mind played tricks on her, her body remained healthy. One day, she walked fifteen miles in search of my grandfather. "My husband should have been home hours ago!" she told the cops who found her wandering along the side of a road outside town. "I am not the missing person. I know exactly where I am! It's my husband you should be looking for." It was a cold December day, and she was searching for Gramps in her housedress and an old sweater. When they called my mother from the hospital, the nurse said Nana had a mild case of hypothermia.

From the hospital, she was admitted to what they called a rehab facility, a nicer name for what was essentially a nursing home with a physician-staffed medical wing. I visited her there, frightened by the sight of the silent, staring elderly populating the halls in wheelchairs and chaise longues. Were the green-tiled walls of the corridor somehow more interesting than their rooms? Insulated in my youthful ego, I felt almost offended by their willingness to be seen. I was grateful that my grandmother never joined them. She stayed in her room most of the time, only taking occasional forays outdoors when we coaxed her.

As hard as it was for me to see her in that place, I am not sure, in retrospect, that it was that difficult for Nana to be there, because she wasn't there, most of the time. She spent hours in her childhood and would often mistake her visitors for her young siblings. My mother, she thought, more often than not, was her mother. In that scheme of relations, I was simply a kind young woman who stopped by from time to time.

As much as I wanted to spare her the present reality of her situation, I searched for ways to bring her back. I think I held out hope that if we could retrieve her lost mind, we could take her home again, save her life. One day, I brought her a portable tape player, a set of headphones, and some cassettes of my grandfather's ancient recordings. I dropped in a tape and placed the earphones on her head so as not to muss her newly coifed lavender-tint hair. When I pressed play, she responded immediately. "Jacob." she said, looking right into my eyes.

"Yes."

She didn't say another word that day. She just sat and listened to the music. When it stopped, I showed her how to turn the tape over and how to put it into the player. I showed her the big green Play button. I knew the technology would be difficult for her; the small motor coordination required would be hard also. She'd suffered frostbite during her fruitless search for Gramps, and her hands never fully recovered. But she was highly motivated, and she could not rely on the nurses to change her tapes. After a few lessons, she learned to manage them herself, listening to her music whenever she liked.

I brought more tapes every time I visited. Some came from her original 78's, and some were copies of old BSO recordings that were being reissued. Any recording that included Gramps was welcome. I wasn't sure if I was only feeding an obsession, or whether the tapes were doing some good, but I felt as though she engaged with the music in a way that she could no longer engage with us.

She was always excited when I brought new tapes for her. She sat up straighter in her bed and summoned her powers of concentration as the music began. I slipped a recording of my own into her player on one visit. "Hannah," she pronounced proudly, after a few notes. There was not a moment of hesitation or confusion. She knew Hannah as surely as she had known Jacob on the day I'd brought the first tape to her. She looked over at me, and removed one earpiece, held it up and pointed to it. "This is you," she said matter-of-factly. She repositioned her headphones and listened while I wiped the tears that were leaking from my eyes.

***

I found it hard to reconcile the strong-willed, decisive Nana of my childhood with the confused and hesitant old woman in the nursing home. Every time I made the trip, I hoped against hope she might surprise me with her lucidity, or with sheer outrageousness. And sometimes she did. It was as if she journeyed back to her former self, if only for the span of a morning.

I will never forget the day I stopped to visit Nana on my way to my first Boston appearance. I'd had some publicity shots taken late that morning, and I was still wearing my concert attire. I walked into Nana's room.

"Don't you look lovely," she said, "I am so glad you were able to make it."

She was seated in the chair by the window, and she was wearing a scarlet wool suit. Her hair was fresh from the hairdressers, shiny with spray. She had her teeth in, and her lipstick matched her suit.

"Nana—you look great! Why are you all dressed up?"

"Do you think I would go to one of your concerts in my bathrobe?"

"No—but—"

"Aren't you conducting the Boston Symphony tonight?"

"Yes—but—"

"One of the nurses read me the *Globe* story. Very nice picture of you. I'd like a copy of that one for my table here." She patted the table beside the chair, pausing to make sure I was registering her request.

She continued: "The first woman on the podium since Miss Boulanger! I am so proud of you. I haven't been to Symphony Hall in years. I don't think we'll have time for dinner, but you'd probably rather eat afterwards anyway. I remember Jacob never liked to eat too much before a performance. I don't know any of the restaurants in Boston anymore. Perhaps you can ask someone from the orchestra for a suggestion."

She paused, looking at me. I felt like I needed to sit down. She filled my silence. "I feel a little hungry now. Maybe we could pick up a snack on the way, and then eat a big dinner later?" This was a question. She wanted me to make the decision.

"You're coming to the concert with me?" I finally managed.

"Yes, I hope you haven't given away all your house seats."

Her awareness was startling: *house seats*. Where is this information stored? This awareness?

Why can't you be like this all the time? I wanted to ask her, as if she could turn on this clarity like a light switch. What happened? What was the trigger? *If I conducted every night at Symphony Hall, would you dress up and be this woman for every concert?*

"Don't you two look beautiful!" The nurse walked into Nana's room, smiling. "Are you all set for your big night out, Rose? That suit is a lovely shade on you. Doesn't she look great?" she asked me.

"Great," I said.

"She's been looking forward to this evening all week."

"Me too." I said it out of politeness before I realized I *had* been looking forward to a day when Nana would be this clear.

"I think it's a good idea for Mrs. Serapin to stay overnight with you; it will be a late night."

"My bag is packed," Nana declared, and she glanced toward a neat little tapestry patterned suitcase in the corner of her room. I wondered which version of Nana would wake up in my hotel room the next morning. I was still having trouble adjusting to this situation. The nurse and my grandmother were looking at me, waiting for my cue. I stood.

"We better get on the road if we are going to stop for a snack on the way." I picked up her suitcase with one hand, and gave my grandmother my other arm, and we walked through the long halls together, red and black, heels clicking, chins high; two ladies on their way to Symphony.

***

In the car, she was full of questions, questions she thought the reporter from the *Globe* should have asked.

"They only have so much space for a story, Nana. By the way, does Audrey know you're coming tonight?"

"Audrey?" she queried back to me.

"Oh, no." I said it out loud without meaning to. I imagined her falling back into forgetfulness as the night wore on.

"Audrey," she said, declarative this time. "No, I thought we would surprise her."

Shock her, I thought. We stopped for soup and grilled cheese sandwiches on the way into town, checked into the hotel where I showered and changed my clothes for the third time that day, and still, we arrived early to Symphony Hall. The guard smiled at Nana as he let us in the stage door. "My grandmother," I said to him.

"I read about you in the *Globe*," he said to her with a wink at me.

"Oh, not about me—about my husband, and my granddaughter, here."

"I am pretty sure they mentioned you too," he said. "I don't know why they didn't put in your picture with that fine red suit!"

"Not my picture, no, no, but it would have been nice if they had enough space to put a little picture of my husband Jacob alongside Hannah. He was her first teacher, you know.

"Don't you think that would have been nice, a picture of your grandfather with his violin?" she asked me.

"Sure," I said, as I tried to gauge how much help she needed from me on the stairs.

They had played up the hometown girl angle in the piece. "How does it feel to know you will be conducting the same orchestra your grandfather played in all those years ago?" the interviewer had asked me. I was annoyed by the question. It *wasn't* the same orchestra thirty-something years later. I answered the question by remembering rehearsals that I had attended here as a little girl. Alone in the vast hall, watching my grandfather, taking in the motions of the conductor.

"And now you are the conductor!' The interviewer was clearly happy with this nostalgic turn. I smiled in response, dying for the allotted forty-five minutes to be over.

I gave my grandmother a backstage tour before I turned her over to the head usher for seating. "I need a little time to prep."

"Of course you do, dear. Don't you worry about me. I'll be watching your back!" She chuckled as I took in this beautiful, amazing woman who was my grandmother, full of humor and life. *Appreciate the moment*, I instructed myself, as I offered up a little prayer that this version of Nana could make it through the evening.

I don't usually look at the audience when I take my opening bow, but rather past them, beyond them, into the place where I know I must find the music. But that night, I looked right at Nana—orchestra, tenth row, center. There would be an empty seat next to her. Dad and Joanne were planning to come on Saturday evening, and my mother preferred to sit in the balcony. I spotted my grandmother right away, sitting up straight in her seat. She was smiling, almost glowing in the darkened house. But the seat beside her wasn't empty. It was occupied by my grandfather, who was wearing his concert tux, and tuning his violin. I resisted the urge to shake the image out of my head. I flashed a smile at Nana. To Gramps, I gave the same sort of subtle nod I would give to the concertmaster when I turned to face the orchestra.

—35—

"Who's the guy?"

That's what Mel asked after Luke passed me the phone. It was one of the few times a call was for me during Luke's ten-day stay. He set up a command post in my living room. He slept on the couch, and at some point, he must have brought over a suitcase, because he was always freshly showered and dressed to solve crimes, ready to aid damsels in distress.

Ten days, Mademoiselle.

He may have left the apartment while I was sleeping. I did a lot of that. But he was on hand to wake me every few hours for our apartment walk.

"This reminds me of being a kid—the circuits around the apartment. It's what they always made me do at Rue Ballu."

"They say it is the best way to keep the pneumonia from settling in the lungs. The doctor told me this was almost as important as getting the antibiotics into you."

"Why are you here?" I asked him.

"Ah, you must be feeling better. You are beginning to ask me existential questions."

"No—really."

"I am willing to walk you around this apartment six or seven times a day. But I refuse to discuss philosophy after 3 a.m."

"Luke—" I tugged on his arm.

"See—you are growing stronger!"

"Can we sit for a few minutes in the living room? I'm bored with my walls."

"Another good sign."

"I will never be able to thank you enough for what you've done for me this past week. But I'm getting better now. I feel terrible about you missing work—"

"You forget, in France we have many more holidays, more than I can ever use on my own. You have made my boss very happy. He always complains I don't take enough time off—that I make him look bad."

"But you have been taking calls—"

"Oh yes, I told them they could call me here. I hope the ringing has not been bothering you?"

"Not at all …" Once again, he had sidetracked me in my line of inquiry. "You haven't answered my original question."

"You need someone here with you, whether you like it or not. The doctor told me you required surveillance. Otherwise, the hospital."

"But you can't take all that time off."

"We do get weekends. Please don't worry. Everything is taken care of. And you're getting tired. It's back to bed with you."

I gave in. I let the mystery man, the angel-cop, lead me back to the bedroom. I let him pull up my covers like I was his child.

"*Merci.*"

"*De rien.*"

It's *not* nothing. But I let that go, too.

The next day, the doctor declared me *acceptable*. "But she still must be walked. And watched. In fact, I suspect she still has some pneumonia in her left lung, but the antibiotics are clearing it."

"All that walking, and I have pneumonia, how could this be?" I heard myself, my inflections. I was sounding like a truly indignant Frenchwoman.

"I cannot be sure without taking a film, but when I listen,

the percussion is not right. You are improved from earlier in the week, however."

Damn. I'd had pneumonia, and I didn't even know it. It explained the exhaustion, the weakness, the falling asleep in the tub.

"You will remain?" she asked Luke.

He assured her he would. Then, more whispered consultations in the hallway. Meanwhile, I was sitting up in bed and feeling annoyed. Why? Luke was caring for me, and so well. I felt like a bad-tempered ingrate.

"Would you like to eat in the kitchen, for a change of scenery?"

Half a grapefruit, a small round of goat cheese, some miso soup and English muffins. I remember telling him once that I missed English muffins in France.

I burst into tears. Do you believe it? I mean, what is *up* with me?

"*Mouchoir,*" I choked out. I hate the way my nose always starts running when I cry. It only adds to the embarrassment.

He returned from the bedroom with the box of tissues and set it on the kitchen table. "No crying in your soup," he said. "Isn't that an American expression, crying in your soup? And then there is crying over milk, too. What is that one? No point to cry over milk spilt already? Something like that. You Americans have the funniest expressions. I remember wanting to collect them all when I was over there." He paused to see if his monologue was having its desired effect.

I blew my nose about six more times.

"Try some soup. "I'll reheat the muffins. Do you want butter and jam?"

"I'm sorry I've been crabby with you. As soon as I start to feel better, I begin to feel irritated with being confined like this. And mad at you for being in charge of me. Then I feel guilty. I mean—how could I be mad at someone who is caring for me so well? I feel like a horrible person."

"You've been very sick. Sick enough to worry us all. Me, Marcel, Emil, Elaine—"

"Elaine? How does she know I am sick?"

"She called; said she would call back when you were feeling better."

Sitting across from Luke, I wasn't only worried that Elaine would jump to conclusions. I could easily set her straight the next time we spoke. I was worried about what she might have spilled to Luke, with all good intentions, for my own good. Damn, all these people deciding what was good for me. That was the root of my anger, this feeling of powerlessness. This feeling that everybody else was making decisions for me. It was like—it was like—being a kid again! Like living at Rue Ballu. Having my days and nights choreographed for me.

A shrink would have a field day with this, right?

I squelched my inclination to quiz Luke about their call, and focused on the explanation I still owed him. "It isn't that I don't appreciate everything you are doing. I really, truly do. I just hate to be this vulnerable, to relinquish all control over my daily life."

"Is that what it feels like?"

"I feel like a child, but it's worse because I understand that I have no choice. I need your help."

"You really hate depending on me, don't you?"

Before I could tell him that it wasn't personal, he said, "It's only for a few more days." He took the muffins out of the oven, pulled two plates down from the cabinet. Then, he sat down, passed me a jar of jam and a knife, and told me his wife had died six years ago. Lung cancer.

"Oh—God. I'm so sorry."

"It's been a long time, and I have learned to live with it—or more accurately, without—her. I am okay. But this week, when I discovered you were sick, and worse, that it was your lungs, I was scared."

"Oh, Luke—"

He held his hand up to silence me. "But I understand that what you have, though serious, will pass. You are strong at the core; we caught the infection in plenty of time, and the doctor assures me you will be fine.

"I cared for my wife while she was ill. I had help of course, but as much as possible, I took care of her myself. I took time from work, and I stayed near her. It was an awful disease—cancer always is—and it was a horrible time for me. Especially towards the end. It reached a point when she didn't always know who I was. The morphine, I guess. Yet I felt compelled to be there with her. I did not want her to die, and I trusted only myself to be with her—as if I could keep her alive. Crazy," he said, shaking his head.

"I have realized, sitting in your living room, thinking and making connections. Taking care of you reminds me: not everybody dies young."

His honesty, his clarity. I didn't have a clue what to say. We were both quiet for a minute, staring down at our plates.

"*Merci*. Thanks for telling me. Thanks for *everything*. Really."

That's when the phone rang in the living room. Mel.

I wasn't ready for his high energy and cajoling ways. "Can I call you back?"

"Schaeffer, you've been holding out on me. A French guy, too."

"No—that's not it—"

"Look—I'll only take a minute of your time. I need to give an answer to London by the end of the week. We're doing this, right? You'll conduct, and you'll have the piece ready by March?"

"Uhh—"

"You love that Glass piece—and oh—more good news: you can program the whole concert—anything you like. Complete creative control, *plus* a commission. It's a no-brainer, right? They'll need you to confirm your selections in the next few weeks—you know, the librarian will need to sort everything out, and of course they want to get the program into the printed materials."

"But Mel—"

"You know you do your best work when you have a deadline. And you told me last week that you were working on a horn thing—"

"I was thinking horn and cello and violin, maybe."

"See you're thinking—you're halfway there. Shit, what's up with that cough?"

"I've had bronchitis."

"Oh, why didn't you say something? We could have talked another time."

"You kept interrupting me."

"Yeah, I do that. Sorry. Oh—one more thing: We'll need a title for your work. Soon on that. Now, are you sure everything's okay with you? Have you been checked out by a doctor there?"

"Yup. I'll be fine. Before we hang up—anything from L.A.?"

"Radio silence. I haven't sent anything in writing. I just let them know that you were considering offers."

"Right. Imaginary offers."

"This London thing is real. And once we put the word out—those offers will start coming. Don't worry. We'll get it all worked out—now get back to bed, and feel better. Oh—and watch your email, okay?"

Mel's right about me and deadlines. Remember when you talked to me about that seed of inner necessity? You said I had it and my mother didn't, and that's why she could give up music so easily? I think you were only partly right about me. I do need to make music—one way or the other—but I'm not as deeply seeded with the necessity to create it from scratch.

I know you would see this as weakness, but it matters to me if somebody *cares*. That may have been the hardest thing about losing you. And Lenny—too soon after you. I do have Mel. And he's more than an agent. After all these years, he's part of my musical family. And he does push. But it's not because he's dying to hear a new composition by Hannah Schaeffer. Chances are the people in London aren't either.

It has to come from me.

I get that.

But do I have it—really? Or have I lost it? Along with my orchestra?

Right now, even thinking about writing something makes me tired. And my sessions at Sainte-Chapelle are on hold, too. The doctor said it will take months to be back to my usual strength—months! But I am improving, day-to-day. The cat food in my pack didn't feel as heavy, and I talked Luke into letting me take the bus up the hill. (Police escort back—a compromise.)

Tomorrow, I'll bring you flowers.

—36—

"Breakfast is coming, Maestro. And I have the reviews ready."

Was I inventing this vision at my doorway? I glanced across to the other bed, half-expecting to see the real Nana sleeping there. The bed was made. Her bag sat open on the bedspread. Someone from room service was already knocking the outer door to the suite.

"I'll get that," she said. "Don't fall back to sleep!"

I heard her accepting the delivery as I stretched and rubbed my eyes. I threw some water on my face. I don't know where my hair goes after hours to get itself in such a tangle by morning.

"Hurry—before your breakfast gets cold!"

I put down the brush, wrapped the hotel bathrobe around me. I was longing for a shower and feeling just the slightest bit irritated at my grandmother's renewed efficiency.

I joined Nana in the outer room and sat across the little table from her, feeling unkempt. In a turquoise pant suit that matched her eyes, Nana looked ready to meet the world. It was hard not to feel a little self-conscious, the way you do when someone visits you in the hospital. The subtle hierarchy of human costuming.

She didn't eat much, but instead read the concert reviews aloud as I ate, inserting her own opinions as she went along. As I came into consciousness, I listened, not paying too much attention to the words, but reveling in the sound of my grandmother's strong voice. Might it be that somehow my conducting the BSO has brought her back? Has some door been opened, some shaft of light entered? Could her awareness be regained in an evening? Triggered by a single event?

It seemed too good to be true. I found myself waiting for her to make some small mistake, to forget a detail. I feared that one slip would lead to another, and that by the time we headed back to her nursing home, she would be the Nana I'd come to expect—and almost accept.

But she maintained her awareness for the four days that she ended up staying with me in Boston. She wasn't satisfied with just one concert, she said. So, she came to every performance, and we took small shopping expeditions by day, eating lunch together. My mother joined us one day. I could tell she was as uneasy as I'd been at the beginning of the week. Being the good daughter to an aging mother requires some mothering; in a strange generational twist, my confused grandmother had become the grandchild that I had failed to produce.

At lunch, my mother was fidgety, twisting napkins, playing with placemats, anxious as a teenager to be excused from the table. She took me aside in the ladies' room. "How long do you think she can maintain this?"

"I don't know. I guess we can only enjoy it while it lasts."

"Yes," she said, removing the cap and turning the tube to reveal lipstick that matched her coppery nails. "But—" she held her lipstick like a pointer, her little mirrored case still poised in front of her— "don't you think it is a little—uh—creepy?"

"Would you rather have her befuddled and frightened like she was? Fading away in her old housedress in that awful place?" I said it too fiercely. I saw my mother shrink back even as she finished applying her lipstick.

"Of course not." Her words were clipped, punctuated by the closing snap of her lipstick case. There was a moment when I might have apologized for what I had implied, but I let the moment pass. We walked back to the table together, and

Audrey leaned down to kiss Nana on the cheek. "Have to go now, Ma. An appointment. Hope you enjoy your afternoon."

As she made her exit, I felt slightly annoyed that Audrey had once more left me with the bill. Even though I'd intended to cover lunch, it irked me that she expected me to pay. On my last visit home, after I'd paid for dinner, she'd said, "This is so nice, having you treat me now." She placed dual emphasis on the words, "you" and "me." The implication was that she had always treated me. "Not all parents get their efforts returned. They make sacrifices for years, save and scrimp, and send their kids to the best schools, and the kids grow up and they don't give anything back. That isn't right."

"I guess not," I said tentatively. I didn't point out that my education had been paid for by patrons, my expenses from scholarships and grants and paid performances. Nor did I mention that with her thriving clothing design business, she could easily afford to treat me.

"It's nice when a child returns the favor, don't you think? Even in a small way like buying dinner." I was replaying that conversation in my head as I watched my mother leave the restaurant. Her back looked angry to me. She hadn't said goodbye.

"Hannah, honey," my grandmother said from across the table. "What are you thinking about?"

"Oh—my mother," I said.

"Oh, you don't need to think about Audrey. She thinks about herself enough for all of us." Then she grinned a sly grin before she lifted her hand to her lips, feigning shock at what had just come out of her mouth.

"Shopping?" I asked, as if I hadn't heard a thing.

"I'm ready. I want to pick out another suit."

She said she didn't want to be seen wearing the same outfit she'd just worn on Thursday. I understood this impulse. Even I liked some variation in my black and white conductor gear.

Sometimes a ruffled blouse to set off a specially cut tuxedo, sometimes a long skirt instead of pants, occasionally all black, and once, conducting a new music concert, I'd worn an all-white ensemble. The look gave the critics something to discuss with certainty, in the way that the music did not.

We found something lovely in a pale coral at a shop on Newbury Street. Even on sale, it was outrageously expensive, but she produced a wad of cash, and the deal was done. "I would appreciate it if you would see that I am buried in this suit. With my anniversary pearls for the wake, but make sure you take them off before the funeral. I feel bad enough letting this beautiful suit go to the worms."

"Nana--"

"But it wouldn't do to go into the ground naked, either." She continued, ignoring my attempt to interrupt this morbid train of thought. "I've been meaning to go shopping for my funeral for some time. I wasn't happy with any of the choices in my closet. And don't you think it's better to be able to decide what you wear at your own wake?"

I had to admit that I saw the logic of her thinking.

"The pearls—they aren't much, but your grandfather gave them to me. Please make sure you take them. Don't let some nasty funeral director snatch them before they lower me into the ground."

"Do you have to be so graphic? If I promise to see to the dress, will you promise to stop talking about the dirt and the worms on this wonderful suit that I am sure you will have many more occasions to wear before your demise?"

"I'll wear it tonight. Do we have time for tea?"

***

In the end, it was Nana's heart that failed her, and not long after the final concert at Symphony Hall. After the last performance, over a late-night room service dinner, we talked about our time in Boston together.

"I am so glad you were able to come."

"I wouldn't have missed it for the world. To see you conduct in Symphony Hall. Jacob and I are so proud of you." My grandfather, in the present tense again.

"And it's been nice to get away from all those sick people." She grew more serious. "I guess I had quite an episode at that home. Just disappeared for a while." I'd wondered how she had felt leaping back into gear this past week. I was never sure that she knew there was a "before" and "after" Nana. I'd been afraid to bring it up.

"You did go missing for a bit. We're so glad to have you back."

"Oh, I'm happy to be here," she said. "But you know something? I don't mean to hurt your feelings dear—you know I love you with all my heart—but I didn't really miss anybody while I was gone."

"Did you have company there?" I asked her, wondering if she'd been spending time with my grandfather.

"I don't know; it isn't that specific. But I can tell you—in case I ever wander back there—I was not unhappy in that place. It was pleasant really. And lovely music." I wondered if she meant the tapes I'd brought her, or if the music came from some other, deeper place.

"Time for bed," she announced. I was exhausted. The six-concert series, and the journey back with my grandmother had taken a lot out of me. I made my way into the bedroom, and she followed me. She planted a grandmotherly kiss on the middle of my forehead and smoothed out my brow. "Don't worry, honey. All will be for the best."

***

When I think back upon that last goodnight, I wonder if Nana knew. In a movie, she would have died that night. I would have awakened to find her slipped away forever. But my grandmother was far too considerate to die in a hotel suite, with only me to find her in the morning. She waited.

She complained a little about some heartburn on the way back to the nursing home, and said she wasn't in the mood to eat. But she seemed fine, if a little quiet. I thought she was probably dreading her return, and I was certainly wishing I could whisk her away with me. I spent many silent moments on that car ride, trying to figure out how I could manage to care for her.

When we arrived, the receptionist was welcoming and pleasant. A nurse escorted us over to the hospital wing for a "readmission exam." "You've been gone almost a week, Mrs. Serapin; we have to check you out!" she said, as she settled my grandmother into a wheelchair.

"Of course," Nana said, sounding absent-minded already. I wanted to pull her out of the chair. Take her back to the city. *We've been walking all over Boston*, I wanted to say. *She doesn't need a wheelchair to get to the other side of the building!*

It was while they were checking Nana's pulse that they first realized something was wrong. It was erratic, and her blood pressure—usually on the high side—was dropping rapidly. The attending nurse pushed the red button on the wall before she even put the stethoscope in her ears. Medical alert, it said underneath. My grandmother said, "Do you mind if I lie down?" Then, before she got an answer, she collapsed back onto the table. I was whisked out of the room. The curtain was drawn. I watched one doctor, then another doctor and three nurses run into the room. Their rubber soles squeaked against the linoleum. Someone sat me down in an orange chair and held my hand.

"What is happening to her?"

"Your grandmother is having a heart attack." She said it gently and firmly, almost the way Nana would have said it to me. I realized that she was the nurse who had complimented my grandmother on her red suit when we'd left the nursing home the week before. "Did you have a good time together in Boston?" she asked.

"Wonderful," I said.

"That's great. I'm sure it was a real treat for her to see you conduct the Boston Symphony. She must have been so proud of you."

"I was proud of her too."

"She is quite a woman."

"Will this kill her?"

"Well," she paused and looked at me, determining, I think, how much I could handle, and whether or not I would want the truth. "Maybe," she said. The word hung in the air between us.

One of the doctors came out of the room. I watched him walk toward us, and I knew he'd come with bad news. By the time he was in front of me, it seemed a swarm of bees was in my head, buzzing, drowning out all sound. His mouth formed words I could not hear. He took my hand, then glanced at the nurse beside me. More lip-moving, a nod from her before he turned to walk down the long corridor.

I fell back into my chair, felt the hard molded plastic against my legs. Another nurse materialized beside me with a glass of water. I accepted it, drank, set it down, picked it up, drank again. The bees were settling down to a persistent hum. "Would you like a cold compress? Sometimes that helps." My hearing was back.

A cold compress? I didn't understand how a cold compress could help my dead grandmother. I stared at her, uncomprehendingly. Now that I could hear the words, they made no sense. Had Nana died, just like that? No warning? Gone?

"Here we go." She was adjusting my collar, applying something moist and chilly to the back of my neck. "Have another sip of water."

I sipped obediently. I was overreacting. Maybe Nana wasn't dead. I felt embarrassed that I hadn't heard the news the doctor had come to give me. "Can I see her?" I asked, figuring it was the only way to know for sure.

"Let's just sit a little longer till you regain your strength. Then you can say goodbye." Oh, there was my answer. And as soon as they heard the word, *goodbye*, the bees were back.

"She's dead."

The nurse, still holding my hand, squeezed it, nodding, "Yes. I'm sorry."

I heard it that time, got the bees to quiet down just long enough to confirm my fears. The bees were still active when I called Audrey to tell her. I don't remember a word that I said, but I got the point across. She arrived at the nursing home in record time, taking the situation in hand. The staff seemed relieved to see her, relieved that she would take care of things, relieved that she was prepared for this eventuality, relieved that she wasn't the emotional wreck that I seemed to be. Had I moved from the orange chair?

Audrey made calls and made decisions. I was glad to be free of responsibility and happy to remain seated. It wasn't until an aide brought me Nana's little blue purse that I realized I had some work to do. There was a note attached to the bottom of it. "Please return to Hannah Schaeffer," it said, listing my address and telephone number. Inside the zipper compartment, I found the pearls and another note:

Dear Hannah,

Please remember that I want to wear the coral suit with these pearls. Don't forget to take the pearls after the wake. I want you to wear them when you get married.

I will always love you.
Nana

I sat for a few minutes, working to collect myself before I got up to locate Audrey. I found her at the nurses' station, just hanging up the phone. "Making arrangements," she said as I approached.

"She wants to wear the coral suit and these pearls." I said it the way I imagined Nana would have said it if she were here, in a way that brooked no argument.

"Oh, I'd been thinking maybe the light pink dress—" She looked at me, saw, I think, that I would stand my ground on this issue. Or maybe she realized that once again, she was outnumbered by the generation who produced her and the generation she'd produced. She shrugged. "Okay, coral. If that's what she said. Where is it?"

"It's still in the trunk of my car," I remembered. "And here are the pearls." I passed her the envelope. She read the note, nodded.

"She always said she was saving those pearls for your wedding day. They have already taken —her," she said. Would you mind dropping the pearls and the suit at the funeral home while I finish up here?"

I said I wouldn't mind, but I was lying. I sat in my car a long, long time before I followed my mother's directions to Mahoney's Funeral Home. They received my offerings with gracious care. Then, I drove to Audrey's, relieved to find the house empty. I let myself in, climbed the stairs to the guest room, shed my clothes, and crawled into bed.

I listened to the bees until I fell asleep.

—37—

Good morning, Mademoiselle. I'm feeling so much stronger. Still napping at odd hours, and no sessions yet at Sainte-Chapelle. Oh, I'm not hauling my own groceries, either. Luke's doing that for me—or sometimes sending Marie over with snacks and carryout. Now that I'm not confined to the apartment, I'm much more pleasant to be around. I worry I could get used to this personalized food delivery service. In L.A., the orchestra paid for a personal chef when we were in season—do you believe it? I didn't use him all the time, but I had this on-call cook and shopper. Also a driver to ferry me to and from the hall.

I was spoiled.

And I'm getting spoiled again.

Luke showed up Saturday morning with three bags of groceries from Rue des Martyrs. "We will feed you well this weekend," he said, unpacking his shopping: some lamb, a fish I didn't recognize, lots of fruit, spices to fill out my limited supply, and flowers—a purple and yellow and white bouquet, which he artfully arranged and set atop the bureau in my bedroom.

"You're not ready yet for the little orchestra—kids, germs, too much exertion. But do you feel strong enough to give me a conducting lesson so I can take the group on Monday night? And perhaps help me make a rehearsal plan? Last week we canceled, but it means so much to the kids to get out, and if you're not there watching, I think I can stumble through a rehearsal or two."

He set to making lunch: perfectly seasoned lamb chops, roasted potatoes, bright green beans just shy of crunchy, mixed with walnuts. Lime ice for desert— "without milk— better for your lungs."

As we settled into our meal, he told me that his wife had taught him to cook. "We'd spend hours together—chopping and slicing and talking—and finally—eating. Sometimes just the two of us, sometimes with company. She told me once that to cook for someone is to tell that person how much you love them. 'Cooking with another person,' Françoise said, 'is just like making love.'

"We always meant to have children. But then, her first cancer. She was in her early thirties. Breast cancer. She went through all the treatments and came through with a good prognosis. She was young, strong. There was a year and a half when we thought everything was okay. We started to talk about the future again. She was feeling fine when she went back for her check-up, but they found the indicators in her blood test. Within months, she was in a great deal of pain. The cancer must have been in her lungs from the start, just not big enough to see. That's what the doctors said.

"We did everything—chemotherapy, radiation, vitamins. I read up on nutrition and cooked all the food they said helped with cancer. But she could barely eat with all the chemicals pulsing through her system. Her tumors were inoperable, and as they said, 'aggressive.' She was a small woman. As the months passed, it seemed to me the tumors were bigger than she was."

He began to clear the table, insisting that I stay still while he cleaned up. "Begin planning my lesson," he said.

I listened to him rinse the pans and load the dishwasher. I thought about Françoise, small and unable to fight any-more. About how badly Luke wanted her to live. But wishing wasn't enough, praying wasn't enough; nothing could fight the tumors that were bigger than she was. When Luke had spoken of Françoise, I heard the traces of sorrow. He missed her, still. I can recognize the timbre of loss as easily as I can hear a middle *c*.

Even as I heard the pain in Luke's voice, as I tried to comprehend his loss, I felt a weird sort of envy. That he loved someone that hard, that deeply.

The music, I can hear you saying. *Give it to the music.*

"I still miss her, all these years later. But I learned to live. Lovers like to say they cannot live without the other, but you know, we can. Especially when there is no other choice." His tone was matter of fact. "So what do you want me to rehearse on Monday?" He spread out the scores on the coffee table.

I showed him some trouble spots; we made a schedule, allowing time for warm-up scales. "I don't want them to fall out of practice."

"Do you have any energy left to help me with my conducting?"

"Sure. You'll be the one swinging the baton!"

We began with 4/4, which he conducted serviceably well until I asked him to switch to 2/4. "That's where I get in trouble—changing meters. I am afraid to conduct that silly folk song medley Monday night—so many changes in time signatures."

"As far as Monday night goes, you don't need to play anything all the way through—I'm sure you've noticed how intently I have been breaking everything down into little sections. The group needs to understand and play all parts before we play everything start to finish."

"Still, I'd like to be able to change meters if I had to. I can conduct 4/4, and I can conduct 2/4 separately, but when one follows the other and I have to change—what am I doing wrong?"

"First of all, it's hard to conduct out of context. Put the

score on the music stand, the one that has that shift in it, and hum the melody line as you conduct. Or just hear it in your head, and the time change will be easier."

When he reached the shift in the music, he dropped a beat. "Still not right," he sighed, shaking his head.

"*Bien sûr*! Do you think you would have played this piece perfectly when you were a beginner on your horn? When's the last time you picked up a baton?"

"Never, actually. I mean, I held it together two weeks ago when you were missing, and all the kids were waiting. But mostly I drilled them on sections, and I counted out loud more than I moved my hands around."

"Look, you're a fine musician. You understand the basics of conducting because you have watched conductors for so many years. Go slowly. And be easy with yourself. It takes as much practice to conduct well as it does to play well. Think of the baton as a new instrument. You have the musical knowledge, a foundation to build on, but imagine if I handed you a flute and expected you to play it as well as you play trumpet."

"We already know that outcome." He'd asked to try a flute one Friday a few weeks ago, and eventually, he had produced a sound—something resembling a high-pitched trombone.

"Luckily, you don't have to worry about tone with a baton."

He smiled.

"But you do have lots of other things to worry about. Even if we could perfect your technique in a weekend, you have all the players in front of you to hear and correct."

"Are you sure you aren't well enough to take this rehearsal? No—I'm just kidding. The doctor says you are staying put. And I will make it through somehow."

"Yes, you will. You'll do fine. But do you really want to learn conducting?"

"I think I do. You won't be here indefinitely to lead our orchestra. I like working with the kids." He paused. "I've even considered returning to school, finishing my music degree. I'd love to teach music at a *lycée*."

I nodded, as though the idea of the Chief *Inspecteur* leaving his job to lead a high school band were not strange at all.

"Okay, let's think about the placement of the beats in the air. Put down the baton, but move your arm with me on this." I stood beside him.

"*One*, in 4/4 is a straight line, vertical. *Two* moves out of the bottom of *One*, sweeping to your left, curving up a bit in anticipation of *Three*. *Three* sweeps to your right, moving down, through the bottom of *One*. *Four* moves up in a curve to the left, the preparation for *One* again."

"The key is in the preparatory beat. In this case, the imagined *Four* that precedes the downbeat of the very first measure. It speaks of tempo and style. In the same way, the last beat before you change meters signals your intentions for the next section. Do you follow me?"

"Yes." He reached for the baton.

"No—not yet. I want you to draw it. There's a ream of paper beside the piano, and lots of pencils around."

"Draw it?"

"Yes. Draw how you would conduct four beats to the bar, moving your pencil as if it were your baton. Your pencil should never stop or leave the paper. Draw in 4/4 for—oh, say thirty-two measures. Then draw 2/4, for sixteen measures before you return to 4/4. Repeat until you don't feel yourself pausing on the transitions.

"After you have that down, look at the score and draw the medley. You can conduct the 6/8 in six or in two. Medium tempo. Maybe try it both ways and see which works better."

"Draw the music."

"Yes—and as smoothly as possible, too. A softer point on the pencil will help. Cover the table with paper. Wake me in a few hours to show me your work."

"This will help me on Monday?" he asked, doubt in his tone.

"Immeasurably," I assured him, but I am not sure he got my musical joke.

—38—

Some part of me died with my grandmother. I gave away a minor conducting gig, knowing that Nana would have scolded me for such behavior. I knew how proud she was of me, how much my debut in Boston had meant to her. But we'd paid with her life for those few days of lucidity. I felt angry, sad, and unmotivated in the face of what seemed a horrendous bargain.

I remember Mel, impatient with my uniform lack of enthusiasm. "We have to build on Boston. You got rave reviews there. Don't you see?"

"Sure," I said, a mumble, an affirmative, but with zero energy behind it.

"I can get you Philadelphia or Vienna, no problem. But you keep telling me you don't want to travel."

"I don't."

"But—*Philadelphia*? You can take the friggin' train. Pardon my French."

"That was French?"

"Oh, I forgot, my little French-trained client would recognize my faux pas." He said it like this: *folks pass*. I had to laugh.

"That's better, a laugh from the young Maestro. Now when are you going to let me book you a gig? We're talking about engagements at least a year, two, even three years away. You'll have time. But you know I gotta book while the iron is hot."

"Soon. I'm just not ready to think about all this right now."

"I'm sorry for your loss, I really mean that. But sometimes it's better just to get on with life."

"I'm sure it is."

"Oh, the young Maestro's stop-minding-my-business voice. Well, since I'm already pissing you off, let me ask you another question. Are you still hanging out with that trumpet player?"

"Trombone."

"Brass family. Right? Absolutely none of my business, but in your agent's respectful opinion, he isn't helping matters, you know."

"Oh, Mel—what makes you say that?"

"He's a brooder, a late-night jazz existentialist. You don't need to be around that right now. You need to lighten up."

"Funny, I don't remember hiring you to run my love life, too."

"You're right. You're right." I could picture him in his office, cigarette hanging out of his mouth, a hand up in protest, a movement that said he was backing off. "I'm glad to hear you have enough spunk in you to know when I'm stepping over the line."

"I'm not wasting this time off. I'm writing something."

"Great news! I knew you couldn't just hang out with that guy being depressed together."

I let that one pass. It was a little too close for comfort, and absolutely none of Mel's business.

"When will it be ready?"

"Damn it, Mel! I don't know!"

"Okay, okay. I didn't mean to rush you. But remember, this *is* what you hired me to do."

He had a point. I'd hired Mel that morning at the Bernsteins' breakfast table, and he'd stuck with me ever since. Not only did he handle my conducting and my composing careers, but Mel didn't mind negotiating the occasional recording contract when I was in the mood for some flute-playing. He was consistently good to me, patient, and able to put up with my moods, and he always kept two goals in mind: a career for me, and cash, for both of us.

"Earth to Hannah?"

"That line's getting tired."

"Can't help it if you spend more time in outer space than the astronauts. Tell me what you're thinking. Philadelphia? Vienna? Berlin?"

"Berlin?" I repeated. That got my attention.

"I think we can manage it, on the strength of these reviews and my excellent contacts. Probably three seasons out. But Schaeffer—you gotta be willing to play the game."

He was talking about the all-male club to which I was an honorary—and if some had their way, temporary—member. Mel knew I wasn't comfortable exchanging favors and swapping orchestras as if they were cards in a game of gin rummy. I had this compelling urge to make music. Oh, that isn't fair, either. Most of those guys are truly committed to their work. But the careerism, and the social climbing. I had no taste for it. And no talent. "Isn't showing up and doing the work good enough?" I asked. This was a theme we'd touched upon many times.

"It could be. Who knows? That's all you did in Boston, and I'm getting calls. But if they want a private reception, if they want to interview you, if they want to annoy you with their insipid questions, I need you to stay cool. We're trying to find you a home, and this is the only way I know to do it."

Home was a podium of my own, a permanent gig with a world-class orchestra. It had always been a long shot, and we both knew it. Guest conductor jobs were one thing, even with orchestras like Boston and Berlin. But to grant an American woman a podium of her own on the world stage would be a much larger break with convention. With every passing year,

I understood this more clearly. At first, I thought—and Lenny believed it too—that the strength of my debut would push away the barriers. When that didn't happen, we remained convinced that the steady accumulation of good reviews would land me a major orchestra all my own. But after more than ten years of strong performances, excellent reviews, and even a few prestigious composing commissions, I had yet to consider a serious offer.

"Do you really think it can happen in my lifetime?" I was having my doubts.

"Yours is the only lifetime we've got."

"Okay. Just don't overbook me. You know how cranky I get when I'm jet lagged."

"I'll call you in two weeks with an update."

"Thanks, Mel."

"*De rien*," he said, just before we hung up, and this time he said it with a perfect French accent.

***

Lenny hadn't made it to Nana's funeral. He sent a giant spray of white roses. "You know I'd be there if I could be—but Felicia—"

"I know. Please don't worry. How is she doing?" Felicia had been diagnosed with cancer a few months earlier, and the prognosis was grim.

"Oh—not well." He sounded like he was going to break down.

"I'm so sorry." Since my early studies with Lenny, I had worshipped Felicia—her lively, knowing ways, her grace under pressure, her gentleness with me, her love and acceptance of her not-so-easy husband, not to mention her infallible fashion sense. The last time I visited, I was startled by her diminished size, her white-gray skin, the hollowness behind the once-dancing eyes. It was as if life were being extracted from her; drawn, like blood. Felicia tried to summon cheerfulness for my visit—asked me about my career, my love life, my wardrobe. But she couldn't sustain it. In the end, we sat together without speaking, holding hands. I could see the silence was easier for her, and I could feel the resignation in her hand. She was moving away from life. As I watched her drift into a troubled morphine sleep, I wondered for a moment if living were the disease, death the cure.

"She's put up a good fight, but—well—she's stopped fighting," Lenny said.

"But you haven't."

"How can I give in, dammit? I can't let her go. I haven't been the ideal husband, and we have had our share of troubles, to be sure, but I have always loved her. Always."

"And she knows it."

"Does she?"

"Without a doubt. I am sure of it." And I was. Theirs was never a traditional marriage, but the bond between them was deep and lasting. He was quiet, taking in the certainty of my words before he changed the subject.

"I'm so sorry about Rose. That's why I called. How are *you* doing?"

"Okay. I'm functioning. I filled him in on Nana's last few days, the trip to Boston, the way she had returned to life, only to depart suddenly, finally.

"Heartbreaking."

"Thank you for not saying that at least she didn't suffer, or that she had a wonderful last week of her life."

"Those things are true," he said. "But it's too soon for you to count blessings. Just feel bad—and write."

"Write?"

"Some music. Something. Anything. It will help."

There was a pause I couldn't fill.

"Did you get in touch with Nadia?' he asked.

"Mel called her."

"How's she been doing?"

"Not bad for a –how do you say it—nonagenarian?

"She's ninety? And holding up?"

"Well, she's frail, and her eyesight is pretty much gone. She's lost a lot of her hearing, too. I think that pains her more than anything else."

"Oh, it would. I don't want to live long enough to go deaf. Whatever you want to say about Beethoven, I wouldn't want to be him. She's not teaching, then?"

"She is. She has some private students, and she still holds her Thursday classes. And she's obsessed with a project to republish her sister Lili's work. She's been making all the corrections herself. She enlisted some help from me the last time I saw her. Really, for her age, she's amazing."

"Nadia has always been amazing. You should go visit her."

Following Lenny's advice, I found Mademoiselle to be almost as indomitable as she was ill. Her body was weakening daily, but her mind and spirit remained strong. After my experience with Nana, I was convinced it was the mind that mattered most. Mademoiselle wasn't letting go. And neither was I. I told Mel to take every European booking we were offered and to leave me room after each series to stay a few extra days in Paris. I brought new recordings and played Mademoiselle the pieces I was working on. Frustrated with her hearing aids, she began to listen with her hands and feet. Positioning her wheelchair in the curve of the grand piano, she told me, "I can hear the bass in the floorboards, treble through my fingertips." When we listened to recordings, she would sit close enough to stretch her hands across the speakers of her walnut stereo console. Her voice grew louder in her deafness, and she spoke more slowly, but hers was still the voice of authority, especially when we spoke of my career, or when I confronted her with a musical dilemma. But she was also the voice of my heart, my past. We talked about my grandmother, my grandfather, her days in Boston, my childhood at Rue Ballu. When I pressed her, she told me stories about her life that I had never heard before, but more often we told each other stories we both knew well, the kind of retelling that reminds us how important we are to one another, the kind of repetition that secures love.

I was in Paris when I got word that Felicia had died. I flew back to New York right away. Lenny was inconsolable, lost. We spent a week of late nights together, talking about life and death and love and loss. And crying. Nana had died only six months earlier, and I was still grieving myself. But there was something in me—some instinct for self-preservation—that Lenny seemed to be lacking. As summer turned to fall, Felicia became every loss he'd suffered, the sum of his sorrows. He seemed to be drinking all the time. I remembered Felicia once telling me that Lenny used alcohol as a form of insulation. "It protects him from the world, from rejection, and from himself," she'd told me. Now, it seemed to me that he was moving beyond insulation. He was administering his own form of anesthesia. When I told him I was worried, he asked me why it mattered. Unprepared for his question, I had to wait until my next visit before I told him to stop drinking and start writing some music.

"Remember what you told me?" He gave no response. "You told me to write something—anything. You told me it would help me feel better. Maybe you ought to take your own advice."

"Did you take my advice?"

"I did. And it worked."

"I have written too many elegies already." I watched his hands shake as he poured himself another whisky.

"You know, it bugged the hell out of me when people said

to me after Nana died, *Oh your grandmother would have wanted you to*—fill in the blank, usually with whatever *they* wanted me to do. I'm not going to presume to know what Felicia would want for you, or how she would want you to be, now that's she's gone. But I can tell you this: Felicia loved you for the way you lived, Lenny. She loved all that *life* inside you, and your generosity—the way you let the life come bubbling up."

He took this in without comment. We sat in silence for several minutes before I revealed my true mission. "Come with me to Paris," I suggested. "I have a concert; you have nothing on your schedule, and it's Nadia's birthday on Tuesday. You know she was in the hospital for a while this summer, but she's back in her apartment again. Let's surprise her with a visit."

When he agreed—whether under the influence of my inspirational speech or, more likely, the half-bottle he'd polished off that night—I picked up the phone to book the flight, not wanting to give him a chance to reconsider. We left the next evening, arriving in Paris on the morning Mademoiselle turned ninety-one. Karen answered the door. Another former student, Karen was a nurse and an important addition to the aging household at Rue Ballu. I'd met her on an earlier trip and liked her on sight.

I put my index finger to my lips before I leaned in for a two-sided kiss. "Don't tell her we're here. It's a surprise," I whispered.

"Karen? Who is there?" Mademoiselle called from down the hall.

"Oh—just the rat man. *Pour deratization*," Karen shouted.

"Tell him to scare all the pests away before my birthday party." I could picture Mademoiselle grinning to herself after that remark.

"*Bien sûr*, Nadia."

"Are there plans for a party?" I asked.

"Nothing like last year. But Emil and Ghislaine will come

over. A few others."

I debated whether we should surprise her now or later.

"Now," Lenny said. "That way, we will have her all to ourselves." He grinned. "I have an idea." He winked and motioned for me to follow him to the piano. The trip was having its desired effect. His mischievous nature had begun to reassert itself, and I was thrilled to follow the crook of his finger. "Piano four hands," he whispered. "Happy Birthday."

"Bach, Mozart, Beethoven?" I asked.

"Beethoven. High drama. And loud, so she hears it! You play the introduction, and I'll join in once I catch your drift."

I began with deep, open chords in the left hand, the happy birthday notes out of order in my right hand. Lenny joined in. Crashing, slow. Blocks of notes in both hands: "Happy Birthday to You." He threw his head back, laughing. I reached across Lenny to answer with a tiny high-pitched melody: "Happy Birthday" interrupted with sixteenth note runs. He answered with "Twinkle, Twinkle, Little Star" — "a little Schubert," he whispered. We played the two tunes against each other, quiet harmonies between them. Almost a pastoral. Until I reprised the crashing block chords, lower now. Lenny slid up the bench to give me more room, while he occupied himself with playing a combination of "Twinkle, Twinkle" and "Happy Birthday" in the upper reaches of instrument. We played like this for another minute, then looked at each other, and with a nod, moved in for the finale. First a unison, gentle, *hap-py-birth-day* in octaves, a growing crescendo, adding fifths, fourths, seconds, moving toward heat, intensity and then, symphonic resolution the way Ludwig Von B. would have wanted it: Chord, chord, rest. Chord, rest. Chord. Rest. Chord. *Hap-py-Birth-day-to*—a trill in the upper voices, descending chords in the bottom, and finally, one giant, crashing chord: *You!*

"In old age, nothing is sacred." Mademoiselle, smiling,

sardonic. She was at the doorway in a wheelchair. Her hearing aids were conspicuous, and her head was listing to one side. She had aged years, it seemed, in a period of weeks.

"Nadia, Happy Birthday!" Lenny rushed to her side, kneeling to hug her.

"Lenny. I should have known. My eyesight is so bad now. I wasn't sure who was seated next to Hannah."

"But you knew Hannah," he said.

"Even blind—even almost deaf—I can always hear her bass line."

"Beethoven's baseline," I said, as I kissed her hello.

"Beethoven as conceived by Hannah Schaeffer. None other." She touched my hair. "I have trouble seeing any detail, but I can see colors—I recognized your lovely hair, *marron*."

"Barely a review goes by that doesn't mention my chestnut locks. It gets annoying."

"Have you brought me any new reviews? Where have you been playing?"

We settled into our usual conversation: work and music, conducting and composing. Lenny sat out for a few minutes, but I drew him in, asked him to tell Mademoiselle about the new recording of his Mass.

"Did you bring me a copy? I want to hear it."

"I did," I said, pulling an album out of my bag. I put the LP on the stereo and moved her close enough to touch the sound. It occurred to me that of the three of us, only Mademoiselle, even with her faulty hearing, was fully inhabiting the music. Lenny was filled with thoughts of loss. He told me once that the Mass had come out of an earlier piece of his, *Kaddish*, based in the Hebrew tradition of honoring the dead. He had dedicated it to the memory of JFK. "A Jewish memorial for a Catholic president," he joked. "I realized I ought to write a Mass." Lenny was working on it when I was his apprentice. He recruited me to assist, asked technical questions, presuming my attendance at so many masses with Mademoiselle would give me insights he lacked. "You have that Jewish strain in you, too—which means you can explain it to me in ways I'll understand. And all those years with Nadia and Bach. How can you tell me you aren't an expert in the Mass form?"

"I could be more helpful orchestrating the woodwinds," I had said to him, laughing.

He handed me staff paper. "Go to it. And this line, here—make sure you give it to the flute. I want to hear you play it."

I played the part at the premiere—an emotional affair at the opening of the Kennedy Center—and played it again on the recording. The recording we made while Felicia was dying, the recording we made just after Nana died. A symphony of losses, this version of his Mass. Another kind of *kaddish*.

It was Mademoiselle and her connection to the music that brought us both back into the room. She was full of questions for Lenny, questions that seemed to spill from her like so many notes on a page. She drew him in, and soon he was at the piano, explaining, instructing, playing. Her wheelchair was tucked in close to him. She was nodding, laughing. I smiled, thinking of the first night I'd met Lenny, here at Rue Ballu. They were seated at the piano that night too.

"What's making Hannah Schaeffer smile?" Lenny asked me.

"I was thinking how we never finished that conversation about the Ravel—that night we met and you two—"

"I remember." He launched into the Ravel. "You were to arbitrate the problem. Do you remember, Nadia?" He played the passage in question, reminding her of their dispute. You never told us who was right." They both looked my way.

"Play it again," I said. He complied. I was standing in the curve of the grand, close enough so Mademoiselle would hear my judgment.

"Tell us who you thought was right then—and who you

think is right now. And no hedging." He winked at me.

"Then—and now," I announced. "Mademoiselle Nadia Boulanger."

Lenny clapped his hands together. "Yes, yes," he said. He turned to Mademoiselle, took her ancient, weathered hand into his and brought her fingertips to his lips. "*Bien sûr*. Nadia is always right!"

—39—

Forget the personal chef or the on-call driver or any of the other perks. Even forget the orchestra and the hall for a minute. Let's talk about the weather in L.A.: warm, sunny, predictable. That's where I'm truly spoiled.

Contrast with winter in Paris: damp, gray, cold.

And pelting rain this morning.

I would never admit this to Luke—he would have me chauffeured to all my appointments—but I haven't fully regained my stamina. Even on the rare days when the sun shines, I've been taking the bus up the hill.

Today, the cats are hiding again.

Not far from here, someone has hung a heavy brown blanket across an open doorway, weighing it down with a rock. The big bowl inside is filled with chunks of meat and buzzing with flies. That means Estelle came in early. She is more of a chef than a feeder. The first time I ran into her, she was wearing long blue rubber gloves and up to her elbows in ground beef. She complimented me on my choice of canned food as she cracked an egg on the side of a gravestone.

Estelle is one of the four regulars I've met so far. There is Jean-Paul—an artist who stops to chat whenever he sees me—who comes down from the 18th at least four times a week, and Robert—large and bald and a little stern—who arrives with two buckets of fish parts most every morning. And there is Yvonne from Versailles. She's usually an afternoon feeder. "It's a long commute," she explained to me the first time we spoke.

I am younger than the principal feeders by ten or twenty years. Any one of them could disappear without warning. How would the cats cope? They don't count on my small offerings to survive, but they depend on human kindness.

Maybe that's why I decided to introduce Marie to the cemetery cats. I worried at first about taking her here. Would she find it frightening or peaceful? Would the wild kitties make her happy or sad? I have discovered that nothing is so black and white with Marie. She worries about the cats, as I do, and yet she is happy to see them, thrilled that some of them recognize her now and come to her when she calls.

Something happened this week. With Marie. Or really, about her. It was nothing she did. It was one of the housemothers who pulled me aside. "You are spending more time with Marie, I have noticed. She isn't a bad child, but you are aware of her history? Have you read her book?" She was referring to the plastic binders that contain each child's case history. I'd been told that, as her teacher, I was welcome to review her records.

"No—I've been getting to know her as she is."

"That's very idealistic, but completely naïve of you. Do you realize she is a fire-starter?"

"Marie starts fires?" I asked, for clarification. I thought I may have been translating incorrectly.

"Yes, she is not allowed in the kitchen, and we search her room routinely for matches, lighters, anything that she could use to start a fire.

"I mention this for your own good." She shrugged. "You really should read her book."

I felt shaken by the information and outraged for Marie's sake. I called Luke from the phone booth by the home. "We need to talk about Marie."

"Is she okay?"

"As okay as it gets in that horrible place. We're both fine.

I just need to talk."

"It's five o'clock now. How about dinner at eight? Your Indian restaurant, maybe?" Luke was reading me right. I wanted the comfort of a steaming curry.

"Do you think I should review Marie's case book?"

"You haven't yet." A statement, not a question.

"No. But this woman today, when I dropped off Marie, told me to be careful, that she was a fire-starter."

"You understand that if I thought there were any danger I would never have suggested you be alone with her?"

"Luke—yes—of course. That isn't what I'm worried about." Or was it? Marie and I made lunch together in my kitchen last Saturday. Inches from the stove.

"I wanted to get to know her in the here and now. I didn't want to be influenced by her history. And now this woman—I didn't feel she was looking out for my own good, or Marie's, either!"

"Oh, it's possible she meant well. And it is good for you to read the book. You're becoming important to her. It's time you knew her story."

I walked back a block, picked up the green plastic binder from the superintendent's office. On the bus, I was oblivious to the crowd, conscious only of the sharp corner of Marie's history pressing into my hip.

Luke was already at the restaurant when I arrived. Emil was there, too.

"I used to teach in the program, myself—until I had to be carted around everywhere," Emil explained. "Jean-Luc thought I might have some insights."

Over dal, lamb saag, and aloo gobi, Emil asked me how the lessons were going with Marie.

"She has talent, and she's a hard worker."

"Now, Hannah has two students. It's a shame her conducting student isn't as talented as Marie."

"Oh, you're plenty talented," I said to Luke. "We just get sidetracked with the discussion points."

During his conducting lessons, Luke has asked me some questions I've never been asked—and some questions I've answered a thousand times before. But all of our conversations feel fresh to me. He is curious about my experience in a personal way that isn't intrusive. I find myself giving voice to many ideas I've never shared. Even with you or Lenny.

The subject of Bernstein fascinates Luke. "Everything I've ever read about him, and the few times I've heard him conduct—he's just so American," he said over dinner.

"What do you mean?" asked Emil.

"He seemed so open, so transparent, unafraid to share the way he felt in the moment. He had charisma, I guess. Hannah has it too."

Emil agreed.

"It's a job requirement. We'll be doing the charisma class as soon as you can conduct a subdivided adagio 6/8."

Luke looked serious. "I don't think I'll do so well on the charisma lessons—if we ever get past 6/8 in six."

"Oh—Jean-Luc—you have plenty of personal magnetism," Emil said.

"I agree. He just hasn't brought it to the podium yet."

"Are you being my teacher right now, or my friend?" Luke asked. "No—don't answer that! It's just—well—I've always admired Leonard Bernstein. I know he's been criticized for being too emotional, for over-interpreting classic works, all that. But he's always seemed real to me. And I know I've only seen you conduct on TV or film, but you do, too."

"I was lucky to be able to study with Lenny."

"And Marie and I are lucky to study with you," he said, pouring me a cup of mint tea.

"Speaking of Marie—shall we all go to Hannah's and have a look at her book?" asked Emil.

At my apartment, we switched to coffee, American style. We all sat in the living room, Luke and me side-by-side on the little couch while Emil, transferred by Luke, sank into the comfy armchair.

"We can't read it all in one night, and I know her case pretty well. Why don't I read you both the summary? Then, I can talk you through the highlights."

Luke read aloud, stopping every so often so he or Emil could translate the social service terminology that eluded me.

"'The subject has been in the custody of the state since age six, when her mother was jailed for drug charges. Father unknown. Foster care was provided. She was removed from first foster environment at the request of foster parents who reported she could not get along with others in their care. Second foster care experience also unsatisfactory. School work generally far below average, though test scores indicate high level of intelligence. Subject showed improvement in third foster family but was removed due to illness of the foster mother, who became unable to care for her.'"

"God, how old was she by this time? Eight? Nine?"

"Something like that."

"And she's lost her father, her mother, and the one foster parent who might have been at all nurturing."

When he nodded, I could see the sadness he feels when he thinks about the life of this young girl, his student, and now mine.

"Shall I continue?" Without waiting, he read the worst of it. "'Mother released from prison in 1988; she requests visitation rights, but states she is incapable of providing a home for subject.'"

"Do you have any more details?" Emil asked.

"Like, did she just outright reject her daughter, or were there circumstances or—?"

"First, let's go over the broad outlines. Then maybe I can

answer your questions. I'm pretty familiar with her history."

He continued reading: "'First suspected fire-starting incident occurred during meeting with mother. Subject is believed to have set fire in trash receptacle in the park where she and mother were visiting. A lighter traced to mother was discovered in subject's room. Mother accepted all responsibility for incident, received additional months of probation and was prohibited from further visitation.'"

"Oh, that's the perfect bureaucratic solution," Emil said.

"'Two known fire-starting incidents occurred in backyard of fifth foster home. Subject was removed from foster system after second fire and placed in detention facility.'"

"Where she is now?" I asked.

"Oui."

"But does anyone care *why* she started these fires?"

Luke sighed, flipped forward a few pages. "'Subsequent incidents in this foster home led to further investigation, resulting in child pornography charges.'"

"No—that is just too much for one kid to take. Of course she started fires! I would too!"

"As would I," Luke said, closing the book.

"And why is Marie in detention? Shouldn't *they* be the ones in jail? Have all the kids in that little orchestra had it this bad growing up?"

"None of them have had an easy time."

"*Les pauvre petits*," Emil shook his head. He looked as sad as I've ever seen him. It made me think we should find a way to get him and his wheelchair into that old school building or get some students to him. I know he must have done a world of good for those kids.

The coffee was stone cold. "Shall I heat these up?"

"Hannah, do you have the makings for *chocolat chaud*?" Emil asked, knowing I would, and knowing it would be of comfort to me.

"Great idea. I'll make it." Luke said. He knows his way around the kitchen now, thanks to his extended surveillance period. "You can read more of this," he said as he filled the kettle, "but it doesn't get any better."

"Luke, was she—used—in the pornography? I mean, has she been sexually abused?"

"That, I don't know." He suggested I meet with Bertrand, the staff psychologist, to get more information.

"Now you see why I was so intent on getting you to take Marie as a student. She needs a woman, a strong, healthy woman in her life." He said this as he delivered three hot chocolates spiked with the brandy he'd insisted I keep on hand "to keep the cold from your lungs."

Emil caught my eye, silently reminding me what he'd said about being a role model.

"But I will leave her, just as her mother has, just as that one decent foster mother did."

"But as long as you are here, you can give her a glimpse into a different kind of life," Luke said.

Is that kind? Or cruel? I wonder.

Anyway, this morning, at the end of our lesson, I told Marie that I'd read some of her book. "I wanted to tell you, to keep things honest between us."

She said nothing, just stared at her flute case, played with the tag on the end of the zipper.

"It's because I want to help."

I thought I caught a shadow of a nod. I kept going.

"I wanted to get to know you without your history between us, but it was recommended that I read your green book if I was going to teach you. I want to say how sorry I am for everything that has happened to you. I don't know what I can do—I'm not really qualified to help. But I can give you music, and maybe the music will be what helps you, not me or anyone else."

She looked up at me.

"Do you understand, Marie?"

"*Mais oui*," she said. There was a pause.

I thought of asking her permission to visit with the staff psychologist as Luke had suggested, but suddenly that seemed like a bad idea. "Maestro Hannah?"

"Oui, Marie."

"*Je vous en prie.*"

It was a more personal thank-you than a simple *merci*. I needed to be careful with my response. "*C'est ma plaisir*," I said. My pleasure.

We walked back to the home in silence. I checked her in, said goodbye, reminded her to practice. I noticed she'd closed down again.

Of course, Emil was right. Luke wanted me to teach Marie more than how to play the flute. I'm not sure what else I am teaching her—introducing her to peanut butter on Ritz crackers, dragging her to the cemetery, inviting her to feed a colony of feral cats, to meet my long-dead teacher.

Oh, now don't get all prickly. I know.

Just because you're dead doesn't mean you've stopped teaching.

—40—

The visit with Mademoiselle seemed to do Lenny good. In her presence, he seemed his old self—funny and engaging, full of music and stories to share. The last night of our trip, we stayed late at her apartment playing piano duets, Mademoiselle stationed between us until Lenny brought her to his side, arranging the piano bench so he could pull her wheelchair in close to the keyboard. "Help me," he said to her.

"I can barely play," she said. "And my ears—oh my ears. Forgive me if I am hearing another version of you playing this section, but I think you may be playing the upper voices too heavily. "Light as air—right here," she said. "My hands are too old. But let me try." The notes in her head guiding what her ears couldn't hear, the memory in her hands pushing her fingers beyond their limits, she played the upper voices—a perfect, airy dance of notes. Eight measures of music that seemed a gift from God.

On the way back to our hotel, Lenny reminded me of an earlier conversation. "Remember when you told me that we the living have a duty to the dead, a duty to live, to be alive? It's something I've always told myself. And believed too. But losing Felicia. God, I felt as if my duty were exactly the opposite. To stop living in her honor. Maybe because I lived too much when she was alive. I hurt her—repeatedly. And she forgave me—again and again. But what kind of life was that for her? And then, damn it, she dies. Why should I get to keep on living my own selfish life?"

"Lenny, it isn't selfish to bring music to millions of people.

It's selfish not to do it. It's selfish to cancel your engagements."

"Yes. I'm starting to believe that again. I still wish I could be a better person—but maybe the music comes at a price. Nadia traded her life for it, never married. Never had a family. I had it all. And now, I'm feeling sorry for myself. Proof of my deep selfishness, I guess. When I look at Nadia—ninety-one—my God. She's still an inspiration to me. She never gives up."

She didn't—or at least not easily. It was the following August that Annette called to tell me Mademoiselle was no longer eating, barely speaking. She was confined to her bed. Mademoiselle, I knew, wouldn't suffer stillness for very long. She was not one to lie around waiting for anyone—even Death—to claim her. I rearranged my schedule, flew to Paris right away, took a taxi straight from the airport to her apartment. Of course, she surprised me.

"Hannah, *chère*, I am so glad you came, but I can see you are overtired. Go back to your hotel and get some rest. Come see me tomorrow afternoon, and we will talk. I won't die today, I promise." She smiled. Blind, toothless, tiny, and near death, Mademoiselle was pleased with herself and her little joke. I began to cry.

"No tears today. Go rest. Come tomorrow and come with music." I was dismissed.

The next day, she was ready for me with questions. How was my career progressing? What was I conducting next season? What was I writing? "Did you get Berlin?"

"Yes. A subscription series in October. I'll premiere *Three Elegies* there. It's a big step—a commission to compose, and an engagement to conduct the premiere," I told her. "But there still isn't a major orchestra in the world that is ready to hire me on a permanent basis."

"It may be just as well, Hannah; a full-time music director doesn't have enough time to compose. You mustn't let yourself get sidetracked. How is your work coming? What have you written lately?"

"Since *Three Elegies*—nothing much," I mumbled, feeling like that eleven-year-old who hadn't done her theory homework.

"Why—nothing much?"

Only Mademoiselle took an interest in my composing life. The rest of the world was indifferent. If I wrote a masterwork, fine. If I gave up conducting and waited tables in Brooklyn, someone might notice, but no one would mourn my loss. I was inconvenient as a female conductor, and barely noticed as a composer. Sure, I had a big premiere coming in Berlin. But really—no one cared—at least not the way she did. To my teacher, my music mattered.

"Tears are tiring for a dying woman. Here is what I want you to do. Blow your nose and listen. Write me something and play it for me tomorrow."

"Tomorrow?"

"I do not have a lot of time. As quickly as possible. Please. May I remind you that the Hannah of eleven years would have composed a symphony in a day? No, I am exaggerating. Some chamber music, then. Should I arrange for a reader? You know I can't see to read the music anymore; someone must play it for me. And play it loudly!" She laughed, then coughed at her own joke.

"Mademoiselle—"

"No more discussion. Start writing. You know I am without mercy when it comes to missing deadlines. I'll see you tomorrow."

On my way back to my hotel, I picked up some score sheets. I began working over lunch, and I stayed up late into the night, writing. Three movements, scored for six winds. In the morning, I called the *Conservatoire* and arranged for some players. We had a quick rehearsal before we trooped over to Rue Ballu, surprising Mademoiselle with a private chamber concert. We set up just outside her doorway. Annette made sure Mademoiselle's hearing aids were operational.

"The bass is tremendous."

"Only because I was writing it for you." We laughed.

"I never expected a concert. What a precious one you are!" She paused for a minute, and I thought perhaps she was weakening. "But the oboe part. I'm not sure I'm hearing it right. This transition—she hummed it back to me note-perfect—it seems a little forced—or sudden, that's it. Am I wrong?"

"No. You're absolutely right. I'll work on that tonight."

Fiddling with the oboe part led me to write another piece for oboe and cello, and playing Scheherazade to Mademoiselle's sultan, I wrote music to keep her alive. I thought that if I could keep writing, she would keep breathing, and if she would keep breathing, I knew that I could keep writing. For two weeks, I wrote like a fiend and brought music to her room every day. Sometimes I would play parts for her on the piano. Sometimes I would haul out my flute and play solo, which she loved.

"Do you remember when I said you were the smallest person with the largest talent in my class at Fontainebleau?"

"*Bien sûr.* I was mortified. And worried that everyone would hate me until you gave them a lecture about how hard my life would be and told them I couldn't hear a bass line and was ignorant in the department of chord progressions."

She half-smiled, but I could tell she was not joking today. "Your talent is still very large, and so, I am afraid, is your heart. Put your heart in your music, Hannah. It is the only safe place for it. And as for your music—why are you wasting it on an old woman who can barely hear it? It's your life that needs saving, not mine."

I knew she was dismissing me, but I wasn't willing to go, not yet. "One more piece? I have been working on it for you."

"Just one more."

***

The next day when I arrived at Rue Ballu, Karen took me aside. "She is having a particularly bad day."

I didn't know what to say. "Is it okay for me to go in?" I asked. I was carrying a flute. I'd planned to play for her again today.

Karen nodded. "But do not expect too much of her." I knocked lightly on the bedroom door and received no response. I turned the doorknob, carefully, so as not to wake her. She didn't move when I walked into the room.

"Hannah?" she asked. She was turned away from me, on her side; her voice was positively tiny.

"Yes, I am here."

"Very weak today," she said.

"You don't need to speak," I said. "Save your strength."

"For what?" It was a good question. It hung in the air between us. "Sleeping a lot," she said. She was speaking in shorthand and in French. Sentence fragments—meant to convey meaning without taking too much breath.

"Thinking about Rose," she said.

My grandmother. So was I. Thinking about losing her. Thinking about how I could not bear to lose Mademoiselle, too. And thinking about how inevitable it all felt in this moment. I thought about the way Nana had almost packed her bags for death, how she became ready to go, almost determined to leave. The months in the nursing home, those miraculous days in Boston. I thought then that she'd come back to us; I believed she'd decided to stay on a bit longer. But Nana had other plans. She bought her funeral dress, saw me conduct at Symphony Hall, and returned to the nursing home, dying there as if she had to rush to an important appointment, one scheduled long in advance. Then six months later, Felicia. She slipped away more slowly, but at the end, Lenny, too, had the sense that his wife had somewhere she would rather be.

"Mademoiselle, do you ever feel as though you are somewhere else?" I was thinking again of my grandmother—those times when she seemed to be locked in the past, not able to recognize us or be certain of where she was. It had been so disturbing to me until she had told me the place where she'd been was a pleasant place. A place she liked to visit.

"Yes." A pause. "I believe I have been there," she said softly, a full sentence.

"Is my grandmother there?" I asked, and immediately I regretted the question.

"Jacob, too." A few beats of silence. She took a big, ragged breath and continued. "Your grandmother told you the truth. It is an agreeable place."

"Is there music there?"

She answered right away. "Yes, beautiful music. Some of it might be yours."

Before I could ask her what she meant, she drifted off. I moved to the other side of her bed, sat in the straight chair facing her. She looked so tiny, so frail. It struck me that she was shrinking away, that her death would be a disappearance, that one day soon, Karen would go in to check on her, and Mademoiselle would simply be gone, no trace.

She was lying on her side, her mouth open with effort of breathing. I stared at her knobby hands, gnarled with arthritis. They held onto the white coverlet. I thought of my lessons, of sitting beside her, admiring her reach, her strength. I remembered being upstairs, hearing her play the organ on the floor below. She made it sound so easy. Such grace at the keyboard, certainty in the pedal.

Her strong, powerful fingers were born to play the piano. Hands, now, that were out of proportion with the rest of her, as if someone put the wrong hands on the tiny-bodied old woman next to me. Her nails were short and neat and very clean, pale, too. Someone must clip her fingernails; Mademoiselle could never stand to have let her nails grow past the tips of her fingers. She said they would ache. I keep mine only a little longer.

In that moment of staring at my teacher's hands, hands that could no longer stretch even an octave, I realized that she would leave me soon, that I was selfish to want her to stay. I could recognize her readiness. There was no fight left in this tiny body, no music left in these outsized hands. Tears leaked out, but I swallowed them, not wanting to wake her.

I wondered about the sounds she was hearing. Beautiful music, she had said, and some of it could be mine. What did she mean by that? Did she hear music I have written, music she remembered as mine? That seemed unlikely. With all the music she still carries in her head: the music of masters. Music she has played and analyzed and conducted. Music she has known all her ninety-something years. I cannot imagine that Mademoiselle would carry Hannah Schaeffer with her, when she could take Bach, Monteverdi, even her friend Stravinsky.

"Some of it might be yours." Might be mine. Was I translating her correctly? Maybe she meant music I haven't written yet?

Her breathing eased; her face relaxed. I wondered if she had arrived at the pleasant place. The place where there was music. I adjusted her covers, bent down to give her a kiss on the forehead. She didn't stir. I crept out of her bedroom and into the living room, where I set up my music stand and played my heart out. Perhaps some of what I play will drift into Mademoiselle's dreams, I thought. I wanted to let her know that I planned to make every effort to locate the beautiful music she thought might be mine.

***

An hour later, I packed up my flute and tiptoed back into Mademoiselle's bedroom.

I watched her sleep.

"The doctors say it won't be much longer." Annette had appeared at the doorway. "She's been in and out of a coma for most of the past two months. Her awareness with you these two weeks has been really remarkable—superhuman, almost."

I nodded but said nothing. It seemed wrong to talk about Mademosielle as if she weren't even in the room, when only yesterday she had been so present. I felt an urge to shield her from all discussions of her own condition. Just in case she could hear more than the music. I pushed a strand of her snow-white hair back behind her ears as I bent down to give her one last kiss.

"*Au revoir, Mademoiselle*," I whispered, before I left the room.

"I have a concert series in Berlin this week," I said to Annette, when I joined her in the salon. "I'd like to stay, but—"

"Out of the question." Annette's tone had something of my teacher's own authority in it. She'd come to Mademoiselle as a student herself almost seventy years ago. Young, immensely talented, a prize student, Annette had become the teacher's assistant—helping to ease the load. Starting in the 1920s, pretty much everyone who studied with Nadia Boulanger also studied with Annette Dieudonne. I was a notable exception. Mademoiselle supervised my musical education personally, in much the same way I imagine she had supervised Annette's. I suspect this fact was at the heart of the tension between us. We never grew to know each other as we might have as student and teacher; still, each of us was a mirror for the other. She saw in me a younger version of herself, and I saw in her the person I might become. But I left Mademoiselle's studio; she never did. She envied my expansive musical life; I envied her intimate world of music and Mademoiselle.

"Did you hear me? Nadia would never forgive you—or herself—if you missed Berlin. What's on the program? How many nights?"

"I'm conducting the premiere of a new piece of mine. *Three Elegies*. I started working on it when Felicia Bernstein was dying. I wanted to say something about how much we lose, even before we die. And then my grandmother died, and I wanted to say something about how death can take us suddenly—but also something about how sometimes—like in Nana's case, we can rally just before the end. I finished it a few days after Felicia's funeral. And now—"

"Now it will be the perfect piece to play for Nadia."

There. She'd said it.

***

In Berlin, there were interviews and photographs—the management had arranged plenty of press coverage for this event. A woman conductor; a world premiere; an American composer with ties to Europe; a student of Bernstein. There were plenty of angles. I did my best to keep my focus, but my thoughts kept drifting back to Paris, back to Mademoiselle's bedside. I called daily, to speak with Karen or Annette, and heard the same words on every call: "No change."

Sleeping late into the morning of the premiere date, I was dreaming of a younger Mademoiselle and a younger Hannah, who was orchestrating something she had written, troubled by some difficult harmonies.

"I know you can do it," my teacher was telling my dream-child self, just as I realized the phone was ringing in the real world.

I picked it up, expecting the hotel desk, my wake-up call.

Instead, Annette's voice, softer than I had ever heard it: "She is gone."

"When?" I asked, and she gave me the details, explained the funeral arrangements, and told me—emphatically—to stay right where I was.

"You must play your *Elegies* for Nadia tonight."

She was right. Mademoiselle would want music for her memorial; my music in Berlin would be a more meaningful tribute than my physical presence in Paris.

That evening at Philharmonic Hall, I spoke to the audience before playing the piece. "Today, Nadia Boulanger passed away at the age of ninety-two. She was a great musician and teacher of music. Her loss will be felt throughout the musical world by the thousands of students—now performers, composers, conductors and teachers themselves—who were schooled by Nadia Boulanger. As a teacher, she was strict, demanding, unyielding, and never easy to please—several members of this very orchestra can attest to that. I was only ten years old when I began my studies with Mademoiselle Boulanger. For me, she was a mentor, an inspiration, and—although she may not have approved of my saying so—my musical mother."

"I wrote the first movement of *Three Elegies* for Felicia Bernstein—Leonard Bernstein's wife and a dear friend; the second, for my grandmother, Rose Serapin. The third movement wrote itself. It was insistent and mysterious to me, and I wrote it with an energy and conviction that seemed to say more about life than death. Recently—visiting Mademoiselle Boulanger a few days ago—I realized that the third movement was written to honor her, the woman who heard the music in me before I could hear it myself. Tonight's premiere performance of *Three Elegies* is dedicated to the loving, living memory of Nadia Boulanger."

—41—

Purple and white asters for you, and the promise of spring in the air. But wait—there's a bouquet already here. Without a card. Only the stick-on emblem of the florist, Messieurs Poulaine. They are, it seems, in charge of you; caring for the grave *à perpétuité*, it says on the back of the family headstone. Forever.

Let's see: six roses—two red, two pink, and two yellow; bunches of daisies—pink and yellow and white; some baby's breath, and something tall and yellow that I can't name. But it will die all wrapped in plastic—no water, no air. I'll make a bouquet for your vase, mixing the mystery flowers with mine. There are *a lot* of flowers here. I wonder—oh—wait—March 15! The day Lili died. The flowers are from you, Mademoiselle. I'd bet anything that you made the arrangements with the Messieurs Poulaine to send Lili an annual bouquet.

March 15. How could I have forgotten? Those interminable Masses, your mourning clothes taken out and pressed the day before. Every year. *Every year*! You practically took attendance at the door, making sure that Lili's memory was honored. There were friendships lost over this ritual, relationships severed with anyone who did not understand the importance of your sister's shortened life, who did not know that attendance was mandatory. Miss a performance, even miss a lesson, and eventually we would be forgiven, so long as we did excellent work. But to miss Lili's anniversary Mass at Trinité was a crime without adequate punishment on earth.

In a way, this is perfect timing for me to tell you how I

programmed the London concert. When I was trying to find a common theme between Phillip's work and mine, I realized that you were the connection, the bridge between us. We share *you*. So I programmed Glass, Schaeffer and *Les Soeurs* Boulanger. I knew you would disown me if I didn't include Lili. But you have work that should be heard more often, too. I did some arranging, Mademoiselle. I hope you'll approve.

For my premiere, I ended up writing a trio sonata with orchestra, horn, violin, and cello: Emil, his grandson Marcel, and Emmanuel, the very fine cellist in Marcel's quartet. I won't have to worry about coaching them. Emil will make sure they practice to perfection. All I have to do is to study the score as if I didn't write it. Become the interpreter doing her best to understand the intentions of the composer. Yesterday, I sent off the score and all the orchestral parts to London. The concert's in three and a half weeks.

Maybe Mel is right. I work best with a tight deadline. Or maybe Emil, the official Love Champion, was right about me. When he asked me to finish that half-written piece—well, I would have done that for him, concert or no concert. Does that mean I write from love, just like he said? In this case, I think yes. Do you think he's right about love outlasting us, outlasting everything? I have no idea.

But I think he did pinpoint the moment when I stopped hearing my own music. It was around the time my mother died. I thought the music had just stopped—and maybe it did. Or maybe I just couldn't hear it. Either way, it scared me. I was afraid it was gone forever. And losing the music felt even worse—I think—than losing my mother. And losing everyone before her. Including you. None of that helped. Then I learn I'm losing L.A. too? Without my own music, without my orchestra, where was I? Who was I? It's all so tangled up together.

But Emil knew the music wasn't lost, or even stopped. And

now I realize that my silence was a pause, a *caesura*. "Don't cross the railroad tracks!" I said to the little orchestra last week, pointing out the two parallel lines that stretch above the staff, separating one measure from the next. "You need to watch up here! Don't play the next note until I do!"

When I am conducting, I know—even in the silence—when the next note will sound. But it's trickier with the music that isn't written yet. Is that what stopped me? Is that why losing my podium has felt like the end of the world?

While I was finishing the orchestration on the trio concerto, I started to sketch something for three trumpets, cello, and string bass. I've never written much for brass, but hearing Luke's smooth sound has given me a new appreciation for the possibilities. A good thing, too, because his young trumpeters in the wayward orchestra would send me running out of the room. But they are Luke's students, so they will improve. They are trying hard, and we must give credit for that.

I don't know how well I'm doing with the *petit ensemble*, but together, we persevere. They are learning their scales, and they are listening more carefully with every rehearsal. But I'm not sure an outsider would be able to detect much difference in the end result. I have written a few little pieces for them to play. It spices up rehearsals and gives them a chance to complain about my parts, handwritten, and not always legible.

"Maestro Hannah, *venez, voyez*!"

Oh, Marie's calling me.

***

"*Là—regardez*." Marie pointed to a dark, low shape, ahead of us on the cobblestone path.

"*Une petite noire*? One of the black cats?" I asked.

She laughed. "No—look! Open your eyes." I moved a little closer. Definitely not a cat. But what? The thing lifted its scrawny neck and fixed one red eye on me.

"*Qu'est-ce que c'est?*" I asked, conscious of the squeak in my voice. Frankly, for all my days with you at the cemetery, for all the time I've spent roaming among tombs, I found this living creature in the path spookier than any spirit presence I could conjure.

Marie giggled. "*Une dinde*."

"A turkey? Here! Why?"

"*Je ne sais pas*." She was enjoying my reaction. "Should we feed him?"

"Cat food?" I heard my voice pitch upwards as I imagined getting any closer to this beady-eyed creature. He was still staring at me.

"What else do we have?"

"Oh, I don't know. He's so—oh, ummm—"

"But he still must be fed, yes? Next time we will bring bird food." She said it definitively, in a way I could not contradict. I am not sure I want there to be a next time with this particular creature, but I am weirdly pleased that Marie is so ready to adopt him.

"Do you think the cats bother him?" she asked me.

For an evil moment, I pictured six or seven cats having Thanksgiving dinner, *la dinde* at the center, before I reassured her. "He's bigger than they are. And he doesn't seem distressed."

We have decided to become turkey feeders. But we won't feed the crows or the nosy magpies. They find their food themselves. The doves—coveted, but rarely captured by the cats—we also plan to leave to their own devices. There is only so much of this bizarre ecosystem we want to disrupt.

Post-turkey, on our way down the hill, we walked by Rue Ballu, and I pointed out your apartment.

"You lived there?" I knew Marie was trying to imagine what it would be like to live in a large apartment with a room of her own, a place that must feel so far from her experience, though only blocks away from the detention home.

"Yes, from the time I was eleven, until I was eighteen."

"Is it beautiful inside?"

"I don't know now, but it was."

Really, I hadn't thought of it that way when I was a kid. I took all the original art and the antique furniture for granted. For me, the piano and the organ were the center of the apartment. It was a place filled with music, written and read, practiced, played and heard. Bookcases jammed with scores, students coming and going at all hours. You, at the piano, reading your way through a new piece, sometimes at the same time that I would be upstairs playing my flute. I would pause to replay a phrase and hear that you had stopped too. I knew you were making a note on the score; I could almost see you through the walls, shaking your head. "Is this correct?" you would ask the student when he came for his next lesson, and it was always a trick question.

You never imposed your own hearing on your students. You never told us exactly where the phrase should go, but instead asked us to listen, to feel where each note was leading us.

"It is not your choice or mine, but the place where the music wants us to go, the place that is *required*. That's what you must discover. You will know it when you pay attention, *n'est-ce pas*?"

Your favorite theme: paying attention. Every moment of inattention is a moment lost. "We have a limited number of moments in our lives. Whether you are creating music or eating your breakfast, pay attention!"

It was a strict decree for the dreamy teenager I was. I lost moments, hours at a time. Spacing out—an expression that you would neither appreciate nor understand.

Marie does it, too. I've seen her sitting on a bench at the

cemetery, or perched on a stone, staring at nothing, contemplating—dare I say—everything. I remember enough of my own adolescence to keep myself from asking her any questions. There is no reason to invite a shrug to hang between us. I think the dreaminess is good for Marie. Here in the cemetery, she can be alone with her thoughts, without worry of her thieving, teasing neighbors at the home.

"Would you ever come here at night, Maestro?" she asked me during one of our cemetery visits.

"It's all locked up at night, and I imagine the cats are prowling, other animals too. I think it would be a little scary."

"What about ghosts?"

"Oh, the ghosts don't wait for the nighttime to come out."

She looked at me sideways, trying to gauge my seriousness.

"You believe in ghosts then?"

"Well, not the unhappy kind that drag balls and chains around, no I don't. But I believe we have souls, and I can imagine there are some souls here after dark, looking after the kitties just like we do in the daylight."

"*Vraiment*?"

"*Oui*. You didn't know your flute teacher was so weird, did you?"

"Well, she does come every day to the cemetery to feed cats and talk to a dead person. That is not so typical."

We laughed, but I could tell Marie was turning over what I'd said.

"Have you ever been to church?"

"But of course. They take us every Sunday to Mass."

"Does it mean anything to you?"

She looked at me. She had no idea how to answer my question. At her age, was I contemplating the guiding spirits around us? Doubtful. I attended weekly Mass only because it was part of my prescribed regimen. It was your faith, not mine that brought me to church each Sunday, but I guess some of it rubbed off. You talked so much of souls, especially of mine, and how it was filled with music. My indifference to Catholicism notwithstanding, I had to take souls under some consideration.

I've come to believe that you're right about my soul: it's the home of the imperative that you always told me I had to find. It's a place that doesn't change; it's the core of who I am. But—for all the talk about the contents of my soul, Mademoiselle, you never once mentioned the existence—or desires—of my heart.

It's my heart that goes out to Marie. And little by little, I think her heart is opening to me, and especially to Luke. She thinks the world of him. Marie was as reluctant to study with me as I was to teach her. She was happy enough with her trumpet-playing instructor, but he told her she needed *une spécialiste*. She came to me to please him.

Now, I can see in her eyes and her posture and in the careful way she answers me in a lesson that she genuinely wants to please me too. While this is a kind of progress, I hope Marie will one day want to please herself. Am I asking for *insoumission*? Perhaps. The only rebellion Marie has known has been born of self-preservation, never self-indulgence. Perhaps what I really wish for my student is comfort and love, enough stability in her life to find the security in herself. I want her to want something, something all her own, on her own.

Oh, here she comes—walking towards me, with the youngest black cat following her. She lifts her finger to her lips, asking for silence, as she tilts her head back in the direction of *La Petite Noire Nouvelle*. I nod to indicate that I see she has a young charge in tow. Marie smiles back at me—a big, unrestrained grin—a smile that tells me she is, in this moment, entirely happy.

—42—

I conducted the Berlin series and moved through several more engagements with a heavy heart. Lenny reminded me of what I'd told him, that it was my duty to live, "especially for Nadia," he said. "Keep working." I had little choice. Mel had come through with lots of bookings, per my original instructions. Canceling an engagement—no matter what the reason—was not a career-building option.

"You're doing the right thing," Mel assured me. "I think we may have an offer in the works—Principal Guest Conductor, The Concertgebouw. You want it, right?"

"Of course." Amsterdam wasn't my first choice—I didn't want to be reminded that I'd lost Peter, too. But a Principal Guest Conductor job was an important step—and a European post wouldn't hurt, either. I welcomed the offer, and the orchestra welcomed me. I'd conducted them regularly for the past several years, and we'd always played well together. Mel finalized the contract, and I signed it on New Year's Eve, 1979, in the company of Mel, Lenny, my father, and Joanne.

"To the 1980s." Lenny proposed, lifting a glass of champagne.

"The 1980s!" A chorus. All of us wanting to look ahead. To look past the sadness of the last couple of years.

"I predict this will be Hannah's dynamic decade," Lenny said, grinning at my father. They'd met several times during the years I had worked with Lenny, but their real bonding had occurred earlier that afternoon, after Lenny found out that my father played clarinet.

"Oh, I played a lot when I was younger, but gave it up for years. But recently—having this musical genius in the family—and more time on my hands, I decided I'd pick it up again. I mean, maybe just a little of Hannah's talent could have come from my side of the family, right?"

"Oh, Frank. Don't be so modest." Joanne smiled at my father before she directed her words to Lenny. "He plays in a jazz combo, you know, and they even have gigs."

"You play jazz? Oh, we have to play together!" The way Lenny said it, you could almost forget who he was. "We'll have so much fun." Phone calls were made, a clarinet was borrowed: very fine clarinet owned by a member of the New York Philharmonic. "He's selling it anyway. We'll let him think you are a customer."

Within an hour, my father and Lenny were playing their way through the American songbook, trading solos and riffs. Their musical chemistry was instantaneous; they sounded as if they had been playing together for years. By the end of the afternoon, they were fast friends, and my father was the proud custodian of a new clarinet. Lenny had made the purchase, claiming that he needed a last-minute tax write-off. He quelled my father's objections. Told him it was an instrumental loan for the life of the instrumentalist, that he'd have his attorney draft the papers and send them along. "Really, you're doing me a favor. You only have to promise to bring this instrument with you every time you come to New York, so we can play."

"Dynamic decade. I like that," my father said.

"Have you made any resolutions?" Lenny asked me.

"Resolutions?"

"Yes. I could never keep up with them on an annual basis." He smiled at me for a quick beat. "But I do like to make them at the turn of every decade. For you: I resolve you will have your own orchestra—as Music Director—within the next ten years."

"I like that. Do I get to make one for you?"

"As long as it doesn't involve my quitting smoking."

"Damn. How about this? You'll live these next ten years as a tribute to Felicia's memory."

"Does that imply I have to be good?"

"Only at living. At being fully alive, at being the man she loved. Tenors optional," I added, with a wink.

"Ah. In that case, yes. I resolve to be done with sadness—but not to forget Felicia."

"Never."

"We should toast her—and Nadia—and Rose," Lenny said. "To our lost ladies. We miss you and we love you."

"Here, here," my father said, lifting his glass. We stretched our arms to the center of the table, each of us careful to clink every glass before we took our first sip.

***

For me, the next decade unfolded in much the way Lenny had predicted. I conducted my first concert as Principal Guest Conductor the following fall. Five years later, the offer came from Los Angeles. Music Director of the L.A. Philharmonic. I would start in the fall of 1987. "You'll get in there while you're still in your thirties," Mel declared.

"Barely."

"Don't get all picky on me. You told me you wanted your own podium before you turned forty, and guess what, Schaeffer—you got it."

"Thank you, Mel."

"You know better than to thank me. Just show up, and keep those compositions coming. They like the idea they are getting a conductor who composes, so we have to hold their feet to the fire. They need to come up with a schedule that gives you time to write."

"What about the Concertgebouw?"

"We're fine. You have that opt-out clause that your genius agent got into that contract. You get a music director offer, you give them a season's notice, and you are free."

"I should have had you write one of those clauses for my love life, too." Spending more time in Peter's home city had led to spending more time with Peter, and over the past four and a half years, we'd moved into something almost resembling a traditional relationship.

"I distinctly recall you telling me to stay out of your love life, Maestro Schaeffer."

"Yeah."

"Are you worried about telling Peter?"

"Yes. No. I mean, I know he'll be happy for me—for my career—but it just seems like we're in this endless cycle. Split up. Get back. Split up. Get back. And almost all the split-ups have to do with my career. Here we go again."

"Maybe he'll move with you?"

"He'd move to the moon before he moved to Los Angeles. Don't worry. I shouldn't have said anything. I want this gig. There's no question in my mind. I want my own orchestra. We've been working on this for what—fifteen years—longer? I'll do whatever I need to do to make this happen."

***

Opening night in Los Angeles was a media circus. The woman-conductor angle was huge—evidently all of the citizens of the city took personal pride that their symphony board was open-minded enough to hire me. Then there was the Hollywood factor. The Dorothy Chandler Pavilion, home of the Los Angeles Philharmonic, was also home to the annual Academy Awards. Backstage, a television was tuned to a local station. I watched live coverage of the scene just outside the hall. The celebrities were filing in; cameras were flashing, microphones were shoved into faces.

"You'd think we were hosting a fashion show," the stage manager said to me, as I stood beside him, listening to the TV reporter describe a steady stream of designer outfits.

"Not only that, but I am beginning to feel seriously underdressed."

He laughed. "Do you have a before-concert ritual I need to know about? It's thirty minutes to show time."

"I like twenty minutes of my own—undisturbed, in the inner office."

"And I need you in the wings three minutes before you walk out there. So, I'll send someone to get you." He checked his watch. "You better go if you want your full twenty minutes."

I walked downstairs, past the dressing rooms for visiting soloists, past the giant room filled with lockers for the orchestra members, past the sound of violins, cellos, horns. Moving beyond the dueling scales and long tones, the snippets of solo passages, I opened the door to the conductor's headquarters. I had yet to redecorate the outer office, but the tiny inner office was already mine. I lighted my candle—in a tribute to my permanence, I'd bought myself a cut glass holder. I stared at my photograph of Mademoiselle, conducting the New York Philharmonic nearly fifty years ago. The frame was worn from years of packing and unpacking. I should get a new one, I thought. Something heavier, something that will stay put.

I wished she were still alive, sitting out there, as I thought about who was in the audience for me—my own VIPs. My mother, Bill, my father and Joanne, Peter. From the remains of so many break-ups, we had, in my last year in Amsterdam, found our way to the surer ground of friendship. He'd be sitting next to Elaine, who had managed to unchain herself from her family and her busy veterinary practice to come to this opening concert. Mel would be on the other side of Elaine. And in the middle of the row, in the best seat in the house: Lenny. "I missed your debut as guest conductor when you subbed for me in New York; I wouldn't miss your debut as Music Director for the world."

I closed my eyes. I felt my nerves. *We get nervous because it matters to us*. Who had told me that? I took several deep breaths, locating the butterflies and sending them out on a warm wind. When I'd cleared out everything except the music, I heard the opening bars of the same Stravinsky piece that I'd conducted during my surprise debut with the New York Philharmonic. I had programmed it tonight as a thank-you to Lenny. For Mademoiselle, Felicia, and Nana—and also for the board, who had requested I program an original composition for opening night—we would play *Three Elegies*. The Copland, the Fauré—they were programmed for Mademosielle, too. Aaron Copland was her student, Fauré, her colleague. And really the Stravinsky was as much hers as Lenny's. I'd first conducted it at Fontainebleau.

"It's all for you," I whispered to the woman in the photograph.

A knock on the door. "Seven minutes, Maestro."

I opened my eyes, blew out my candle, adjusted my ruffles, ran a brush through my hair. Then I walked upstairs to wait in the wings, preparing to inhabit my future.

—43—

The cats are fed, and I have distributed yesterday's floral excess, dividing it into three bouquets—one for Emil, one for Marie, one for my place. I stopped first at Emil's to see if he had any questions about his part. We went over a few things, and I gave him a copy of the score.

"Let's have dinner tonight—you, me and Jean-Luc. Something not as spicy as Indian. I suffered for that dinner."

I felt terrible. I had no idea.

"Don't get me wrong. I love a good curry. But not every curry loves me back. Let the old man make the reservation this time. I know how you study up before a big premiere. This will be a farewell dinner—until London."

We ended up going to the same place where I'd met Emil and Luke last summer when I'd first arrived in Paris.

"Maestro," he said, smiling, standing until I was seated.

"Luke," I said. "We Americans like a strong vowel."

"Ah, I remember that," Emil said. "You two just refused to give up the titles. What was that about?"

Luke shrugged in that way he does.

Oh—you'll be proud of me, Mademoiselle—I finally apologized for the way I'd behaved that night. "I'd just been so looking forward to seeing Emil again, and I was mad I had to share."

"*Pas de probleme*, I just assumed you were a bigot."

"Oh my God—you didn't—"

"Well, I couldn't imagine you would be, but in my skin, I can never be sure. I was glad I was the cop, not you."

That's the thing, Mademoiselle. I don't know what it's like for Luke or Marie—that extra layer of worry, the need to be always on alert, simply because they happened to be born not-white. You lived in pretty much an all-white world, and my life hasn't been that much different, at least at work. As long as it's taken the upper echelons of classical music to become a little less male-dominated, it's taking at least as long to become a little less white.

Luke smiled, smoothing out the conversation the way Emil had done that first night. "We were just talking about how you'll have three new pieces on the London program—including yours. And the concert is just three weeks away. Now I understand why you plan to hole up in your apartment until you leave. Well, at least the Glass is in your arm." He smiled, knowing he was using Lenny's expression.

"Actually, it's the Glass that worries me the most," I heard myself saying.

I hadn't realized it until that moment. It's a combination of factors. The brilliance of the premiere in L.A. and every amazing concert of that series. The distance—almost a decade—between performances. And yes, the soloist. I am nervous about seeing Geoffrey Lassman again. Ridiculous, you say. I know! On so many counts.

"Because he'll be there," Emil said. "That's why?"

For a deluded quarter-minute, I thought Emil was talking about Geoffrey. "Huh? Who? Oh—you mean Philip. Right. Um—maybe. But—it's more that the premiere of that piece was one of those rare musical moments, you know?"

"A moment of transcendence," Luke said, recalling our café conversation about the life of a Maestro.

"Yes—that," I agreed.

"And the orchestra—it isn't yours this time," Luke added—supplying, he thought, another reason why I might be worried.

I looked at Emil. He nodded, as if to say it was okay to tell Luke, that I could trust him. But that wasn't my hesitation. I keep returning to the denial stage of this particular loss.

"Well," I said, "that's true. But I don't actually have an orchestra anymore—except for the little delinquent orchestra, which you know, we really should name."

"What? What do you mean?" Luke asked.

Emil did the nodding thing again, this time in Luke's direction, as if to confirm the truth of what I'd just said.

"The Phil didn't renew my contract. Or more accurately, Mel—my agent—determined they were not planning to renew. So, I plan to resign—pre-emptively."

Luke looked shocked, almost shaken. "What idiots!" he finally managed. "And how are you feeling about it?"

"Well, I was a bit of a wreck. Emil can vouch for that. But working on the sonata and getting ready for the concert, and daily practice in a beautiful space, running the little orchestra, getting to know you and Marie—it's all helped. And I'm trying to persuade myself that being without my own podium will free me to do more composing."

"It will," Emil said. "Look—it already has—and you know Nadia would say it's about time, too!"

"I know—it's just—"

"That you love it," supplied Luke. "I can see how much, even with the kids."

"You'll still guest, right?" Emil sensed, correctly, that Luke's observation wasn't exactly what I needed to hear.

"But that's not the same, right, Hannah?"

It seemed to me that Luke was at once reading my mind and also depressing the hell out of me. I've been working all these weeks on coming to terms with this. On being okay—or kind of okay—with leaving L.A. Sure, maybe I'm doing a lousy job of letting go, but at least I'm not bursting into tears every other day anymore.

"Give it time—if you decide you want a music director position somewhere else, I'm sure you'll get offers as soon as the word is out," Emil said. "Now, where is our entrée?" he wondered aloud, probably hoping for a change in subject. I sure was.

But not Luke. He was a well-dressed French bulldog.

"Why wait for an offer?" he asked.

Emil and I just looked at him. I was beginning to remember how much *Inspecteur* Bourlou had annoyed me at our first meal together. Was it the restaurant?

"I mean, if you want your own orchestra, why can't you just make one?"

"Form a symphony orchestra," Emil repeated, checking on translation.

"Sure, maybe it would be a chamber orchestra, and a shorter season or something—but look—isn't that what Philip Glass did? He has the Glass Ensemble, right? Why can't you do something like that? The Schaeffer Orchestra."

"God, what an awful name," I said.

"*D'accord*—maybe it's not the right name. But do you know what I mean?"

"The Glass Ensemble only plays Philip Glass."

"You could play your own work, too—which would keep you composing—but maybe also other people's work—twentieth and twenty-first century—like you're doing at this concert. That's what would make the Schaeffer Orchestra unique."

"I really—*really*—hate that name."

"But you don't hate the idea, do you?"

"Maybe you could ask Mel about it," Emil offered.

"I suppose I could," I said, just as the waiter showed up with the appetizers.

What do you think, Mademoiselle? It's kind of crazy, right? And it would take money—money I don't have. Mel pointed that out to me as soon as I sprung it on him.

"So, you think it's a bad idea?" I asked him.

"No, I think it's a brilliant idea that will require several shitloads of cash."

"I could sell my place in L.A., and as soon as I'm fifty-nine-and-a-half, I could cash out my retirement from the Philharmonic, right? And I have been banking my residuals."

"Schaeffer, the markets have tanked—stock and real estate—especially in California. Now isn't time to cash out anything. No, you'll need backing. I can call your patron's attorney. I don't know how deep those pockets are, but the stipulation is that the funds support the composition of your own work."

"And I'd be composing new work for the group to perform. But I wouldn't have to give up conducting either."

"We'd probably need more than whatever the patron would provide. Then there's the matter of the orchestra—where would it be, and how would you recruit players?"

"I've been thinking maybe instead of creating the orchestra, I could borrow one."

"How do you borrow an orchestra?"

"Well—think about it. In L.A., I programmed a lot more contemporary work than most orchestras do. Especially after we moved into Disney Hall. It was the perfect space. And now the Phil has that reputation. Unless the Board and the new director decide to change course in a big way, I can't borrow L.A. But I might be able to find an orchestra somewhere—"

"That would let you create a contemporary series—or season—that runs in tandem?"

"Yes, something like that—maybe. Or even a couple of orchestras that wouldn't mind lending me players because these concerts would be so different from what they're doing."

"Any idea where?"

"None—not yet."

"Contractually, you may be on to something. And it would save on start-up costs, for sure."

"So—not crazy?"

"Just crazy enough. Let me make some calls. Maybe we can announce something—bare bones—but something about your intentions—that would help the whole L.A. thing make more sense in terms of your career, too."

"I'd be lying if I said I hadn't thought of that. I wouldn't feel so much like a symphonic Little Bo Peep."

"That's funny. And P.S., only you could pair the word *symphonic* with a nursery rhyme character. Let me work on this, Schaeffer. You focus on London. Oh—do you have a name for this group?"

"When Luke brought it up, he called it the Schaeffer Orchestra."

"God, that sucks." Then: "Oh—you don't like it, do you?"

"Not at all."

We hung up laughing.

—44—

I loved my new job in Los Angeles. I loved working with the same orchestra day after day. I loved staying in one place for weeks, even months on end. Mel said it was essential that I accept the occasional guest conductor engagement, but L.A. came first and foremost, both on my calendar and in my mind.

"You still love it?" Lenny asked me on the telephone. It was early in my second season.

"I do."

"I miss those days. There's nothing like having your own orchestra."

"I have trouble thinking of the orchestra as mine. I love working with them day-in, day-out, but these great musicians—really it is their orchestra—"

"And so, New York wasn't mine?"

"Oh, they were. Definitely."

"But L.A. isn't yours?"

"Well—"

"Hannah Schaeffer, I think your conducting mentor forgot to give you ego lessons. It isn't enough to conduct a killer Brahms, you have to be able to puff up your chest and act territorial."

"Puff up my chest? I mean, really. There must be some better way to express female ego."

He laughed, and then he started coughing. It seemed recently that we couldn't get through a phone call without Lenny having a coughing fit. "Are you okay?" It was stupid question. Clearly, he wasn't okay. He admitted the last time that I visited him that he'd been diagnosed with chronic lung obstruction, another way of saying emphysema. Still, he hadn't stopped smoking.

"A second," he said. I heard him swallowing liquid. I hoped it wasn't whisky. "Hang on, okay?" I could picture him, glass in hand, going to the kitchen where he kept the pills on the counter. "Tell me a story," he said, when he picked up the phone again, hoping that I wouldn't notice his shortness of breath.

I obliged with a complicated tale of back-office politics. "Just to remind you that the duties off the podium are never much fun."

"It's true. I don't miss that part of it. I don't miss the battle between the music and the money—though I was pretty good at getting my way."

"You were. You're my role model."

"But I'm done with fighting now." There was a pause that felt ominous, or was it the words that felt that way? I remembered him telling me ten years ago that Felicia had stopped fighting.

"Oh, you're not even close to done, Lenny. Plenty more battles for you to wage—and to win." It was a reassurance—for him, and for me, too.

"You're kind, but—hey, I need to ask you something. Would you play my *Mass* for me as a memorial?"

"Lenny!"

"I know it's a little egocentric of me to try to control the music at my own memorial, not to mention to ask for my own work to be played. But then, *I* got the ego lessons from *my* conducting teacher." He laughed, coughed.

"It's not egocentric. It's morbid. What makes you think—"

"That you'd play it? Because you are the kind of woman who respects a dying man's wishes." He laughed again.

"This isn't something to joke about."

"I am asking you in all seriousness. Now will you just say yes so I can change the subject?"

"Yes, Lenny. I'll conduct the *Mass*. At a special concert in your honor. Maybe I'll even plan a series—a Bernstein retrospective. And I'll write something just for you. But between the planning on the retrospective, my responsibilities here in L.A., and my composing backlog, I will need about twenty years to pull this off. So, you better stick around another couple of decades. Okay?"

"Thanks," he said, "but just the *Mass* will be fine."

***

The following spring, he was diagnosed with a rare form of lung cancer that is typically the result of asbestos exposure. I'd been right about his willingness to keep on fighting; he managed to conduct several more concerts before he died that next October. When I conducted Lenny's *Mass* on November 14, it was the forty-seventh anniversary of his debut with the New York Philharmonic. The musicians came from orchestras around the globe—men and women who had worked with the Maestro in London, Paris, Tel Aviv, Berlin, Vienna—to join members of the New York Philharmonic. Under other circumstances, it would have been a difficult group to conduct; there were twelve concertmasters playing first violin; principal players occupied every chair in the orchestra. But we were there for Lenny. These were people whose lives he had touched, and this was the smallest, easiest thing to do, to give some music back to the man who had brought so much of it to the world.

I cut parts of the *Mass* and rearranged some sections a bit. They were changes Lenny and I had discussed through the years, changes he told me he intended to make when his conducting schedule slowed down and he had more time to rewrite. But his conducting schedule never slowed, only his breath, his heart.

When Schuyler Chapin had called me to tell me that Lenny had died, I felt dumb and dull and as if I were falling in slow motion, or in a dream. Then, I remembered Lenny's request. Damn him, he *was* a dying man. And he was right: I would absolutely respect his wishes. After a minute, I broke my own silence. "He told me he wanted me to play his Mass."

"I know. He mentioned it to me, too."

"I need to do some rewrites before we play it. Stuff Lenny always talked about doing but he never did."

"Hannah, are you okay?"

"Yes. But this is important. Let's put the call out to all the major orchestras to send us representatives. Let's do the concert at Avery Fisher Hall. Let's use the proceeds to start a Bernstein Educational Foundation—"

"Are you alright? I mean, these are all great ideas, but do you really want to do all that planning right now?"

"Not the planning. That's your department. But I am going to hang up this phone and take down my score and get to work. Right now."

I knew the approach—throw everything into the work, into the music. I worked on Lenny's *Mass*, and I worked on a tribute piece of my own. I wasn't sure when it would be done, or when I'd be able to slip it into a program in L.A., but I worked like I was months past deadline. And to fill any remaining space—any space where I might notice how alone I felt without our dead-of-the-night phone calls, the endless conversations about musical interpretation—I wrote an arrangement of his theatre work, *Bernstein on Broadway*. I conducted the premiere with the Boston Pops on his birthday that next summer.

The keep-busy medicine worked its magic. I poured my

heart into music, and I began to believe Mademoiselle was right. "Your fate, like mine, is musical," she had told me. As long as I did good work, created something of artistic, musical value, mine would be a life well-lived. And so I kept living it. Years zipped by, *presto*.

My father died.

Then, my mother.

But I kept busy—almost busy enough not to notice that none of the music, anymore, was mine.

Then, I lost my orchestra.

—45—

Elaine was right about the heather. It's starting to bloom now, pale purple against the gray-white of your headstone. I moved it at least four times, trying to figure out the right location. I've learned this year that plants work best in groups of three, so I set them in a forward triangle. Yes, I have been continuing my consultations with the flower vendor by la Cité and with the gentleman at Messieurs Poulaine—is it terrible that I think of him as the florist for the dead? Oh, and not only about your grave garden, but about the window boxes at the apartment, too. They were just a weedy mess. And it turns out I wasn't kidding about planting vegetables. Last month, when I was returning Marie's book to the detention home, I saw a courtyard out the office windows. I learned it belongs to the building—and Luke jumped on board when I suggested we get the kids to plant a garden there.

There's something about getting my hands in the dirt that makes me feel satisfied. Elaine says it's "grounding" me, although my efforts so far are in containers—your grave, my window boxes. I'm thinking the kids will get some sense of accomplishment from digging in dirt and planting seeds, watering, tending to something that is their own. Voltaire, right?

Do you know if Voltaire had a cat? The little black—who is a lot bigger now, but still *une petite*—she's been rubbing up against me the entire time. She wants a petting. Now—almost every day after she eats, she comes to me, asks to be held. She purrs and settles into my lap, and sometimes she even begins to groom—which is awkward, as I'm not a solid surface, but it's as if she has these two dueling impulses—that cat-instinct to clean after eating and the need to catch a cuddle while I am here. And you know what? I don't care what Luke says. I'm going to take her home with me one day soon.

***

I've always pictured you tending this grave when you were alive. Were you the one that planted the unruly groundcover? I'm constantly trimming it back, pulling it up to make room for more color. But it's important to have that year-round green. Was that what you had in mind? It's a kind of bass line. Providing support for all the seasonal notes. Gardening feels a little like arranging to me—not composing exactly, but something like orchestration.

Speaking of, I hope you approve of what I've done with your piece. I'm so looking forward to presenting something of Nadia Boulanger's to the world. Why did you stop composing? I know—you always said Lili was more talented—but you stopped after she died, didn't you? Maybe it's because I've been thinking about what stopped me—or almost stopped me—and I guess I just wish there had been someone around to say to you, *Don't.*

I mentioned the title of your piece to Luke in passing—it was on Monday night. We'd had a small recital at Sainte-Chapelle for the little orchestra—still unnamed, as is my imaginary contemporary music ensemble—and afterward, he and I grabbed a bite at the café.

"Vers La Vie Nouvelle: Toward the New Life," he said, a literal translation of the title. "Appropriate. That's where you've been moving, isn't it?"

"I hadn't thought of it that way, but—yes, I guess I am. I don't know where it will be or exactly what it will be."

"You think you will create the contemporary music orchestra?"

"Mel's working on getting some funding. We'll see. But I still haven't figured out a name—or where the ensemble might be based. I told you about the idea of borrowing musicians, right?"

"You did—it's inspired. Almost as inspired as the original idea, *non*?" He smiled.

"*Non*—the original idea was beyond inspired. Truly, Luke, I'm not sure I would have thought of it on my own. I was so stuck in the idea of losing L.A., and I've lived inside this classical music world for so long—well, I'd lost all perspective. I guess—here's an Americanism for you: I couldn't see the forest for the trees."

"But now you do. And I have an idea for where. How about *à Paris*?

"Here?"

"Think about it—a European base makes the most sense—it gives you better borrowing power. You could recruit from several major orchestras. Everyone has an EU passport. Your players could just hop on a train to Paris."

I'd been thinking New York.

"And you could keep the little orchestra if you want, and continue working with Marie and keep visiting the cats, and help with the garden, right? I mean, haven't you been building *la vie nouvelle* this year in Paris?"

The question hung in the air for a moment.

"And then, there's me. It would be hard for me to run away with you to the States right now, especially since I'm in the middle of adopting your most promising student."

"You're going to adopt Marie?"

"I'm working on it—but—did you hear the part about me wanting to run away with you?"

I didn't know what to say.

"So serious," he said, brushing a strand of hair off my cheek. He sat back and lifted his hands in his signature French shrug. "I had to say it. After preaching to you over so many meals about following your heart, I felt I ought to reveal the contents of mine."

He laughed, and I smiled a reflexive, professional smile, a smile that would pass among strangers. But someone like Luke could read the false set of my jaw, the mismatch between my eyes and my mouth. I looked down at my lap.

Sometimes at Sainte-Chapelle, I've caught him staring at me as I put away my instruments—or coming out of the ladies' room at a café, I've noticed him, watching me move across the dining room. But through our Friday lunches and Monday dinners, our rehearsals with the little orchestra, and our recent Sundays spent with Marie, and even during our forced cohabitation when I was sick, Luke has offered his easy friendship, and asked for nothing from me.

"Hannah?"

Looking up, I rearranged my face into what I hoped was a more convincing smile.

"It was unfair for me to say that to you tonight, days before a big concert, an important concert. Selfish too. I got carried away at the wrong moment. Please forgive me."

"Forgiveness is not required, " I managed. "You've been a wonderful friend, Luke. It's just that—"

"I know," he said. His turn to look down.

But he doesn't know—not at all, because in that moment of watching him fold and refold his dinner napkin, I finally saw him: the man who had cared for me when I was sick; the man who had challenged me to think about music in ways I hadn't—maybe ever; the man who had helped me to open my own heart to Marie; the man who had made me understand that I could teach music without giving myself away; the man who had inspired me to write—for God's sake—a trumpet trio. And the man who saw a way for me to have it all, right when I thought I'd lost everything that mattered.

No, he doesn't know, and really, I don't know, myself.

I wanted to reassure him then, to thank him. I wanted to touch him. But I didn't move.

We skipped dessert, both of us claiming a fullness that neither of us felt. When he dropped me off, he passed on our usual cup of tea. He got out of the car and walked me to the entrance. He entered the *digicode* for me, opened the door.

"Hannah—*attendez*."

I spun around, surprised by his use of the *vous* form. I looked up at him—expecting advice, or a parting word.

Instead, he kissed me.

It was not a peck, but a soft graze of his lips. As if he thought I were a fragile object, as if he believed that a more determined kiss might break me. Before I could hear the notes of that kiss, he was stepping away, holding the door, making certain I had my keys, instructing me to turn my living room light off and on again to signal all was well in my apartment.

Upstairs, in the few seconds of darkness, I noticed the blinking green on the answering machine.

"Hi, Hannah, it's Geoffrey—Geoffrey Lassman. Phillip gave me the number. I hope it's okay to call. I just wanted to say how much I am looking forward to playing the *Serenade* with you again in London. And I hear you're premiering work on the program too. Congratulations. That's great. If you want, you can call me. Or—um, well—well if we don't talk, I guess I will just see you there."

I've decided to go with Option Number Two: See You There.

Because the sad truth is that underneath all the musical armor, I'm still that girl who tried out kissing with Elaine and went on dates with farm management majors hoping to lose my virginity, the girl, who—let's face it—doesn't understand the first thing about adult relationships, who can pine for someone she doesn't even know, for something that never even happened. A girl who dresses up like a boy, so they will let her conduct world-class orchestras.

I have lived the life that you prepared me to live, Mademoiselle. Is it fair to say I have made sacrifices? No. Not really. I have always chosen music.

But you know, sometimes I wonder if I could have chosen music *and*.

Coda

We opened with Boulanger. My arrangement of *Vers la Vie Nouvelle.* I felt good; my hands felt like yours—those strong, sturdy hands that always defied your age, the hands I loved to play alongside—ten years old, and stretching to make a seventh, twenty years later, and still envious of the easy ten-note span between your thumb and pinkie.

The orchestra was responsive. They liked the piece. I could tell right away, in the first rehearsal. They settled into it as if it were a compelling novel, turning the pages, hopeful of the outcome. They were not disappointed. Three bows for your work, Mademoiselle, before I moved toward Emil, waiting in the wings.

"Can I trust them to get my part on the right stand?" he asked.

It was an absurd thing for him to worry about. We were in a world-class venue. And I bet he had it memorized anyway. But I understood his focus on the details that could be controlled. It is the slip of the hand, the slack of the lips, the miscalculated breath that we truly fear. But to voice those worries would give our musical nightmares permission to come true. I reassured him that I would give him time to make sure his music was in order before we began.

"Nervous?"

"Not about you," I answered, promptly.

Marcel and Emmanuel approached, finally satisfied with their tuning. "Are we ready gentlemen?" I was tempted to link arms with my soloists, to cross the stage like Dorothy and her three pals in search of Oz. Emil would be the lion, for sure, always my favorite. But Emil has plenty of courage, and his bravery was catchy as he made his dignified way across the stage, using the fancy cane we found in a pricey antique shop in the 8th *arrondissement.*

On the podium, I took two deep breaths, turned my eyes to my soloists, questioning them with my eyebrows. They answered with barely perceptible nods. I smiled. *We are ready.*

The first note belonged to Emil. I prepped the downbeat, handing off the opening to the long clear tones of his horn.

We played. I fell in love with the music as it moved through us all. It's Emil's piece, Mademoiselle. The horn is the heart of the trio. Even with the flourishes I'd written for Marcel and the beautiful aching cello part that Emmanuel played to perfection. And Emil was in fine form, his sound effortless, true, resonant, and right. The earth to Marcel's sky, the ground beneath the vibrating strings. Emil drew them in, pushing them beyond their limits. They were an orchestra unto themselves, a neighborhood within the larger city of musicians on the stage.

The London players were responsive, interested, calling out to the trio and listening for their response. I'd written a conversation between Emil and the orchestra's horn section, and they were right there, sure speakers in a dialogue that could last all night. A *diminuendo* in the horns, and it was the concertmaster's turn to shine with Marcel and Emmanuel, a mini trio within the trio, expanding into a quartet as the viola joined in. I'd worried about that section because it is such a shift away from the horn, the focus of the work, but as I heard the lively interplay of strings, I realized it is perfect—and exactly what is needed. Emil re-entered, calling his comrades back: first a gentle coaxing, their whispered responses. Then, Emil's sound deepening, the tempo broadening to contain his beautiful round notes.

The ending surprised me almost as much as it surprised the audience: a flurry of notes, fast and loose, trio and orchestra in unison, like so many songbirds set free.

I heard that interval of silence before the applause. I caught Emil's eye. "*Merveilleux*," I mouthed to him. I turned to the audience, sweeping my arm to the soloists, asking them to take their bows. The applause was thunderous. I picked up Emil's hand and walked with him to the center of the stage for his own bow. The audience knew it was the performance of his lifetime because they could imagine nothing more perfect than the sure sound he'd just shared with them. I gestured with my left hand to the orchestra, and they stood. And then, the audience rose, as if I'd waved them to their feet as well.

"*Belle musique*, *chère*," Emil said to me, as I steadied him for the walk offstage.

"Beautiful, thanks to you."

"Thanks to me, only because you wrote such beauty for me to play. And you invited me to play it here, too." Emil shook his head, as if he was having trouble believing where he was. "Are you worried about the Glass?" he asked me as we reached the wings.

Was it that obvious? I wondered, before I remembered who was asking the question. I am a book Emil's been reading since I was ten years old.

I'd worked the piece carefully with the orchestra in three sessions without the soloist. When Geoffrey arrived, the music came together effortlessly on the first run-through. Only my inner perfectionist—whom I have named, incidentally, after you, Mademoiselle—demanded we review a couple of transitional moments. She was in control, and all business—sure and strong.

Perfectionism—required for practice—is not useful in performance. In concert, I must put the inner Mademoiselle to sleep—or distracted, I will stumble in my beats, forget an important cue, lose track of myself, the music, or any one of the musicians in front of me. There are things I can worry about before I walk across the stage to the podium, even as I stand to face the orchestra, but once I give the downbeat, I must erase all ideas of perfection, and only make music. Trusting the years of musical experience seated before me. Trusting the musical understanding, transferred, in that moment—as I sweep the baton up and then down again—from my head to my heart.

Emil reached out and squeezed my shoulder. "Relax," he whispered. "It sounded great in rehearsal."

***

In the guest conductor's quarters, I lighted my traveling candle, stared at the flame. I had twelve minutes of Lili Boulanger to play before I could even think of the Glass. And I knew there would be some sort of psychic hell to pay if I messed that one up. I quieted my mind so I could hear your sister's piece—orchestra, chorus, and soloists—and was lost inside it when the stagehand startled me with the eight-minute warning.

The audience was welcoming, warm, and still there. It is astonishing to me how many audience members pack up and leave in the middle of a contemporary music concert. Perhaps they forgot to read the program before they bought the ticket? Or maybe they can only take so much.

We opened strong, and it wasn't until the applause at the close of *Du Fond de L'abîme* that I felt my nerves rising again. I gestured to the orchestra, moving to the wings.

Geoffrey was there, saxophone strapped around his neck. "That was great," he said, as I made a U-turn, moving back to the stage to acknowledge the continuing applause.

"Your piece was gorgeous." Geoffrey said as I returned

from the second bow. "I listened from the hall."

"Thanks." I smiled and I stepped away from him while the stage was being reset. When it was time to enter, I led the way.

After a welcoming handshake, I turned to the score. I focused on the opening notes, hearing them one by one: bells. I let the audience wait longer than I usually do while I listened to the music in my head. Then I picked up my baton, checking in with a glance at my soloist and my concertmaster, before I swept up and then down, in just the way I'd been teaching Luke.

We were off.

Geoffrey's playing was expressive, mesmerizing—and the orchestra in front of me was ready, attuned. I followed Geoffrey, and they followed me, and we enjoyed a long ride together. It was every bit as good as any one of the performances we'd given in Los Angeles. When I turned to the audience to acknowledge the roaring applause, I saw Emil, ninth row, center aisle, clapping, smiling, nodding. And a few rows behind Emil—Luke—with Marie on his right, Elaine in the seat to his left.

I left the stage with Geoffrey. As we reached the wings, he leaned in.

"Dinner?" he asked me.

I waved him back out for a solo bow. He returned, smiling. "Did you hear me?" he asked as we took the stage again.

It was impossible to reply, impossible even to consider his request. The past had gone careening into the future, colliding into the present. I motioned to the composer—sixth row, center—asking Phillip to stand.

I saw Marie waving at me, just a shy little wave, a secret signal to say *I know you*. I looked right at her and smiled. Elaine turned to say something to Luke, and Luke leaned over to say something to Marie. Then Luke straightened up and grinned while Marie blew me a kiss.

I picked up Geoffrey's hand; we bowed together.

Applause winding down, some of the audience was beginning to head for the exits.

"Time for dinner?" Geoffrey asked me when we reached the wings.

I looked at him, but I saw beyond him. Luke helping Emil through the stage door. Marie just ahead of them, looking for me. I watched the guard, shaking Emil's hand, congratulating him. Marcel introducing himself to Elaine. Luke saying something that made Marie smile. Elaine, laughing, and everyone joining in.

"Thanks for another stellar performance." It was the Maestro speaking to her soloist. Geoffrey thanked me in turn, leaving a pause for me to fill. But I had nothing else to say. I shook his hand before I moved into the circle of laughter and shared congratulations.

Elaine gave me a hug. Emil kissed me on both cheeks.

I squeezed Marie's shoulders before I moved toward Luke.

"There's something I've been wanting to say—I mean, do."

On tiptoes, I leaned in for the kiss.

Accelerando percussion. A fluttering tremolo in the upper voices. A melody I must write down later. And a strong, rhythmic bass line to contain it all.

This time, I think, the music has chosen me.

Together—the music and I—we *are* moving toward a new life. Luke, Emil, Marie, they are coming too. And so are you, Mademoiselle. Not just because I am your aging duckling, or because your voice is always in my head, or because you truly are my musical mother. But because you made it so.

You knew, all along.

I didn't. I never even guessed.

Until Mel forwarded me the email from the patron's attorney, with the provisions of the trust attached. On a slightly crooked scan of a typewritten original, I noticed a correction—a little caret mark, inked in, and pointing to a single missing word.

Compose, it said, in the compact, upright hand I know by heart.

Acknowledgements

My thanks to the fabulous folks at Blackwater Press—the insightful and delightful Elizabeth Ford, the unflappable Maestro of Production, Luca Guariento, and the thoughtful editorial and creative duo of Vivien Williams and Sam Stafford—along with a huge measure of gratitude to artist Inés Gregori Labarta for creating the beautiful cover for this novel.

My thanks to the writers who were kind enough to be readers: David Gillham, Karol Jackowsky, Daphne Kalotay, Mira Lee, Margot Livesey, Rosie Sultan and Amanda Eyre Ward.

My thanks to Hannah's cheering section: Holly Anderson, Helene Atwan, Ghislaine Aubrun, Jack Barney, Leanna James Blackwell, Ginny Breen, Kay Campbell, Jill Christiansen, Dan Cullen, Ginger Curwen, Cindy Donaldson, Guy Ducornet, Jane McDowell Ford, Janet Gauland, Tom Hallock, Joe Heitz, Bob Hugo, Harry Hussey, Mitchell Kaplan, Jay Leutze, Julia Lord, Anna Mantzaris, Tina Maravich, Jennifer Maguire, Bridget Marmion, Kathy Neugent, Heidi Fettig Parton, Andy Ross, Marly Rusoff, Tony Savoie, Suzanne Strempek Shea, Marshall Smith, Andrew Sterman, Vicky Titcomb, Katrina Valenzuela, Theresa Whouley, and Bob Wyatt.

My thanks to Dr. Lawrence Hartzell and his teacher, Mademoiselle Nadia Boulanger.

About the Author

Kate Whouley is the author of two critically acclaimed memoirs: *Remembering the Music, Forgetting the Words*, winner of the 2012 New England Book Award in nonfiction, and *Cottage for Sale, Must Be Moved*, a 2005 BookSense Book of the Year finalist that was recently released in an expanded 20th anniversary edition. Kate directs the MFA program in creative writing at Bay Path University, serves as a writer and contributing editor at *Yankee* magazine, and is the editor-in-chief of *Multiplicity*, the literary journal of the Bay Path MFA. An avocational musician and the managing director of the Cape Cod Concert Band, Kate traces the inspiration for her debut novel, *The Maestro and Her Protégé*, to a long-ago music theory class taught by a demanding professor who was once a student of the famous—and famously formidable—musical master, Nadia Boulanger. Kate lives, writes, plays music, and obeys the current Cat-in-Charge in the cottage that inspired her first memoir.